# DEADMAN'S TOR

The wind was crying like a lost child among the rocks on Deadman's Tor. In his hiding place in the graveyard at the foot of the hill, the pale gentleman cursed the wind and covered his ears with his hands. "Don't trouble me tonight, you angry spirits. I am here on *your* business as much as my own."

The wind died down for a moment. Over the voices in his head came the clamor of approaching hoofbeats on the carriage road leading past the cemetery. He was just able to make out an immense brute of a black stallion, and a dark, powerful figure in a many-caped riding cloak and a wide-brimmed hat.

*So . . . the highwayman will keep his appointment.*

Hastitly abandoning his hiding place behind a tombstone, the pale gentleman pushed aside a rusty gate and whisked inside an open mausoleum. It would not do to be discovered skulking like a dog among the graves.

## DAW titles by Jennifer Roberson

**The Chronicles of the Cheysuli**
SHAPECHANGERS
THE SONG OF HOMANA
LEGACY OF THE SWORD
TRACK OF THE WHITE WOLF
A PRIDE OF PRINCES
DAUGHER OF THE LION
FLIGHT OF THE RAVEN
A TAPESTRY OF LIONS

**The Sword-Dancer Saga**
SWORD-DANCER
SWORD-SINGER
SWORD-MAKER
SWORD-BREAKER
SWORD-BORN*
SWORD-SWORN*

THE GOLDEN KEY
(with Melanie Rawn and Kate Elliott)

THE GLASS KEY*

**Anthologies** (as editor)
RETURN TO AVALON
(a tribute to Marion Zimmer Bradley)

HIGHWAYMEN: ROBBERS AND ROGUES

* forthcoming

# HIGHWAYMEN: ROBBERS & ROGUES

EDITED BY
JENNIFER ROBERSON

*With interior illustrations by Elizabeth Danforth*

DAW BOOKS, INC.
DONALD A. WOLLHEIM, FOUNDER
375 Hudson Street, New York, NY 10014
ELIZABETH R. WOLLHEIM
SHEILA E. GILBERT
PUBLISHERS

***This is dedicated to***
***the Genie Runcibles of SFRT1 Cat43/Top49,***
***without whom this anthology would not exist.***
***Literally.***


Cover art by Yvonne Gilbert.
Interior art copyright 1997 by Elizabeth Danforth

DAW Book Collectors No. 1060.



First Printing, June 1997
1 2 3 4 5 6 7 8 9

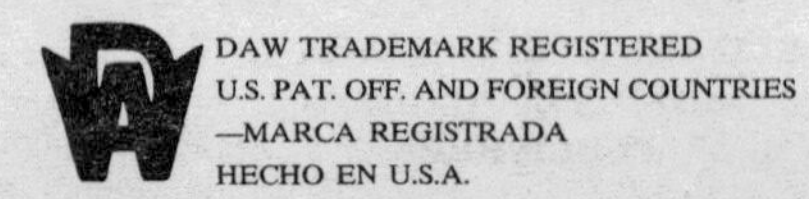

DAW TRADEMARK REGISTERED
U.S. PAT. OFF. AND FOREIGN COUNTRIES
—MARCA REGISTRADA
HECHO EN U.S.A.

PRINTED IN THE U.S.A.

# THE HIGHWAYMAN

## *Alfred Noyes*

PART ONE

The wind was a torrent of darkness among the gusty trees.
The moon was a ghostly galleon tossed upon cloudy seas.
The road was a ribbon of moonlight over the purple moor,
And the highwayman came riding—
  Riding—riding—
The highwayman came riding, up to the old inn-door.

He'd a French cocked-hat on his forehead, a bunch of lace at
  his chin,
A coat of the claret velvet, and breeches of brown doe-skin.
They fitted with never a wrinkle. His boots were up to the
  thigh.
And he rode with a jewelled twinkle,
  His pistol butts a-twinkle,
His rapier hilt a-twinkle, under the jewelled sky.

Over the cobbles he clattered and clashed in the dark inn-
  yard,
He tapped with his whip on the shutters, but all was locked
  and barred.
He whistled a tune to the window, and who should be wait-
  ing there
But the landlord's black-eyed daughter,
  Bess, the landlord's daughter,
Plaiting a dark red love-knot into her long black hair.

And dark in the dark old inn-yard a stable-wicket creaked
Where Tim the ostler listened. His face was white and
  peaked.
His eyes were hollows of madness, his hair like mouldy hay,
But he loved the landlord's daughter.

The landlord's red-lipped daughter.
Dumb as a dog he listened, and he heard the robber say—

"One kiss, my bonny sweetheart, I'm after a prize to-night,
But I shall be back with the yellow gold before the morning light;
Yet, if they press me sharply, and harry me through the day,
Then look for me by moonlight,
Watch for me by moonlight,
I'll come to thee by moonlight, though hell should bar the way."

He rose upright in the stirrups. He scarce could reach her hand,
But she loosened her hair in the casement. His face burnt like a brand
As the black cascade of perfume came tumbling over his breast;
And he kissed its waves in the moonlight,
(Oh, sweet, black waves in the moonlight!)
Then he tugged at his rein in the moonlight, and galloped away to the west.

## PART TWO

He did not come in the dawning. He did not come at noon;
And out of the tawny sunset, before the rise of the moon,
When the road was a gypsy's ribbon, looping the purple moor,
A red-coat troop came marching—
Marching—marching—
King George's men came marching, up to the old inn-door.

They said no word to the landlord. They drank his ale instead.
But they gagged his daughter, and bound her, to the foot of her narrow bed.
Two of them knelt at her casement, with muskets at their side!
There was death at every window;
And hell at one dark window;
For Bess could see, through her casement, the road that he would ride.

They had tied her up to attention, with many a sniggering jest.
They had bound a musket beside her, with the muzzle beneath her breast!
"Now, keep good watch!" and they kissed her. She heard the doomed man say—
*Look for me by moonlight;*
*Watch for me by moonlight;*
*I'll come to thee by moonlight, though hell should bar the way!*

She twisted her hands behind her; but all the knots held good!
She writhed her hands till her fingers were wet with sweat or blood!
They stretched and strained in the darkness, and the hours crawled by like years,
Till, now, on the stroke of midnight,
Cold, on the stroke of midnight,
The tip of one finger touched it! The trigger at least was hers!

The tip of one finger touched it. She strove no more for the rest.
Up, she stood up to attention, with the muzzle beneath her breast,
She would not risk their hearing; she would not strive again;
For the road lay bare in the moonlight;
Blank and bare in the moonlight;
And the blood of her veins, in the moonlight, throbbed to her love's refrain.

*Tlot-tlot; tlot-tlot!* Had they heard it? The horsehoofs ringing clear;
*Tlot-tlot; tlot-tlot,* in the distance? Were they deaf that they did not hear?
Down the ribbon of moonlight, over the brow of the hill,
The highwayman came riding—
Riding—riding—
The red-coats looked to their priming! She stood up, straight and still.

*Tlot-tlot,* in the frosty silence! Tlot-tlot, in the echoing night!
Nearer he came and nearer. Her face was like a light.
Her eyes grew wide for a moment; she drew one last deep breath,

Then her finger moved in the moonlight,
Her musket shattered the moonlight,
Shattered her breast in the moonlight and warned him—with her death.

He turned. He spurred to the west, he did not know who stood
Bowed, with her head o'er the musket, drenched with her own blood!
Not till the dawn he heard it, and his face grew grey to hear
How Bess, the landlord's daughter,
The landlord's black-eyed daughter,
Had watched for her love in the moonlight, and died in the darkness there.

Back, he spurred like a madman, shouting a curse to the sky,
With the white road smoking behind him and his rapier brandished high.
Blood-red were his spurs in the golden noon; wine-red was his velvet coat;
When they shot him down on the highway.
Down like a dog on the highway.
And he lay in his blood on the highway, with the bunch of lace at his throat.

*And still of a winter's night, they say, when the wind is in the trees,*
*When the moon is a ghostly galleon tossed upon cloudy seas,*
*When the road is a ribbon of moonlight over the purple moor,*
*A highway man comes riding—*
*Riding—riding—*
*A highwayman comes riding, up to the old inn-door.*

*Over the cobbles he clatters and clangs in the dark inn-yard.*
*And he taps with his whip on the shutters, but all is locked and barred.*
*He whistles a tune to the window, and who should be waiting there*
*But the landlord's black-eyed daughter,*
*Bess, the landlord's daughter,*
*Plaiting a dark red love-knot into her long black hair.*

# CONTENTS

# WRECKERS, ROOKS, AND BOOKS: AN INTRODUCTION

## *by Jennifer Roberson*

In an industry dominated by novels and nonfiction, anthologies are anomalies, an assemblage of short stories written by many authors about a multiplicity of characters, times, places, and incidents, compiled by one or more editors, and placed between covers to form one finite package. Perhaps they grew out of reader demand for magazine stories bound into one "unit" for ease of reading, collection, and storage; or perhaps a clever publisher recognized the potential in compiling and repackaging old stories into a new venue, to reach an existing audience as well as to explore a new one.

Traditionally, modern anthologies have failed to sell as well as novels. They are difficult to market, according to the publishing industry, because readers prefer to invest time and money in the depth and breadth of the world-building and characterization more common to epic-scope novels and ongoing series. And yet anthologies are also ideal venues for authors who prefer short fiction to long, for writers who wish to challenge themselves and their audience in ways better suited to brevity; and especially for readers who prefer appetizer to entree when taste-testing authors with whom they are unfamiliar.

The fantasy and science fiction genre has always provided a fertile field for anthologies. Many of today's most esteemed and established f&sf authors broke in via stories in magazines and anthologies. But novels allow the opportunity to explore multiple layers in society and character growth, in the evolutions of culture and politics, the resolutions of certain ideas, ideals, and quests, and thus are more seductive to most writers; also, from a strictly pragmatic view, novels pay better than short fiction, and sell better. Thus we see more novels written and published, and far fewer short fiction anthologies.

Some years ago an enterprising individual hit upon an innovation in the subgenre. Called "theme anthologies," each volume features stories on a given subject, primarily original work written specifically for the anthology. Such themes may be generalized by genre—horror, romance, science fiction, mystery, etc.—or more specifically require stories about and/or are limited to such things as animals (*Horse Fantastic, Cat Fantastic,* etc.), quantified issues and agendas such as women warriors or gay/lesbian themes, or anthologies celebrating the work and influence of specific authors (*Return To Avalon,* a tribute to Marion Zimmer Bradley).

Though seemingly self-limiting, theme anthologies have proven both fascinating and enduring in that they provide a creative challenge to the contributors—a chance to write variations, to expound a personal view, or to invent a completely fresh take on a popular idea—as well as to the editors who must define the parameters for the individual themes and assemble the stories. Because one must write about something *specific,* not just exhume a story, idea, or concept that arrives in one's brain and begs to be shown the light of day.

Certain authors, critics, and readers consider theme anthologies bankrupt of originality, projects akin to term papers assigned in college. Well, color me a raving revolutionary, but I always viewed term papers as the ultimate challenge: to perform the assigned task while also interjecting my own individual views and variations in my own voice, not merely to regurgitate dates and data. (Fortunately most of my instructors, including my law professor, found this both intriguing and worth rewarding. A few did not; but then, these professors continue to make their livings regurgitating dates and data, while I and others like me make our livings writing about imaginary worlds and people—which is a lot more fun, I daresay!)

For anthology editors and publishers, as with anything, there are no guarantees that a given theme will prove intriguing to the readership. One develops what one believes is a provocative, appealing, and evocative theme, and one hopes to receive equally provocative, appealing, and evocative stories that not only suit the theme in some respect, but are entertaining to readers.

*Highwaymen: Robbers and Rogues,* however, is an atypical theme anthology. In fact, it's an "accidental" anthology, born not of market and editorial calculations but of the ether, in the phosphors of certain authorial reprobates who hang out in my topic on Genie, an online bulletin-board service that is home to a large proportion of professional fantasy and science fiction writers as well as to readers. Its conception was decidedly prosaic: someone thought perhaps one of my upcoming fantasy novels was about vampires because the title was suggestive of such.

Neither the novel nor the title had anything to do with vampires, but nonetheless the seed was sown. Someone else mentioned a romance novel title similar to mine, but explained it was about a highwayman, not a vampire. My reply was to marry the two vivid and popular images: a vampire highwayman.

The next thing I knew, such topic inhabitants as Susan Shwartz, Jo Clayton, Lois Tilton, Ashley McConnell, Deborah Wheeler, Doris Egan, Doranna Durgin, Bruce Arthurs, Kate Daniel—published professionals all—were chiming in with oddball and off-the-cuff suggestions about highwaymen. Werewolf highwaymen. Zombie and mummy highwaymen. Even, so help me, a *lesbian female transvestite vampire highway "man."*

And of course talk segued into a discussion of Alfred Noyes' incredibly evocative poem "The Highwayman," as those of us who had read it in school waxed effusive over the colorful imagery, the to-die-for romance, the lush language, the tragic outcome of the dashing highwayman's love for black-haired Bess, the landlord's daughter.

From then on it was—madness. Susan Shwartz called dibs on Prince Hal and Falstaff. Esther Friesner, told of the insanity, requested Dick Turpin. The "virus" spread in the space of a few hours: people e-mailed me to say they wanted in—and, by the way, here was the story *they* wanted to tell, about their own personal highwayman.

Within two days I had enough potential participants to fill two volumes. It seemed the very least I could do was *apply* all the energy and talent oozing so happily out of my topic. So I wrote a proposal and sent it to my agent. This anthology, this anomalous marriage of the publishing industry and the electronic communication revolution, is the result.

The highwayman is one of the most beloved and universal of archetypal heroes—or antiheroes, as the case may be. Novels, short stories, ballads, sagas, poems, films, plays, theatrical presentations, and television series are full of such templates as the dashing and romantic gentleman-thief; the loner on the run from the authorities for a crime he didn't commit; the man (or woman) of good birth but impoverished family forced by circumstances to hold up the coaches carrying gentry and nobility (or stagecoaches carrying schoolmarms, saloon girls, ex-gunfighters, and alcoholic doctors); the righteous and right-minded individual who rebels against the system and rises from obscurity/peasant origins to help the poor and less fortunate; or the *rich,* righteous, right-minded—and politically correct—philanthropist who decides to help the poor and less fortunate. Incognito, of course.

Contained herein are twenty-three tales about such right-minded—and wrongheaded!—knights of the road, land-sharks, light-fingered gentry, thimble-riggers and artful dodgers, picaroons, footpads, desperados, and other such miscreants as we could devise. But the roads our creations travel are decidedly unpredictable and vastly divergent: there is the comedic and the tragic, the bizarre and the ironic, the historical, romantical, science fictional and fantastical, plus a wide array of characters, settings, time frames, styles, and takes, from an atmospheric short-story sequel to the Noyes poem through classic bandits such as Robin Hood and Dick Turpin, to, appropriately, a hacker plying his trade on the information superhighway, all strikingly illustrated by Elizabeth Danforth.

As I said in my letter to contributors: *Anything goes.*

Welcome. I and the others invite you to board our coach, our personal "theme ride." We hope you enjoy the journey.

But you might consider leaving your valuables at home.

©'96
danforth

# GIVE A MAN A HORSE HE CAN RIDE

## *by Esther Friesner*

History knows him as Ethelred the Unready. We know *her* as Esther the Ubiquitous. But with sound reason: she's very good, and very funny. Esther Friesner has frequently been nominated for the Nebula and Hugo Awards, and in 1996 she won the short story Nebula for "Death and the Librarian." Recent novels include *The Sword Of Mary,* sequel to *The Psalms Of Herod,* and *Child Of The Eagle.* She is also a contributor to and editor of anthologies, including the infamous *Chicks In Chainmail.* Esther's story is about Dick Turpin and a tree. While Esther has seen the actual tree, she has not to my knowledge seen Dick Turpin. (But then, with Esther, you never know. . . .)

"Knavesmire," said the gaffer, coming to a footsore stop in the lee of a small grove of oak trees. Dusk was falling, the velvet shadows painting the little woodland with the same tender hues they lavished upon the cathedral towers of distant York Minster. "And you won't be finding a place more worthy of its given name, though you travel from Land's End to the Orkneys."

"Thank you very much," said Lady Caroline from her perch atop the docile bay mare, "but such a voyage was not in my plans for the immediate future."

With a daintiness that had made her the belle of more than one rout at Bath (and which had also drawn the Prince Regent's wandering eye too frequently for her peace of mind) the lady descended from her horse unaided and approached her guide on his own level. "You are certain this is the place?" she inquired, looking all about. "For a site as deserving of its name as you paint it, it strikes me as singularly lacking in bogland."

"Oh, quite sure, yer ladyship," the old man replied. He patted the flank of one old oak tree in particular. "Bogs and mires be chancy things at best, and the summers hereabouts been unconscionable dry of late, but this be the place, sure as houses. Matter of fact, it were 'pon this very tree they slung the rope that took Dick Turpin's life."

Lady Caroline's elfin features contracted into a moue of blatant disbelief. She cocked her head now this way, now that, as she regarded the purported hanging oak, until at last she said, "Lie to me again, and I don't care how old you are, I shall have you whipped."

The old man's mouth dropped open, revealing a set of teeth in the leisurely process of rotting from discolored gums. "Yer ladyship, I swear on my mother's grave—!"

"Yes, you're a ready one to speak of graves," said Lady Caroline. She adjusted the set of her redingote and lifted her chin. "For all your fine talk, I'll wager you couldn't find your mother's grave any more than she could find your father's name. I have paid you handsomely to conduct me to the tree where the famous highwayman Dick Turpin was hanged. I did not pay you in clipped or counterfeit coinage, and therefore I do not expect to have a false tree foisted upon me. Either you are as lazy a lump of sheep's kidney as the good city of York ever spawned, or else you fancy that I am stupid. I would strongly caution you against this misapprehension. It will only bring you needless pain." She gave the air a pert slash with her riding crop to emphasize her point.

"Oh, now, yer ladyship—" The old man took off his unfashionable three-cornered hat and wrung the rusty brim between thick-nailed hands. "You haven't got cause to speak to old Jack King like that, an' me the blood descendant of Tom King as was Turpin's master in the gentleman's trade."

"Until Turpin shot him." Lady Caroline relayed this fact in a tone entirely devoid of moral assize. "Some say it was an accident. For myself, I know not and care less."

By now the old man's face had exhausted its full store of false contrition. A canny look came over his features, admixed with a cruel slyness that seemed far more at home there than any previously expressed emotion. "Just so, yer ladyship, just so," he drawled. "And how does it happen that a woman of yer own fine blood and bearing would come to know so much about Dick Turpin's life and death? For that matter, how do you come to say so certain that it wasn't *this* tree from which he danced his final jig?"

And so saying, he dealt the oak's bole a sturdy wallop.

"Ouch!" cried the oak tree.

"By that, for one," said Lady Caroline. Still holding fast to the riding crop in her left hand, she used two fingers of the right to reach into the opposite sleeve of her redingote and drew forth a length of peeled hazel twig. It had been polished to a satiny gloss, its buffed flesh incised with a series of arcane symbols, and yet there were still three tender green leaves flourishing at its tapered end. With this wand she struck the oak thrice upon the trunk, crying out in a foreign tongue as she did so.

When the last echo of those heathen syllables had faded on the twilit air, Jack King contrived to stop shaking in his boots and remark, "You all right?"

"No." Lady Caroline's mouth had become a rosebud of pique. Could eyes indeed shoot daggers, the oak tree of her attentions by now would have resembled a porpentine. "I am gravely disappointed." She shot a surplus glare at the old man. "Unless, of course, you were inquiring after my sanity?"

"Not to cast any doubt over that, yer ladyship—nay, nay, far be it from me an' all that—but there is some that say as how if you keep company with a bedlamite too long, too close, some of the poor wretch's affliction can rub off on you a bit. You see, I don't normally go about hearing oak trees say *ouch* in such a provoked manner, and so I was wondering if maybe—"

By now it was too dark to distinguish Lady Caroline's riding crop from her hazel wand. Therefore Jack King could not tell which one she used to slap his hat from his hands. "You are a fool, sirrah!" the lady pronounced, lovely even in her ire. "Because you have no comprehension whatsoever of my actions, you assume that I am mad. I am *not* mad. I am merely a witch."

"Ah," Jack King said, laying a callused finger aside his bulbous nose and tipping her a comradely wink. "In that case, I'll be begging yer ladyship's pardon, please, an' thank you." And with a low bow as rusty as his hat, he stooped to retrieve the old tricorner and took off into the dusk at remarkable speed for a man of his years and infirmities.

Lady Caroline stamped her small foot and hurled any number of epithets after him, none befitting a gentlewoman's tongue. If she nourished any hopes of the man being shamed into returning under such a shower of abuse, she was swiftly educated otherwise. All that her petty tantrum succeeded in doing was spooking the bay mare. Like old Jack King, that placid animal's outward appearance was also deceiving, for it shifted its oat-fed bulk off and away into the gloaming at a phenomenal rate, leaving the lady alone and stranded. Lady Caroline uttered one last curse concerning horses in general, then slouched back against the oak tree, the spirit and image of frustration and despair.

"Come now, it can't be *that* bad," said the tree. And with those words a slender shape all veiled in green, skin the color of autumn-touched oak leaves, detached itself from the bole of the tree and curtsied before the lady.

"You're here!" Lady Caroline exclaimed, pressing her hands to her bosom in an access of delight. Her riding crop fell unheeded, though she held tight to the hazel wand. "You've come!"

The apparition cocked its head to one side, regarded the lady out of large, green, somewhat upturned eyes, and replied, "Of course. You summoned me. Bark and gall, it would be worth my life if I didn't come when called!"

"Then why didn't you?" Lady Caroline snapped, all her elation translated to pique on the spot. "Why did you leave me standing there so long and never show so much as the tip of your nose? How dared you dawdle?"

"I did not dawdle," the other countered in peevish tones, sore affronted by the lady's charge. "I responded promptly . . . for a tree. I have found that one's sense of time tends to be shaped by one's environment, and when that environment is heartwood—" She shrugged.

Her excuse was insufficient for Lady Caroline. "By heaven, you made me appear to be lacking in my wits, and before a bumpkin such as that ha'penny Methusaleh, Jack King! Creature, you are sorely in want of a whipping!" So saying, she raised the hazel twig high.

The Prince Regent had often spoken in rather terrified admiration of the lady's mercurial personality, although it must be admitted that a man who wishes to woo a woman to his bed is capable of the most monstrous falsehoods. Needless to say, the tree-spirit had no such designs upon Lady Caroline's virtue. The finely made, almost human-shaped hand gestured once, and Lady Caroline let out a whoop as an oak sapling launched itself heavenward from just beneath her petticoats. The bold young tree rushed upward hungrily as though starlight were its rightful meat, and it did not halt until it had carried Lady Caroline clear of the forest crowns.

In the circumstances, it was not unreasonable that the lady dropped her wand. The tree-spirit retrieved it and scrambled up the newborn oak, nimble as a squirrel. "My name is not *creature,*" she said, settling down comfortably on the branch to which Lady Caroline clung. "I am called Damia, a dryad by birth, profession, and personal inclination for going on twenty-five of your mortal centuries." She swung her long legs, prettily crossed at the ankles, and added, "I don't believe we have been properly introduced?"

For all her hotheaded and hoydenish ways, Lady Caroline had vast reserves of composure upon which to draw. She introduced herself to the nymph with as much aplomb as if the two of them had just met at the *levée* of a mutual acquaintance. Having given her name and titles, the lady concluded with the revelation, "—direct lineal descendant of the notorious highwayman, Dick Turpin, on my mother's side."

"Dick . . . Turpin?" The dryad's eyes went wide, then wider still. She knelt upon the branch from which Lady Caroline dangled and brought her face down to stare her unwilling guest right in the eye. "Prove it," she snarled. Her teeth, though small and perfect, were the sickly brownish-green of ripening acorns.

"So I shall, if you will be good enough to convey my person safely to the ground," Lady Caroline said, a trace of the accustomed hauteur sneaking back into her tone. "Do so at once, if you please."

Whatever proof she might be able to offer to validate her claims to Dick Turpin's blood, her devil-may-care attitude in the face of probable death seemed a suitable down payment. The dryad frowned for an instant, then stroked the young oak's bark. The tree gave a little whimper, but it surrendered most of its growth in short order, dwindling earthward until Lady Caroline could easily set her feet upon the forest floor.

Once Lady Caroline had recovered her footing, the oak shot back up to its former stature. The lady was still brushing bits of bark and moss from her redingote when the dryad closed in. "Well?" Damia demanded, twitching Lady Caroline's wand peevishly.

For answer, the lady reached into the neckline of her garments and withdrew a golden locket. Opening it, she revealed a miniature limned upon an ivory lozenge. The artist who had executed this work was not among those of the first water, yet he had contrived to present the lineaments of a more than presentably handsome man just out of his first youth. Damia stared at the painting and gasped in recognition. She made a grab for it, but Lady Caroline sidestepped her onslaught and dropped the object of her desire back into its hiding place.

"I assume from your reaction that you no longer doubt my claims to Dick Turpin's blood?" she asked oversweetly.

The dryad only stood there, pressing one hand to her verdant bosom. As one in a dream, she extended the other, bearing the wand, and offered it wordlessly back to its proper mistress. When she at length recovered the power of speech, all she could say was, "My poor Dickon."

Lady Caroline's eyebrows rose. *So the journals spoke truly,* she thought. *The trees themselves* did *give my forebear warning of his pursuers, and now I know why. Tsk. The splinters—! Well, here's luck for me at last, in any case, to have found the very tree where Turpin's leafy ladylove dwells, albeit it was not my original goal. Still, a useful find, and I do mean to use it! It seems that old Jack King has earned his shilling after all.* A smirk of no little satisfaction touched her lips. She promptly dominated it into a more politic expression of womanly sympathy rather than outright gloating as she stepped near to place one arm around the dryad's shoulders.

"So true a heart, so worthy of his love," she murmured. "Oh, my dear Damia, let us put aside our initial misunderstanding. I have come into this wilderness seeking you solely because of the affection you cherished for my ancestor." Then, to guarantee that the dryad took her meaning, she added, "The very *deep,* very *intimate* affection." And she contrived to blush.

Damia lifted her huge and luminous eyes to Lady Caroline's face. "You mean—you mean you know that he and I were—were—?" Here she burst into a passion of tears.

"There, there, my dear, I understand your confusion," she said gently. "Matters of sentiment in one generation are seldom meat for more than mockery in the next. It is to our shame that we assume that *we* are the first and only souls to have truly loved, meanwhile we treat the *amours* of our forebears as no more than a dated jest. I assure you, I have not come all this way and subjected my dignity to Jack King's abuses merely to laugh at you for what you and my ancestor shared."

"Have you not?" Damia's nose was dripping sap. Lady Caroline passed her a handkerchief without comment. The dryad saw to neatening her appearance and when she was somewhat better composed added, "Then what is your purpose?"

"One which you of all will most appreciate, Damia," the lady replied, twirling her wand like a spindle. "For I mean to bring back the wild, the bold, the wicked highwayman Dick Turpin in flesh as much as in spirit, to our several benefits."

The dryad gasped, a sound like an April breeze riffling new-spring leaves. "You can't mean it! It's against the first law of holy Mother Nature! Oh, you *are* mad!"

Lady Caroline merely twitched her nostrils and gave the dryad a condescending look. "My dear, a little more Bible and a little less bark and you could pass for a Methodist. Really, Damia! Where is the proud, wild, daring pagan spirit that so captivated my ancestor's heart? What would he say if he could hear you now, all flustered and twittering over so small a matter of basic nigromancy?" Her lips curved up into a tempter's smile that Prince Lucifer himself might emulate. "Don't you *want* to have him back?"

"Of course I do," Damia said. "You have no idea how much I loved that man. We met one moonlit night when he was just starting out in the trade. He tethered his horse to my tree and stretched out between my roots to rest. He looked so handsome, drowsing there!" The dryad sighed over the tender memory. "My heart yearned for him immediately; I stepped out of my tree for the first time in centuries. When he opened his eyes, I was lying beside him. Ah, me, I can still hear what he had to say about the moss stains after we—"

"Thank you, my dear, that is assuredly more than I prefer to know," Lady Caroline said briskly, looking most uncomfortable. "If you would be so kind, eschew all further revelations of a carnal nature. The high art of witchcraft which I practice requires its more resolute devotees to maintain a maiden state if we are to master the more difficult spells. I have done this, at some personal sacrifice, and I do not relish hearing about those fleshly delights perforce excluded from my experience."

"I beg your pardon?" the dryad inquired, perplexed by the lady's manner of self-expression.

"Don't talk like a trull," Lady Caroline responded concisely. She slapped the wand into her palm smartly. "Well, then, to work. The night draws on, and I have many pages of grammarye to read through while there is yet light by which to see." She produced a miniature volume from the inner pocket of her redingote, then offered the dryad what could only be termed a saucy smile. "Shall we proceed?"

"Proceed?" the spirit echoed.

"To the proper tree, my dear; the tree whereon my ancestor did breathe his last. The soul is best lured back to earth upon the spot whence it departed. As for the body, when death overtakes it violently there commonly occur a number of, ah, less than elegant muscular reactions. A measure of—" She waved her hand, as if seeking to pluck from thin air some tasteful way of expressing the malodorous truth. "—*control* is lost. Thus also it is easier to conjure up a new—albeit temporary—fleshly shell from earth which has known the taste of the old, even if that taste was only of effluvia."

The dryad gave Lady Caroline a hard, piercing look that as good as declared her skepticism in the face of so much thaumaturgical twaddle. However, like all woodland creatures, Damia was possessed of a good measure of curiosity, and so without much more ado she took the lady where she wished to go.

To do this, they left the woods, for the tree upon which the highwayman Dick Turpin had mounted to Judgment stood lusty yet lone in the midst of a fair greensward, excellent country for the grazing of horses. There were, in fact, a goodly selection of the noble beasts roaming at liberty over the grass, though for the nonce they evinced no interest in the interloping females, human and otherwise. In the distance a modest cottage might be glimpsed, far enough removed to afford the lady-witch as much privacy as her art demanded, and farther off still stood the grand old city of York.

"Are you certain this is it?" Lady Caroline demanded of the nymph who had become her Vergil.

Damia nodded emphatically. "Try your summons on it and you'll see: Not a smidge of life within that trunk, except what's proper to any growing plant. This tree has known a hanging, right enough. You know as well as I that none of my kind can endure inhabiting a tree that has been an accessory to murder."

"My ancestor was not murdered," Lady Caroline corrected her. "My disapproval and regret of the act itself notwithstanding, he was, properly speaking, executed."

Damia sniffed. "Proper speaking changes nothing about the facts. He was murdered, and we dryads will not consort with the spillers of blood."

"Very well, I see no reason not to take you at your word. And should you prove mistaken, we shall have lost nothing but time."

"Mistaken? Ha! I know trees," said Damia. "Let us see if you know as much witchcraft."

Lady Caroline did not deign to respond to the dryad's challenge through words, but through deeds. As calm and self-possessed as any mistress of a dame school, she opened her modest volume of cantrips and conjurations and proceeded to read therefrom in a good, carrying voice. Some of what she uttered made the dryad perk up her ears, as it was an admixture of various Classical languages. Some of her invocations left poor Damia entirely at sea, being either elder tongues or gibberish. All of it appeared to fascinate the horses, who flicked their silky ears forward and took a few cautious steps nearer the ladies and the tree, perhaps in hope of apples or simple adoration.

While Lady Caroline called upon whatever powers attended such esoteric harangues, she paced around the bole of the oak tree widdershins, every now and then closing her book to extract a pinch of dust or a glittering pebble or in one instance a dessicated lizard from the reticule ever at her elbow (There being only so many items one could conceal in the most utilitarian of redingotes). These she tossed into the lower limbs of the tree, her eyes always averted.

Throughout the rite, the dryad observed the mortal woman's doings with a growing measure of intrigue. Being a natural sort of creature, she went where her interests led her, in this case into the branches of the tree itself. From this vantage she had a most satisfactory view of Lady Caroline's perambulations, or at least it was satisfactory until the dried lizard landed in her lap. When this happened, the dryad let loose a shriek that might have done the most missish of parson's daughters proud, and tumbled out of the tree directly upon the lady below.

Lady Caroline's humour at this turn of circumstance was not to be gauged. "Get off me, you tuppenny moss-monger," she snarled, her face on a level with the oak's root. "You've ruined my spells. Run fast and run far. If I catch you, you may account yourself fortunate if you don't spend the rest of your days as a cut-rate topiary arrangement." With a mighty effort, she thrust herself up from the ground and rounded upon the still startled dryad.

"It was an accident," Damia replied with the air of being the wounded party in the case. "Your own fault, what's more. *Some* people watch where they fling their lizards."

"*Some* people know that to raise the dead, one must keep one's eyes to the earth. The spells for revivification are dangerously close kin to those for demonic evocation. Unless *you* feel up to confronting a Prince of the Netherworld and explaining it was all a mistake?"

"Hunh! I think that a *real* witch could handle such trifles. And I think I have nothing to fear from a hedge-witch like you. Topiary indeed!"

"So?" A monitory light crept into Lady Caroline's eyes. She opened her pocket grimoire to its most well-perused section, namely that covering all spells of blasting, blighting, obliterating, and blemishing the complexion of rivals. "Then in deed be it!" And she began to rattle through a series of verses in dog-Mykenean.

Poor Damia! She recognized both the meaning of the words and their intent. She tried to flee, but found herself literally rooted to the spot. Lady Caroline had selected the tried-and-true spell preferred by the Olympians themselves when turning ex-lovers or close relations into plant life. It had been used to good and lasting effect on Hyakynthos, Adonis, Daphne, and a whole seed catalog of others. Having her victim possessed of a pre-existing affinity to vegetation only made the young witch's task all the easier.

It was just as the feathery gray bark reached the dryad's shins that the soil at the oak's root gave a tremendous groan. Dirt humped itself up from below, then fell away in smutty showers. From out of the loamy heart of that unnatural eruption there stepped a naked man. He was tall and lean—although by no means meager-fleshed—just past his first youth, well-formed in all his parts, with long, chestnut hair and laughing eyes. These latter took in the situation at a glance, and without a moment's hesitation he stepped up to the assailed dryad and plucked her from the toils of Lady Caroline's spell as though she were a daisy on the village common.

Damia gazed into his face for a heartbeat, then gave a squeal of rapture and locked arms and legs around him in an embrace as enthusiastic as it was improper. The man endured these attentions with an expression of bemused affection, though eventually he disentangled the nymph from his person and set her feet upon the ground once more.

Lady Caroline could not restrain a look of regal triumph as she stepped forward to present herself to the resurrectee. "Cousin Richard, I presume," she said, with a slight curtsy. His nakedness in no way nonplussed her. Her studies in the forbidden arts had long since accustomed her to the fact that most of the arcane beings one summoned inevitably arrived on the scene in want of haberdashery.

"Cousin, is it?" The man took her hand and raised it to his lips. "Not too close a degree of consanguinity, I hope?" There was no mistaking the earthy intent behind his gallantry, and the sheer power of insinuation in his voice made Lady Caroline blush where his nudity could not. Flustered, she muttered a minor charm which caused him to be instantly clothed in a fine gentleman's ensemble proper to his own time. The effect was both antique and alluring.

"I have not recalled you to life for any such reason," she said hastily.

"There's a pity," he murmured, while behind him Damia stood with hands on hips, a fine steam rising from her lissome body.

"Cousin, I am a practical woman," Lady Caroline began.

"Then there's a waste," the rogue cut in, giving her a goatish glance.

"*Practical,* I said." Lady Caroline subdued the obstreperous beating of her heart, which ungovernable organ had been so stirred by so little as a meaningful glint in the resurrectee's eye. "I do not risk more at the card table than I can afford to lose, nor—much as I adore them—do I frequent the races unless I may comfortably lose every wager I choose to make."

"Oh, *practical,* is it?" Damia sneered. "How clever of you humans to find another word for *dull.*"

"Hush, girl," the bold Turpin snapped at his erstwhile inamorata. He then turned charming eyes upon Lady Caroline and said, "You must forgive the lass her discourtesy, who never had the benefit of your delectable breeding. Her bite's far worse than her bark."

Lady Caroline arched one eyebrow at her ancestor's jape. "*May* I continue?" she inquired coldly.

He cut her a lavish bow. "I should be heartsick if you did not. Pray proceed."

She gave a little sniff and went on: "*I* am practical, as I said. Unfortunately, my late Papa and brothers were *not,* and so when the last of these died of drink and wretched excess, I found myself confronted by the unpleasant fact that my inheritance was equally divided between jewels in pawn, estates mortgaged, and debts outstanding."

"Poor girl." Dick Turpin uttered a lusty sob that lacked both tears and verisimilitude as he hastened to gather Lady Caroline into his embrace. "What a tragedy! You must let me ease your heart." He proceeded to attempt this by reaching for the aforementioned organ, bravely defying all obstacles in his way, such as her bosom.

Lady Caroline gasped at such effrontery and used her knee to some good purpose. The notorious highwayman, so lately returned to the pleasures of the flesh, was now rudely reminded of the attendant pains as well. He doubled over, groaning, while Damia flung herself upon him offering solace.

Lady Caroline glowered at them both and shook her wand sternly. "Cousin Richard, your continued presence upon this earth depends upon my Art which, for your information, depends upon my virginity. To acquire the skills I now possess, I was constrained to pledge myself to three-faced Hecate, who is but another aspect of Diana, chaste goddess of the moon, the hunt, and the crossroads. Her disapproval of those who too readily forfeit their maidenheads is legendary."

"Goddess of spoilsports, you mean," Turpin said. "Let

her lead a mirthless, barren life if she fancies it, but why should she care if someone else has a bit of fun?"

"Perhaps because it's impossible to sneak up on your quarry when you're eight months' gone with child," Damia suggested. The old lovers enjoyed a fine laugh over that sally.

Lady Caroline was not amused. "If you do not keep still," she informed the dryad, "I shall fling you into the next parish."

"You and what catapult?" Damia challenged. She clung to the highwayman and prettily made huge cow's eyes at him. "You won't let her do anything nasty and magical to me, will you, Dickon? You saved me from her sputtery spells once, after all. You *can* do it again?"

Dick Turpin had a reputation for gallantry. This was no great thing, for in the ballads most of the gentlemen of the road were equally assumed to possess a certain inborn gentility, no matter the truth of the situation. Balladeers knew what their audiences expected and they delivered the goods. However, in Turpin's case it was true, especially when it came to defending a lady. This, even when the lady in question was more foliage than flesh.

"Never fear," he told her. "I am your man. At least I know that *you* won't spurn my gentle wooing." He placed one arm protectively around the dryad's shoulders and confronted Lady Caroline with: "If you want anything of me, you proud hussy, you had best respect this lady's person, else all I'll give you by way of aid is my boot to your backside and welcome!"

"And if *you* wish to continue enjoying your return to an earthly existence," Lady Caroline countered with a smile that would send a viper dashing for safety, "you will understand that you are in no position to dictate terms to me. The flesh in which you find yourself this night will melt away like spring frost in the first gray dawnlight. It is a temporary house of earth in which I have stowed your spirit only long enough so that you may answer certain questions which I will put to you."

"Oh, is that the way of things?" Turpin's brow grew dark as an oncoming thunderhead. "I cannot say as I care to have my soul shoved in and out of eternity by a mere chit of a girl like you."

Lady Caroline folded her arms across her bosom and said, "Nevertheless."

"Well, then, ask away, and much good may you have of it!"

"Dear Cousin Richard, I find your company so much more pleasant when you are cooperative," the lady remarked, smug as a cat stuffed to the whiskers with fieldmice *à la crème.* "I will not vex you overmuch, I promise. As with all the best spells, the one which I have used to resurrect you for my inquisition limits the questions which I may pose you to three."

"If any of them touch on the nature of the life after this, save your breath," Turpin sulked. "Whatever knowledge I ever had of that is gone from my skull."

Lady Caroline laughed. "And how practical would such knowledge be? No, no, Cousin Richard, my queries cling very much to *this* world. Tell me now: Do the old songs sing truly when they claim that you hid away a goodly measure of your ill-gotten gains before death claimed you?"

"True enough," Turpin replied grudgingly. He gave Damia's breast a squeeze to relieve his feelings of being ill-used by his headstrong descendant and went on to say: "A man must put something aside for his old age, or so I thought back in the days when I still fancied I'd *have* an old age. That's one of your poxy questions answered." He looked so sullen that poor Damia's heart was moved and she pressed her tawny mouth to his in a kiss to swallow cities.

Lady Caroline viewed this public display of affection in pretty much the same manner as she might observe the progress of a maggot across the rim of her marmalade jar. "Then here's a second for you, if you can spare the breath to answer it," she said crisply. "Where is it?"

"Where's what?" asked Turpin, managing to remove the attentive nymph from his face for that much time, at any rate.

"The treasure, you fool!" Lady Caroline shouted. "The fruits of your illicit career, the booty of the road, the mainstay of the old age you never achieved, the *gold,* you blockheaded ninny, the bloody great heaps of *gold!*"

Turpin clicked his tongue and shook his head in pity and in sorrow. "Such language. And you call yourself a lady. My, my." And that was *all* he said.

Lady Caroline took what time she needed to bank the

fires of passion and recover her icy facade, then said at last, "Well? We haven't got all night. Where is your answer?"

"Right here," said the highwayman, tapping his temple. "And that's three questions asked, so if you don't fancy playing the keyhole-peeper, my sweet lady here and I would prefer to have a bit of privacy for our revels. There's nothing like knowing you're going to die at dawn to add spice to the fleshpots of Egypt."

"Greece," Damia corrected him.

"I guess it doesn't hurt any to add a bit o' grease, too, if that's your pleasure," he admitted, "but I don't know where we're going to get any at this time o'—"

Lady Caroline howled, spooking the horses. As the beasts went galloping away over the fields, Dick Turpin sadly watched them run. "Now what need was there for *that,* woman?" he asked. "So much fine horseflesh, tearing breakneck across the parish, very like to run themselves sick if they don't take a tumble first and have to be shot for what's no fault of their own, poor darlings."

"Forget the damned horses," the lady gritted.

Turpin drew himself up to his full height. "Madam, I'll thank you not to speak so blasphemously of the good beasts that helped to make me what I was."

"You mean a human flitch of bacon, hanged from a tree limb to be cured?" Lady Caroline asked, all treacle and roses. Then, with a pretty lift of her shoulders she added, "Oh, very well, I'll see to the horses."

Her hazel wand pointed off in the direction of their streaming tails and described a figure-of-eight on the air. The plunging herd executed a smooth turn to the right, in perfect unison, and having wheeled about now came back toward the human trio, their gallop diminished to a canter, then to a trot, and last of all to a walk which ended when they encountered the lovely feed of ripe apples which Lady Caroline had so thoughtfully scattered upon the green a stone's throw from the highwayman.

Dick Turpin observed their feasting with a nod of approval. "That's better. There's hope for kindness in you yet, cuz."

"And what about in you?" the lady countered. "Now look, *cuz,* you know and I know that while I asked *three* questions, fairly enough, you only answered *two.* Why not tell me where you've hidden your treasure? It won't be doing *you* any good after this night, heaven knows!"

Dick Turpin regarded his descendant with the cool, hazel eye of disdain. "Even so, I can't see as how I relish the notion of it doing *you* any good either," he stated. "You're a fine wench, but too proud-stomached, your recent kindness to the steeds notwithstanding. If this is how you queen it when you haven't two ha'pennies to rub together, I'd hate to release you onto the world a rich woman!"

Frustrated to the limit, Lady Caroline began to chant a string of perfectly mundane curses, unlike the magical maledictions she had employed against the dryad Damia earlier that night. As for Damia herself, the nymph attended Lady Caroline's vituperative litany first with close attention, then with fading interest, and finally with a boredom so great it led her to inquire at last:

"Why don't you simply *make* him tell you? If you get to ask him three questions, shouldn't you also be guaranteed three answers?"

"Oh, my gracious *thanks,* my lady," Turpin drawled with utmost sarcasm. "What a royal help you are, to be sure!"

Damia shrugged. "It's almost dawn, my dearest, and so far you have put more effort into trying to seduce this mealy-mouthed mortal than to seizing the moment—and my body—while both of us are still alive enough to enjoy it. Athena was right: The only passions upon which a female may depend are the purely cerebral." She returned her attention to Lady Caroline and demanded, "Well?"

"I would compel an answer from him if I could," the lady reluctantly admitted. "Alas, the spell for revivification seems rather to rely on the resurrectee's common gratitude for a fresh taste of life than upon any inherent compulsory power of the spell itself." She scowled blight, boils, and pestilence upon the recalcitrant Turpin, who affected to study his nails in a most diffident manner.

"I . . . *might* be persuaded to be more grateful . . . *and* more cooperative if you might likewise be persuaded to—"

"Would you like my body?" Lady Caroline said with such abruptness that both Damia and her Dickon were fairly bowled over by the rush of words. Even the horses lifted their muzzles from the feast of windfall pippins and pricked their ears forward.

Before any of her astonished listeners could respond to

her unexpected offer, the lady-witch made haste to clarify it thus: "That body into which I have placed your summoned spirit is indeed a mere effigy which will vanish with the dawn, as I told you. However, it is within my power to employ a *second* spell to transfer that same spirit into a body already living. If you will tell me the whereabouts of your treasure, I am willing to share this, my mortal shell, with you." Here she lowered her eyes modestly.

"I don't know." Turpin stroked his chin in thought. "*My* bold spirit in a *woman's* body?"

"Considering *some* of the things you've put into—" Damia began, but her words devolved to mere inarticulate grumblings.

"And where would *your* spirit go?" the highwayman asked the lady.

"Nowhere," she replied mildly. "We would cohabit, unencumbered by the flesh, enjoying all the delights of that supreme union which it is said that only the angels know. And my spirit has no virginity to lose, so Hecate won't have any complaints."

"I don't know . . . I'm rather fond of the, ah, encumbrances of the flesh."

"The spirit is more reliable. It does not tire, nor does it ever shame one by refusing to perform at certain delicate junctures," Lady Caroline wheedled. "Moreover, in the realm of the spirit, size is never a consideration."

"Here, now!" Turpin bridled visibly. "I'll have you know that there never was anything lacking about my—!"

Damia sniggered nastily. Having lost game, set, and match, clearly she had decided to throw over any chance for the Good Sportsmanship award as well.

Hecate on the earth wore the guise of Diana, goddess of the hunt, and now her maiden votary closed in on her prey with skill and vigor enough to make her divine patroness proud. "Think, dear Cousin Richard," Lady Caroline pressed. "Think of what such an arrangement would mean for us both. I am young and hale and avoid physicians; I will enjoy a long life which *you* may share! Moreover, it will be a life of as much luxury and indulgence as your—I mean *our* wealth can buy. Or to put it in a way you will be sure to understand—" (Here the lady moistened her lips and smiled in a most beguiling manner.) "Your money *and* your life."

It is a rule well known in the finest of missionary circles, that one stands the best chance of making converts of the heathen (rather than having the heathen make collops of you) if you address them in a language that they can readily comprehend. Thus, too, with Dick Turpin.

"I'm yours!" cried the lusty highwayman, flinging his arms wide and attempting to fling himself also upon his benefactress.

"O sir, a moment!" she cried, raising one hand to forestall him. "I am unprepared. Only permit me to speak the words of the cantrip which will unite our spirits, and then the first touch of your ensorcelled self will effect the transference."

"As you desire, my dear," he said, stepping back with a gracious bow. "I would I had a glass of wine to hand wherewith I might toast our happy future."

"Here," said the lady, with a twiddle of her wand, and a brimming pewter beaker materialized in the gentleman's grasp. "Now shush. I have to concentrate."

And she did. A very pretty picture she made, too, with her violet-shaded lids lowered fully over her bright eyes, her finely sculpted nose tilted heavenward, little dapples of moonshine falling over her upturned face, and her lips moving rapidly over the syllables of the spell. As for her worthy ancestor, for all that he was an admirer of womanflesh second only to horseflesh, his first love was and had ever been the grape. He buried his nose so deeply in the first wine he had tasted for decades that he did not notice his scorned dryad mistress stalking off in the direction of the horses.

They stampeded just as Lady Caroline spoke the last word of her incantation. Having a field of fallen apples sprout into an orchard mere inches from your muzzle will tend to panic the most placid of steeds. Dick Turpin never even got a glimpse of the horse that trampled him just as the sky over York silvered with the first hint of dawn.

"Yer got a guest, yer ladyship." Old Jack King—older and crustier with years and wear—came into his mistress' presence trailed by an aging sprig of the British nobility. "Lord Penrose, as is."

"Thank you, Jack, he is expected. You may go," said her ladyship. Time had done little to dim her charming smile, and had added only a few threads of gray to her hair.

The living relic tugged his forelock and shambled off around the corner of the manor house stables without another word, leaving a somewhat miffed and disconcerted Lord Penrose glaring after him. "Really, Lady Caroline, a woman of your fortune might hire a better breed of servant," he sniffed.

"My taste in servants, as my fortune, answers to none but myself," the lady replied genially. "In Jack King's case, I confess to a frail, feminine sentimentality. I could not possibly dismiss him. And the old fellow *does* have a way with horses."

"Ah!" At the mention of the word *horses,* Lord Penrose's flabby face lit up, even to the wen at the tip of his nose. "Then you have guessed the cause of my visit."

"Of course." The lady signaled to one of the many grooms in attendance. The lad scampered into the shadows of the great manorhouse's capacious stables and returned leading a fine bay stallion. "Newgate's Pride by Turpy out of Moll Flanders," her ladyship announced. She regarded Lord Penrose the way a butcher might consider a waiting side of beef and added, "You have brought the payment?"

Lord Penrose could only nod, stricken wordless with admiration for the magnificent animal, son of that famous steed whose prowess on the British turf had won back for his lady-owner her lost patrimony more than tenfold. (And if envious tongues disparaged a woman for lowering herself to the racecourse, more philosophical observers deemed it only fitting that a fortune lost at gambling might be regained by the same means.)

"And you agree to the *other* terms?" Lady Caroline inquired. For answer, Lord Penrose plumped a chamois bag of golden guineas into the lady's hand and said, "I swear to care for him as close as if he were my own son, and never to show my face before you again should I allow any ill to befall him."

"Brooks? You heard?" Lady Caroline turned to one of her grooms.

"That I did, milady, and I'll stand witness to it," he replied in an accent that was startling in that it betrayed more of Oxford than of oxen.

Seeing Lord Penrose's astonishment, Lady Caroline demurely explained, "Brooks was always a bright lad. I sent him to University at my own expense. He is now our local magistrate—a wonderful position for one so young, and certainly a convenient return on my initial investment. And, like old Jack King, he is wonderful with the horses." The lady and her false groom exchanged a smile.

Lord Penrose's face darkened. "You have no need to resort to the law to keep me to my word. I have said that I accept your terms and I have made full payment for the animal. Count it out, if you like."

"Oh, no, my lord," the lady replied sweetly. "I see no need for that; I trust you. When it comes to the sale of any one of Turpy's foals, it is not the money that matters."

"You'd never tell that from the price," his lordship grumbled.

Lady Caroline affected not to hear him. "You see, it is to the noble Turpy that I owe all I have. Though he was no thoroughbred, he was a champion. I treated him like a member of the family while he was yet alive, and now I cannot help but think of his sons in the same manner. I only sell them to those willing to cherish them as much as I would. And now, my lord Penrose, if it would please you to sign this trifling document which Brooks has prepared—?"

While Lord Penrose grudgingly signed the trifling iron-clad contract in which his oath to watch and ward Newgate's Pride was given written underpinning, one of Lady Caroline's actual grooms saddled the animal for him. The last stroke of the pen was still wet on the paper when his lordship mounted to the saddle and rode proudly off on the splendid son of a champion sire, his dear-bought hope for the future of the Penrose stud.

Lady Caroline was still at the stables, to all apearances supervising the grooming of another of her steeds, when Lord Penrose came limping back about an hour later, bruised and tattered, attended by solicitous servants, and waving his riding crop like a madman. "What manner of demon did you sell me, witch?" he bellowed. "That limb of Old Harry hadn't gone half a mile before he took the bit in his teeth, tore out cross-country, and pitched me into a furze bush!"

Lady Caroline regarded him coldly. "And where is the creature now, my lord?"

"Damned if I know. Back at the bottom of the pit that

spawned him, for all I care. I want my money back and I want it now!"

"I see." The lady patted the sleek neck of the white horse before her and added, "I will thank you to leave my property at once, according to the terms of our contract."

"What?" Lord Penrose spluttered.

"I said leave," the lady repeated. "If you cannot even bring your horse home safely, you have obviously failed to care for him as promised. I owe you nothing but my prayers for your success in finding him again. Is that not so, Brooks?"

Brooks avowed that it was, and was backed in this avowal by a company of bullyboys from the village who had somehow contrived to materialize out of the shadows of Lady Caroline's stables. Lord Penrose did a quick tally of their strength and numbers, compared this to that of his attendants, and decided that force never solved anything.

"A *real* lady would not cower behind the law," he sniped as he mounted the same animal which had originally conveyed him to Lady Caroline's estate.

"A *real* lady would have been your breakfast," Lady Caroline replied evenly. "A *true* lady makes the best of what life gives her, even if that gift does not conform to her original plans. If it is any consolation to you, my lord, I promise to use the price of my poor lost Newgate's Pride to purchase some new shade trees for what was his favorite meadow. For some reason I simply can*not* get oaks to thrive on my property." She feigned a deep sigh and directed the groom to apply a bit more energy to the sponging of the white horse.

Lord Penrose glowered down on her from the saddle, wearing his wounded dignity like a cloak. "And *I* promise you this, milady: That I will have justice!"

"How nice for you," said Lady Caroline distractedly. She took up the sponge from the inept groom and with her own hands rubbed at what might have been a stubborn spot of bay-colored dirt on the white horse's left flank.

"Justice!" Lord Penrose thundered as he rode away. "I *will* have justice! To take a man's money thus— Why, it's—it's—it's nothing less than highway robbery!"

The white horse rested his muzzle on Lady Caroline's shoulder and laughed.

135F932A1750B1694431D1023C8F019531116571127AC588
100111101101
3A0267401BF77909DFAA61034CAB57933DE497B54401251

# KID BINARY AND THE TWO-BIT GANG

## *by Michael A. Stackpole*

Mike Stackpole is one of those authors at home in any universe, be they self-created or franchised. He is perhaps best known in the f&sf field for his "Rogue Squadron" *Star Wars* books, and novels set in FASA's Battletech universe, but Mike also writes in his own unique worlds. Fantasy novels include *Once A Hero,* the upcoming *Talion: Revenant,* and *Eyes of Silver.* Short fiction has appeared in several anthologies, including the tribute volume for Roger Zelazny, *Friends of Roger.* But Mike is more than a writer; he's also a *raconteur par excellence,* and a consultant and expert witness for the oft-beleaguered game industry. This story proves his versatility, his unique view through hackers' glasses of the world-to-be, his wit, and his wordplay.

I crashed into his domain though a back door, leaking data as I went. I quick-slapped a patch on the hole in my side, but that still left golden letters and symbols hanging in the air. I glanced at it fast, making sure it was ascii and not hex. As nearly as I could tell I'd taken the hit through a trolling ascii buffer—I'd have to go back out and recover the data at some point, but it wasn't important, and the damage was far from serious.

I stood up slowly and dusted off my avatar. If I'd walked into the Bitter Root Saloon in the real world, I'd have called it seedy. Here in OutLAW territory, the grunge just meant the proprietor hadn't upgraded his graphics package recently. It wasn't bad, probably only a couple of revs old.

I tipped my hat to the man behind the bar. "Howdy, partner. Sorry about hacking in this way, but I was in something of a hurry." I flipped him a gold Ike and he snapped the icon out of the air in his right hand. It represented a keycode to a discreet deposit on a Swiss cyberbank and would more than pay for the damage I'd done to his domain.

"Obliged." The man's avatar had golden eyes, which were novel the first hundred times I'd seen the same on others, but his were a bit close-set. "You hunting or hiding?"

"I was one, now I'm the other, I guess." I looked around the domain. It looked pretty small, but it had a stairway leading up to some doorways off a corridor, and I imagined there were hidden rooms beyond them. Through the windows I saw more buildings outside, but no other avatars wandering the streets. If it weren't for the age of the graphics, I would have figured his domain for a new start-up—a start-up that was going to fall to bits fairly soon. "Get much traffic out here?"

"Not really." He flashed my Ike. "Don't need much if folks pay well enough."

I fished another of the coin icons from my pocket. "I pay well. Set me up."

"Bourbon or beer?"

"Bourbon. I'll need the hard stuff."

The bartender's avatar arched an eyebrow at me. "Bad men must be coming after you."

"Yeah. Kid Binary and the Two-Bit Gang."

"Oh," he said. "You'll be wanting doubles."

Time had once been that ranging out on the information superhighway hadn't required fortification, but those were back in the early days before governments decided the nets couldn't be allowed to go unregulated. Regulations were set in place all over the world, creating Licensed Access Wards, or LAWs, in which behavior was proscribed and the average user was well protected. Corporations sponsored many of the early LAWs, with things like Disney-LAW and Six-Flags LAW still proving very popular.

To make the regulations and enforcement workable, the governments looked to software providers to create environments that could be controlled. Microsoft immediately released its Iconographic Domain Format products, setting a standard for LAWs everywhere. With IDF software, every user could create a graphic avatar through which he would interface with the LAW environment. Microsoft's first release featured a Wild West graphics package, and that quickly became the standard for much of the Western world. While some corporations and some nations created their own proprietary images, pretty much everyone built on Microsoft's IDF architecture, so MS icons could find their way into any LAW.

The main problem with the LAWs was the fact that the environments were perfectly safe because government E-rangers went everywhere and looked into everything. If a corporation wanted to conclude a deal of questionable legality, or wanted to transfer data of a proprietary nature between sites, doing so through an environment that lent itself to scrutiny wasn't wise.

OutLAW territory was born. Anyone with access to an IDF package, a computer, and a landline or cel-modem could create his own Personal Access Domain. PADs took the place of web pages pretty quickly. Many folks maintained them like a hobby: having one was like having an aquarium through which all sorts of odd things could swim. Provide access to interesting data files, create shortcuts to other PADs or LAWs, do on-the-fly icon modifications, and your PAD would become popular. In some cases the PADs became popular enough that a prop could make enough money collecting Ikes to pay for the upkeep of the domain.

The PAD I'd crashed into wasn't really that unusual, except that it seemed a lot more quiet than most others. I actually found that to be something of a relief since Microsoft had recently released Circus Maxx 3.2—a circus-based IDF—and I was sick and tired of seeing clowns running around. But the fact was that if this place didn't have a lot of traffic and the prop was running it as a commercial enterprise, he had to be providing services that folks were willing to pay for.

My avatar consumed the bourbon. I couldn't taste it, of course, and didn't get a buzz off it—though there were software patches that did allow for sensory disorientation. The bourbon here acted as temporary armor against shots taken by my enemies. Each ounce of the bourbon formed a data buffer through which another avatar's hunter-killer programs would have to chew before they got to vital data.

Most folks learned early on that if they're going to run through OutLAW territories, they'd best be working on a dedicated machine and keep nothing on it they weren't ready to lose. Combat in the cyberwest boiled down to sending modified virus programs out to trash the other avatar's system. When Microsoft released the Wild West IDF, it included guns and bullets—the latter being viruses that just logged a user off when she was hit too many times. Guns were the virus launchers and limited the number and size of the bullets any user could have ready to fire at any one time.

Of course that sort of Marquis de Queensberry combat lasted about as long as it took for the first hacker to pirate a copy of the IDF software. Now bullets varied in caliber and impact. A derringer might shoot something that logged a user off, or added donkey ears to his avatar, while a Sharps 5.6 Buffalo Gun would head-crash a drive or cause a power surge that would burn out a scanning laser on a CD-ROM.

The bartender looked at my avatar carefully. "You've been around a while. You should know better than to be going after Kid Binary."

"Oh?" I gave him a smile. "You know something about him?"

"I might."

"Like?"

"Like the reason they call him Kid Binary." The bartender mimed drawing a gun. "When he's on, you're *off.*"

I laughed. "Heard it before, but I've always liked it. What else do you know?"

"Something."

"You gonna be telling, or selling?"

The bartender winked at me. "A story told is just a story, but a story *sold* has facts in it."

I fished into my pocket and pulled out a big gold double-eagle Ike. I had them minted especially for me at my bank. The bartender immediately recognized how rare the icon was. I slid it across the bar to him, and it disappeared. "Give me the full Geraldo on this guy."

The bartender poured me another bourbon. "Kid Binary is a coach-poacher who works the Badlands. I don't get a lot of newsgroups out here, but word has it that he was once an E-ranger from the States who found out that some of the alphabet agencies were running black data through covert channels layered into LAWs. He took off some of their ones-and-zeroes as evidence and they set him up for a big wet-delete. They missed him, and he's been working from breaks to stop them and their pals in the military-industrial complex from taking over the world."

"I see." He hadn't told me anything I hadn't heard in slightly altered forms elsewhere. The Badlands were Business Access Domains (local area networks, downloads and security) which were a lot like PADs, but with nasty software packages that could hurt folks who weren't meant to be interfacing with them. To transfer data between Badlands sites, corps would "coach" them: layer them with shells of protective software that made them as appealing to deal with as a Bengal tiger crossed with a porcupine. Picking them off wasn't easy, and the list of Kid Binary's successful targets read like the Fortune 500.

The fact that Kid Binary worked from breaks explained how he had lasted so long, and could easily be seen as confirmation of an assassination attempt in the real world. While programs could disco a user or trash a system, data hijacked on the net had real world uses. Some corps, if they had a line on a user's true identity, would try to disconnect him from life, which tended to hurt a lot, and was usually very messy.

Breaks were cracks in the system that allowed covert entry. Every LAW and PAD required a basic address—the minimum being the phone number through which it connected to a server that provided access to the net. Going in through a break meant Kid Binary either hardwired access into a net or hacked his way into the phone company and gave himself temporary access points though numbers that were, thanks to his work, unlisted and untraceable.

"What's the story with the Two-Bit Gang?"

"Small-time data-sifters and code-pokers mostly." The bartender shrugged. "They mostly prey on nubes who leave the LAWs and go ranging. A couple of them—Doc and Hurrikane—are vets of the Samurai Invasion, but the rest aren't very good codeslingers."

I took another look at the saloon. "You get hit in the Invasion?"

"Not hard—I had protection."

"Right. Doc and Hurrikane?"

"Right."

I winced. "I think Doc is the one that got a piece of me."

The bartender nodded. "Like as not. Learned good during the invasion, that one did."

Of that I had no doubt. Executives in Kotei Software's Tokyo headquarters decided to dispute Microsoft's domination of the net about five revs back. They launched their Shogun IDF with an invasion. Ninja hackers infiltrated PADs and unleashed viruses that redrew the icons in the IDF software. A suit became a kimono, a ten-gallon hat became a helmet, and bourbon bottles became sake flasks. The Chicago Stockyards LAW became a fish market in nanoseconds. The assault came as a complete surprise, as did the strength of the reaction from the States.

Most of the folks in the States couldn't have cared less about Microsoft and their domination of the IDF market, but they resented the hell out of Kotei launching this invasion on December 7th. Nubes and vets flooded the Out-LAW territories and made up for with enthusiasm what they lacked in skill and software. The world's phone system locked up tight and would have melted down except some cybergenius unloaded a virus called "Fat Man" on the Kotei mainframe and the scent of melting silicon could be smelled across the ocean.

I held my hands up. "I don't want to cause you any trouble, but the Two-Bit Gang has gone and done something they shouldn't have."

"No surprise. They just use my place as a dead-drop for information, so they don't really mean that much to me. They long ago burned the goodwill they earned keeping them samurai out of here." The bartender smiled carefully and leaned forward. "If you want, I have some arcs on them. I'll let you have them cheap."

I nearly went for what he was offering because archived files about the Two-Bit Gang would be useful, and any data on Kid Binary might help me sort fact from fiction concerning what was out there. The problem was that to download the files, I'd have to lower my guard and accept data into my system. If I did that, I'd leave myself open to a virus attack or a sneak shot. "You tempt me, friend, but I'll pass."

"I understand." The bartender nodded and poured me another bourbon. "So, you an E-ranger or something?"

"Could be." I narrowed my avatar's malachite eyes. "You hear anything about their hitting a coach containing a code key?"

"Maybe." The bartender didn't meet my stare. "What was it for?"

"Scientists at a research lab in Kolwezi completed the DNA sequencing of the Ebola-Zaire B virus. They encrypted the genetic code and sent that to AMRID, with the code key to follow. Without the key, AMRID's people can't use the sequence."

The bartender shook his head. "Have the researchers send the code key again."

"Can't. Katangese guerrillas hit the lab because they thought the researchers were part of a government program to spread the epidemic, which they think the government has used to wipe their people out. The truck-bomb disco took out the lab and two city blocks around it."

The bartender poured himself a bourbon and tossed it off quickly. "Sounds like this code key could be really valuable."

"A reasonable offer might be made for its recovery."

"Pair it with the virus code, and you'd have quite a package."

My avatar nodded. Doing a DNA sequence on a virus was a great help in finding a cure for it, but advances in sequencing meant the technology became cheaper and more abundant. For next to nothing, a dissident force could manufacture a vial of some hideous plague and introduce it into a major metropolitan water system. Chechens were rumored to have done that to cause the Winter Fever that killed 250,000 people in Moscow during the winter of '07. That had been a gene-engineered version of the Marburg virus, and the harsh winter kept folks indoors, limiting the spread. Had it been summer or a mild winter, Chechnya would have had its independence.

"I can't let that happen." I shook my head. "From everything I've heard of Kid Binary, I don't see him pulling that sort of job off. I always thought he was kind of a Robin Hood."

The bartender shrugged. "Maybe they didn't know what it was they were getting, or maybe Kid Binary decided to get something for himself. Times a man gets tired of just making do."

"Anything's possible."

The bartender nodded toward the batwing doors at the front of the saloon. "They're incoming. Doc may be inclined to be reasonable. Watch out for Tenniel. He's just crazy mean."

"Thanks." I checked the two six-guns I wore, one to a hip. I had more bullets in my pockets and on my belt. I began to wish I had brought my Winchester .44 because it was more accurate at range, but its lack meant I was faster. That was the tradeoff with avatars—the more software options and armor you packed, the slower your processing time. Granted, running on a fast system could give you an edge, but in the Territories, you could only see an appreciable difference when going up against some Nintendo Cowboy thinking he's Dooming in God Mode.

My Colts would suit, I figured. Walking over to the doors, I noticed that the floorboard creaked and the doors themselves needed oiling. Even a tumbleweed skitter-click-clacked along the boardwalk and a dust-devil hissed as it sprayed sand against the saloon's windows. I smiled. What this domain lacked in graphics it more than made up for in sound.

Down toward the far end of the small town setting that defined the rest of the domain, the Two-Bit Gang arrayed itself and waited for me. Doc was almost pure MSWest: tall, slender, black jeans, duster, hat, handlebar mustache, pointy boots, with a six gun on his right hip and a shotgun cradled in his arms. The only variation that separated him from every nube was the pair of samurai swords whose hilts peeked up over his left shoulder. The blades weren't particularly powerful weapons in cyberspace, but wearing them openly was a death warrant since many Japanese wanted to win them back. The fact that he had them meant he was good.

Next to him stood Hurrikane. The basic avatar had come from one of the fantasy IDFs that were popular with kids. Hurrikane had dressed a huge, hulking troll up in samurai armor; all of which meant he was armored through and through. He'd be slow, but he'd take a lot of codecracking before he logged. The weapon he carried was a flame-thrower—it made up in punch what it lacked in precision and elegance. Once it started burning code, you could lose a lot of protection fast.

I assumed the next person was Tenniel. He was pretty much stock MSWest, wiry and cocky enough to carry only one gun. Boots, jeans, a red-checked shirt, buckskin jacket, and brown hat completed his outfit. It didn't look like he was carrying much more protection than I was, so he was relying on speed, too, to keep him safe.

The guy next to him looked like a riverboat gambler, and I pegged him as Webster. He usually caused trouble by going into PADs that allowed wagering and cheating the nubes out of Ikes. At best he sported a derringer. He was probably the least of my worries, but I knew better than to dismiss him.

The last member of the gang looked, from moccasins and beaded loincloth to the feathers in her hair, to be every inch a Native American Princess. Betty.Drivekiller started with a DisneyLAW Pocahontas avatar, swapped sex appeal for modesty, and had slapped digitized butterflies on the halter top that strained to contain her sex appeal. She sported a knife and a tomahawk on her belt, carried a Winchester, and had a bandoleer of shells for the rifle looped over her right shoulder.

I'd have been impressed and even intrigued, but the way Betty kept checking out her reflection in the general store's window, I figured that behind that avatar was some adolescent boy who was correctly thinking that this was as close as he'd ever get to a pair of tits. His reflexes might be quick, but he was outfitted more for show than action. It struck me that Betty was really some whizzer nube they'd picked up to help them crack the coach with the code.

I nodded toward them and swept my jacket back to show both of my pistols. "Where's Kid Binary?"

Doc took a half-step forward. "I'm here. You deal with me."

"Fine. You've got something I want, and something you really don't want to be keeping. Hand it over, and I'll see to it that you don't get hurt."

"You think I was digitized last rev? I've been around." Doc jerked a thumb at the swords. "I've learned that information is power and power is always a seller's market. You want the code key we got? A million double-eagle Ikes will get it for you."

"A million for each of us," Betty added.

Doc shot Betty a frown, then turned back toward me. "You give me the money, Kid Binary gives you the code."

I shook my head. "Be reasonable. That code key gets

into the wrong hands and a lot of people end up dead—really dead, not bit-dead."

"Then take up a collection among them and pay us."

"Not enough time." I smiled. "I guess some bits are going to be flipped before we resolve this."

Doc looked down the line of his compatriots. "You'd go against us, all of us?"

"So many targets, I can hardly miss." My hands dropped to my guns as Doc's shotgun started to come up. I cleared leather and sent my first three shots at him. The first bullet under the hammer in each pistol was a dum-dum—meant to hit hard, which they did. The general effect was to engage Doc's armor and chew up some processing time as his software tried to blunt the trauma. The third bullet was a stinger. It punched through the crumbling armor and exploded into a hail of tiny viruses that immediately ate into Doc's face. His avatar's surprised expression evaporated into a cloud of golden hexadecimal gobbledygook, then his body flopped down on the dusty street with a delicious meaty thwack.

The prop really did have good sound files.

And the rest of the Two-Bit Gang gave them a good workout. Hurrikane's flamethrower roared as a stream of burning fluid jetted out toward me. I dove to my right, away from the saloon and beneath a wagon parked in front of the hardware store. I found my flight aided by a tug on my left hip, but I had no time to examine the wound because Hurrikane torched the wagon.

Hoping the fire and black cloud of data would cover me, I rolled to my feet and sprinted as best I could across the boardwalk and through the hardware store's plate glass window. It sounded better than it looked when it broke, and it had been coded with safety glass, so I didn't get sliced to ribbons going through it. I got up and started toward the back of the store, but the limp I'd developed slowed me down.

I hunkered down behind the counter and took a moment to look at where I'd been shot. I was leaking mostly ascii, but I caught some hex strings in the output. I was able to patch the wound on the fly, but what I'd seen told me who'd shot me and why he'd been so confident. Tenniel was using viper rounds. They get their name from an acronym for Virtual Intelligence Program ERaser. They seek out the little bits of virtually intelligent code that allow avatars to do extraordinary things. Viper rounds became very popular after the first comic book company released an IDF package based on their superhero universe. Various VI code packages were popular in the territories and I suspected Tenniel was loaded with code that, at the very least, increased his speed and helped his aim.

The hardware store's interior brightened as the snapping growl of the troll's flamethrower grew louder. With one twitch of his trigger finger he could turn the building into an inferno. A viper round might have helped take Hurrikane down, but since I hadn't been expecting to hunt superhumans, I'd not packed any code-kryptonite. Instead I rotated the cylinder on my right-hand gun to the fourth round, popped up as Hurrikane framed himself in the broken window, and shot him point blank with a parvo round.

Parvo is one of the nastier anti-avatar viruses available, and was big enough that I only carried one round with me at a time. The name is another acronym: Programmed Asymmetric Recursion/Variable Operation. It's also known as a palsy round because what it does is pump different values to the paired variables that make an avatar work, and puts the avatar through rapid repeats of operations. It wouldn't kill him, but it would take him out of the fight for a while.

As Hurrikane did a flaming Macarena out into the street, I ran for the back of the hardware store and jerked the door open. I glanced out, saw nothing, then came out running. Further up the alley, running behind the buildings, I saw Webster. I'd started to draw a bead on him when a bullet smashed me flat and left me to crawl to the cover of some discarded crates and a watering trough behind the jail.

The bullet had hit me in the back and punched out through my flank. It was only an ascii wound and the bullet had been a simple ripper round. It was a little more sophisticated than a dum-dum, but not as elegant as a stinger. I knew Betty.Drivekiller had to have put it in me, but I didn't know where she was, and that was trouble.

The crates and water trough offered me rather weak cover. They were basically icons—not as sophisticated as an avatar, but made up of the same sorts of ones and zeros. A virus would have to chew through them before it could get to me, but most of the atmosphere icons in a domain wouldn't slow down the sort of viruses we were slinging around. All they really did was to hide targets, which was exactly what I didn't want.

I glanced out past my crates to see if I could catch a glimpse of Webster, but he was less of a gambling man than I thought and didn't show himself. I swore and decided to reload, when I heard a heavy footfall behind me. I whirled back and leveled both of my pistols at the avatar behind me, but didn't fire.

A blonde little girl whose hair fell in curls over the shoulders of her red dress looked at me with concern. "Are you hurt, Mister?"

"Get away from here, little girl. This is not a place you want to be in."

She held a hand out toward me as she inched closer. "I can help you."

"Look, I don't want to be rude, but beat it." I holstered my left gun and dug into my jacket pocket. "Will you go if I give you something? Would you like some candy, little girl?"

Her eyes brightened as my left hand came out with a red gummy bear in it. The candy was an icon just like the coins I'd given the bartender, and in the real world could be exchanged for a coupon that would buy the users the candy they got on the net. Corporations had pioneered this sort of thing, and I kept candy with me because some netheads always remained in character no matter where they ended up.

"Cherry. My favorite," she giggled.

"Your lucky day." I flipped the gummy bear to her, and she plucked it out of the air with a certain amount of elan. Her proud smile dissolved into shock as the gummy bear's upper body grew to life-size proportions. Its arms reached out, pulling her close, then it snapped her head off with one bite.

I winked at her as her head floated down through the bear's jellied insides. "That, Tenniel, is why you shouldn't take candy from strangers." The girl's body collapsed, and the gummy bear melted over her.

Tenniel had been running a Proteus VIP that allowed him to shift to a new icon. If I'd let little Alice help me with my injury, I'd have been letting her in past my defenses to mess with my core code. She made the mistake I wouldn't by accepting the candy from me, and paid the price I'd have been charged for her help.

Tenniel had been good, though. His only mistake had been in being lazy. His Proteus program swapped bit-maps, but didn't change sound files. While he looked like all sugar-and-spice, he had the heavy tramp of a codeslinger's booted feet.

I took a moment to reload my guns, slipping stingers into the empty chambers. It occurred to me that my biggest threat at the moment was Betty.Drivekiller, and she'd been armed with a Winchester. That was a good launcher, especially if the user didn't want to get close to his target—the size of the launcher reflected the complexity of the code used to acquire its target. The kid wearing the avatar was using nube ammo, so I chose to assume he was using nube strategy, too.

That put her on top of the general store, hidden behind the lip of the roof. I rolled to my feet and stood behind the crates. "You're mine, Webster," I shouted and fired a shot at several stacked crates farther down the alley, back behind the general store.

Two things happened at once. Webster danced out from behind the crate I'd shot at and fired at me with his derringer. The slug took me in the right shoulder and scored hex. His shot ruined the second one I took in his direction, but I'd corrected my aim by the third shot and nailed him with a stinger right over his heart. He pitched backward, strings of hex spurting up into the air as if the avatar's holed heart were pumping alphabet soup.

Betty.Drivekiller popped up on the General Store's roof and triggered a shot at me. One of the crates at my feet exploded into golden alphanumerics. My first return shot went high, causing Betty to duck down behind cover, assuming out of sight was out of danger.

Big mistake.

Firing my pistols in tandem, I peppered the roof lip with stingers. They blew great honking holes in the clapboard siding, spraying data-lethal splinters everywhere. Betty jumped up and tried to backpedal away from the bullets, but a stinger caught her in the left leg. The avatar spun around, then tumbled from the roof and landed hard accompanied by a broken-bone cacophony.

I jogged over to where she lay and kicked the Winchester from her hand. "You weren't bad, kid, just not good enough. You need experience."

"I've had plenty of experience," she snarled at me.

"Okay, my mistake. No hard feelings." I dug into my pocket. "Here, have a piece of candy."

Betty smiled at me. She caught the candy in her left hand as her right hand was going for the knife she wore. It didn't help her.

I think she found it a *new* experience.

I limped back toward the hardware store, reloading as I went. I knew I had to deal with Hurrikane, so I pulled out the nastiest bullet I had and loaded it into my left-hand pistol. I spun the cylinder to put the aphid round next in line to be shot. Like the parvo round I'd pumped into him earlier, it wasn't really designed to be a killer, but Hurrikane had set himself up to be particularly vulnerable to it.

Dozens of little bonfires burned in the street in front of the hardware store. The hotel and restaurant next to the saloon was already fully engaged in a blaze. Golden symbols floated on the domain's ether to land on the smithy and stable's roofs, starting them to smolder. In no time the whole domain would go up, and replacing the graphics files would cost someone money or a lot of time.

Being a civic-minded individual, I decided to fight the fire. With fire.

Hurrikane had finally beaten the parvo. The avatar rested on one knee at the far end of the street while his user was undoubtedly working furiously to reset his variables. I closed my right eye, aimed the gun at him, cocked the hammer, and pulled the trigger.

The aphid round is an Armor-Piercing, Heuristic Interface Disrupter. As avatars perform tasks, the VIPs driving them accumulate experience—they literally amass trial-and-error data that gets factored in with user input to make the avatar function to the best of its abilities. Because of this limited learning capability, an experienced avatar in the hands of even a nube can be very effective.

The aphid round effectively cuts the avatar off from its accumulated experience and kicks the heuristic portions of the program into problem-solving overdrive. The program quickly cycles through all sorts of behaviors, though it will not do anything self-destructive. All avatars carry that self-preservation coding.

Hurrikane's flamethrower did not. The aphid round hit it and immediately started its tiny VIP running through problem-solving situations. Pretty quickly it explored the consequences of a simultaneous detonation of all the fuel it had left in the twin tanks. The resulting supernova immediately reduced the south end of the domain to twitching characters dancing like water droplets on a hot skillet.

Of the Two-Bit Gang and everything from the general store back there was no trace.

In the aftermath of the blast's tremendous thunder, I heard the sharp click of a double-barreled shotgun's twin hammers being drawn back. I dropped my guns and slowly raised my hands. "Kid Binary, I presume?"

"Right the first time out." The voice came strong and rich. "Turn around slow."

I limped around in a circle and found myself staring at an avatar I'd seen thousands of times before. It was stock MSWest, the Avatar with No Name. From the stubby cheroot to trademark squint and serape, it was one of the more popular avatars roaming around. The shotgun wasn't standard equipment, but it didn't add many gigs to the package, so this wasn't the first time I'd seen ANN hauling one around.

"So that's your secret, Kid? You choose a dead common avatar so you're hard to track?"

Kid Binary nodded.

I winced. "Wrong answer."

"What?"

"I know Kid Binary." I shook my head. "You're no Kid Binary."

"Yeah?" The shotgun's barrels came up at my face. "Process this."

He pulled the triggers, and the hammers fell. Two flags shot from the ends of the barrels and unfurled to reveal the message, "Bang!" The sound file that played was a raspberry, which seemed somehow seredipitously appropriate.

I hooked a toe beneath one of my pistols and kicked it up into the air, then snatched it with my left hand. "As I said, you're no Kid Binary."

ANN's face slackened and the cheroot fell to the ground. "You really know Kid Binary?"

"Yup. All my life." I smiled. "And the secret to my success is not picking one common avatar, but to change common avatars the way other folks change clothes." I gestured with the pistol. "And I believe you're wearing one of my hand-me-downs."

The avatar snapped its fingers and the ANN facade puddled at his feet like a silk gown. "I found it. I didn't know what it was or how to use it until Betty.Drivekiller started checking out some of the coach-cracking code you had there."

"That's kind of what I figured." In taking off a data-coach a couple of revs ago, I got hit with a tracer round. I stayed online long enough to pull the coach's data onto an opdat disk, then crude-coded an evasion VIP for my avatar. I let it run while I did a hard-disco—I literally yanked the cable from wall—before agency apes could find me and peel me like a banana.

The bartender kept his hands up. "How'd you gimmick the shotgun? You never touched it."

"Nope, but you took a double-eagle from me. I like to guarantee that those who take my money aren't going to be taking shots at me." I nodded toward his saloon. "I assumed you were the one using my old avatar when you started drinking, and confirmed that guess when Doc started asking for double-eagle Ikes, which he shouldn't have known I was carrying. Next time you communicate covertly with him, remember he can't keep a secret."

"Right."

"So, where did you find this thing?" I kicked the sloughed-off avatar onto the burning remains of the wagon and watched it melt.

"It was here. I was going to be out of touch for a while, so I set up a bunch of Guardian programs to keep hackers out. When I came back, I found there had been many attempts to get in, but only one had succeeded. It was your avatar. He was here in my saloon, downing bourbon after bourbon."

"No surprise. Self-preservation programming had taken over."

"That's some great code you've got if an abandoned avatar can survive being hunted."

"I like to think it's good." I frowned. "What disturbs me is that the avatar had a destruct timer. He should have been nothing more than a corpse when you found him."

The bartender smiled and leaned back, hooking a heel over the bar rail. "I put the Guardians in the perimeter and street here, but null-timed the building interiors, so I wouldn't have to repair the entropic decay when I got back."

"I guess that's it, then."

The man waved a hand at me. "Come back any time you want."

"I think you're forgetting something." I held my right hand out. "The code key." As he started to slip behind the bar, I added, "Just set it on the bar and move away from it."

Pain washed over the bartender's face as he set the glowing green cylinder next to the bourbon bottle. "Look, at least give me some of the money you'll get for it. How about ten percent?"

"You already have it."

"How's that?"

I shrugged and reached for the key. "Ten percent of nothing is nothing."

"But it's going to take forever to repair the damage out there." The bartender shook his head. "With money I could get a new IDF package."

"It was your people who blitzed your bits, not me." I frowned. "You still gonna let them log-in here if you fix the place up?"

"They're friends." The bartender shrugged. "What can I do?"

"Give them a place where they'll fit in."

Poaching a Circus Maxx 3.2 demo-coach wasn't that tough, and kluging it together with what was left of Bitter Root worked fairly well. It took a while to debug things, but pretty soon The Two-bit Circus and Wild West Extravaganza became a popular PAD. I thought it was kind of cute, the prop liked the business and the Two-Bit Gang, well, they protested at first, but after a couple of revs, those clowns felt right at home.

UBCVACE
ISOEPIL
DANFORT

# THE MOONLIGHT FLIT

## *by Rosemary Edghill*

This author is two people. Rosemary Edghill's recent titles include *The Bowl Of Night, The Cloak Of Night And Daggers,* and the X-Men novel *Smoke and Mirrors.* As eluki bes shahar, she has published the Hellflower science fiction trilogy. Both authors have contributed short fiction to various anthologies. (Other incarnations may have published more.) As editor, I published eluki bes shahar in *Return To Avalon.* For this particular anthology, I am moved to say a rose(mary) by any name reads as sweet.

There were two things that defined Morgan ap Twdr's life. One was the ability—it had been with him almost since he'd been able to walk—to speak to horses with almost more facility than he could communicate with his fellow villagers. The other was his passionate desire not to dig coal.

The new century ran on the fuel dug from the earth. From the lights that turned London's night into day to the new looms that were turning the midland weavers out of their cottages to starve—men and machines alike looked to coal to turn possibility into reality. And across Britain—and especially in Wales—men answered the call, toiling for pennies, investing their lives in a world that never saw the sun, a world that killed with casual cruelty through black-lung and cave-in.

If he did not wish to go to the mines—and he didn't—Morgan could take the King's shilling, follow the drum off to the Continent to fight for the English in their foreign war. But he was no petted noble boy with two thousand guineas burning a hole in his pocket. If Morgan went to war, it would be on foot.

Without horses.

So that left the need to find something that wouldn't

involve either mines or muskets, and that led him, on that raw spring night, to the library of a Shropshire country house.

The iron manacles hung heavily on his bare wrists. Laid in irons for a felon, and not even the hope of transportation or impressment awaiting him. The Magistrate wasted no mercy on grubby Welsh boys who'd had the temerity to make off with prime bloodstock. Had it been his fault they'd left the beast running free in his paddock for the night? An afternoon of drinking at the local alehouse had told him that they never brought the horse in for the night. Too wild to catch, they said.

*He'd* had no trouble.

It'd been rotten bad luck that had led him—barebacked and bare-headed—directly into a troop of militia boys being moved on the double up to Birmingham to suppress the hijinks of Captain Swing and his Luddite followers. Their colonel had been local enough to recognize the stallion, damn the luck—and worse than that, knew that Morgan was no groom to be out at this hour and riding where he should have led. He'd faced down the captain's pistols as one of the lobsterbacks ran for the Justice of the Peace—they'd gotten the man out of his bed to bind Morgan over, which had *not* improved the man's temper.

Now he was going to swing for it, like as not. Morgan sighed ruefully. Still, he didn't see what else he could have done. The horse had been just *begging* to be stolen, to run free of the ministrations of these chowder-witted English who didn't know how to care for prime cattle. And Morgan, who knew what a flicked ear or a cocked hoof was *really* saying, had felt it his Christian duty to oblige the beast.

As he waited for whatever came, he looked about the room. It was finer than any he'd ever seen before in his life—silver and crystal and not all of it together worth that prime bit of bloodstock he'd backed. He'd bet anything you cared to name that if he'd been able to get out from under their pistols, the beast would have left those job-cattle in the dust. The stallion was meant to run—anyone could see that.

"If you're quite through gawking?" a voice said.

There'd been someone here all along—someone he'd overlooked. Morgan turned toward the sound of the voice.

The man was sitting in a chair before the fire. He was dressed like a nob—fawn knee-breeches and blue tail-coat and no more jewelry than a few fobs and a cravat-pin—and a ring on his finger with a sapphire so fine that it would buy every man in Morgan's home village a fine dinner of French wine and roast goose every day for a year.

"Aye," he said briefly. The gentry—and this man was more than that by a long stare—liked it if you were properly humble, but for the life of him, Morgan couldn't see the point. He was going to swing next market day, he'd bet—well, he'd bet his life on it. He smiled again at the thought.

"I am Malhythe," the man said, standing. Morgan's heart sank. Even he had heard of Malhythe.

Colworth Rudwell, Earl of Malhythe, was a rich man, a Whig, and a man who suffered no fools gladly, even his own son. If he was not Prime Minister, it was only because he did not want to be. Both Mad King George and his feckless heir sought Malhythe's advice, and occasionally even followed it.

What could a man like that want with him?

Morgan stared. Malhythe regarded him balefully. The silence stretched. Malhythe finally broke it.

"It might be considered customary, in circumstances such as these, to inquire into the reasons for your presence in this house," Malhythe remarked.

"I imagine, m'lord, that you'll come round to telling me," Morgan said. He shifted slightly, and was annoyed to hear his chains clink. It was an unpleasant reminder.

"You are impertinent, sir," Malhythe observed, but not as if he were annoyed.

"And I'm thinking you might do a man the courtesy of offering him a drop, seeing as the man's to be hanged not three days hence."

"There's whiskey on the sideboard. Do help yourself." Malhythe turned and gazed into the fire, and his next words were addressed to the flames. "Are you quite set on being hanged, Mr. Tudor?"

"You're known to be quite a pernicious horse thief," Lord Malhythe observed a few moments later. He'd seated himself again, and invited Morgan to sit—an easy familiarity that Morgan mistrusted.

"Am I?" Morgan asked, pleased. Still, here he was, and the fire was warm and the whiskey neat. And there was nothing worse they could do to him than hang him.

"Clever, resourceful—and usually uncatchable. Whatever possessed you to try to make off with Halliwell's prize stud on a full moon night? Templeton-bred, half-brother to Torchlight, out of Witchfire . . . you can't have imagined he'd just *overlook* the beast's disappearance?"

Morgan ignored the discussion of his prize's breeding—although anyone in his line of work had at least heard of Marcus Templeton's Sussex stud—he wouldn't have been able to sell the animal as itself, so why know who its parents were? "I can't imagine what came over me, sir," he said piously.

Malhythe gave him a sour look and took a sip from his glass before he went on. "It was exceptionally foolish of you. Still, it's brought you to my hand—and I've need of a man like you."

Now they came to it. Morgan leaned forward in his chair, the drink in his hand and the bands on his wrists forgotten.

"I am a man who likes to know what's going on around him, especially among that class of people who might, shall we say, be prepared to be less than exact in their observance of the law."

"You want me to turn informant," Morgan said, intrigued and revolted at the same time. It wasn't a new concept to him. Didn't the mine owners have their informants among the miners, to warn them of troublemakers and the possibility of strikes?

But Morgan didn't work in the mines. And he was damned if he would, even to keep from hanging.

"Not precisely. I'll want you to pass me what information comes your way in the course of your duties, but I'm not asking you to spy. I'm asking you to steal."

There was a pause, then Morgan burst out laughing. "Me? Steal? For *you?* What in the good Lord's name is there you could want that you couldn't have for the asking?"

Malhythe smiled thinly. "It's a quizzing glass. And a young lady has just lost it at cards."

The Mirror Rose had been in the Hanaper family since before anyone could quite remember. An antiquary who'd seen it suggested that the stone itself was possibly Roman—a disk of ruby roughly two inches in diameter, with a silvery flaw in the center of the stone whose shape had given the gem its name. It had been reset several times, though always as a quizzing glass. The present setting was believed to be Jacobean.

The Mirror Rose belonged, at present, to Sir Geoffrey Hanaper, principal private secretary to Endymion Childwall, Marquess of Rutledge. My lord had occasion, in the course of his work for the Crown, to communicate in code—long letters which his secretary carefully encrypted into a code which the French had thus far not been able to break.

As might be assumed, this cipher was a hotly sought-after item. A prudent man would keep it in a safe place, and so Sir Geoffrey did: in plain sight. He carried the Mirror Rose whenever he attended upon Lord Rutledge—no one would be surprised at the presence of so notorious a family treasure about its owner's person; neither would they be surprised that so valuable an object reposed in the Hanaper safe when it was not actually being worn.

Unfortunately, Sir Geoffrey rejoiced in the possession of two lovely children: Griffin and Vanessa.

It was Vanessa who'd begged to wear the Mirror Rose to Gabriel Daltrey's card party, and Vanessa's mother who'd acquiesced. Stockford, the butler, had been the only inhabitant of Hannay House possessed of the safe's combination, but Stockford was a fond elderly man, grown old in the Hanaper service, who saw no reason not to do as Her Ladyship directed. Sir Geoffrey was safely away on a flying visit to Town while all of this transpired, or that worthy's good physician could hardly have answered for the strain upon Sir Geoffrey's heart—especially when it would come time to break the news to him that his beloved daughter had staked the family heirloom upon a hand of whist . . . and lost.

While it is true that Mr. Daltrey should not have encouraged such a bet, and, it having been made, was nearly honor-bound to return the stake, some fault must also append to the Minerva Press, for publishing the works which Vanessa devoured with such assiduousness, containing as they did heroines by the score prone to make such hasty pledges with little thought of the explanations that would come due thereafter.

"We have had our eye upon Daltrey for quite some time, and suspect that he knew what he was doing when he romanced the silly chit into making her grand gesture. Now he has the Mirror Rose, and should he succeed in sending it home to France, not only those communications already dispatched, but those which cannot now be sent securely, will be imperiled."

Morgan leaned back in his chair. He basked in the warmth of the fire and thought about pouring himself another whiskey. "So you're wanting me to go after this Daltrey and snabble the sparkler and the codebook back. But what I don't ken is why you're wanting me for the job; it sounds simple enough for even an Englishman to manage it. Daltrey can't be a very bright lad, letting you know he'd rumbled you. Why didn't he just take the what'd'ye'callit out of the thing and give the girl her pretty back?"

"It can't be done. The codebook isn't inside the quizzing glass—it *is* the quizzing glass. The five bands along the handle are engraved with letters in the Hebrew, Greek, and Latin alphabets. Once the rings are set in whatever combination, it becomes the key to the cipher. The Mirror Rose is the key in the most literal sense—who has the key has Hanaper's code," Malhythe said.

Morgan considered this. "Well, all I can say is that it all sounds deuced smoky to me. Still, if you want me to noddle off and lift this gentry-cove's bawbees—what's in it for me?"

Malhythe studied his gleaming fingernails by the fire's light for a moment. "You are to be hanged on market day," he observed mildly.

"Indeed I am," Morgan said amiably. "And if I am, the women in every valley for miles around will weep for me. And your pretty toy will be on its way to Boney."

Malhythe smiled, as if in some way Morgan's answer had pleased him. "Very true. And it would be . . . convenient to me if young Gabriel was not entirely certain *why* he had been relieved of this particular piece of jewelry. So I will provide to you four things: the key to your manacles, the open door of this study, unfettered access to that stallion you seem to have taken such an interest in—and a place at which you may exchange Hanaper's Mirror Rose for gold once you've obtained it."

Morgan considered the matter. There'd been no mention of a pardon, and now this fine English lord was asking him to commit highway robbery, a crime for which the Redbreasts were often brought in by the parish in which the crime had been committed—and Bow Street's famous Runners were more than happy to oblige, with the fat reward of golden guineas (mandated by Royal warrant) in the offing. On the other hand, his only other choice was to dance at the rope's end Wednesday next. Not appealing.

"I'm your man," Morgan said enthusiastically, standing and holding out his hands to be unshackled.

Malhythe held up the key. It sparkled in the firelight, as hard and unyielding as his lordship's damnable eyes. "I shall only observe," he said, fitting the key into the lock, "that should you fail of performance in this small matter, I shall have you in hand again within a fortnight—though, if you would care for some advice, it would be much better for you had you put a period to your own existence long before that."

For a long moment, Morgan stood frozen. The irons dropped from his wrists, and still he didn't move.

"Don't worry yourself, m'lord," Morgan said, his voice slightly hoarse. He'd heard the words that Malhythe had said—and, more, he *believed* them. "You'll have your pretty. Only tell me where and when you want it lifted."

"Go to this address—can you read?" Malhythe demanded, producing a paper from within his coat. Morgan nodded numbly, blessing his schoolmaster father who'd given him his letters—not only in English, but in his native French. The Welsh tongue had been his mother's only legacy to him, and a poor one in an age that had made its very utterance punishable by fine and imprisonment.

"Good."

Malhythe held out the scrap; Morgan took it and stuffed it into a pocket of his battered moleskin coat.

"The butler at that house will give you the rest of your instructions—including where to find Mr. Daltrey. Now go. The moon will set in a few hours, and you'd best be out of the county before the hue and cry is raised." For an escaped horse thief—which was what he was about to become.

But Morgan, turning his back on his strange mentor and striding toward the uncurtained French doors that even now stood ajar, thought it would be much better to be a horse thief that the Earl of Malhythe had some use for than a Duke that he did not.

*"And may the devil be in heaven an hour before YOU'RE dead,"* he added in his mother's tongue as he stepped through the doors and headed in the direction of the stables.

Gabriel Daltrey had every reason to be pleased with himself this soft spring night—not the least of which being that he was no longer buried in the country, pitching woo at that sheep-eyed Hanaper girl. Her father was Rutledge's man—everyone in Daltrey's set knew that—but access to state secrets, even thirdhand, had not rendered the silly chit one whit more agreeable.

And he hadn't gotten the state secrets either—the silly chit was remarkably deaf to suggestions that her father's study might be an agreeable place to spend an hour or two. He hadn't been able even to procure an invitation to dinner at Hannay House in his entire month here.

No, that covert had been drawn to no good effect, and now he must go to meet Tallyrand's courier all-but-empty handed. Well, he would send him the Mirror Rose. Perhaps the story of how Daltrey had tricked an English family out of its heirloom treasure would turn the French spymaster up sweet, and certainly Daltrey needed goodwill from that quarter far more than he needed the few thousand pounds the sale of the relic could bring him.

The coach rocked gently across Hounslow Heath in the direction of London. Daltrey was returning from a party at the little house of one of *bas* society's most famous—or infamous—hostesses, the woman known simply as Aspasia. No one knew who had her in keeping, but whoever the old devil was—and no amount of coaxing could induce the charming barque of frailty to say—he kept her on a light rein. An invitation to Aspasia's delightful house in St. John's Wood promised an evening of deep play, the company of a number of charming not-quite-ladies, and a number of other inducements as well. Aspasia's little house was where Buck and Blood, Pink and Corinthian, met on an equal footing. It was fertile ground for one who hunted such game as Daltrey did, and he had taken several scents tonight that promised good hunting later.

But that wouldn't save him tonight when the clock struck three.

Daltrey's good mood faded as the hour for the meeting drew nearer—by the watch in his pocket, as well as with every revolution of the coach's wheels. He'd spent too much time this spring trying to gain entry to Rutledge's set, and it had failed. He didn't believe that Hanaper knew anything of moment in the first place—and whose fault was that? Not his. Daltrey could only course what he was set upon. The days when half of London knew the identity of the Scarlet Pimpernel and held its tongue were gone—this was 1805, for God's sake, not the middle of the Dark Ages!

"Stand and deliver!"

The shout went up just as his team of well-bred grays shied to a halt, yanking the carriage this way and that, and knocking Daltrey to the floor. He heard the guard on the box discharge his musket fruitlessly into the air; he heard the crisper pop of a pistol, and a thin scream. The dispatch he meant to deliver in Covent Garden an hour hence spilled from its case, and he was still scrabbling for the papers when the coach door was yanked open.

"Stand and deliver," a lilting voice said.

Daltrey looked up, into a face out of . . . history.

The apparition wore a dusty gold-laced tricorn upon his head, pulled well down over his eyes. The lower part of his face was swathed in a muffler of purple silk, and he wore a scarlet coat with deep cuffs, gleaming satin facings, and row after row of tarnished silver-gilt buttons. It was such a coat as Daltrey's grandfather might have worn.

Just as highwaymen were an affliction from that time, not this.

Where was Bow Street's Mounted Patrol, that should have saved him from this? Where was the militia, whose quartering within the very town was supposed to discourage brigands? Daltrey stared into the gleaming barrel of an all-too-modern Manton and wondered in despair how he could ever have worried about Talleyrand's displeasure when there was such a clear and present danger here at hand.

The coach rocked as the guard and coachman, witlessly following the armed man's bidding, unharnessed the team. Daltrey groaned. Those tits would be in Scotland by morning, and he'd be stranded here—just as the highwayman intended.

"Well, m'lord? Will you hand over your pretties? Or do I blow your head off and loot the body?" From the amiable sound of his voice, either alternative was acceptable.

"You'll never get away with this," Daltrey groaned.

The stranger appeared to consider this.

"It's very likely that you're right, m'lord, and no mistake. Prigging the ginger on the High Toby is no life for a man as wishes to make old bones," he said with regret. "But if you'd be so kind as to hand it over at once; it's a raw night out, and I don't like to make the horse stand any longer than I must."

A volley of shouts and the thunder of hooves assured Daltrey that some horses, at least, were not standing at all. He ground his teeth. He only hoped the highwayman's horse had run off as well—no, he hoped that the animal would bolt with its master aboard and break both their necks—or, better—

"And you!" the highwayman shouted over his shoulder. "You lot be off—'tis a long walk to Town to fetch help for your good master here."

His pistol did not waver as he spoke, and Daltrey saw a bulge in his deep coat pocket that must be at least one more. Loaded, and if the lead ball didn't end your days, then the attentions of a Harley Street surgeon afterward were surely enough to make any man stick his spoon in the wall.

"Your blunt, m'lord," the highwayman said again. "And your seals and fobs, your rings, that diamond you've got stuck there in your cravat—and that bauble around your neck. If you please."

It wasn't that much. He could win its equivalent at the tables any night his luck was in. The only mercy in all of this, Daltrey reflected, was that the man didn't know who he was—nor that the papers at his feet were as good as a charge of High Treason any day of the week.

Hands shaking with resigned fury, Daltrey lifted the chain of the Mirror Rose over his head. He'd have to find some other way to turn his French masters up sweet, but the story should still amuse—even if now he was the butt of it.

Who the devil would have thought he'd meet a highwayman in this day and age?

"You didn't take the papers?" the Earl of Malhythe said.

"D'ye think I'm quite addlepated? Your man told me to leave any writing I saw, and so I did. It was a shabby trick you played me with these scarecrow traps, though. I ought to have served you back and taken the lot."

"But that would not have pleased me," Malhythe said simply, "and this surely does." He held the Mirror Rose up to the candle that sat between them on the table, and the light struck through the ruby lens, making the silver rose blossom.

The two men sat in the kitchen of a house in Stepney. This house was not a house known to belong to the Earl of Malhythe, though it was one of several properties he owned. Officially, Malhythe was not yet in Town, though the Season was already fairly begun. But Malhythe's own fashionable house did not yet have its knocker upon the door, and its fine Adam and Hepplewhite furniture was still swathed in veils of Holland cloth, awaiting its master's arrival.

There were other things to occupy Malhythe's attention.

Morgan had been here once before; its steward was a remarkably stubborn and close-mouthed man, but there'd been good stabling for the stallion and a warm bed for its master, and Morgan had learned in a hard school to concentrate on essentials and avoid useless questions.

"You have the quizzing glass, and whatever else Daltrey had upon his person. He retains the report that is . . . perhaps less accurate than its recipient might hope for. A good night's work, all in all," Malhythe said. From his pocket he took a small bag and set it on the table. It clinked when he did so. Morgan didn't touch it.

"Then I'm free to go?" he suggested, although he doubted it.

Malhythe didn't answer directly. "You'd better give me the jewels; he'll report them stolen, or their former owners will, and I shouldn't like to see you taken up too quickly."

"At all," Morgan amended. There was little point in arguing about the other—he dug into the pocket of that ridiculous scarlet coat and dumped the glittering golden litter on the table. It didn't matter what Malhythe was paying;

the fistful of yellow boys he'd harvested would more than pay their scratch—his and the stallion's—at some inn to the north and west where the innkeeper knew better than to ask too many questions of a man with a matched set of pistols.

"At all, I suppose," Malhythe agreed. "But as you've done me good service this evening, I confess myself inclined to look kindly on you in the future."

*May that day never come.* Morgan prayed fervently. "So our business is done. And I get to keep Moonlight?" Morgan confirmed.

"Of course. But there will be other favors—from time to time—that you will be able to perform for me." Malhythe smiled coolly. "And I thought you might like to see this." He produced a folded handbill from within his coat.

It was newly come from the printer; the paper still reeked of ink and the print itself was slightly smudged from the page's rough handling. As Morgan glanced over it, his heart sank. *"Wanted—highwayman—armed robbery—dangerous—wears a violet scarf—black horse—"*

The old devil must have been having them printed at the same time Morgan was robbing the coach. Maybe even before.

*"Fifty guineas reward?"* Morgan said in outrage. *"Mad Merlin?"*

"One must call you something," Malhythe said imperturbably, "and I dare say you would not wish to be known the length of England as Morgan ap Twdr. I think it is a rather good likeness," he added mildly.

Both men gazed respectfully at the smudged and nearly unrecognizable image of a glowering man in a tricorn with a scarf pulled well up over the lower part of his face.

"And now, there is one last task you must perform for me to finish this business," Malhythe said.

Vanessa Hanaper lay upon her bed long after the rest of the household had returned for the night. She was too exhausted even to consider how unbecoming she must look with her eyes red-blotched with tears. She had kept to her room all this past week since returning home from that disastrous party—but Papa would be home tomorrow, and the headache that would answer for Mama and even for Griffin would not put him off for a moment. Mama would tell him that she had lost the Mirror Rose, and Papa would send for her to demand a full explanation.

She could *not* tell him that she had lost the gem to Gabriel Daltrey over a hand of cards. She could not!

Only Papa would be here tomorrow—and the Mirror Rose would not. Mr. Daltrey had most disobligingly refused to return it after the party, even when she'd offered to buy it back with a kiss. Her tiresome brother Griffin—who, even Vanessa had to admit, was a crack shot with a pistol and *ought* to be the terror of any person of breeding or sense—had gone to see Mr. Daltrey the following day, with no pleasant results; Vanessa was forced to the painful conclusion that Mama had been right in refusing him the invitation to dine at Hannay House—Gabriel Daltrey was not truly a person of breeding.

Last night Grif had come to her again—Vanessa was keeping to her rooms, in hopes that news of her indisposition would reach Mr. Daltrey and wring his withers with remorse enough to induce the return of the quizzing glass—and promised that he would obtain the Mirror Rose without fail. But no one had seen Griffin today at all—not Stockford, who knew everything, nor even the indispensable Roberts, abigail to both Lady Hanaper and her daughter. Griffin had not come home last night at all.

Vanessa wondered hopefully if Griffin might not have met with a shocking accident. Surely that would distract Papa from inquiries into the whereabouts of the family treasure—and news of the family's bereavement must naturally induce Mr. Daltrey to come forward with a tangible token of his share in their grief. . . .

There was a sound at the window.

It took several moments for Vanessa to recognize it. Pebbles, flung from the gravel drive at the leaded panes of her window.

Griffin! It must be he! Vanessa scrambled from her bed—not even pausing to collect the cashmere shawl at the foot of it—and flung open the casement windows at the foot of her bed. She leaned out, into the moonlit night.

There was a stranger in a many-caped greatcoat and a tricorn hat standing beneath her window, holding the reins of the most magnificent gray she'd ever seen in her life. For a moment Vanessa was distracted from her own troubles by contemplation of the beast.

"Don't you want this?" the stranger asked. He held up a familiar object by its handle. The ruby lens glittered in the moonlight.

"Yes!" Vanessa gasped, feeling her heart leap within her breast. "But—where's Griffin?"

"Is there no female capable of restraining herself from idle chatter at moments like this?" the stranger growled. "I have no idea where Griffin is—in fact, I wish him at the devil. Now, d'ye want this or not, girl?"

"Oh, yes!" Vanessa said fervently. "But . . ." she continued, confused. If he wasn't a friend of Griffin's, how had he known to bring it here? Who was he? Had Mr. Daltrey perhaps sent him?

"Ah . . . long had I heard rumors of your beauty, fair maiden, and when rumors came to me in my low boozing ken of your trouble, it was a swift night's work to set right what had gone wrong at the hands of this foul rogue," the stranger recited, rather in the fashion of one delivering a memorized message.

Vanessa didn't care. "Is Daltrey dead?" she demanded hopefully.

"It's a bloodthirsty child, so it is!" the stranger exclaimed. "No, the beautiful Daltrey yet breathes—and if you'll leave off playing cards with him, I dare say he'll trouble you no more. Now give us a kiss, and you can have your bauble."

"Kiss?" Vanessa said blankly.

The stranger heaved a deep sigh, swinging the quizzing glass by its chain. "As I'm a highwayman, I can hardly give it to you for free, can I? I have my professional reputation to consider. Now give us a kiss, and I'll be on my way."

"Well . . . all right," Vanessa said doubtfully. She leaned out over the sill as far as she could.

The stranger—a highwayman!—remounted and brought his horse as close beneath the window as possible. He stood in his stirrups, and when he stretched his hand up to her, Vanessa saw that he was wearing a gold-laced scarlet coat in the style of a previous age. She plucked the Mirror Rose from his hand as his lips brushed her cheek. She heard him chuckle, and a heat suffused her, composed in equal parts of delight at her own daring and relief that there would be nothing, after all, to report to Papa tomorrow.

"Oh, *thank* you, kind stranger!" Vanessa cried. "But how can I ever repay you?"

The stranger seemed to be having some difficulty keeping his countenance after the benison of such close proximity to the goddess he had long worshiped from afar, but mastered it at last. "Ah, fair maid, your kiss is enough to sustain me through a thousand perils. I shall carry the memory of it to my grave." He settled himself in the saddle and drew on his gloves, taking up the reins again. Before she could quite catch her breath, he was moving down the gravel drive, his horse's footfalls a loud heartbeat in the stillness of the night.

"But—but—when will I see you again?" she cried after his retreating figure.

He paused. The horse reared up, and the highwayman swept off his tricorn in a dashing bow.

"Just look for me by moonlight," he said, laughing. And then he turned his horse and it galloped away.

It was only sometime later that it occurred to Morgan that Malhythe had probably been after him particularly, and had probably been the man responsible for penning Moonlight out in that oh-so-enticing fashion in the first place as well—but by then he'd seen enough of the Earl's cold-blooded manipulations in the service of England not to care overmuch. His pockets were filled with gold and his nights with excitement, and while someday he might yet swing, he would certainly have escaped both the Army and the mines. Beyond that, Mad Merlin had little interest in Malhythe's ambitions, and less in the mad Corsican who was drenching Europe in blood.

But in his work?

Ah, a man could take *pride* in his work.

danForth ©96

# THE BANDIDO OF POZOSECO

## *by Kate Daniel*

Until recently, Kate Daniel wrote primarily for teenagers, with various titles published in the *Babysitter's Nightmare* series. But she is a fine short story author for adults as well, as exemplified by contributions to *The Shimmering Door, Enchanted Forests*, and to this anthology. She's also a cook: Katie has *two* recipes included in Anne McCaffrey's cookbook *Serve It Forth.* (Readers may thus enjoy her work as well as her food!) As a fellow Arizonan, I was particularly pleased by the Hispanic setting and atmosphere of this story, as well as by its timeliness and topicality.

*Heat, thirst, so thirsty, Santa Maria, agua, oh, please I need water, I beg of you, Virgen Santisima, Madre de Dios, my son, water for him at least, you were a mother, Blessed Virgin . . . now and in the hour of our deaths . . . our deaths . . .*

The voice was so distorted, forced through a parched throat from a body with no moisture to spare for tears, that Rhonda Zimmerman had trouble recognizing it as her own. She clicked off the tape recorder. There was more, another three minutes of increasingly unintelligible Spanish and dry coughs, but she couldn't stand to listen to it. Hearing it made her throat ache, even though she couldn't remember making it. She picked up her cup and drained half the overly sweet mint tea. It helped. She rewound the tape.

It was no help anyway. No matter what method she used, she hadn't been able to contact the right spirit. There were plenty of ghosts in the area, which wasn't surprising; thirty-four years in Arizona had taught her how treacherous the desert could be. But she had found no ectoplasmic trace of her target, the one she'd been hired to exorcise after a local Catholic priest had failed. A bigger mystery was why this region of northern Mexico had been settled in the first place. Although "settled" might be the wrong word, she thought. Rancho de Pozoseco had no close neighbors; it was over sixty kilometers by road to the nearest town.

"*Perdoneme*, Doña Rhonda." She hadn't heard him knock. Her employer stood framed now in the doorway, one hand still on the knob, the unlit hallway behind him a dark backdrop to his almost theatrical good looks. It was a dramatic pose. Felipe Luis Maldonado Alvarez had a gift for dramatic poses.

He smiled at her with conscious warmth and advanced into the room. "Forgive me, I did not mean to interrupt your work. Do you make any progress?" Again the smile beneath the heavy mustache. The mustache was flecked with gray, as was the dark hair at his temples, the faintest hint of aging. His smile was all gallantry and flirtation.

One hand flew up to pat her hair automatically. She knew what she looked like: short and ball-shaped, with frizzy gray hair straggling its way out of an untidy bun. Turning back to her notes with an effort, she shook her head. "Mr. Maldonado, I can't find a trace of your ghost. This does seem to be a locus of great power, but there are no ghostly bandits and absolutely no malignant influences. I haven't even had a nightmare."

"I did not imagine the attacks, Miss Zimmerman." The suave manner cracked for a moment, and fear showed through. "A bandit of a century ago has shot me twice now, and even though it did no physical harm . . ."

"Certainly, certainly! My dear Mr. Maldonado, surely you don't think I'm questioning your word? Not at all, not at all. A *great* many bandits in this part of Mexico, what with Pancho Villa and the revolution, poor people desperate for a change—I read *all* about it before I came, of course—this manifestation is obviously *quite* focused, as though the unhappy soul felt a particular animosity toward you. Perhaps an ancestor, some ancient grudge against your family . . . well, I shall simply have to see what I can discover." She was dithering worse than usual, she knew, fogging her lack of progress in a cloud of nonsense.

He smiled ironically and inclined his head slightly. "I suppose I expected a miracle from my personal ghostbuster." She kept her face still with an effort; Rhonda had hated that movie from the moment it came out, and every client she'd had since then had referred to it at least once. "You have been here less than a week. But this . . . haunting . . . it's disrupted my life, my sleep, my business. Surely you can understand why I am so anxious for you to succeed."

"Oh, of course! Now, there's this one poor soul, quite recent—a widow with a nine-year-old son, age about twenty-seven, I think—there's a very strong connection with this location, although I don't believe she lived here. Maybe she died near here—anyway, she manifests *quite* strongly, and I thought, perhaps a seance, nothing elaborate, just the two of us, possibly you knew her . . ."

"Dear lady, I am interested in only one ghost. This poor widow—pardon, but she does not sound like anyone I would know, alive or otherwise. So, another dead end. If you will forgive such a tasteless joke." He stepped to the door and bowed slightly in his most charming manner. "Concepción will bring you a tray if you wish, but I hope you will do me the honor of dining with me."

"Oh . . ." She shook her head, knowing how fluttery she sounded. "I'm afraid not. I intend to fast tonight, and try another working when the moon sets. Perhaps tomorrow?"

"As you wish, Doña Rhonda. You are the expert, after all." He bowed once more, like an old-fashioned courtier, and withdrew, softly closing the door behind him.

She waited a full minute by her watch, then tiptoed to the door and laid an ear against it. No sound, but it was a solid door. She opened it a crack and looked out. The hall was dark and untenanted.

She closed it again and let out the breath she'd been holding. "How the hell I get into these things. . . ?" Muttering to herself, she pulled out the yarn-decorated straw bag that served as her briefcase. Good thing she always carried rations. A handful of trail mix, an orange she'd picked up earlier in the day, two rolls left over from breakfast, a little jerky . . . it was an odd meal, but it kept her from having to sit through Maldonado's attempts to charm a stupid *gringa* getting on toward Social Security. Besides, clients always liked the idea that their medium was fasting.

She did fast sometimes, of course; her gifts were quite genuine, and many of the traditional practices worked. But when she moved to Sedona in the '60s, she had discovered that a certain amount of showmanship helped even the most trusting clients. Then she had been pale and thin and intense, with hair dyed a premature silver. Now she was, to all appearances, a fluffy old lady. There was even a faint trace of an English accent she had no right to in her voice, since it made people think of cups of tea and cats and Sybil Leek. Showmanship, all of it. Only the power was real.

She sorted through the tapes while eating. Technology was wonderful; tape recorders were much simpler than automatic writing. She wasn't sure why that particular ghost affected her more deeply than the other troubled souls here, but no doubt she'd find out. The woman (her name was Teresa; Rhonda didn't know how she knew this, but then she often didn't know how she knew things) would be back. But she was a modern ghost; she'd probably died within the past year. There was no apparent connection between her and the classic Mexican bandit Maldonado had reported.

Ah, here was the tape of their original interview. She'd listened to it a dozen times, but perhaps she'd missed some clue, some hint of background. She started it and closed her eyes to concentrate, absently licking her lips where sugar from the dates in the trail mix had frosted them.

*. . . rifle looked like something out of an old Western. But he handled it like he knew what he was doing, so I gave him my money. And then he just faded away. A ghost, dammit. I looked for my money, but I couldn't find it anywhere . . .* Rhonda hit pause and sat there, replaying the memory of her own reaction to his words and his immediate search for his money. There was something about Maldonado that bothered her, a smell of rot. He wasn't in the drug trade; that smell she knew, and she never missed it no matter how surface-respectable a person was. Not an abuser of women or children, or . . . stop it, she told herself; hidden evils are not the issue here. She simply distrusted men as charming as Maldonado seemed to be.

*Since I knew it was just a damned ghost* (his English was idiomatic, she noted, but it was an interesting turn of phrase), *this time I told it to get back to hell; I wasn't going to throw more money away.* (What *had* happened to the money? It was unusual for a ghost to affect the material world so directly.) *It aimed the rifle at me, but I just laughed. It was a ghost, right? It couldn't touch me. Then it fired. Pain . . . I couldn't believe the pain. I thought I was dying! Then it reloaded, so I threw it my wallet. As soon as I did, it faded just like the first time, and the pain went with it. I couldn't stand up at first, I was shaking too hard. No trace of the wallet.*

Still concerned about the money. Perhaps it was just an excess of greed she smelled? No, she'd been around that often enough to recognize the smell. She started the tape again. There were more incidents, a month's worth. After the ghost shot him for having no money, he made a point of always carrying some. Like mugger money, she thought. No special location triggered the haunting; it had happened both here on the ranch and when he'd been away on business. Finally she clicked off the machine and rewound the tape. Nothing there she hadn't noticed before.

She put in a blank tape, set it to record, then got the rest of her working tools out. Chief among them was a cheap kitchen timer. It was an unlikely object for a medium, but over the years she had trained herself to come out of trance at its loud bell. It made working alone safer, if not ideal. Paper and pens of several colors, a candle for focus, and she was ready. She lit the candle and turned off the lamp, leaving the room shadowed. Seating herself in front of the candle, she gazed into its yellow-white heart and slipped easily into the waking sleep of her job.

The tape from her session that night was worthless, as were the ones she made over the next two days. On the third morning, however, she awoke with the memory of a dream and a conviction. Maldonado's elusive bandido had finally paid her a visit, and now she knew she'd make no progress as long as she remained here. The answer to the haunting awaited her someplace away from the Rancho de Pozoseco.

Over the years, she had learned to never question such guidance. Maldonado was away on a business trip, saving her the trouble of inventing appropriate patter to explain her sudden urge to go exploring. By ten A.M. she was in her Trooper, easing over the ruts in the road leading to the distant highway. It took over an hour to reach it, and the heat grew fierce as the elevation dropped. Once she reached the highway, she stopped, uncertain of how to proceed. She had a map, given her by Maldonado when she had agreed to come, but it was crude, the road to the ranch marked in with pen. Finally she turned left, toward distant Caborca and Nogales, the way she had entered Mexico eight days before. Maybe the ghost was just trying to get rid of her. It didn't feel that way, but some spirits were tricky. As she drove, she tried to remember her dream. The figure she'd seen had worn the ragged white pants, straw hat, and poncho of the poorest *campesinos,* crossed with a bandoleer. Just as Maldonado had described him. Young, though, with a much slighter build than her client. Hardly more than a youth, in fact, lacking even the traditional mustache. There was something about the figure that bothered her, but she didn't think it was trying to lead her astray.

The small town of Los Tajitos gave her a chance to fill up on gas and buy a map. The ranch road wasn't shown, but there was far more detail, including a road leading up to a town named Sasabe, right on the U.S. border. A matching town was shown in Arizona, like the better known and larger pair of towns named Nogales and Sonora, some distance east. Maybe she would go home that way; it was a much shorter route than going through Nogales. It wasn't until she found herself turning onto a road marked with the sign "Sasabe" that she realized this was her looked-for guidance.

If the ghost *was* trying to get rid of her, this would be a good way of doing it. The sign indicated a distance of some eighty kilometers to the small border town, and the road wasn't exactly an interstate. When the pavement came to an end a short distance outside of town, second thoughts became shouts in her mind. The monsoon, the summer rain, was almost at an end, but cloudbursts and flash floods were a serious danger on these back roads. Despite the persona she assumed for customers, Rhonda had too much sense to take off across strange country without telling someone of her plans. Normally, that is. But she had followed the promptings of her gut for almost fifty years; she wasn't going to ignore it this time. Besides, she had both a CB radio and a cell phone, as well as a five-gallon plastic jug of water and an equal amount of extra gasoline. She kept on driving.

The road grew worse, and she apologized out loud to the Trooper. Rhonda believed in being polite to inanimate objects, since she was never entirely sure just how *in*animate they might turn out to be. Despite the road, it was a beautiful drive. As she headed northeast, the ground rose once more, until she was driving through low hills that climbed ahead of her. The rainy season had left a desert transformed, high grasslands that rolled like a carpet to the horizons, lush green covering the hills and hiding the dead, sere grasses of previous seasons. Always so amazing, the effect a small amount of water could have in this harsh-seeming land, she thought. Thirty years of living in the desert wasn't enough to dim the wonder.

Several times she considered turning back, but each time her instincts argued with her common sense and won. By the time she reached Sasabe, over two hours later, she was exhausted. She parked near the tiny *zócalo,* the public square at the heart of every Mexican town. The brickwork around it was freshly painted, a cheerful blue and white, in better repair than most of the town. Her hope of finding a café dimmed as she looked around. From the stares she was collecting, tourists were not common here.

She got back in the Trooper, wondering for the first time in her life if a spirit had misled her. There was nothing here worth seeing, no clues, no voices. The thought of the road back made her ache; her bones would feel those ruts for a week. But she could think of nothing else to do.

Turning around under the collective stares of several little boys, she started back down the road to the south. Near the edge of town, a faint track climbed one of the hills to the west, barely visible through the long grass. On impulse, she turned to follow it. At least it was smoother than the collection of ruts that passed for the main road. It led over the hill, along a wash, past the end of a barbed wire fence, then climbed again, this time a long smooth slope to the west. Except for the twin tire paths, there was no sign of human life, no houses, not even any cattle. She shifted down as the grade increased near the top of the slope, and stopped at the crest. The throb of the engine sounded too loud, and she turned off the key and got out. Very faintly from the town behind her, she could hear the sound of a radio playing salsa. North of her, in the United States, the thumblike volcanic core of Baboquiviri was visible. Rhonda stared at it; she'd seen the peak, sacred to the Tohono O'odham people, from the patio of the ranch that morning as she ate breakfast. It was a prominent landmark, but it wasn't that high. The ranch must not be far away. She hadn't realized it was so close to the border. The map Maldonado had given her showed the ranch well south of the frontier. It might have been a simple error, but she wondered about it.

A light breeze blew wisps of hair around her face, carrying the scent of sun-warmed grasses. A sprinkling of late poppies, paler than the ones that bloomed in the spring, was scattered through the wild grass, almost lost to sight. Rhonda took a deep breath. At her feet, a tangle of wild gourd-vine spilled around the base of a yucca. Her eyes followed the faint road up the hill to the west, higher than the one on which she stood. A hawk circled above it, and someplace a locust buzzed like a dentist's drill.

With the sound came a tingle along her spine. "Well, it's about time," she muttered. Perhaps the trip hadn't been a waste of time after all. She stared at the hilltop with eyes that saw and discounted everything, listened with ears that filtered out the sounds of insect and distant music. Someone . . .

*"Venga acá."*

The whispered words were soundless, a voice she'd never heard but recognized instantly. Teresa. Not whom she'd been expecting, but surely there would be an explanation soon. Rhonda started the engine and drove on, up the far slope. The nameless track continued, kilometer after kilometer, never quite fading away, never leading her into a spot she couldn't get out of. A few times the road crossed washes that tested the Trooper's capabilities, with loose sand or, in one case, a boulder as big as a small car, sitting on top of the tire tracks that were the only assurance that someone had driven this way before. Rhonda had to pick her way through the jumble of loose rock paving the wash before she could rejoin the somewhat-beaten path on the far side.

Low spots in the road were still muddy from the last rain. She'd been driving for some time at a speed no faster than a brisk walk when she spotted fresh tire prints in mud, along a wash. She stopped and got out. Truck, she decided. A big, heavy pickup, at least. The tracks to the west looked fresher, as though someone had driven along this route recently. If they could get this far, she could follow the tracks back to . . . Pozoseco? She didn't know, but it was the right direction. She went back to the Trooper and stopped. It felt—*wrong.*

She scanned the horizon, close here in the depression of the wash. Nothing visible. Once more she reached for the door, but the feeling of wrongness persisted. "All right, who's here? Teresa?" Eyes closed, she looked with her other vision. There . . . her physical eyes snapped open, as a misty form appeared. Not Teresa. The figure from her dream. Maldonado's bandit.

"Now why here?" she asked it. There was no reply.

Something about the figure tugged at her memory. Something . . . there was something not quite *right* about that ghost. No question that it was a ghost, she could see the hillside quite clearly through it, but something . . .

"Why here?" she repeated. "What do you want? How can I help?" These weren't ideal working conditions, but if the spirit chose to manifest itself here, she would manage.

The figure's mouth didn't move, but again she heard the voiceless whisper, *Venga acá,* Come here. The same voice she had heard before. "Teresa?" she said aloud, startled, but knew the answer before the ghost shook its head. This wasn't Teresa. Yet it was Teresa's spirit that she heard. Interesting; the two *were* linked, then.

The ghost raised the rifle—shotgun? Rhonda didn't know enough about guns to identify it—and motioned for her to follow, up the wash along the tracks left by the truck. She started to climb into the Trooper, and was hit by a feeling of wrongness so strong it left her dizzy. Right, then. On foot. "I don't know what you want, my friend," she called, "but I am still of the flesh. Just a moment." She rummaged around in the back until she found the canteen she kept there for emergencies. This entire expedition was insane, but that was no excuse for ignoring basic precautions. "All right, I'm ready."

It was a good thing Rhonda had spent years hiking around Sedona. She would have given up within a kilometer without that training. The trail followed the wash roughly, and at intervals she could see traces left by the truck. The ghost stayed ahead of her, leading the way, waiting impatiently as she scrambled over rocks it floated over effortlessly. She stopped to catch her breath, and the figure of the bandit hovered near, showing every sign of a most unghostlike impatience. "You might try to remember what it was like when *you* still had a body," she grumbled, and it backed off a short distance. But beyond the—body language? surely that couldn't be the right term—of the ghost, Rhonda was aware of a need for haste. Haste and silence. Hurriedly she took a swig from the canteen, then scrambled on.

The figure of the *bandido* turned aside from the wash and drifted up a small hill. It motioned her to follow and she did, with a sense of approaching climax. As she neared the top, the figure flickered like the image on a TV when the power fluctuates. Then, in an ectoplasmic power failure, it thinned and vanished completely.

"After bringing me all this way . . ." Rhonda muttered, but her voice was as silent as the one that had led her here. Whatever was beyond the hill, she knew this wasn't a wild goose. She took five more steps, realizing as she did that she was holding her breath in the proper clichéd fashion. She looked down to where the wash doubled back below her.

She'd been right; a large pickup had left the tracks. More specifically, a very familiar, dark blue Dodge half-ton pickup, parked beneath a mesquite hanging over the wash. She'd seen it before, although not for the last few days. It was Maldonado's truck, and her client himself was standing about a hundred feet away, his back to her. Beyond him, a man was crawling under a fence across the wash, the last of a group, at least a dozen. The men vanished into the mesquite thickets beyond the fence. Baboquiviri, looking like a blunted arrowhead from this angle, thrust skyward some miles beyond them. *Coyote,* she thought. *He's a coyote. That's what I smelled.*

Coyote in this case didn't mean the four-legged kind, an animal that Rhonda rather admired. It was the term used for smugglers of human contraband. The fence over the wash must mark the U.S.-Mexican border. America's golden streets still lured immigrants eager to make money at menial jobs no one else wanted: maids, agricultural workers. These days they were usually illegal, unfortunately. She sympathized with them, but the crooks who took advantage of them were another matter. Scavengers, preying on the weak and desperate.

The last of the men moved out of sight, and Maldonado turned back toward his truck. Belatedly Rhonda realized she was in plain view. The realization was forced on her by the way he swore and pulled out a gun, aiming it right at her.

"Doña Rhonda. You should have stayed at the ranch."

The gun looked enormous. Possibly she could turn and run . . . but he was scrambling up the hillside as easily as a burro, never taking his eyes off her. She remained where she was, trying to act as if it were completely normal to meet at gunpoint, miles from anyplace. If the situation hadn't been so dangerous, Rhonda would have been ashamed of herself; she positively *chirped* a response. "Mr. Maldonado! This truly must have been *meant.* That poor restless soul I told you about, the widow, called me here, a spirit guide in the *truest* sense of . . ."

"Save it." He was at her side now, and shoved the gun under her nose in a manner the fluffiest old fool would have to notice. Obligingly, she chopped off the spiritualist patter. Instead, she pointed beside him.

"I followed them. You didn't tell me there were so many." It was like watching mist forming over a lake. A thickening in the air, and suddenly figures took shape, some wavering, some so solid it was hard to believe they'd been nothing but air a moment before. Many figures, over a dozen. She couldn't count them precisely; they seemed to drift and melt into one another as she shifted her eyes. The bandit was in front, closest to Maldonado. The coyote saw the ghost and swore.

"I owe you an apology," Maldonado said to Rhonda, his eyes fixed on the ghostly highwayman. "I'd just about decided you were as phony as that British accent. You did me a favor; this is the first time I've been able to get a group across in a month without *him* interfering." He grinned, an appropriately predatory grin. Reaching into his pocket, he pulled out a fistful of bills and threw them at the ghost. They drifted through the silent form like autumn leaves. "There's your damned payoff, and it's the last. Get rid of this damned soul for me once and for all, Señorita Zimmerman, and we should be able to work things out. A bonus of some sort. You'll even live long enough to spend it."

Not bloody likely, she thought, considering what she'd seen. But curiosity outweighed concern for her own fate at the moment. She could see an entire group, a veritable swarm, of ghosts surrounding Maldonado, hate and fear and rage that reached beyond death made visible. "Can't you see the others?" she asked. She started describing what she saw. "That one, his name is Carlos I think, very short, and the one behind him, Roberto—is that it? yes—Muñoz Ramirez, and next to him, right in the middle of that yucca—could you move, do you think? It makes me queasy, looking at that stalk coming out the top of your head. Thanks, dear. Manuel, isn't it? Yes. And next to Manuel . . ."

She rattled on, describing and naming those she could distinguish, aware as she did that she was babbling again, sounding like the most feather-headed of New Age Old Ladies. She couldn't help it; the patter had been part of her for so long it came out automatically. It was obvious Maldonado recognized many of the descriptions. His eyes narrowed as he looked around him, searching for the figures she saw so clearly, and clearly seeing none of them.

"And finally, right next to our *bandido* . . . why Teresa, so this is what you look like! And your son . . ." Rhonda turned to the most corporeal of the ghosts and her voice faltered. Teresa was a young woman, just as Rhonda had thought, but with a face that was almost a twin to another specter. She looked back to the figure of the bandit, which held its antique rifle aimed steadily at Maldonado. "You . . ." Rhonda swayed as a double image formed for a moment, coalescing into the same ragged figure. "No wonder I couldn't summon you! Mr. Maldonado, are you aware of the drawbacks of gendered languages? They shape one's impressions so. You referred to the *bandido* haunting you so often, I never thought to look for a *bandida.*"

"What?" He turned to glare at her for a moment, then looked back at the ghost. He—no, *she,* and Rhonda suddenly knew that her name was Mariana—smiled and with her left hand pulled the thin fabric of her worn poncho tightly against her body, revealing the slight but unmistakable curve of a breast underneath.

"Like *La Carambada,*" Rhonda said, aware she was babbling but unable to stop herself. "Back around 1860, around Querétero, a woman bandit who dressed like a man, she use to bare a breast after she'd gotten the money, rubbing her victims' macho noses in the fact she was a woman . . ." She stopped speaking abruptly in order to duck the backhanded blow Maldonado aimed at her.

"Look, I don't make these things up, you know!" She waved wildly at Mariana. "She's a woman! Or, well, she was . . . can you see the others yet?"

"No." He made as if to move toward Mariana, but the ghost raised her very unspectral rifle and he stopped. "All right, so it's a woman, dammit. Just get rid of it."

"I do not simply *get rid of* restless spirits. I try to help them find peace, solve the problems which bind them to this plane and keep them from moving on . . ." The patter started again, every word of it true this time, as she tried desperately to think of what to do next. Judging by the resemblance between the two ghosts, Teresa and Mariana, she had a good idea of what was holding them. Teresa had been one of Maldonado's "customers," abandoned to wander lost and without water in the desert. She had died somewhere north of here with her son, on American soil, their bodies still undiscovered. A desire for justice and decent burial had drawn them back. But why couldn't Maldonado see them?

"Shut up, damn you! Just get rid of that bitch!"

"She is—" And here came the rest of it, so obvious now, so heartbreakingly simple. There were times when Rhonda regretted her gift. Mariana's history, the poverty, her husband dead at the hands of the *rurales,* the Federal police—it was all there in her mind now. None of it mattered, though, except for one fact. Teresa had been Mariana's descendant, the last of her family, and she and her son had died while Mariana watched, helpless to help the living. No wonder she'd come after Maldonado.

Rhonda took a deep breath. "She is the grandmother—great-grandmother? I'm not sure—of Teresa. The ghost I told you about before. Right there, not three feet away from you. And they want justice. I can't banish your *bandida* without it."

"That's too bad. I hired you to do a job."

*Click.* There was a metallic snap as the ghost cocked her rifle, still aimed at Maldonado's chest. He brought his own gun up smoothly in answer. "I don't think so. Not if you don't want to see this one die right now."

Rhonda didn't remember until afterward that Maldonado couldn't see the other ghosts. Her reaction was foolish anyway, as young Tomas, Teresa's son, was already dead. But he was a very solid-looking ghost, and for a crucial moment, all she could see was a gun being brought to bear on a child. She gasped and dove forward, trying to take the boy in her arms, and tumbled down the hill, somersaulting through the brush as a gun roared over her head.

A tangle of mesquite broke her fall. For a few breaths she could think of nothing beyond breaking free of the thorns. *The earth does spin,* she thought hazily; *it's spinning right now.*

Then another gun went off, and she stared back up the hill. A curl of smoke came from the barrel of Mariana's rifle as she backed away from Maldonado. His teeth were bared in a scavenger's smile. If the noncorporeal blast had harmed him this time, he showed no sign of it. "*Puta!* Ghost or not, I've had enough of you and your interfering."

Mariana backed up a few more steps, and the rest of the spirits crowded behind Maldonado, a nontangible pressure. A detached observer in Rhonda's mind took note of the fact that Mariana's feet were firmly planted in thin air, and she realized that the ground had looked solid beyond her own feet right up until the moment when she'd found herself falling. If the ghosts were clouding perception . . . the ghost moved back again, almost as if she were afraid of the mortal, then turned as if to flee. Maldonado's triumphant shout as he grabbed for her turned into a scream as he plunged over a sharp drop-off. Rhonda thought the spirits gave one final shove as he went over.

It was a clear drop instead of the steep slope she'd fallen down, but it wasn't that high. She got ready to run, then realized she couldn't hear him. No sound. On the hillside, figures wavered, dissolving like mist on the breeze. She stood up, wincing as the mesquite snagged her once more, and looked around. Maldonado lay in a crumpled heap at the base of the short cliff, his head bent at an impossible angle against a rock. "I wonder if he'll haunt anyone," she said aloud. Probably not, she decided. His cares had all been for this plane, for his money and his evil little business, to the point that he had only seen the one ghost who could hurt him by taking his money.

All the ghosts were gone except for Mariana and her family. Rhonda spoke aloud. "I'll see you get decent burial, with a priest. I promise." Teresa smiled and, together with her son, faded like the Cheshire cat. Rhonda headed back toward the Trooper, and Mariana stayed with her until it was in sight. Then she spoke for the first time, a husky voice that could easily be mistaken for a man's. *"Gracias, señora. Por la causa. Viva la revolución!"* She raised her rifle in salute, and was gone.

A revolutionary after all. Not surprising; many of the Mexican bandits had been. Well, better honest highwaymen, or highway*women,* than bloodsuckers like Maldonado. There was a small pile of paper where the ghost had stood; the breeze was playing with it. Rhonda picked it up, snagging one brightly colored piece as it started to blow away. Money, over a thousand dollars from the look of it. Maldonado's, no doubt. She picked it up, then got into the Trooper and realized she'd lost her canteen someplace back on the hillside. No matter. She turned the vehicle carefully and headed back toward Sasabe. It would be dusk by the time she got there, but she thought the border crossing would still be open, and with luck she could be in Tucson by nine. She'd get some proper maps of the area, find Teresa and Tomas and keep her promise. *For the cause . . .* Madera's revolution was dead, but she could give the money to one of the groups that worked with illegal immigrants. "Rest now," she whispered, to the ghost no longer there. "Viva la revolution indeed."

[illegible]

[illegible]

© 96
danforth

# WE MET UPON THE ROAD

## *by Jane Emerson*

*Jane Emerson, as Doris Egan, has published several fantasy novels, among them the wonderful "Ivory" books featuring the clever, amusing, and seemingly mismatched pair of lovers Thea and Ran. Doris, as Jane, writes short fiction (including an upcoming story featuring this same protagonist), and hugely complex, fascinating novels of interstellar politics and adventure such as* City Of Diamond. *Either Jane or Doris—or perhaps both—is also dabbling in television. Here is a sampling of Jane* and *Doris: an exquisitely rendered classic tale of upper-crust society, stiff upper lips, spies, assassins, and intrigue.*

The devil sent him to Castle Saint-Cloud. It was not Stephen Price's own idea, but then, little of his life had been his own idea for many years now.

The devil was incarnate, as was his wont, in the person of Sir John, who received him in his sun-washed room high above the waters of Herse Harbor. Outside, Stephen could hear the sounds of the Royal Engineers as they worked on the new docking facilities. The Adriatic breeze that stole through the window was rich with the tang of summer and salt.

Stephen did not relax. He never relaxed in the presence of Sir John. He sat warily in the bare wooden chair, his back as stiff as his Engineer's uniform, his face unnaturally calm. But that was not unusual; Lieutenant Stephen Price's twenty-five years had destroyed his capacity for open displays of emotion. This, together with his sandy hair and unlined face, gave him the appearance of any young gentleman out of Oxford on a bought commission.

"Stephen, my own dear boy," said Sir John, looking up from his papers, and the warmth of his greeting made Stephen nervous. Sir John smiled, removing his spectacles in

a gently civilized way that disturbed his guest even furthe
"How good that Captain Kenmore could spare you."
"Captain Kenmore's always very obliging."
"He is, is he not? Tell me, do you like my new office
It rather reminds me of our first interview together—" h
paused, "—in the warden's office on Tanmore. Sir Joh
was a plump, cheerful, gray-haired man in a civilian coa
of blue superfine and exquisitely tied silk cravat—the mo
temperate man in the city of Herse, Uncle Jack to half th
children on the docks. His hands were as delicate as
young girl's. "Another lovely room above the sea." H
gazed down at his papers musingly. "Of course, his wa
better decorated than mine. He could afford the labor."
It was best to ignore references to Tanmore Prison fro
Uncle Jack. Stephen waited.
Sir John laid his papers on the table before him with th
mild air of a country schoolmaster. He smiled. "You de
serve a holiday, Stephen. Travel broadens the mind."
You could not tell Stephen was startled from his so
voice. "I thought you wanted me to stay in Herse."
"A few days of rest in the mountains will do you a worl
of good. I'm delivering you to the Baron Kouris; he's eage
for dinner guests. A very lonely man. I'm sure you ca
sympathize."
"Delivering?" inquired Stephen with his habitual gentle
ness. "Am I to be tied up with a ribbon?"
"Only if you prefer it, dear boy. You're to go and mak
yourself agreeable to the family Kouris; I'll give you a lette
of introduction. And while there, you're to become ac
quainted with the children."
"Children," said Stephen warily.
"Aged twenty-one, nineteen, and sixteen. Michae
Clothilde, and Ilyest." Sir John's smile quirked. "The Ba
on's first wife was English, the second French, and the thir
a native mountain girl."
"Will I have the honor of meeting the Baroness?"
"Alas, no. The Baron would seem to run profligatel
through his loved ones."
Stephen said only, "I trust he is more careful with h
guests."
"Dear Stephen. Your obliging nature recommends itse
to me as always. May I tell you a story?" Sir John offere

him snuff. Stephen shook his head. Sir John said, in a voice that suddenly hinted of adamantine steel, "Take it."

Stephen opened the gold clasp of the enamel box with a flawless snap of his fingers and inserted a pinch of snuff in each nostril with the mechanical perfection he'd been taught, one year ago. He hated snuff, but his hate for Tanmore was greater. As Sir John talked on, Stephen could feel the vapors permeating his skull like a thousand steel pins. But he held the powder there in prescribed fashion, postponing the vulgar punctuation of the sneeze.

"My story begins in Paris," said Sir John, once again friendly. "Or, really, it begins in Italy, where General Bonaparte has been so active. After the Battle of Marengo, Bonaparte offered terms of peace to the Austrians, but the best he could get was an armistice."

Stephen could hold back the sneeze no longer. It burst forth. Sir John raised an eyebrow and continued, "At the end of June the First Consul returned to Paris, where he consulted with his Minister of Foreign Affairs on how best to proceed. On Talleyrand's advice, they decided to follow the fashion of late and offer peace terms based on a split of territory neither of them presently own. Is that handkerchief monogrammed?"

Stephen froze, the white linen square half out of his pocket. "Yes. Lieutenant Foster's handkerchiefs were monogrammed, so I thought—"

"A nice touch. I approve. One of the duly apportioned territories would be Viume itself. Specifically, the French would allow Herse to be taken by sea, since the mountains have defended it so well by land."

"Allow? Surely the British ships here in Herse Harbor would have something to say about it? And Viume has been an independent monarchy for centuries."

"Well, you know—it was to be a *secret* agreement." Sir John's eyes gleamed with quiet merriment.

This was understandable to Stephen, for he had not yet found the eggshell of a secret that Sir John had not picked his way to the yolk of with his sharp, well-tended fingernails.

"As you may not have heard, the Turkish Sultan was a great friend of France before this recent unpleasantness in Egypt. His money assures him that he still has friends in France, in fact. One of these friends got hold of a copy of the agreement—which, as there were only two, showed great resourcefulness, I'm sure you'll agree. Travel by sea being the chancy thing it is these days, he was transporting the document overland to Constantinople, when—right here in Viume—"

He cut himself off. "Have I mentioned the Baron's children?"

Stephen waited.

"Poor things, they must be tormented with boredom. One of them has taken to riding the roads."

He fixed Stephen with a glance like a weight of pressed glass.

"Bothering passing travelers."

It took a moment. "A highwayman?"

"Tiresome, is it not? Stand and deliver, over and over again? Well, he relieved the Sultan's agent of this document, which must be a disappointment to the Sultan, did he know about it. Missing the chance to hear what France and Austria are planning to do on his very borders . . ."

"And the agent?"

Sir John made a dismissive gesture. "Made it as far as Herse, poor chap."

"Of course, to the city of secrets. But no farther."

"The young Kouris has put the document up for sale. Buyers from France and Austria are already on the way; you will get there first." Sir John gazed down at his papers. "I'll send two tickets for the morning coach around to your rooms, with any further instructions. The rest of the day is yours; go home and pack your things."

Stephen sat there, bewildered, for a second.

Sir John looked up. "You'll make yourself useful, won't you, Stephen?"

*Useful.*

"Am I to kill the Baron, sir? If he proves to be the seller of the document?"

"Stephen! I hope my past requests of you have not caused you to form a false estimate of my character. Surely you don't imagine I'd ask you to practice your formidable knifework on a citizen of another country, over whom we have no jurisdiction."

Stephen was silent.

Sir John shrugged. "In any case, it's not necessary. The

seller is one of the Baron's children—this I have from witnesses. Determine which of the young aristocrats it is."

"And . . . purchase the document?"

Sir John seemed mildly shocked. "Dear fellow. Where do you get your ideas of my budget? *Procure* the document."

"May I ask how, sir?"

"Really, Stephen, have I troubled you with details before?"

He spoke in a dismissive way. Stephen remained seated. Sir John looked up. "Well?"

"Sir, may I have an advance on my salary? I've been creeping up the stairs past my landlady for nearly a week."

Sir John regarded him for a moment, then said, "Four shillings. Pick it up from the secretary on your way out." When Stephen still didn't move, he said, "What else?"

Stephen hesitated. "Captain Kenmore said that he wished me to help with his project to expand the western seawall."

Sir John tilted back in his chair and folded his beautiful hands across his plump chest. He watched Stephen with the amused sadness that might be given to an erring child. Stephen felt his face flush. "My boy," said Sir John, in his rich baritone, "it's not as if you could do him the least amount of good, you know. It's not as if you were really an engineer—"

For a moment Stephen felt himself swamped with acute embarrassment, as though he'd been pretending to be something he weren't; as though it were *his* idea.

And then, more than half the time, he believed he truly was an engineer, working on an equal footing with the men around him. Until someone asked him a question, and the huge blank space in his mind forced him to temporize—damn Sir John. *You have the gift of adaptability,* he heard the voice echo in the warden's room. *You drop like an obedient felled tree into whatever ravine it pleases fate to send you. Like a raindrop into a pitcher of washwater; until even the other drops of water don't know who you are.*

"Captain Kenmore only needs me to carry his instruments and assist him. I might learn something of—"

Sir John was shaking his head. "Don't do yourself an injustice, Stephen, you're quite remarkable enough in your way; you needn't feel the lack of higher arithmetic." He bestowed on Stephen a smile of what seemed genuine affection. "No, your talents lie elsewhere. I have no desire to make a sow's purse out of a silk ear." He picked up the paper he'd been perusing earlier. "Six shillings. Close the door as you leave, dear boy."

He clattered down the stairs and stepped into the white Mediterranean sunlight. Around him was the noisy, masculine world of Herse Harbor: dockworkers, sailors, Royal Engineers and their fetchers-and-carriers. The squawking of seagulls as they dove for the blue-green water. There were a few maids scurrying here and there on quick errands to the waterfront shops, but that was all. The women of the British community stayed indoors during the summer day, emerging in the evening like late-blooming flowers.

He walked up the hill from the harbor in his lying Engineer's uniform with its sword he had no notion of how to use.

*You'll make yourself useful, won't you, Stephen?*

As though he'd been larking, playing, luxuriating in being . . . almost . . . a normal person. Perhaps he had.

Herse in summer: gray-gold houses and red roofs illuminated by the sun like a candle in a golden jar. Walks at twilight on the promenade beyond the docks. Taverns spilling music and violence into the street at all hours, or till the morning watch came and the owners shut the doors to sleep. Pungent smoke hanging interminably in the air around the Arab coffeehouses.

And too many flies. Stephen bought a quarter-wheel of cheese from a merchant in Sesha Street; even inside the shop, doors and windows shut, there were a dozen flies.

In fact there were fourteen. He amused himself by counting them as his cheese was wrapped in brown paper. Outside he opened one end and cut off a piece, which he dropped in the gutter for the flies since they had already claimed it back in the shop.

He'd become more fastidious since Tanmore. More vulnerable.

On that chilling thought he turned into the higher slope of Gradka Street, passed through the archway, and climbed the steps past the rows of flowerpots and drowsing cats. Marigolds, anemone lilies, summer roses in white and red. The ubiquitous green-and-blue shutters of Herse.

Once inside the house he moved silently for the stairs.

He could hear Mrs. Tosti moving about the kitchen, arguing with her cook, and he had no desire to hand over any of his shillings just yet.

He took the first two steps.

"Why, Mr. Price, sir! You're back early."

He nearly jumped. It was only Nita, the housemaid, a mountain girl come to Herse for work, who helped Mrs. Tosti with the cleaning. She had the moss-dark eyes of the mountains. She hurried past him down the curve of the stairs.

"I must go! The pig is drunk again!"

Stephen was not surprised by this extraordinary statement, taking it to mean that the black-and-tan sow quartered in the back yard had once again broken into the still kept by their enterprising landlady. He *was* surprised, however, when the girl stopped, walked back to him, frowning, and examined him in the light of the dusty stair window.

"You're going on a journey," she said. She smiled. "Good. It will teach you to laugh."

She whirled and hurried out to minister to the pig. He stared after her for a moment, then started up the stairs.

Inside his rooms he went at once to the bathroom, with its old Roman-style bathing tub of chipped marble. He poured water from the pitcher to the washbowl and splashed his face. The small surprises of his life were like a continuing series of slaps, some painful, some merely awakening. He'd given up any pretense of expectation for what reality ought to be.

He emerged from the bathroom into the comfortable sitting room. *His* room, his territory, where a few shillings meant no one could put him out. Essentially, therefore, it was a lie. He glanced at the empty hearth and old chairs of leather and worn velvet, and suddenly he wanted sunlight and clarity again. He crossed to the balcony, opened the shutters, and stepped out into the white brightness.

The table had been cleared from breakfast. Balconies were a penny a dozen in Herse, but he liked this one; he could just see, down at the end of the slope of Jacquard Street, a slice of bay with the packet *Louisa* in dock. And far over the red slate roofs, the blue of the Mediterranean spread in a peaceful liquid blanket across the horizon.

He stared as though he could see beyond it to the fortress prison of Tanmore, lapped by these same peaceful blue waves.

There were footsteps behind him. Without turning, he said, "Forgive me my impertinence, Nicholas, but is there any reason you cannot go to the mountains?"

Nicholas Reims was a small, neat, dark man, three years older than Stephen, or so he said. But then, he also said he was French.

Nicholas set a cup of chocolate on the table. "Viume is a country of mountains. Where in the mountains?"

"Castle Saint-Cloud. The home of Baron Kouris."

Nicholas stepped away from the cup and shrugged. "Why should I not be able to go to the mountains?" He turned to go inside.

Stephen sighed. It would be good to have a valet who was less cryptic. He sat at the table, lifted the cup and drank a few sips.

*You'll make yourself useful, won't you?*

Three flies had already gathered in the tiny pool of chocolate in the saucer. Stephen pushed out his chair, rose, and opened the shutters. "Nicholas!"

He stood, a dark figure in the shadows of the sitting room. "Sir?" said Nicholas, with the tinge of irony he habitually gave the word, so subtle it was reproachless.

"Are there flies in the mountains, Nicholas?"

"Not as there are here."

"Then, by God," Stephen said savagely, "the sooner we get there, the better."

Stephen went to bed early, expecting to rise before dawn for the coach. Summer in Herse brought mosquitoes by night, so he made certain the candle was out before opening the window to the blessed night breeze. It was cool and clean on his cheek as he lay under the sheets. He loved this room. It was a minor thing to love, but he did.

The inner shell of Tanmore had had no guards, no assigned cells; the prisoners were left to keep order however they chose. Stephen—his name was not Price in those days—had found a place to sleep, a niche in the rock high above a shaft they called the Well; no one knew he was there or bothered him. All night long he heard the murmur of the sea far below in the dark. It was the only memory of Tanmore he didn't mind revisiting.

He called it back now, and rode the gentle waves until he fell asleep.

Their coach was the mail coach to Treves, which passed out through Herse along a road lined with cypresses and olives. Shreds of clouds feathered the blue sky behind them, and the wind off the sea pushed them along. Stephen and Nicholas sat inside, buried under packs of mail and baggage. Sir John had insisted he bring a dress uniform, to please the Baron, and an actual hatbox to contain his black bicorne with its stiff white plume. A *hatbox.* As though there would be any reason to wear the thing within the castle.

Nicholas' silences grew darker, if that were possible, as their coach crawled into the shadows of the mountains.

"You're not a keen traveler, I perceive," Stephen remarked. "Have you any reason to think we may not be welcome in the mountains?"

"Fortune-telling is not among my duties as valet."

Nicholas was not very free with his "sirs" when they were out of company, and Stephen had no wish to press so talented an assassin on his manners. He did, however, suspect that Nicholas knew far more about native politics than he pretended, so Stephen shrugged. "You might try. The housemaid did as much."

"You will go on a long journey," said Nicholas, with a marked lack of enthusiasm. "You will meet a dark stranger—"

"Very well, Nicholas. You make your point."

"You will come into an inheritance—"

"She didn't say that."

"Don't trust the stories the women of the mountains tell you."

"And how would you know, Nicholas? I thought you came to Tanmore from France."

Nicholas was silent.

Stephen smiled.

By late afternoon they were far into the mountains, and Stephen had, for his sanity, ceased looking out the window to see how close the coach wheels came to the edge of each precipice. The trees had a bleaker look, and the closeness of the nearby peaks cast a shade over the road. The coach had stopped once, for a herd of goats, but beyond that single herder there was not a person to be seen on the road.

He and Nicholas were dozing when a pistol shot snapped them awake. Stephen turned to Nicholas at once, alarm on his face, and said, "Tanmore luck! Heed me, if this is a highwayman, it is most urgent that we *not* kill him."

Nicholas, whose pistol was half out of his waistcoat, gave his employer a look composed of disbelieving patience and slid the weapon back inside.

Stephen unlatched the window and stuck out his head warily. No one—a barren landscape grouping of rocks and trees. "Coachman!" he called. "Did you fire? Are we near Castle Saint-Cloud?" For, he thought, perhaps he should not assume that any particular robber of the mountains was *their* robber.

Either the coachman was dead, or he considered Stephen's sanity on even a lower par than Nicholas's estimate, for he made no answer.

But another voice came. A young man's voice. "Will it please you to descend from the coach, sir? And your companions?"

Stephen heard Nicholas sigh, but he ignored this, opened the door, and stepped out.

What he faced was no longer a landscape grouping, but a painting out of Ingres or David. A few yards away, on a magnificent black steed, sat a young man in an open coat of floral and lozenge silk, with matching waistcoat and breeches, all trimmed with silver gimp and buttons. He wore a lace-edged cravat, and there was lace at the ends of his sleeves. His mask was a black velvet domino, and there was a silver periwig atop his head. A sword with a jeweled pommel sparkled at his side.

Stephen stared, nonplussed. It was as though a ghost from their grandfather's time had appeared on the road to challenge them. Hessian boots, V-fronted, with tassels completed the picture of what the well-dressed highwayman was wearing this year.

"Sir?" called the robber, in the voice of a well-spoken youth. He spoke in English, which, considering Stephen's uniform, was not inappropriate—if one knew English. "Have you nothing to say?"

*Sir John would like to meet your tailor,* he thought. Then

he pulled himself together. "My travel money is at your disposal, but I fear you will be disappointed in it."

The mouth beneath the domino curved into a smile. "Do not do yourself such an injustice, sir, before I have inspected the treasure." Treasure. As though he were a privateer and Stephen's pocketbook a ship overtaken in the night.

Stephen turned out his pockets ostentatiously, then handed over his coin. "Six shillings?" inquired the gilded apparition. "Unenterprising traveler, you make me feel I should be adding gold to your own treasury."

"It would not be refused," said Stephen, with a wryness that made the robber laugh.

Stephen liked the sound of the laugh. So this well-bred ghost was one of the Baron's sons. Was it Michael or Ilyest?

A rougher voice interrupted. "A cheap traveler's trick, my lord. The money's hidden in the coach among the mailbags. I say that we blow the head off this lying rascal and—"

The sound of a pistol being cocked made Stephen whirl around. "No! Nicholas—"

He turned back, obedient to the touch of cool metal on his throat. The Baron's son was fast. The point of the jeweled sword was a hairsbreadth from his windpipe.

"Tell your companion to put down his pistol." The Baron's son was breathing hard, beneath the brocade coat. *He might well cut my throat,* Stephen thought, seeing that hand tremble with . . . anger? Fear? Excitement?

"Nicholas," he said carefully. "Put down your pistol."

He could not turn back to see. Would Nicholas obey? He was an enigma, but surely not the sort of man given to laying down his life for anything beyond himself. And Nicholas could shoot the second robber and fling a knife deep in the throat of the first in an instant. *He* would survive, whatever happened to Stephen.

But miraculously, the sword was taken away. Stephen glanced back and saw that Nicholas had placed the pistol on the floor of the coach and stepped down.

The highwayman moved back, the sword still in his hand. "We are friends again," he said lightly. Stephen could see the second horseman now; a stocky man with an older voice, in a dusty riding coat. He lacked the lace and silk of his companion.

Keeping the sword positioned carefully, the Baron's son (Michael or Ilyest? Michael or Ilyest?) began going through Stephen's pockets himself. "Friends sometimes insist on knowing things about each other," he said apologetically. He slid a hand inside Stephen's waistcoat, and checked around the belt for a pouch.

She had to lean in to do so. Stephen felt her breasts through the coat of silk brocade.

Not Michael or Ilyest. *Clothilde.*

Stephen was not shocked at this news, he was simply pleased. He liked women. For a goodly portion of his life, the only ones he'd seen were the whores rowed out to Tanmore; they were a cheerful bunch, far easier to get along with than the inmates.

The highwayman drew back, a sparkle in the dark eyes that shone through the slits of the domino.

*She suspects that she gave herself away with that,* he thought. *But either she doesn't care, or it was deliberate.*

*Very well, then. We pretend.* Stephen leafed through the books of his training and the memories of his childhood. *It is not for a gentleman to claim greater acquaintance with a lady than she may be willing to allow.*

"What necessity brings you to so lonely a road, sir?" inquired the jeweled and laced horseman, in his clear, well-spoken voice.

"The devil," said Stephen promptly, and the horseman laughed.

"You come from Herse, then," said the youth. "For my parents have told me many times that the devil lives there."

"And they are right," said Stephen, inclining his head with a smile.

"And, of course, this road goes nowhere else but to Herse."

"There is that," said Stephen, in his soft, agreeable voice.

"Which leaves only the question of where you are going," said the highwayman. He walked lightly back to his black horse and mounted.

"Very true."

"Well?"

"Our aims are as open as a sheet of window glass," said

Stephen. "We are traveling to Castle Saint-Cloud, where I am to enjoy the hospitality of the family Kouris."

The dark eyes sparkled further at the "hospitality of the family Kouris." The horse felt his rider's amusement and danced a step or two to the left, eager to be off and galloping. "You're a guest at the Baron's table? My sympathies, sir—a regular Dover Court, all talkers and no hearers!"

"Then they have bad need of me," said Stephen, bowing, "for I intend to listen."

The horseman laughed. He signaled to his companion, and they turned and cantered away. Hoofbeats echoed down the mountain road.

Stephen stood silently for a moment. Then he looked up at the coachman, still frozen like a Greek statue. "Have a good heart sir," Stephen reassured him. "Think how quickly we've been robbed. You will arrive in Treves well according to schedule."

Nicholas climbed into the coach, and he followed. They seated themselves among the bags once again, and after a few moments—long enough for the coachman to relieve himself, Stephen estimated—the wheels creaked below them and they moved forward.

"Clothilde," he said after a moment. Nicholas looked at him. "That was the Baron's second child," he explained.

"Really. Down in Herse, the young ladies paint screens. I, too, recognized one of the horsemen—the stocky gentleman with the deep voice."

"He was masked."

"But his hands were ungloved, and I recognized his tattoo." He paused. "From Tanmore."

Stephen's eyes widened. "We will avoid him," he said firmly.

Nicholas nodded.

Stephen settled back in the seat. *Clothilde.* That would make life easier. Stephen had never yet failed in any request Sir John had made of him, and felt it would be unwise to start.

He knew the point of attack. The rest should be simple. *Your pardon, Lady Clothilde. We met upon the road—*

He could relax. Almost.

"What else did she say?" asked Nicholas suddenly.

"What? You heard all she said to me."

"No, the housemaid. At home. What else did she say, beyond that you'd take a journey?"

"That it would teach me to laugh," said Stephen, his chin on the window of the coach as he watched the waning sun turn the mountaintops the color of old blood.

Nicholas looked at him silently. "I may be forgiven for doubting it," he muttered at last.

Castle Saint-Cloud was old and sturdy, perched halfway above a plunge that ran straight down to the center of the world. It was of massive blocks of mountain granite, well-built to defend against centuries of attackers. The doors were wooden, Stephen saw, and new. He showed his letter to the gatekeeper and he and Nicholas walked in, carrying their bags and the hatbox.

It was cooler up here. He should have brought his great-coat. But his jacket would do well enough, as long as they were indoors.

Nicholas was sent to the kitchen for a meal and wine, and Stephen heartily envied him. He himself had to follow a servant old enough to have buried Abraham through miles of castle hallways, until he came to the Baron's study.

"Wait here," said the old man, and Stephen waited among the old books and odd busts of unfamiliar people until the door at last opened again.

"Mr. Price?" Stephen stood tiredly as a friendly voice boomed, "My apologies for making you wait! Tukrest only just gave me your letter."

The Baron was a big man, wide and tall, with jet black hair. He was also an eccentric. He wore a long banyan gown, embroidered with Persian designs, and a set of Turkish slippers. It occurred to Stephen that he could see where his daughter got her sense of fashion.

"You're welcome, sir, welcome!" The Baron wrung his hand. "We don't get many visitors up here, so you're doubly welcome! Sir John tells me you're in need of a few days of rest. Overwork, sir! The curse of you British! I hate to see so young a gentleman fall prey to it. Sit down, we don't want you on your feet!"

Stephen sat, feeling himself in the grip of a force of nature. It would be best to simply cooperate until the friendly tornado passed.

"Have you eaten yet? I hope not!" cried the Baron, ignoring Stephen's shake of the head. "We don't keep country hours here, sir! Why, it's barely nine o'clock, on a fine summer's day! A feast awaits you! Go to your room, Mr. Price, and—" The Baron paused to fling open the door. "*Tukrest!*—By the time you've washed and rested a bit, you'll find—*Tukrest!*—you'll find mountain hospitality laid out and ready."

He'd grasped Stephen's hand and pulled him to the door. Stephen's gaze happened upon a portrait above the lintel, and the Baron saw his glance. "My third Baroness. A woman of infinite wisdom and patience. She put up with much, sir." She looked to be a girl of fourteen, but perhaps it was the light.

*"Tukrest!"* Stephen tried not to jump. "Ah, there, you are. Conduct Mr. Price to the room over the armory. Mr. Price, delighted! Sir John writes such praises of you in his letter! I look forward to your judgment of my wine."

Stephen cursed Sir John, who, of course, had the devil's own sense of humor. But with any luck, the Baron would continue to require little in the way of conversation.

Once in his room, he waited impatiently until Nicholas appeared from below. Stephen nearly yanked him through the door. "Thank God! Tell me about wine."

Nicholas said, "It's a solace to mankind."

"Damn it, man, seriously. The Baron thinks I'm an expert."

Nicholas shrugged. "The best wine is in the kitchens, and if I may judge by what I just sampled, the Baron has a fine cellar."

"But what should I say when he asks?"

"Look at the bottle—if it's French, tell him good things about French vineyards. Cheat."

"But see here, Nicholas—he's very likely to have decanted before I see it."

"You're a British spy entrusted with the welfare of a nation, but you can't arrange a glimpse of a bottle of wine? You need more help than mine. Sir."

Stephen gave him a sour look. "You know very well I'm entrusted with as bloody little as possible."

Nicholas glanced around the room. "I see they brought up our bags. Good." He lifted Stephen's bag, set it on the cedar chest at the foot of the bed, opened it, and began laying out his things. As he worked, he said, "If it's served with a sweet, tell him he's achieved the perfect balance between the poles of taste. If it's served with a savory . . ."

"Yes?"

"Hmm. Tell him the same thing, I suppose. Shouldn't you be more concerned with the assignment that brought you here?"

Stephen paced the room. "That much is under control, whereas the wine could prove embarrassing."

There was a knock on the door, and he opened it to find old Tukrest standing there uncertainly. "Dinner is nearly ready to be served, Mr. Price. May I conduct you?"

Damn. Stephen changed quickly while Nicholas made a clucking sound. "Late to table, not a good start."

"I don't think the Baron is the sort to keep to the proprieties. But it's a pity if I can't escort Lady Clothilde in to dinner; I'm looking forward to that."

They had not waited for him, which both relieved and annoyed him. A British house would not have begun the meal without the guest being seated. He entered the dining room, a formal smile on his lips.

It was a banquet hall, with the mahogany table of a king. The family was grouped about one end, an empty chair placed among them. Candelabra lighted the sideboards, and everyone was dressed as though for a ball. His first thought was that he was glad he'd brought the clean uniform after all.

"Mr. Price!" boomed the Baron's voice from across the hall. "Join us! Let me make you known to my dear children!"

Stephen walked forward. Three faces turned to him. Three pairs of dark, sparkling eyes, three heads of dark hair framed by artful curls, three lily-necks emerging from gowns of sheer Paris cut.

The Baron was an eccentric. His French wife had insisted on a feminine name for her infant, but he'd carried his own way with the others.

"Michael," said the Baron, and his oldest daughter nodded. Her lips curved in a smile that was familiar to him.

"Clothilde." But Clothilde's smile was also familiar.

"And dear Ilyest." The youngest daughter did not smile, but this fact did nothing to comfort him.

For once Stephen's ready tongue deserted him.

"Dear me," said the Baron, "our guest is rooted to the spot by your beauty. Damien! Wine for Mr. Price! Let us coax him to the table!"

The servitor poured a glass and handed it to Stephen, who received it mechanically. As their hands touched, Stephen noted the blue collar of a Tanmore tattoo at the wrist. He looked up involuntarily, meeting the man's eyes, and saw there the stare of a confused recognition.

"Mr. Price?" inquired the Baron.

And for the first time in eight years, Stephen began to laugh.

# WHERE ANGELS FEAR TO TREAD

## *by Laura Anne Gilman*

Though best known as a science fiction and fantasy editor, a role which enables her to select and refine the books we buy (and to understand the agonies writers undergo), Laura Anne Gilman is also an author who understands the creative muse—or at least how powerful that muse may be! She has published short fiction in *Amazing Stories,* and a number of anthologies, one of which earned her an honorable mention in 1996's *Year's Best Fantasy and Horror.* She has also cowritten a Quantum Leap novel, *Double Or Nothing.* The story debuting here is a powerful tale of the future—or possibly of the present. If we're not careful.

"We'd like to hire you." Her voice was shaky—not on the surface, but underneath. Where the sharks can smell it. She knew it, could hear it in her own voice, and shifted to the attack. "If you think that you can handle the job, that is."

The lady had style, I'd give her that. I wasn't surprised that Walt had given her my contact number—he was always a sucker for damsels in distress. Now we just had to hope that *la policia* hadn't begun recruiting social workers as bait.

That's what she was, this Annie McCarthy. A social worker. A doer-of-good. And she and her coworkers wanted to hire me for a job as-of-yet unspecified. Knowing better, I was still intrigued. What do social workers need with *a ladrón*—a thief—like myself? Somehow I didn't think they were looking to add to their funding by boosting a few pretties from Gracie Mansion. Not that this would be a bad idea. . . .

I was tempted to *=push=* her for the information, but didn't have the energy to spare. I keep my particular skills for the jobs, and let negotiations handle themselves. No remnant of fair play, just common sense. If you blow all that psychic energy up front, you've got nothing left in reserve. So I sat back, leaned the wooden chair against the wall like I had nothing better to do and nowhere in particular to go, and waited

"Children, Mister—" She waited for me to cue her. I hadn't given them my name, and wasn't about to now. Giving me a have-it-your-way look, she continued. "We're talking about children. Stolen from their homes, broken, and used for labor in some of the worst hellholes we've ever encountered. And we can't do anything for them."

I raised an eyebrow at that. Wasn't that—saving the world—what social workers were for? Social workers and cops and judges, oh my. Another woman noticed my near-sneer, and took over the narrative.

"Oh, there are laws, and we can bring charges against the bastards—but they're gone before the warrants can be filled out. They close up shop, and disappear into the night. And they take the children with them." The new speaker was Ilene, a broad-shouldered black woman of perhaps fifty. She'd been in what she called the "used kid biz" for twenty years, and to be honest there probably wasn't a horror that she hadn't seen, not a sob story she hadn't heard. The rest of the women in the room, seven total, were much the same. Tough cases, with the hard-eyed look that spoke of too much seen, and too little done. They were the system—and the system didn't work. Big surprise. I wasn't going to cry into my coffee in sympathy. But I was beginning to understand that turning to me might not have been such a big step for them after all.

Ilene's hand trembled as she downed another holly-and-ivy decorated Styrofoam cup of coffee. The other women pretended not to notice. She was telling me about their last attempt, which had ended with two cops and three kids wounded, and none of the slavers captured. That was her word, not mine. Slavers. It sounded so . . . Gothic. Or did I mean medieval? My education's sadly lacking. A voice I try to listen to was telling me that not all the money in the world was worth this—and these ladies weren't likely to come up with anything near that amount. But they had come well-recommended, and that meant they had to have at least some cash on hand. So I put my instincts on the back burner and settled down for a long listen.

"It was purely by luck we found out about this." Annie had taken the story back up. She was their leader, obviously. "One girl came in, a runaway, who told her caseworker about kids who were disappearing off the street. Not going home, not OD'ing. Disappearing. Wholesale numbers. That was unusual, so my office looked into it."

"And?" I prompted her, accepting another cup of what was passing for coffee from the one Asian woman in the group, a tiny thing with the unlikely name of Gertie.

"And we found two of the girls in an empty warehouse, chained to a wall. Stinking in their own shit. Their 'master' had left them there, they said. Because they spoke to outsiders. So now they won't say word one. They just sit there, and stare at the wall, and whimper for their 'master.' "

Uh-huh. Better and better. Every inch of my gut was screaming to get out, and get out now. This was *not* my kind of job. I've never been fitted for shining armor, and the only time I got near a horse I broke out in hives from the smell of cop all over it. "So you've all pooled your knowledge, and come up with . . . what?"

Ilene took the lead again. "This job's tough, and civilians can't always handle that. So we all tend to hang together socially as well as professionally. And the topic—came up." She stopped to take a breath. "Once Margaret and Annie mentioned it, we all found similar cases, all in the New York area. Four times, in four different cities, children between the ages of seven and fifteen have been found, chained and abandoned."

Ilene got up to refill her cup from the pot of coffee warming on the table. The small meeting room was chilly. Apparently the Y didn't believe in heating basements. Cold must be good for the souls of young Christian women. Didn't do much for mine, but I wasn't young, Christian, or a woman. Which thoughts meant I was letting my mind wander again, and as the saying goes, it's far too little to be let out alone.

The rest of the story was pretty much what I'd expected: children sold for the price of crack, or to satisfy a debt, or simply to get them out from underfoot of parents with too many children, too many bills, and too few options. What was interesting was that *la policia* had found records, bills of sale, during that failed raid. The younger the child, the higher the price, apparently. Male, female, black or white or Asian didn't seem to matter. Just age, and the fact that the parent freely relinquished all rights to the child. Interesting. Why go to such lengths to ensure the kids were free-and-clear?

I didn't immediately think witchcraft, or satanic worship, or any of that other crap that The Public has been trained to immediately suspect. I have a much more cynical view of human nature and needs. More likely, whoever was behind this was using that information to break these kids. Tough to hear that mamá and papá didn't want you any more.

But none of that mattered to me. It wasn't my job to figure out the whys and wherefores. My job, which being a smart boy I had managed to figure out by now, was to get them back. Without, of course, getting caught by either the cops or my target. Or getting killed, natch.

I'd have to be *loco, un estrafalario*, to take this job. But hey, what's life without a challenge?

"Ey, Crannie, time to wakies, wakies!" I know she hates that. It's why I do it. My not-so-faithful assistant poked her tousled head over the loft and bleared down at me.

"For chrissakes, Miguel, I hope like hell you've got a job, to be waking me this goddamn early."

I stood and admired the line of neck into shoulder that her pose afforded me. "Yes, my precious, we have ourselves a job."

"Uh-huh." I tensed, knowing that voice. "And is this the come-kiss-me heist somewhere warm you promised me last winter, or are we stuck in lovely Jersey City again?"

Uh-oh. Busted.

"Goddamnit!" she roared, throwing off the covers and shimmying down the loft's ladder with a grace I could both admire and fear. She continued to question my birth, my sanity, and the status of my genitalia, all the way to the main floor, even while pulling my robe off its hook and wrapping it around herself. I keep the studio well-heated, so it was more to show her displeasure than to protect herself from drafts. I took this disappointment in stride.

"Now, now, Crannie, that's hardly polite language for one of your social status."

She added a few comments on my own status as gutter filth to her tirade, at which point I gave up and went to make some coffee. That swill the night before had been worthless except as engine lubricant. When she finally ran down, and came into the kitchenette after me, I was settled with a double-sized cup, a bagel, and the late-edition *News*.

"Okay," she said, braiding her hair off her face with quick movements that never ceased to fascinate me. "Gimme."

Finding Crannie—Angelina Cranford of the Manhattan Cranfords to her peers—bored out of her stoned little wits during a High Society party I was crashing, was definitely a case of the good Lord looking out for children, drunks and fools. She understood the fascination of the Game, but never got so caught up in it that she made mistakes. That was why I took her on as an apprentice, once the appeal of banging each other senseless had worn off. That, and the fact that she's as mercenary as they come. I wasn't more than five words into my story before she cut to the chase.

"This is going to be one of *those* jobs, isn't it? Have you forgotten that this is supposed to be a business? You know, get a contract, get the item, get the money?"

I stared into my half-empty mug, wanting very badly to deny her words.

"Isn't it?"

I looked up then, gave a little half-shrug. "Two out of three ain't bad?"

She glared at me, threw up her hands, and perched herself with a little hop onto the minuscule counter space left next to the coffee maker. "Hired by social workers. Christ Almighty. So, Han Solo, why're we 'doing a favor' for the system *this* time?"

I recounted my previous evening, not leaving out any of the particularly gritty details. The perfectly maintained mask she uses for a face didn't so much as twitch, but I saw a definite flicker of interest. Maybe she wouldn't leave my *cojones* in the dust for the crows after all.

"My gut tells me that this guy's weeding the kids out, abandoning the ones who still had some fight left in them. The ones they've been able to locate were sold to dealers who needed cheap labor, or sweatshops not even willing to spend the money it would cost to hire illegals. They've been keeping about a third of their inventory. I figure—"

"So, what? We find the goods on these guys, then what? Wrap them up nice and neat for the cops? Christ, we're the bad guys, remember?" She was tapping one perfectly manicured nail against the newly whitewashed cabinet, the only sign that she was—against her mother's advice—thinking.

"We're not the bad guys," I reproved her, watching that finger the way seismologists consider their monitors. "We're the underdogs. The champion of the have-nots. The whiff of excitement into their normally dull and dreary media-driven days."

"Careful," she said dryly, leaving off that infernal tap-tapping, "you're giving yourself a boner."

Be damned if she wasn't right.

"The shit/has/hit/the fan."

That brilliantly poetic observation came from my cohort. Fortunately, I don't keep her around for the quality of her conversation. I grabbed the night-vision binoculars from her and took in the scene.

"Oh, shit."

"Isn't that what I said?"

Even as we squabbled, Crannie and I were moving into action, packing up the 'nocs and the assorted debris of our stakeout. While she made sure that we had left no trace of our stay there, I hefted the leather weight of my workman's belt to a more comfortable position, making sure that my tools were in order. One job, I had forgotten to secure the penlight, and spent five minutes searching for the lock in order to pick it. I try not to make the same mistake twice. New ones—hell, yes—all the time. But repetition is so boring.

Crannie whacked me on the ass, not lightly. "Move it, boss."

Sliding out the second-story window of the abandoned warehouse where we had been stationed for too many cold hours, I kept one eye on the activity in the building while the other watched my footing on the icy fire escape steps. Damn damn damn damn. From the activity we were seeing, they were moving the kids too early. My employees claimed that the shipments went out with the early morning rush hour, hidden in the traffic. Their information was wrong, by at least two hours. Dodging homeless bodies, I jumped onto the running board of the Toyota pickup parked in the alleyway below us.

"I hate it when a plan doesn't come together."

That was Crannie, squirming into the driver's seat, swearing when the seatbelt didn't pull smoothly. She started the engine, careful not to give it too much gas and attract attention.

The social justice squad had wanted me to take the kids away as soon as possible, to avoid the risk of them being spirited away again. I let them natter, advice running over me and none of it sinking through. Even before I'd scoped out the place these goons were keeping the current crop, I knew that was a good way to get myself killed, something I try very hard to avoid.

Instead, Crannie and I were going to run a variant of our highwayman routine. The old "stand and deliver" bit. You'd be amazed, even in this day and age of personal security, how many folk carry pretties on them without even half-assed precautions. Clean, fast, and lucrative. And when I let Crannie do the up-front work, some of the guys even think it's worth the cost to their wallets.

But for this, we needed something more subtle. Reclaiming a dozen kids, some of them likely drugged to the gills, needed a bit more cover than usual. I'd spent a few days with road maps and an old trucker friend of mine, and come up with a plan that should work. If nothing went wrong, the stars were aligned properly, and the gods were kind.

In my line of work, however, the gods are more likely to look down upon me and snicker. By moving the kids early, these bastards were sending my entire well-thought-out plan to pieces. Nothing too unusual, as Crannie was fond of reminding me, but in this case the loss wouldn't be a handful of pretties going on to their rightful and legal owner rather than myself, but twelve kids for all practical purposes disappearing from the face of this earth.

Goddamn it. I'm not the Salvation Army. Why couldn't I have passed on this job, maybe taken the holidays off? I pushed my fingers more securely into the black leather of my gloves, and thought dire thoughts about my ego, and the unhealthy urge to show off.

We sat there in the pre-dawn gloom, the engine idling, until they'd finished loading the eighteen wheeler pulled into a garbage-strewn loading bay. The front end of the vehicle stuck out into the deserted street so that we had a good view of the cab, and a bad view of the rear. I'd spent some time in the back of a truck like that, when I was a punk trying to heist a few loads of cigs before they were stamped and sealed by the tax man. Unless some serious money padded that hold, their cargo was in for a long, uncomfortable ride. And somehow I didn't see the bosses passing out any cash that wasn't essential to the upkeep of their merchandise. Good business sense, after all. Something Crannie never tired of telling me I lacked.

But after she got a decent glimpse of the bodies being pushed up the ramp, my protégée was conspicuously silent. These weren't children. They were wraiths, obviously unwashed and underfed even at this distance. Shrunken, silent, and barely human. I dropped the 'nocs to the seat and stared out the window while dawn made its first acquaintance with the snow-crusted street.

There was a news article I had read some months ago, about a young boy in Pakistan who was sold to a carpet maker to pay for his brother's wedding costs. Sold for $12. How much, I wondered, were these *niños* going for? I knew the streets, knew the price people put on flesh and what they used it for, and not much shocked me any more. But those kids were broken, worse than anything I'd ever seen. The kind of people who could do that weren't human. Not to my way of thinking about it.

Out of the corner of my eye I saw Crannie unlock the glove compartment and pull out our sole means of self-defense. I didn't say anything as she loaded it.

The obscene parade ended, and the ramp was removed, the heavy doors swinging together. Although at that distance we couldn't hear anything, I knew the instant the doors slammed shut and the insides were plunged into blackness. Beside me, Crannie said something rude under her breath, and placed her hands at ten and two on the steering wheel.

"Steady," I cued her, more for the need to hear my own voice than because she needed reminding. "Let them turn the corner first."

"Teach your gramma to suck eggs," she snarled. Her gaze fastened on the back end of the truck. One man on the sidewalk waved the driver off, indicating an all-clear, and the truck pulled out into the street.

The moment the truck finished turning and headed down the street away from us, Crannie pulled out of our hiding spot, every movement smooth and silent. There was a reason I let her drive.

The truck did the expected thing, rumbling though the back streets of Jersey City, heading toward Route 1. Southward. Philly, then, and not Manhattan. All to the good—Manhattan gives me hives. I pulled out my map and started marking off spots with a red wax pencil, overriding previously penciled-in marks. The waxed-paper map had been my sole Christmas present from Crannie. I had given her a pair of black spike heels. We were both reasonably pleased with our loot.

"One thing in our favor," I said now. "Likely, they're not going to call in the troopers for backup."

Crannie grunted, not really listening to me. She tends to shut me out when she's concentrating. Could be why our sex life never went very far.

After twenty minutes of pothole-ridden road, I was tapping my hand against my thigh, the slick nylon running pants a comfortingly familiar sensation. Some wear black denim on a job, or sweats, but I got caught in a drainpipe one night, and the sensation of wet denim against your skin is enough to drive a soul into honest work. This material slicked off all but the worst rain, and didn't reflect light the way a raincoat would. And best of all, if caught—I was merely out for a jog. Everyone knows joggers are crazy, right?

I reached for the volume knob of the CB radio, installed where a stereo would be in anyone else's car. If the driver currently cruising six lengths ahead of us noticed something off, we had to know immediately. I had the police scanner tuned in as well, and only training allowed me to keep the noises from both straight in my head. All was clear, just the usual post-holiday traffic on the road. I do so love New Year's. All those wonderful hangovers making people forget to put their jewelry back in the safe, or neglect to hit the "alarm" button on the security sensor. Just the thought of how much money I could have made this weekend made my teeth ache, and the roof of my mouth water.

I forced my attention back to the map, making several

more marks before folding it to show the current territory and letting it lie flat on my lap. We had a while to go before our first opportunity, and I was bushed.

"Wake me when we reach the first marker." I directed my driver, and let my head slump back. With fine-honed skill, I was asleep in seconds.

True to the plan, Crannie woke me just as we passed the sign for North Brunswick. Any longer a nap, and I would be too groggy to be much use. Rush hour traffic was rumbling along, the eighteen wheeler moving at a steady clip just within eyesight. Crannie was keeping pace with another red pickup, occasionally making eye contact with the driver, a scruffy-bearded blondie with muscles where his brains should be. My waking up put an end to that game. I needed coffee. And a plate of *huevos*, but that would have to wait. Coffee was in the thermos just at my feet. A long gulp, and I felt almost human again.

"According to Dale"—that was my trucker friend—"the only weigh station open is just past Lawrence, before we hit Trenton proper. So we've got another thirty miles or so." That was a blessing. Let the tension build too much before a job, and you're more likely to make stupid mistakes. And stupid mistakes get you permanently unemployed.

Crannie nodded, shifting her position slightly. "Only two of them in the cab. You still want to take them after the station? I'd be happier if we were out of sight of that many boys with popguns."

I shook my head. "I'd rather them be relaxed, think they've cleared the last hurdle before delivery."

Crannie harumphed softly. She wasn't convinced, but I was boss. She ever took to arguing with me during a job, that was when she went solo.

"Think we can count on the kids to help out, once we spring them?"

I looked at her with disbelief. Had she seen the same kids I had? "No."

"Didn't think so," she said softly.

North Jersey has its share of hills and rises, and even a few things that a millennia ago were mountains. But the farther south you go, the flatter and flatter the landscape becomes. It's pretty, but boring. And the early-morning view from Route 1 wasn't even all that pretty. By the time we reached signs for Lawrenceville, I was ready to scream. Loudly.

"We're on deck," Crannie said softly, glancing down to where the loaded gun lay next to her thigh. Two dangerous weapons. She'd dressed for the part before we left the loft this morning. The weather conditions had worked against her usual leather mini, but the black velvet leggings and high-heeled boots should work just as well, if not better. Leather might set off warning lights for our boys. Velvet and durasteel, and she'd have them trussed for dinner before they could spit.

The rest was my job.

The sign for the weigh station came up before I was ready for it. Gnawing my lower lip, I double checked my toolkit yet again, wishing for something more useful to do with my hands. Slowing the truck, Crannie shut off the CB—too much static from the line of truckers bored out of their skulls—and turned up the police scanner. From here on in, that scanner would be our metronome, ticking off the pace of this job.

From Dale's description, I followed our target mentally as they joined the line of truckers waiting in line to be weighed by equally bored guys in cheap polyester khaki uniforms. If we were lucky, they'd be so bored our target would slip right through. If the local gendarmes whiffed something wrong, they'd have that truck unloaded in a matter of minutes, and that would be the end of that.

Sometimes Crannie can read my mind. Parking on the shoulder a mile ahead of the entrance ramp from the station, she put her blinkers on and turned to me. "Why don't we just tip the cops? You'd still have sprung them—still collect the money. And we wouldn't run the risk of getting our asses shot off."

I closed my eyes, wishing that it were that easy—that I had never seen the "package" I had been hired to deliver to safety. "Yah, they'd still pay us. And your pretty little ass would be much safer. But that's not what I was hired on to do, and that's not what I'm going to do."

Crannie looked at me then, her blue eyes wide. "What are you going to do?"

I didn't answer her. I wasn't sure myself. But there was

a hard, painful voice telling me it had something to do with justice. Retribution. Something violent, and unfamiliar, that felt good in my gut. It didn't feel like a job any more.

Raising the 'nocs to my eyes. I waited for endless moments, until I saw the now-familiar truck coming down the exit ramp from the weigh station. Apparently, they'd managed to slip by without attracting attention. Why did that not surprise me? How many times had they done this, after all. It must be routine. They were confident. And confidence made for casualties. Hopefully, theirs.

Indicating the truck to Crannie, I slid down in the seat as she flicked on the flashers and got out of the car, her pout already in place. Stalking to the front of the car, she threw open the hood, then moved herself into the road, innocent face and devil's body ready to flag down the first red-blooded male to come her way.

If this didn't work, we were screwed.

Fortunately, God was gracious. I must remember to sacrifice a goat sometime soon. The eighteen wheeler slowed just enough for Crannie to make eye contact. That was all I needed. While my assistant did her best to exude come-fuck-me helplessness, I did what has made me such a valued employee of any number of organizations and individuals. I *=pushed.=*

The truck slowed even further, and one of the goons jumped down to saunter over to the damsel in distress. Damn. I was hoping to catch both of them. Oh, well. What can't be helped, as my *abuela* used to say, must be kicked in the ass.

*Abuela* was a tough old broad.

Picking up the gun off the seat and sliding out the side door while goon #1 was preoccupied with my now-ditzy assistant, I strolled to the back of the truck, all the while keeping up a steady whisper of no-see-me's. I like to think of it like the old cone of silence from "Get Smart," where the Chief and Smart would have a conversation that anyone with half a talent at reading lips could pick up. If you knew what I was doing, the gig was up. But with a little distraction I could walk up to a mark and take cash from his hand.

Easing myself to the back of the eighteen wheeler, I took a deep breath, held it, then let it out slowly. This was the sticky part. The mark didn't see me because he wasn't expecting to see me. Shifting his mind away from me was just a matter of letting it believe what it expected to believe. But they would be looking for any motion from the cargo area. Taking another deep breath, I *=pushed=* against the mind of goon #2. He wasn't a dummy, which made my job easier, not harder. Dummies question their brains—smart people rarely do. After all, if it works, why second-guess it? I told him that he saw nothing in his rearview mirror, felt nothing through the cushioning of his vinyl seat. I thought about throwing in the suggestion that his partner and that chickie were going to put on a show any minute now, to make sure that his attention remained focused in front of him, but decided against it. The more balls you have in the air, the more likely it is that one of them's going to knock you senseless.

Taking a woman's compact out of the leather pouch at my waist, I wedged it in the truck's trim so that I could see the driver's side reflected back at me. If that door opened, I had to know immediately. Satisfied that the mirror was secure, I turned my attention to the doors in front of me. The lock was a good one, but nothing that would give me cause to sweat. Taking the essential tools, I had the hasp open in seconds. My hand on the bar, I hesitated one last time. Once I started to open this door, the job couldn't be called off. This was the sticking point. Either I did it or I didn't.

I could hear a truck rumble past us, and rested my head against the cold metal, wishing that I'd had the luxury of doing this job in full darkness. But, with any luck, not even the sight of kids fleeing across the highway like deer in the dusk would be enough to stop truckers intent on getting to their destination and catching some shuteye.

Not giving myself any more time to think about it, I slid the bar back and cracked open one of the doors. All of my concentration was on keeping goon #2 from hearing what I was doing, so I had almost forgotten what I was going to see when I got the door open all the way.

It wouldn't have mattered. No matter what I had expected, it wouldn't have prepared me.

Past the boxes piled for camouflage, bodies sat on the floor, each chained by one leg to a small hook set into the walls of the truck. Matchstick arms were crossed over protruding knees, and ribs etched themselves against too-pale skin. Their eyes flashed a yellowed-white in the daylight, and they tried to hide against the bare metal walls. All of them had been stripped of their clothing once they entered, I realized. Gritting my jaw until it ached, I heaved myself into the fetid darkness and closed the door behind me, making sure to hook one end of a braided elastic cord on the outer handle and attach the other end to my belt prevent me from locking myself in with the merchandise. Just call me a Boy Scout.

Clicking on a mini flashlight. I ran the pale light over the bodies, not daring to speak for fear that the sound would carry into the cab. Sound's a bitch to disguise. The bodies followed me with their gaze, not moving or making a sound themselves. Even from here I could see unhealthy bruises. I approached the largest of them, a boy of perhaps twelve, although it was difficult to tell. He had no facial hair, and damn little on his arms and legs either, but that could have been from malnutrition as well. He stared at me, barely moving, as I ran my hand over the chain, up to where it connected to the wall. Holding the penlight in my mouth, I went to work. This was tougher than the door had been—they didn't have to worry about nosy inspectors wondering about reinforcements here. His chain fell away into my hand, and I lowered it slowly to the floor. I waited to see how he reacted, but he just sat there, staring at me. Terrific.

Moving to the next body, I repeated my maneuver, then again, until all ten were unchained. By now, the first ones freed were starting to move slightly, lifting their arms and twisting their bodies as though expecting to be beaten for the mere act of movement. Dammit, I had no time for pity. Any minute now, Crannie was going to have to either back off, or put out. And if it came to the latter she wouldn't talk to me for a week. Better to get out now, and hope we were still on schedule.

Tapping the first body on the shoulder, I jerked my head toward the door, where a faint slant of light came in through the opening. He stared at me, uncomprehending. I swore silently. What did they want, an engraved invitation? It looked like I was on to Plan B. I damn well hate Plan B.

Sticking my head and shoulders out the door, I saw in my mirror that Crannie had both goons out now, heads down in the engine of the pickup. Good girl. Pulling myself back into the cover of the cargo area, I took a deep breath and closed my eyes. I hated this. I really, really hated this.

*=Pushing=* gently with my mind, I reached out for the ten minds sharing my space, gently weaving a web around them. Slowly, trying not to jolt their abused selves any more than I needed to, I created a compulsion to follow me without questions. Without sound. Without hesitation. I also, for good measure, threw in an image of the chilly basement where I had met with my employers. If I could get them out of here, they might eventually make their way someplace safe. That would complete the terms of my agreement. Clothing they'd have to find themselves. My skills had limits, dammit.

Tugging on my mental leash, I pushed open the doors and sat on the edge of the raised bumper.

*=time=*

*=time please=*

In the mirror I saw Crannie give one of the goons a pat on the shoulder, then climb into the cab of the pickup and start the engine. It turned once, then caught like the finely tuned machine it was. Shaking the fall of perfectly coiffed hair, she smiled and waved at the goons, who suddenly realized that they had given their windfall a way home that didn't involve sitting on their laps. They looked goonishly crestfallen. Idiots. If I'd been hired to transport deeply illegal goods, I wouldn't be so willing to take on an unknown passenger. But then, that was why I was now in possession of their cargo, and they were headed for a bad fall.

Timing the goons' movements, I *=tugged=* on the leash, bringing the oldest boy to my side. Indicating the pickup, I pasted an encouraging smile on my sweat-slicked face, and sent him on his way. Two more followed in swift order, clambering into the covered back and ducking under the blankets I'd thrown there hours before.

The truck vibrated from the slam of cab doors shutting, and I double-timed the next three bodies. It was time to be grateful for their conditioning—not one of them broke stride or looked around.

Two more, and the massive engine under my ass roared to life. Damn. If we started to move, I was going to lose something concentration-wise, and that was going to get us all killed.

*=go=*

*=go=*

Not waiting for Crannie to respond, I scooted backward and closed the doors behind me.

"Sorry, folks, but it looks like the freedom train's gonna be delayed a while."

They stared at me, uncomprehending. I stared back at them, my penlight the only illumination and only enough to cast them into shadows.

Half an hour by my watch, and my ass was killing me. How did they stand it? Answer: They didn't have a hell of a lot of choice. Idiot. The silence in the cargo area was worse than the discomfort; kids shouldn't be this quiet. Measuring the risk, I began to talk to them, quietly, the way you would a dog you weren't sure about. If you were to ask me five minutes later, I couldn't have told you what I said, probably something I thought would be soothing that was merely inane. It didn't seem to matter. I was talking just to hear myself blow wind.

Another glance at my watch, and I realized that I was going to have to do something fast. If I let them reach their destination, more goons would be opening those doors, and I didn't doubt that they'd have nasty little shooting things.

"Okay, here's the plan. I'm gonna throw you out of a moving truck. How's that?"

No response. Great. Nothing like a little enthusiasm. Leaning my head against the cold metal, I closed my eyes and tried to summon a little energy. I felt like a busted flush, but there wasn't a hell of a lot I could do about it. I still had four kids to recover, not to mention my own highly prized if aching ass.

There was a scuffing noise, and one of the bodies started across the metal floor toward me. Tensing despite myself, I wasn't ready for the tiny little hand that curled into mine.

Oh, hell.

A little head, hair stringy and soiled, leaned against my side. Such trust. What the hell had I done to earn such trust from this battered little bird?

Taking off my jacket, I draped it around bony shoulders. "Okay, troops. Here's the plan. They stop, and we scatter. Where, you ask? Damnifiknow. And what do we do if they start shooting at us?" I would have laughed if I thought that I had the energy to cover the sound. "Then, *niños*, you duck."

Dislodging my limpet, I dragged myself over to the door and pushed it back open, careful not to let it swing away from me. Peering out, I saw unfamiliar roads rolling past in the sunlight. Damn. We weren't going into Philly, then, or we were using routes I wasn't familiar with. That was a problem—we could be ending up anywhere, and quite possibly soon. On the other hand, these near-empty fields would make for better escape routes than a cement-lined interstate. I felt bodies pressing against me, and squared my shoulders.

"Hang on just a second longer." I told my troops, then lifted my hand to my mouth, took the flesh between thumb and forefinger into my mouth, and bit down hard. The pain cleared my brain for just long enough to *=yell=* at the goons that their front tire had just blown out.

The truck swerved, then straightened, rolling to a stop at the side of the road. Throwing the door open, I tossed the jacket-covered bundle off, followed in quick succession by the remaining three bodies. They moved without my prompting, dashing in four different directions. It would have been easier for me to cover up movement in one direction, but I couldn't fault their instincts. Two goons, four possible targets. If they could just keep working at that level, some of them might live long enough to grow up.

I heard a shout, then the goons came running. I slammed the door and slumped against the wall, too exhausted to do more than wish my charges well.

"Go after them, dammit! I'm going to check the back." Goon #2, giving orders. Coming to the side of the truck. Heading toward the doors.

I rolled over onto my side and breathed heavily, my head aching and my lungs burning. Terrific. I'd panicked, closing that door without my gewgaw there to prop it open. Which meant that I was now trapped inside this tin can. In the backwoods of Pennsylvania, with a partner who had no way of finding me, and me without the reserves left to *=push=* a mouse.

I reached for the pouch on my hip, touching the heavy leather like some folk would pray the rosary. Removing the pistol slowly, the cold metal seemed to burn my fingers with static. I didn't like guns. This one came off a retired cop who'd tried too hard to bust me when we were both younger. I'd taken it as a souvenir before he moved to Hawaii.

I'd never done more than shoot a few practice rounds in the alley. Never tried to point it at another person. Never needed to.

Not much point now either. Talent running on fumes, even if I started shooting the moment they opened this door, I'd still be taken out before I got ten paces. Fifteen if they couldn't shoot straight. I laughed, my voice strained like a smoker's hack. At least taking these bastards wouldn't be a bad way to go.

"Sorry, Crannie," I whispered. "Should have listened to you, just like you always said. Take good care of my business now, you hear me?"

Cuddling the pistol like a teddy bear, I wrapped my free hand around one of the chains set in the wall and braced myself for the inevitable opening of the doors.

© 96
danforth

# DIANA'S FORESTERS

## *by Susan Shwartz*

Susan Shwartz, five-time Nebula Award nominee and two-time Hugo nominee, has published several historical fantasies, including the recent *Shards of Empire*, and the upcoming *Cross and Crescent*; and has cowritten with Josepha Sherman the *Star Trek* novel *Vulcan's Forge*. Short story credits include contributions to *The Shimmering Door, Enchanted Forests, Dinofantastic, Chicks in Chainmail, Return To Avalon,* and many others; she edited the *Sisters In Fantasy* anthology series. As always with Susan's work, this story is created out of the truths of history, beautifully embroidered with her own special talent.

Shakespeare struggled up Gad's Hill. Settling his aching bones on the soft grass beneath an oak, he gazed down the road for Canterbury. Sweet Jesus, he was weary of this world.

He scooped up water from a nearby pool that reflected the moon's face and sighed. The walk from London had not been long, but he was scant of breath. *You're getting soft, my lad,* he chided himself. He had promised his company a play that would make angry Majesty laugh. If he failed, they could face worse than the plague years when, the theaters shut, honest city actors had to venture out on tour.

How long since he had truly rested? Not since last August when his Hamnet died. The grant of arms had arrived some months later to proclaim him, heirless though he now was, a gentleman.

He breathed in the country air. The midsummer night was filled with noises. Here on Gad's Hill, the city subsided into remembrance of burned-out fires, slops, bear-baitings, and the occasional charnel reek of a head crowning a pike on London Bridge.

"Why slog out to Gad's Hill, a twenty devils' way, Will?

You must be moonstruck!" Burbage protested when Shakespeare confided where he would go to seek rest and inspiration. "Midsummer night's short, robbers ply the road, God knows what else skulks in the woods, and you'd needs be wandering alone?"

*I am* never *alone.*

He might never have met proud Titania by moonlight in the forest, but, then, he was no Oberon—just, by the liberty of some very wretched clerks, Will Shaxper, Shagsper, or whatever. Prosperous, balding, dignified, with a share in a cry of players and the style of gentleman. None of which he could support unless he could *write* again.

Besides, he carried nothing that a highwayman might covet, except his knife, except his knife, except his knife. Nice rhythm: he must remember it.

He cast a loving glimpse at the shadowed forest behind him. Truly, his heart lay in the countryside: young Will, tanned and lithe, quick of foot or tongue, knowing in the ways of woods or rivers. In the shadows of Avon, he had snared coneys and tickled trout or a willing woman's thighs apart.

*Outwitted yourself there, didn't you?*

Oh, well, from that bargain pricked in the leaves, he had his pearl, Susanna, and he had had his twins, of whom Judith yet survived. And the children's mother, a good manager, a good woman, he supposed, God save the mark.

If he could have stayed in Stratford, perhaps at this very moment, he and Hamnet would be slipping out of the fine house—no, there would have been no London money to build it—well, they would have been slipping away from *some* house or other through the forest. His son. Shakespeare had been an unsatisfactory son. Perhaps Hamnet, had he lived, would have been equally unsatisfactory to him.

King Henry, whose history he aspired to write, had a noble father, old John of Gaunt, time-honored Lancaster. Had he ever lost a cherished heir, he would not have treated his son, Prince Hal, with such contempt. But surely a hero-king demanded a muse of fire, not a worn-out playwright. A fine irony: The bereaved father must write about a father who squandered the love of a good son.

*Next time, Will, try writing something easy?*

Shakespeare propped his chin on his knees where the

darns puckered his hosen and stared at the road. Now, how far had he gotten in what envious rivals who jeered at "Shake-scene" would surely call his latest highway robbery upon Holinshed? An old king, a cold king, tormented by guilt for the death of Richard of Bordeaux (about whom the less said the better for fear of Her Majesty's fears); the prince; Ned Poins; assorted rude mechanicals, and a meaty comic part he dare not name after Sir John Oldcastle, for Oldcastle died a martyr, and Shakespeare had gotten into enough trouble with great families already.

Now what? It was known the king had kept Prince Hal short of funds. Lollards such as Oldcastle were austere, which would hardly do. Make it not austerity, but debt. Shakespeare's Oldcastle . . . no, what was that other name? Fastolfe . . . Falstaff? Good: use it.

Make Falstaff always in debt from riotous living. Shakespeare smiled to himself. That would mean at least one fine wild scene in an inn. He could write such scenes in his sleep and often had. Trickier would be the episode chroniclers had always been at such pains to explain away: Prince Hal's highway robbery.

Shall the son of England prove a thief and take purses? A question to be asked—and most likely a line he would use. But why? And how would he depict in the confines of a wooden **O** a prince turned highwayman?

Seeking inspiration, Will tried to summon up that veritable prince's guard of characters and creatures that spilled from his consciousness into his plays. Lately, that riot of invention had failed. *I am most dreadfully attended,* he had once heard a gentleman of the court say. Another useful line.

He cupped his hand in the pool, bright with the full moon, and sipped again. Falstaff would have sack and sherry and nut-brown ale to wash down his pork and his pasties and the venison he would not have been especially careful about poaching.

Back to his play.

His characters would meet at Gad's Hill. Falstaff would boast of his thefts. What should Prince Hal do?

Well, Gad's Hill provided an answer to one problem: Falstaff's quarry. Why not Canterbury pilgrims? That would provoke a laugh and prove the Lord Chamberlain's Men were no nest of Papists.

Bells jingled down the road, growing nearer, sweeter, louder: bold pilgrims, traveling by night. Well, they would soon pass by Shakespeare's oak. A cloud seemed to wreathe the pilgrims: not dust, in this damp air, but a kind of light.

Shakespeare blinked. Had his fancy of an entourage of his own characters finally made him mad as the sea and wind when both contend which is the mightier?

He *knew* those pilgrims. A prosperous innkeeper, much pleased with himself and his company. A knight, a worthy man and well-tried, judging by his posture and how he sat his horse, served by a squire whose elegance would have been absurd if not for something firm about the jaw that marked him as the knight's son. A bold-eyed merchant woman whose riding dress had hiked up to expose a shapely ankle in red hosen.

Other pilgrims jingled by. Monks, priests, nuns, including a prioress, her elegantly draped black robes neatly arranged in one of the sidesaddles that Richard's Queen Anne had brought from Bohemia, fingering beads that looked more fit for dalliance than prayer. Yet the monasteries had been dissolved by order of Good King Henry.

The clothes on those pilgrims! Shakespeare had worked with enough court garments in the company's wardrobe to know that clothing could last for generations, especially if metal threads were woven in. Those dagged sleeves, the quaint headdresses . . . no one in London had worn such garb for generations; yet these seemed newly stitched.

Most frightening was how the pilgrims' lips moved as if they laughed and spoke, but he heard only the sweet bells on their horses' harness.

Sweat prickled beneath Shakespeare's old shirt. Who were these people—or what?

A man in sober mouse-gray velvet, a hat that covered all his head, and a discreet forked beard, reined in his horse and rose in the saddle, his head up like a hound sniffing the air. Shakespeare met the stranger's eyes and glanced quickly away, shocked by how those eyes pierced behind surfaces in a way, yet held such a kindly merriment. . . .

"Friend?" he called. Shakespeare had heard such accents on tour, when his company passed through villages so tiny that people seldom saw newcomers and, as a consequence, spoke a language quainter by far than London's speech. "I spy a kinsman out there."

The mouse-gray man's gaze fixed on Shakespeare like a forest archer stalking the Queen's deer. The man held up his hand. The pilgrims stopped. Even the bells fell silent. Dismounting, the stranger walked to the foot of Gad's Hill.

"I am coming up."

Shakespeare leaped from the grass. His bones protested, and he turned the twinges into a yelp. "I'll cross thee though ye blast me," he cried. He drew his knife and held it up, turning its hilt into a cross.

"Stay, illusion!" he commanded grandly. Herod in the old pageants could have thundered no more loudly. Words spilled from his mouth: *"If there be any good thing to be done that may to thee do ease and grace to me, speak to me. By heaven, I charge thee, speak!"*

"Well," said the gray man, *"Benedicite."* Making the sign of the cross, he smiled.

As his wife Anne had often told Shakespeare, curiosity would be his undoing. Still, the stranger had blessed himself.

"No smoke," said the man, "no turning upside down and vanishing in a gust of flame. I am no damned wight. By the bye," he added, "your exorcism was finely done, though your language is sorely changed from mine own."

Shakespeare saw himself in the other man's eyes: the domed forehead, the one earring, the eyes that loved to look on life or beyond it. There were indeed more things in heaven and earth than the university scholars' philosophy had ever dreamt of.

"You should write those lines down and use them later." The stranger fumbled in his pouch. "No tablets with you? These may serve."

He produced a wad of—parchment?—and rustled through it.

"Jesu, how I suffered for these records. Robbed three times in under a week," he muttered to himself. He chose out a few leaves and handed them over. "I can spare these, I think. The parchment's still quite usable."

Shakespeare looked down at it: scraped almost to the membrane in places, overwritten in others, and, in the old spiky hand replaced by the Italic script by scholars of the New Learning, a name. Galfridus Chaucier . . .

Or, as anyone who had ever blotted half a line knew him, Geoffrey Chaucer.

Shakespeare thought of making the sign of the cross himself, then bowed instead.

"The language has changed sorely from when I walked beneath the sun," Chaucer observed amiably. " *'The lif so short, the craft so long to lerne.'* " How do you this changed speech to write in?"

Of all the questions Shakespeare might ever have expected to hear from a fugitive of a Faery Rade, that was surely the strangest. Placing hands on his hips (one clutching the wadded parchment), he burst out laughing. "Here is God's plenty, Master Chaucer."

The man raised an eyebrow, and Shakespeare remembered that he had been schooled in the courts of England, France, and Italy. Another bow was called for and an introduction. "One William Shakespeare, late of Stratford-on-Avon, shareholder in the Lord Chamberlain's Men, bearing the style of gentleman."

Chaucer bowed in return, those deceptively mild gray eyes *placing* Shakespeare for all time. "Excellent well; we are both gentlemen. What is more to the point: we are both poets, though you are of the quick and I . . . ah . . . nonetheless, we are brother poets, and your need summoned me this Midsummer Night."

Shakespeare had summoned him? Day and night, this was stranger than even he had dreamed in his play of Midsummer Night.

"It is you who can command me," said Shakespeare. "You who are brother-in-law to the Duke of Lancaster."

"Ah, bless his third wife, the Lady Katherine," said Master Geoffrey. "Sweet Kate and her sister, my Philippa, a very sour pippin indeed. But a good woman for all that God rest her soul."

A little weak in the knees, Shakespeare sat again anc gestured to the grass beside him. Chaucer pulled a cuj from that capacious purse of his, scooped up water, anc offered it to Shakespeare. The moon in miniature bobbec in the cup like a toasted crab, and the water's taste wa sweet.

"What is it that you write?" asked Chaucer.

"Words, words, words," said Shakespeare. "Some poem in the mode of Petrarch—" Chaucer inclined his head, "— but mostly plays."

"Pageants?" Chaucer raised a brow.

"Far more than that." Shakespeare gestured, trying to create for this poet lost in time the playhouse that he loved, the crowds of groundlings, the dangerous young gentlemen seated on the stage, vying with the actors. "I seek to tell the tale of Prince Hal, Henry, fifth of his name."

Chaucer crossed himself. "I served his great-grandfather," He paused. "Who is the king now?" he inquired, circumspect as a practiced courtier.

"A virgin queen," said Shakespeare, enthusiastic as all London. "A great and puissant lady, descended from King Arthur himself."

*"In the'olde dayes of the Kyng Arthour, of which that Britons speken greet honour, Al was this land fulfild of fayerye."* Chaucer's eyes twinkled as he recited his own verse. So that was how the old tongue sounded!

"It is not Faery or such vanity that I write but history. Her Majesty was not precisely pleased with my last play about the fall of King Richard."

Chaucer shook his head. "I would think not. Well, then, what is the news? One night a year of liberty does not give me fresh news. Does England still fight the French?"

"We fought Spain," Shakespeare told him, striving to compress the long, long tale of years into a prologue clever enough to offer the old master.

"Ah, the world is much changed from my own. I am glad I walk no more beneath the sun. Tell me, this play of yours: Henry, you said, ruled France as well as England?" Chaucer's face lit. "I knew him as a boy—a promising lad, much favored by his grandsire."

"It is a hard tale to write," Shakespeare faltered, oddly shy.

"Well, what do you have, sir? Show me!" Chaucer gestured. "Otherwise, why summon me? Show me your work the way I have shown you mine!"

He gestured at the pilgrims on the road below: silent, motionless, frozen in a spell of dreaming. Even the stars seemed to pause in their twinkling.

"Come, man," coaxed Chaucer. "I'm safely dead, I cannot steal your play. Show me. Use the moonlight."

Stranger things *had* happened at Midsummer. How the moonlight glimmered in the pond, on the road, even haloing Chaucer's pilgrims. The light seemed palpable. Shakespeare put his hand out into its beams. Flesh and bone tingled.

He gestured. The moonlight coalesced, and a character began to form. Tall. Lean. Shabby, but possessing some smatch of honor. Shakespeare gestured again, lightening its hair.

"Edward Poins," said Shakespeare. "My Ned. Companion to the prince. A fork, feeding Prince Hal his lines."

Chaucer again raised a brow. "You make him Plantagenet in seeming. Come, sir, would you defame a king?"

"I defame a prince, making him a highway robber."

The Chaucer-apparition almost choked on another sip of the moonlight-laced water. "I would hear that story."

Shakespeare looked up at the moonlit sky.

"Have we not all night?"

"Show me your other players," Chaucer demanded.

Shakespeare's hand on the moonlight was surer now. Peto appeared and Bardolph, down at heels, at knees, at elbows, grotesque of nose and codpiece, and poorly armed. Chaucer grinned.

"Excellent. And their master? I knew Sir John Oldcastle, a very worthy man."

Lovingly, Shakespeare gestured. A stocky figure formed, sagged, grew gor-bellied, bowed of leg, fat of rump, bulging in a stained, torn doublet that had surely once seen court service. A hat with a tarnished feather perched on hair combed to hide its thinning: crafty little eyes, much reddened, but dimmed to embers by the magnificent crimson bulbous nose, its purple veins mapping their owner's dissipation. If a gypsy's bear could guzzle sack in human guise, this was surely he.

"Falstaff," breathed Shakespeare, proud as the first time he held his son.

Chaucer studied this last, best creation, his face expressionless by design, the ancient rogue.

Subtly, Shakespeare gestured. The character turned and winked at the two poets. A monumental belch emerged somewhere from the depths of that belly, shaking Jack Falstaff's frame.

"Now, Hal," he boomed, "what time of day is it, lad?"

Chaucer slapped his thigh and chortled, holding up hand. "I beg you, spare us! You'll set him farting nex and the night is far too sweet. Set your fat, aging misrule to act!"

"I thought," Shakespeare began, "I would have him rob some Canterbury pilgrims."

"What?" demanded Chaucer. "My young prince, a robber? I thought you cozened me. Did that happen in good sooth?"

Shakespeare shrugged. "In legend."

"Think, man. What turns a good man into a robber?" He looked at Shakespeare, then whistled a ballad he had known since boyhood.

"Robin Hood!" he exclaimed. "You can rob from a robber . . . so . . ." He slapped his knee. "Falstaff robs the pilgrims. Then the prince robs him!"

Shakespeare gestured. The figures moved, arguing, laughing, drinking.

"Let the prince protest, at least," said Master Geoffrey. "I know he is no robber."

"But the scheme for him to rob Falstaff?" Shakespeare would regret discarding that.

"You have your fork, Ned Poins. Have him feed it to the prince."

Shakespeare set his head upon one side. "How like you this? 'I have a jest to execute that I cannot manage alone.' "

Chaucer nodded. "Now, draw the action out."

How much easier it was to block a scene in moonlight than with living, breathing, *arguing* actors. Ned Poins proposed the jest: He and the prince would hide, disguised in buckram, wearing masks. Invention was easy enough to come by in such small things, but . . .

"Wherefore, you ask," Chaucer broke in, making the moonlit figures quiver, "should they do this?"

Shakespeare laughed as he had not laughed since word had come of his son's death. "I have it!"

He drew breath and spoke again, in a high, young man's voice, mimicking a young blade trying to ape the better-born. "The virtue of this jest will be the incomprehensible lies that this same fat rogue will tell us when we meet at supper: how thirty, at least, he fought . . ."

Chaucer nodded. "Write those words *down,* man."

Shakespeare bent his head and scribbled, aware of the old dead poet peering over his shoulder: So that was how pens looked now and that was how men wrote? Such small matters, yet so fascinating.

"I have it!" he cried "We start with Jack Falstaff. He's fat and scant of breath, the young men press him hard, they hide his horse, and he can walk no farther."

The moonlight figure staggered, lurched, threatened to break wind, and bellowed for his horse.

Chaucer laughed. "Now what?"

"Now," said Shakespeare, "enters the prince."

A sudden hesitation seized his hand: Chaucer had known Prince Henry. Gently, he stretched out his hand. A new figure materialized: young, handsome, grinning now, but with hints of resolve about the mouth.

"His father was taller," said Chaucer. "His grandsire taller yet."

"Look ye if the man who retakes France prove not every inch a king," Shakespeare replied. "Now, let it work. Mischief, thou art afoot!"

He gestured again. Prince and Poins slipped away, hands over their mouths so they would not giggle like the mad boys they had been scant years before, withdrawing into the woods for their buckram and their vizards, masking themselves, drawing swords, each shaking his head at the other when laughter threatened to overwhelm them.

"You would bring Jack Falstaff forward on your stage . . ."

"And off, still complaining. Then, just as he thinks he has gotten safely away . . ."

Shakespeare brought down his hand as if commanding a charge.

Poins and the Prince leaped forward.

"Your money!" cried the Prince.

"Villains!" shouted Poins.

Shakespeare swore and cried in the deep cracked Falstaff's voice he knew his company's best comic would use. Words bubbled from his lips, a fountain of lines to set the groundlings in a roar and bits of business that would even make the gentles laugh. He gestured, demonstrating to Chaucer how the actors would shout and chase around in circles, then run out. They would come crashing through the "woods" on stage, fatter and sloppier than Demetrius and Lysander, bemused by Puck. A pity he could not brin the wanderers of the night into the play, but it must be the history of a great prince, not some mad tale of Faery.

The prince pulled off his mask. He turned away from the running figures and spoke to Poins. "Got with much ease. Now merrily to horse. The thieves are all scattered, and possessed with fear so strongly that they dare not meet each other: each takes his fellow for an officer. Anyway, good Ned. Falstaff sweats to death and lards the lean earth as he walks along. Were't not for laughing, I should pity him."

"That's my prince!" Chaucer laughed until tears glistened in the moonlight on his face and fell onto the earth .

"Who's there?" the prince's voice went from laughter to a taut watchfulness. He had served, Shakespeare remembered, on the Border when he was barely more than a lad.

"Your change of tone was too abrupt there," Chaucer whispered to Shakespeare.

Shakespeare shook his head. "I did not write that line."

"I asked, 'Who's there'!" the prince repeated. He drew his sword and started up the hill. It was clear from the way he held it now how lax he had been in the mock assault on Falstaff. "If you are thieves in truth, surrender to a true-born prince."

"I never wrote those lines," said Shakespeare. He looked down at his knife. What use was cold steel against a spirit? And how would he dare draw on a true-born prince?

Assuming that he had time and skill: the young man who started up the hill was schooled in war. Robbing Falstaff was a jest: this was business.

Shakespeare flashed a glance at Chaucer, who gestured, *Let me handle this.*

*With all my heart,* Shakespeare gestured back.

The older poet rose and bowed deeply. The angry prince recoiled.

"Master Chaucer?" he exclaimed and crossed himself. "I lit mass-candles for you myself. What prodigy is this?"

"No prodigy, my prince," said Chaucer. "A poet at Midsummer."

Prince Hal glanced about. "The land is sadly changed. And that gangrel creature beside you . . ."

Chaucer laughed. "The poet who summoned me."

Prince Hal raised his sword. "You! Can you call spirits from the vasty deep?"

Shakespeare shook his head at the line. Just let him survive the night and he would appropriate it for Glendower, whose talk of the moldwarp and the eagle harked back to Merlin's prophecies.

"They never answered if I did, my lord," he told the apparition. "At least not until this Midsummer's Night."

Chaucer had started down the slope. He started to sink to one knee, reaching for his prince's hand, but Hal swept him instead into an impetuous boy's hug.

"Midsummer Night, my prince. Spirits walk abroad. And you, of Arthur's blood, are cloaked in magic."

"You look no different from when I was a boy," the prince told Chaucer. "No older. Yet I am now a man . . . sweet Lord, how long?" Awareness and the beginnings of fear dawned in his eyes.

"We have lain i' the earth nigh two hundred years," Chaucer told him. Both spirits crossed themselves. The Prince turned toward Shakespeare.

He had summoned magic he had not understood. Let the great ax fall, if fall it must. At least he had seen what he had seen. And he had traded verse with Geoffrey Chaucer. There were worse ways to go.

The air fell silent as he waited for the Prince he had raised to pass sentence upon him. "Lad . . . I mean, my prince," Chaucer began, but Prince Hal waved him off.

"You did not mean to rob me of my rest, but . . ."

Dogs erupted, barking, from the forest. *The little dogs,* something whispered in Shakespeare's consciousness, *Tray, Blanche, and Sweetheart* . . . Please God, he would live to use those words. Those were names for ladies' dogs such as Chaucer's prioress would overfeed. They were not names for the dogs he saw now, lithe ropy things with red ear and green, glowing eyes.

"*Benedicite,*" whispered Geoffrey Chaucer. Prince Ha crossed himself.

Those two were older than Shakespeare, closer to th land. They knew the stories, knew whose red-eared, green eyed dogs coursed the forest at Midsummer. Had Shake speare invoked Oberon and Titania? Older spirits than the and far more potent than the Puck roamed these woods.

He who ruled them emerged from the trees, dressed a a simple hunter except for the crown he wore, wrought twisted horns.

Shakespeare drew his knife. On such as he, cold iron . . .

"Get behind me, masters," came the prince's voice, as cool as on a battlefield.

"My prince, let me shield you!" cried Chaucer, and tried to push between him and the Horned King.

The young prince stepped aside. "I am a belted knight. It is for me to protect men in my grandsire's service. You, too, Master Shake-scene."

Where had he gotten *that* name? Shakespeare wondered.

The prince stepped forward, his gaze never leaving the shadows that masked the Horned King's eyes, and knelt in homage.

He held out his sword across his knee, hilt toward the Master of the Hunt, as if he presented his blade to the king his father.

The Horned King smiled austerely.

"Well done," he said. "And you, master poets. Your creations are strong."

"I thank you, Master," said Chaucer.

Shakespeare laughed somewhat uneasily and made as if to kneel, too.

"See thou do it not!" commanded the Horned King in a voice as sere as the last leaves clinging to a winter bough. "For are we not all England—I to rule its nights, you to shape its dreams?"

Shakespeare bowed his head.

"You, Master Chaucer. You begged leave to answer this man's call. But he has years left, and dawn is near. Are you ready to move on?"

"He is buried at Westminster," Shakespeare protested. For that matter, so was the Prince kneeling in homage before the oldest king of all.

"Ah, yes," said the King, "but once a year, he rides out with me on pilgrimage. How should it be otherwise? He loves this land as he loves his God; and both have their claim on him till world's end. Why should there be any less mercy to the blessed than to the likes of Judas. He, you recall, has leave to cool himself upon the ice each Christmas? Why should my Geoffrey be denied his midsummer night?

"For that matter," he added, "why should you? My court lacks a playwright."

Curiosity spurred Shakespeare hard. But never to see his

plays performed or write another? Never to watch the face of the audience light up and hear the crowds roar, the coin clatter in the till? Or see his daughters smile?

Shakespeare shook his head. The Horned King smiled.

"I wish I might have seen your play," said Maste Geoffrey.

"Come back next year," Shakespeare invited. "We'l have one other gaudy night. You, too," he nodded politely—was he not styled a gentleman?—at the Prince o his creation and the King.

They bowed to one other. The Horned King beckoned The Prince rose, bowed, and withdrew into the forest Chaucer walked down the slope. Shakespeare heard th jangle of bells and harness, fading into silence.

The summer mists rose and brightened. He yawned. Jus a few moments' nap before he returned to town. . . .

Shakespeare woke with a jolt that set every bone to lamenting. "And I awoke," he muttered, "and found me o the cold hillside."

He was too old to sleep out of doors. His scanty hai was matted, his mouth as dry as if he had drunk too much though he had drunk only water from the pool. A battere cup lay nearby, filled with leaves. Oak, ash, and thorn. I a circle around him, the grass had been trodden down. H still could see the pawprints.

"I have had a dream," he murmured to himself, "pas the wit of man to say what dream it was. Methought was—there is no man can tell what. Methought I was, an methought I had—But man is but a patched fool if he wil offer to say what methought I had."

Shakespeare rose, one hand to his back. Strangel enough, it did not ache. Something tumbled out of hi pouch and he bent to pick up . . . a wad of parchmen somewhat greasy and much scraped over so that the morning sun shone through it.

"Galfridus . . ." he read in old-fashioned letters, followe by lines he could not remember having written, but that h knew were his every bit as much as the two children wh lived in Stratford and the heir buried there. He shook hi head.

"The eye of man hath not heard, the ear of man hat

not seen, man's hand is not able to taste, his tongue to conceive, nor his heart to report what my dream was."

He glanced down the page at the words, the wonderful, funny words. More sang and thundered in his head, and he knew he would remember them.

The summer air grew warm. Insects and birds sang as he turned back toward the town. Behind him, more than just the water chuckled.

*Exeunt Omnes.*

# FOOL'S GOLD

## *by Doranna Durgin*

Doranna Durgin debuted in 1995 with a bang: her first novel, *Dun Lady's Jess,* won the Compton Crook Award. She has since published *Changespell,* a sequel, and *Touched By Magic,* the first volume in a new world. Upcoming novels are *Barrenlands, Wolf Justice,* and a short story featured in *Lammas Night.* In this anthology, Doranna (who, like her protagonist, is a mean stall mucker-out herself) marries two popular archetypes—the highwayman and the lycanthrope—with effective results.

The howl wound its way through the hills, echoing off the steep slopes until it reached the village of Silvercliff and was absorbed by fear. Raicha stood outside the inn's livery stable, shivering despite the warm spring air. The wolves were howling too often of late; she couldn't remember when there had ever been so many, and there was even talk of the wolf-kin, slaughtered to extinction as they were. Behind her, the stabled horses snorted, moving restlessly in their stalls. Some of them were passing through, but the inn's own horses certainly knew it was evening feeding time, and it made them all the more easily upset by the noise of wolves.

Raicha wished she had an excuse, too.

*Work,* she reminded herself, rubbing the goose bumps from her arms, and returned to it, though not before touching the protection ward over the door. She watered and fed the horses and the inn's two milk cows before she was interrupted by a polite call from outside the barn. Brushing hay from her shirt, she went to see who it was, knowing he wasn't familiar with Silvercliff if he hesitated to simply come in and bellow her name. She'd been working here for the last twelve years, since she'd reached seventeen summers, and everyone knew her.

She stood in the open door. Yes, a stranger. Long-legged, lean-hipped, with a day or two's growth of black whiskers obscuring the distinct point of his chin but in no way dimming the spark of his unusual amber-brown eyes. Nice. It'd been too long since she'd had a new face to look at, and everyone around here was far too used to looking at her to actually *see* her any more. These eyes were looking at her . . . and seeing her. Yes, very nice.

*Enough of that.* "Help you?" she asked, hoping her blush wouldn't show so much in the shadows of the sun gone over the western ridge, for her plain, freckled features showed her emotions far too clearly.

"I need a horse," he said, offering her a smile.

"What for?"

His smile turned to a frown, as if he hadn't understood that simple question.

"What for?" she repeated. "Hill riding, road riding, carriage pulling—and what's your experience?" Anybody else from Silvercliff asked for a horse by name; the inn had only a handful, and very few people had the pasture space for horses of their own.

His expression cleared. "Ah. Hill riding. Something calm. I'd like to arrange for daily rental starting tomorrow morning."

She turned his little frown back at him. He sure didn't talk as though he was from around here. Nor dress like it. In contrast to her own rough-woven trousers, he wore fine black leather pants, well broken-in and fitting him nicely indeed. Her sash belt looked like a rag next to the narrow, sparingly tooled leather belt riding the angles of his hips. And what she had once considered a sturdy, quality short-sleeved tunic looked like rough-weave next to the drape of his sleeves. The words slipped from her thoughts to her mouth. "You're not from around here, are you?"

"No," he said, unoffended. "Does it matter?"

She shook her head. "I know the horse for you. Mudpie. He's got a sure foot, and a steady pace. You won't get no speed from him, though."

"Mud-pie?" He raised a black eyebrow into the strands of his fallen forelock. In the deepening shadow she thought she saw silver, but he didn't look old enough to be growing out gray.

"It's a Silvercliff horse, not a fancy city horse. Might not be what you're used to, but it suits us out here."

That earned her two eyebrows. "I'm not from the city," he said, his eyes showing deep amusement—although Raicha didn't get the joke, not at all. "Now, who do I pay for this horse?"

"Inside. Big Rees. He ought to be behind the bar. You can come get the horse tomorrow, after the sun hits the top of the hill, there. If that don't suit you, we'll try to change his morning feed till it's timely."

"All right." He gave an odd little gesture, lifting his sharp chin up and over; she'd have missed it if she'd glanced away even a second. "Thank you."

"It's as right," she said, waiting until he'd turned his back and headed for the inn beside the stable. She watched him, admiring; his moderate size did nothing to diminish the powerful ease of his movement.

*Staring again.* Raicha closed her eyes, sighed, and returned to work. Whoever he was, he was just passing through, and she had a barn to sweep. It seemed as though she'd always had a barn to sweep, but in truth, that wasn't so. She'd had plans for a family, once. She'd once dared to love, a young love . . . a love who turned out to be a scoundrel, stealing one of Rees' best horses and running off with a customer's goods. This had been *his* job, and Raicha had stepped into it in a desperate attempt to appease Rees, to pay off the worth of the goods and the horse. She hadn't meant to stay on, not for so many years.

But it hadn't taken her long to learn that along with horse and goods, her young man had also taken her good name and left her tainted. She hadn't been much before, just a girl with plans for a family and a modest homestead—but now she was less. Soon enough, everyone had grown used to Raicha-the-stable-girl, and forgot she was ever anything else. She was a fixture, to be shouted for and handed horses, competent and . . . And nothing. If anyone suspected there was more to her, a woman complete with likes and dislikes and quirks and sometimes even a clean face and softly arranged hair, they never took the trouble to find out.

So Raicha swept, and then she cleaned tack, until the night closed in and the lantern flickered inadequately beside her. She leaned over it, peering through the smoky, wavery-glassed chimney to see if the light was dimming because the wick was short, or if the lantern was running out of fuel. But she jerked upright almost immediately, startled by the sudden shouting outside the barn. Shouting, though not at her; several people, growing louder . . . a wail of distress, a cry of grief; Raicha snatched up the lantern and ran to the front of the barn, hesitating in the doorway to decipher what she saw.

She couldn't even tell who it was, just a handful of people in the darkness, all running toward the inn, leaving a trail of alarm and excitement behind them. "Jinny!" a woman's voice cried out, harsh denial that made Raicha blink. "Jiiinnyyy!" There, there was the grief she'd heard before. But what—?

And then she saw them, coming into the tiny village, darkness-obscured figures running toward the inn. Something bounced off the shoulders of one, in the arms of another. Then she knew, and her grip on the lantern handle tightened until her blunt fingernails cut grooves in her palm.

They'd been due back yesterday, along with two sturdy inn ponies. Those had been for the children; Marnten had ridden his floppy-eared plow mule. And his wife had tried not to worry, had told anyone who would listen that there were plenty of things to have delayed them, especially if business had been good, but oh, how she wished she hadn't agreed to let the children go, even if it was time they learned this part of their fine silversmithing business, even if Jinny was nearly a young woman and Kurn just a year younger. How she wished they'd spent the coin for a good strong protective ward, or even a tiny spell of blessing.

But no one had known there'd be trouble in the hills, not then. The first attack had happened while the smith was gone, traveling to Joinen and then downriver to the big town of Sayerston. Marnten wouldn't have known there was danger in the hills, for there were often isolated incidents of trouble. But with two more attacks, and three deaths altogether now, there was plenty of reason not to trust safety in the hills to his slow-plodding mule, no matter how nimble the ponies.

Raicha watched the men run by, her eyes riveted on the flopping tail of Jinny's gold-blonde braid, dangling from a head too limp; that head had fallen back to stretch her throat to the dark sky, mouth gaping wide and black stains all over her face.

No, not black. Dark, dried red. Raicha couldn't see the color, but she knew it.

Movement at the end of the village caught her eye again—two men, carrying a larger figure. Marnten. Betrayed by his even-tempered, slow-moving mule.

*Mud-pie.* Even-tempered, slow moving. She had to find the stranger, push him to take a more responsive horse—or to stay out of the hills, whatever his business. Abruptly, she turned away from the grief and fear and the filling village street, heading against the stream of all those people pushing their way out of the inn.

There he was. Standing to the side, stiff with anger, his eyes soaking in the light of the lantern and throwing it back at her with an odd gleam. This time, his mouth was set and angry, the muscles of his jaw working.

"Why don't they stay out of the hills?" His voice was a growl, and an accusation. "Can't they figure it out? There are robbers in the mountains!"

Raicha took a step back, surprised at how menacing he suddenly seemed. She reacted as she would to a quarrelsome horse—calmly, smoothly, but not backing down. Not showing the fear. "Where else are we supposed to go? The miners got to get to town for supplies, don't they? Our silversmiths and smelters got to sell their goods somewheres, don't they? What is there around us *but* mountains?" She heard her voice harden. "I come to warn you that maybe reliable old Mud-pie isn't the safest horse for you, after all. But I guess you already knew it. It just don't seem to bother you."

He gave her a startled glance, but his grim expression hardly lightened. "He's fine. I'll pick him up tomorrow morning."

A fresh outburst from the gathering in front of the inn drew Raicha's sudden attention; after a moment of concentrated watching and listening, she realized everyone had learned what she already suspected. Jinny was dead.

Blinking back tears that would only obscure the poor light, she glanced back at the stranger. And then blinked again, for he was gone. It was no use searching shadows, not with the lantern flickering like this. Raicha smeared a forearm across her eyes, and went to see if Jinny's father or brother had survived.

The stranger told Raicha his name was Pheylan, and finally allowed that he was looking for *something* in the ridges and slopes that made up the tightly woven hills around Silvercliff, but not what. He came for Mud-pie early each morning, and returned him late, usually after dark. Raicha kept a close eye on the horse, who was at first uncharacteristically nervous under Pheylan's hands, but that soon eased, and she started watching for Pheylan instead of Mud-pie. He always had a rakish smile for her, while his eyes picked up the light of the lantern and flung it back at her, gleaming almost as brightly as a cat's.

She tried to pretend she wasn't curious, and that she didn't think about him in her quiet moments, or worry that he'd be robbed. At least there were fewer people dying. Instead, they came into town afoot, shocked and empty-handed, babbling about how the man had come from nowhere, but always seemed to have a gaily caparisoned horse waiting beyond the actual ambush. The man himself, they insisted, always came silently from behind. He left them on foot, alive and unharmed, and if they'd had a mount, it eventually wandered into town after them.

The wolves grew closer, and their howling louder . . . and, somehow, angrier. They often woke Raicha in the middle of the night, making her wish it was winter, when she slept at the inn instead of out in the hay loft. She bought herself a small charm and slept with it; she would have bought herself something stronger, a minor magic, if she could have afforded it, but those were rare in Silvercliff. She even thought about asking Rees if she could stay inside, but they were coming into the busy season, when merchants from Sayerston traveled up to buy the silver that had been collecting through the winter months.

Then came a day when one of the miners from the Northridge tunnel came sauntering into town, trailing a donkey well-laden with the rich silver the mine produced.

Raicha took the donkey, but kept an eye on its owner. The man was bursting with something; she couldn't tell what. She was on the verge of asking—a moderate rudeness—when it came bursting right on out of him.

"Met that robber," he declared, sucking noisily on the tobacco in his cheek.

"You what?" Raicha stared at him, thinking of the donkey's undisturbed burden.

"Yep, I sure did meet that fellow. Popped right out of the trees in front of me—right from nowheres!—and demanded my donkey. Waved his big fat knife right in my face."

And then she looked at his face, searching for some slight cut.

"Oh, no, I didn't give him no chance a'tall." The man smiled a gap-toothed grin, and neatly shot a gob of tobacco juice and spit at the side of the stable. "Grabbed me that little bag—there, on top—and fetched that robber such a wallop it laid him flat."

She just gaped at him. "Did you . . . is he . . . ?"

The man shook his head in disgust. "No. Damned donkey got fussed about it all, dragged me around a little. When I got it settled down, the robber was gone. But he's bound and certain to be hurtin'!"

She heard the story again at the inn, over dinner—from a handful of sources who embellished it without shame. They toasted the miner into drunkenness, communally pleased to have had someone strike back at the robbers at last.

That was before the riderless horse trotted down from the dark hills and into town, herded by wolf laughter bouncing around the slopes. No one knew the horse. A stranger, then. Someone who hadn't heard how dangerous Silvercliff's hills had become. Raicha breathed a sigh of relief when the horse was brought to her, and she saw it wasn't Mud-pie. Pheylan had not yet returned the rented horse this day, and it was well past the time he customarily ambled into Silvercliff.

She put up the horse. It was a handsome animal, aside from the fresh, puffy wounds around its hocks that looked more like the work of the wolves she was hearing than any robber's blade. What was going on in those hills? And where was Pheylan? Raicha found excuses to hang around the stable, forgoing the company in the inn. When she ran out of chores, she simply lingered at the stable door, letting the rare breeze play across her face, trying to tug straggles out of her sensibly braided, red-brown hair. She tried to pretend it was the breeze that drew her, and not any hope that she might spot Pheylan and Mud-pie.

But the moon rose high, the wolves howled faintly, and eventually, Raicha had to leave her post and climb into the loft for sleep.

Come morning, Pheylan greeted her at the door. Mud-pie crowded him, his neck stretched as if he could suck up the grain in his stall without actually entering the stable.

"You weren't supposed to keep him out all night!" Raicha pushed past Pheylan to inspect the horse, forgetting she was barefoot and wearing only a long tunic, her freshly washed hair damping the material.

"I was delayed," Pheylan said, not looking at her. "He's fine. I won't need him today, and you can keep the day's rental in return for last night."

Raicha ran her hand down the last of Mud-pie's legs and stood. There wasn't a mark on the horse, not even dried sweat under the saddle pad. He certainly hadn't been used hard. "He's fine," she agreed, and took the reins, leading Mud-pie into his stall where he plunged his nose into his grain bucket and only grudgingly let her pull it out long enough to remove the bridle. She dumped his saddle onto the half-door of an empty stall, stomping-around mad that she'd let herself worry so much.

Pheylan's cleared throat suddenly made her more than aware that although he was silhouetted against the light shining on the face of the opposite ridge, she was probably perfectly visible to him. In her tunic and bare feet, and long, wet hair. She felt the tunic's dampness against her chest, and crossed her arms in front of herself, staring back at him.

"Why are you here?" Pheylan asked suddenly.

She just stared at his silhouette, astounded.

"This is a job for the young. You shouldn't be sleeping in a barn loft, you should have your own home, and . . . and a family." He hesitated, as if he'd only then realized how rude the question was.

"I'm good with the horses," Raicha said, flat-voiced.

Pheylan gave her a moment's silence before he said, "That's not what I meant." He leaned against the thick timber of the door frame. "That's all right. It wasn't a proper question. I just . . . looking at you, I had to ask. There's more to you than this."

"There was, once," she said, all the angrier that he'd stirred up those ancient feelings again.

He didn't reply.

She eased out of the shadowed doorway, hearing in retrospect how worn he'd sounded. She saw it then, the great bloom of a bruise across the side of his face, split over one eye with dried blood still marking a trail down his face to the sharp line of his jaw, now obscured by swelling. There was more, too, an odd, angry red flush around it all. She couldn't hold back a small sound of dismay.

He met her gaze. "It's all right. Just looks nasty."

*Bound and certain to be hurtin'.*

"Don't bother to come back for Mud-pie," she said, letting the cold anger that filled her heart come out in her voice. "He won't be available for you no more."

"What?" His expression was total bafflement.

She stared pointedly at his face. "I should've known anyone as full of pretty words as you was no good."

"Raicha—"

"No." She hardened herself to the pain that showed in his eyes, to his obvious misery. She only hoped it hurt as much as she did now, feeling betrayed all over again. "You tell me this one thing," she demanded, because he was still giving her that look, that particular hurt of someone who believes he's been wrongly judged. "Did you kill Jinny? Did you kill Marnten? And what about that horse that came out of the hills last night?"

"That's three things," he said, but winced when she glared at him. "Raicha . . . I arrived *after* the robbing started, remember? I didn't kill anybody. That's not what I'm here for."

"I don't know when you arrived—I only know when you needed a horse. I ought to raise my voice this very minute, and bring the town down on you. I ought to—"

"Please," he said. "Don't."

She opened her mouth to do that very thing, and hesitated. He'd caught her gaze, he had, with those golden eyes, the eyes that had made her trust him so quickly in the first place. Gold, here in Silvercliff.

She was a fool. A fool once, for her former love. And now twice, for a man she hardly knew. And this was her punishment, to stay here at this stable until she was too old to climb up to the loft anymore. She closed her eyes, said it out loud. "I'm a fool."

"You're not," he said. She heard his intake of breath, as though he'd started to say something else and changed his mind. Instead, his hand touched the side of her head, followed the damp sheen of her hair to her shoulder. "You're not."

The hand fell away, but Raicha didn't look at him, didn't glance up to acknowledge the words. When she finally did open her eyes, he was halfway out of town. In his step there was none of the graceful power that had first caught her eye. His movements were heavy, as though weighed down by a yoke of fatigue and sadness.

Pheylan didn't return to Silvercliff. The robberies stopped, and Raicha struggled with herself, with what she ought to feel and with what she often felt instead. One moment the man was nothing but a robber, not worth a second's thought, the next she wondered if she'd misjudged him, and if she'd ever see him again, soothing the yearning she couldn't drive away.

But within a six-day of his departure, a bloodied, riderless horse wandered into Silvercliff, trailing broken reins and a desperate hunger. Rees thought it looked like the Regional Justice's horse, and the townfolk decided it was time to go looking for the bandits. A posse rode out, seven capable men on mule and horse.

Only one of the mules returned, its saddle covered with blood, and the town fell into grieving. Raicha mourned with them, and from an additional, private grief. Had Pheylan done this? Had he been some part of it? Or maybe Pheylan wasn't involved at all. No one man could have handled the entire posse, and she'd never seen him with any other.

If only his face hadn't betrayed him, battered by a sack of silver. If only he'd even tried to deny her accusations . . .

But he hadn't.

She was immersed in her silent battle of judgment when Rees took her aside. With a fatherly hand on her shoulder and regret in his voice, he said she was going to have to ride the hills.

That brought her out of her mood fast enough. Ride the hills? The hills where only an idiot traveled nowadays?

Idiots . . . and those who knew no better. That last, Rees told her, they could try to change. They only had so many horses left, and so many men who could ride them. Messages were going out to the three big mines, and they still needed someone to ride to Joinen to announce that the hills were closed to all until the robbers could be found. To tell Joinen, which was big enough to draw actual magic-users, to enforce the closure with strong border wards and warning.

"I wouldn't send you if I didn't think you could make it," Rees said. "You'll have the fastest horse." And the longest distance. "You're the best rider we've got, the best out of all of us to try for Joinen. You can do it."

Thrice a fool, Raicha thought, for she believed him.

She headed for Joinen, where the southern Snakeback River joined with the Sayers River running to the east. It was the last stop for any travelers before they hit these steeply sloped woods, and the best place to stop the traffic. She arrived bruised and scraped by branches and overhanging rocks, unmolested by robbers. She gave her warning, she snapped at their disbelief, and she spent the night shaking over the return ride. In the morning they tried to mollify her, their attitude changed by late night hours spent counting up the number of people who had not yet returned from the Silvercliff area.

Raicha was not mollified. Joinen was warned, and would post their signs and erect their wards; no more of them would die. But Raicha had to make another run through the hills. She choked down half a bowl of porridge and saddled her horse, determined to take the mountain trails twice as fast as the day before.

She almost made it.

With Silvercliff so close Raicha felt she could reach out, grab it, and pull herself to safety, her horse bounded suddenly sideways in the narrow trail, off the trail and onto the steep, slippery slope below them. Raicha shrieked in fear as the horse plunged for balance, panicking. She took the ends of her long reins and quirted him, shouting in his ear, her only goal to become more of a threat than whatever had driven him from secure footing.

Finally, his legs trembling with effort, his hooves carving out chunks of dirt and spitting them out behind, he regained the trail. But she couldn't get him to move. He stood and shook beneath her, half-rearing when she urged him forward. At last she realized that if robbers had been in chase, she'd already be facing them. *Unless they're just laughing themselves silly.*

So she quit yelling and kicking and simply sat there, breathing. After a moment, when she and the horse had both quieted, she felt alarm trickle back.

She could still hear harsh breathing.

Raicha froze. She listened until she could no longer pretend there was nothing to hear, and until she was convinced that whatever it was, it wasn't getting any closer. That was when the whining started. Intermittent and low, like an animal that simply couldn't help itself. *Wolf* came instantly to mind. Badly hurt wolf. A wolf this horse would never walk past, no matter how far uphill it was from them.

She dismounted to discover her legs were unsteady, shaking almost as badly as the horse's. Ignoring them, she haltered the animal and led it back down the trail, securing it to the sturdiest tree limb she could find. Then, knife in hand, she slowly followed the sound of the panting whine, wishing very hard that the horse would just stand still and quit jerking noisily at its tree. But soon enough—too soon—she was within sight of her quarry.

She stopped when she saw the creature, a black wolf with silver-tipped hairs around its head and neck, dusting finely down the line of its back. The fur on one of its back legs was spiky and matted—blood, no doubt. The side of its head and face was the same. Despite its jerky and panicked attempts to rise, its head seemed stuck to the ground. Carefully, she stepped closer, trying to reconcile what she saw with the clothing scattered at the base of the tree, and the small neat pile of supplies.

Its whining faded away. As she moved around to its immobile head, it . . . Was it *wagging* its tail? Before she coul
doubt it, the wolf made a new noise, a deeply throaty plea

She saw, then, that she was safe; it was collared, stake
by a chain so short it could barely lift its head. Throug
the thick hair of its ruff, she thought she saw a gleam o
silver. Real silver.

Collared by mere silver—and, more significantly, held b
it. She thought of the howling that echoed through Sil
vercliff's nights, of the ghastly wounds on their dead, an

on the horses that survived to make it back to town. Of ruthless thieves without much care for who they slaughtered, man or child. *Not wolf.* Wolf-kin.

Raicha's lips pulled back in a wolfish snarl of her own. She didn't care why this one was here, wounded and staked. Once it was dead—once she killed it—there would be one less of the wolf-kin roaming these hills. She hefted her knife, but that would take her too close to the creature. A good stout stick, a couple of hard blows to that chained head . . . that would do it. Then she could heave its body far down the steep hill, below the trail. Her horse would pass above what it wouldn't pass below.

The wolf groveled, placing its head on the ground and twisting to expose its belly, its ears flat back as it rapidly licked the air, not quite meeting her eyes. Even Raicha, stable woman, recognized the submissive gesture. "Don't even get your hopes up," she told it coldly, and went in search of a stick.

The wolf watched her alertly, never shifting from its submissive posture, not even when Raicha moved in again, bearing a branch thicker than her upper arm, and twice as long. The animal trembled before her, sick and weak and hurting, giving a deep whine that expressed clear frustration at its speechlessness. Raicha raised the stick—*Wolf-kin. It and its kind have been killing my people*—and took a deep breath. *Now. Do it . . . now!*

The wolf barked, a short, sharp sound, and Raicha jumped; her determined blow faltered, thunking into the ground as the wolf jerked its head aside. And then it looked her straight in the eye, a long, significant moment, and lifted its chin, shifting to expose its throat in an oddly familiar gesture. She stared at it, her club still resting on the ground, and the wolf repeated the gesture, still holding her gaze.

Its eyes were golden. Familiar.

Raicha stumbled back, jaw agape and knees suddenly wavering. Golden. The eyes of a man she had trusted.

Wolf-kin. Pheylan was wolf-kin. And the wolf-kin needed to be killed, but she could never do it. Not now.

*If I walk away from here, he'll starve to death. I won't have to see it. I won't have to* do *it. All I have to do is* not *do anything.*

But in the end, she couldn't do that either. Slowly, in

dream-movements that would dissolve into panic if she thought about what she was doing, Raicha reached for the silver collar and unclasped it. It fell away from the black wolf's neck, leaving a narrow line of raw and blistered skin.

She'd expected him to jump up, to make himself less vulnerable. But all he did was move closer to her, an effort-filled scrabble over the ground, close enough so she could stroke his head and neck. After the slightest of hesitations, she crouched, sinking her hands deeply into his fur, and rested her cheek against the top of his head.

But only for a moment. Then the wolf rose unsteadily to his feet, wavering in place. There was a look about him, a strange and wild look, and Raicha slowly backed away, wondering if she'd chosen wrongly after all. His hackles rose, and he made a noise deep in his throat, and . . . he changed.

The glow that enveloped him was sharp and painful, flashing randomly like a crystal in the sun, and lingering long in Raicha's vision. When she finally blinked away the dazzles, he was . . . Pheylan. Half covered by a blood-crusted blanket from his supplies, collapsed against the tree, eyes closed . . . but definitely Pheylan.

Raicha closed her eyes a long moment, and spoke into that darkness. "I thought the wolf-kin were all dead."

"No," he said, his voice a croak. Raicha moved over to him, cataloging his injuries and the clear signs of fever—his flushed face, his shallow, panting breaths. Wolf-breathing. "Everyone thinks we're dead, that we have been, for years." His hand went to the open throat of his shirt, where the angry red weal from the collar was starker than ever. "We've just gotten sneakier. We had to, once your kind decided we weren't fit to live among you anymore."

"No wonder we tried to kill *your* kind off, so many years ago. You're here, and you came to rob and kill us."

His face grew tight and angry, wearied as it was. Old bruises from the miner's blow, unhealthy colors of gray and yellow, still lingered under blood from the new cut there. "I didn't come to do anything *to* you. I'm trying to protect you from my own."

"You tried to rob the miner. No way you can deny that. He hit you with crude silver, and it took you down better'n he ever expected. You'd be dead if his donkey hadn't made such a fuss."

Pheylan gave a rueful nod, and leaned his head back on the tree. "Right you are about that. I tried to rob him. And I've robbed others. But I've never harmed anyone. I was doing it to protect you all."

"You got hit just a little too hard, if you think that makes any sense!"

He closed his eyes, and found her hand with unerring accuracy anyway. She thought about jerking it away . . . and didn't. He ran his thumb over her knuckles, and when he spoke, it was with the same ineffable weariness that filled his every movement. "My pack is here, in the hills. We're an old family, and one who remembers the Days of Slaughter very well. Too well. We were trying to make an honest living to the north, until one of us died."

Raicha said nothing. People died; that's the way it was.

"It was an accident. But no one would accept blame, or pay the death price—though we all know very well who caused it." Pheylan shrugged. "My pack was finished with human ways. Struggling to survive, when we could have done quite well if allowed to be true to our nature. We decided to . . . the ranking among us decided . . . they killed the man who caused my sister's riding accident. And then they left, came down here to find the right place where they could turn rogue. They're the ones who rob even the silver it hurts so much to touch. They're the ones who kill when they don't have to."

After a moment, Raicha asked, "And you?"

He gave a short laugh, but cut it short with a grimace. "I've been trying to scare you all away! I've given this particular stretch the worst reputation I could."

Raicha thought of what she'd been told, of the silence of the robber—*a wolf, slipping through the trees*—and of the caparisoned horse. *Mud-pie, made unrecognizable?* It still didn't make sense. "How—"

He gave her a faint grin. "How long do you think it takes a wolf to learn these trails? How hard do you think it is to find someone, then run ahead to place the horse—he was all for looks, just something to keep people from thinking *wolves*—and wait?" The grin faded. "But I wasn't enough; no one person could be. They keep getting past, and they keep getting killed."

Raicha discovered he still had her hand, was still caressing it. She let him, but it didn't stop her frown. "Then, what happened here? Who did this?"

"My pack."

"Your *pack* did this? Your own people?"

"I was working against them . . . and I wasn't careful enough. I'm lucky they found it amusing to give me one last chance. If there'd been another out-pack robbery before I died of silver poisoning, they'd have come to get me . . . but it's been two days now. They won't be back." He closed his hand more tightly over hers. "It was pure perfume to scent you on the breeze."

Raicha looked away, glad his eyes were closed, and thinking of how close she'd come to killing him. Those hard, angry feelings seemed far away, now, replaced by need to help, instead. "Then you've got to rob someone, while they all think you're tied. They'll have no way of knowing I freed you."

He shook his head, once, a weary gesture. "I can't, Raicha. Even if they hadn't run me down first . . . two days with silver . . . Too much."

The roads. "The roads are closed," she said out loud. "There won't be anyone to rob."

"Are they?" He opened his eyes to look at her, for the first time something other than utterly defeated. "It worked? Your people have had enough?"

She nodded.

"The pack won't stay long, then, not now. They'll move on. I . . . I had planned on being with them when that happened." He touched a hand to his neck, and let it fall away. "They need someone to talk them into living the right way again."

Raicha closed her eyes. They were wolf-kin, but they were his people, and he loved them; the pain of losing them was right there on his face. *If he's not with them, they'll just go somewhere else and start the killing again.* She said again, "You've got to rob someone."

"Raicha—"

"Be quiet," she said, fiercely enough to startle even herself. "The word's just gone out . . . there's got to be someone who'll push his luck, and try to get through the hills. I—" she tripped over the words, then said them anyway. "*I'll* do it."

His astonishment turned quickly to objection, just as

fierce as hers. "No! You can't!" But it left him wincing, arm wrapped around bruised ribs with his breath trapped somewhere between.

"I can," she said. "You just ask anyone in town if I'm known for my wisdom. One mistake is all it takes, and I guess it's about time I lived up—or down, I suppose—to my reputation." He just furrowed dark brows at her; she didn't give him time to say anything. "You said you know these hills. That means you've been here long enough to learn the comings and goings from the mines, even the one-man workings. I bet you can set me on a road that ought to get some traffic."

He just shook his head, and very slowly at that, but Raicha saw the glint there, the bit of hope that had been missing before.

"They won't know it's me," she said. "Not if I use the same costume on my horse as you put on Mud-pie. I'll cover my hair, and wear that fine shirt of yours, if it's still in one piece."

"It's not." He sounded bemused. "But I have another."

She moved back to the collar and studied it, finally finding a silver link that had been crimped in Pheylan's struggle against the chain. She broke it and dropped the collar to the ground, a gesture of disdain. "Here," she said. "Now it'll look like it broke, and you crawled away. You're still too puny to rob anyone, that's clear enough."

Pheylan's golden eyes were sober. "It was a close thing."

"It's over." She kept her voice matter-of-fact, although inside, she was anything but. How she'd actually accomplish a robbery, she had no idea. And . . . in saving Pheylan, in leaving him free to rejoin his pack where he might keep them from besieging some other town, she would lose him. She cleared her throat. "When your pack goes . . . you'll be gone, too."

He looked up at her, a different kind of pain on his face. "Yes," he said. "I'll have to do my best to keep them out of trouble. It'll take time before I'm sure everything is well."

Raicha looked away. She'd known it. It would be the price to pay for the folly of caring in the first place.

It took two days of haunting the path that formed from the tributaries of trails coming from a handful of one-man workings. Two days of waiting by the roadside, with Pheylan, the wolf-Pheylan, watching up-path. In between, two nights of anxiety, of hoping the pack wouldn't scent Raicha's hidden horse. They shared the grimy blanket, and while the first night Pheylan was so ill they neither of them slept, the second afforded some peace, and by morning they were lying close against the chill of dawn, quietly savoring the moments together.

He had kissed her that morning, before shifting to his limping wolf-form. It had been gentle and undemanding, and when Pheylan stepped away from her, there had been regret in his eyes. Raicha didn't need to ask. If they found their victim today, she wouldn't see him again.

If she was a fool, then, at least she didn't do things hal heartedly. As if there were any doubt, when she wa crouched here in the trees just uphill of the path. Pheylan' borrowed longknife stuck out of the ground before her, anc the horse was tied in the trees downhill, where she coul easily throw herself onto his tall back. Pheylan, too, waited lurking in the woods, waiting for one of the miners.

One unwolflike bark would be all the warning Pheylan could give her once their quarry crossed his path; it wa almost more than he could do to get there in the first place She worried constantly—he'd barked, and she'd missed i in the rustle of the breeze that swooped up the hill to rustl the upper branches of the trees. He'd weakened again, an a miner had gone by unnoticed, so she'd have no warnin at all.

Ironically, she took comfort in the things Big Rees ha said. *I wouldn't send you if I didn't think you make it.* H thought she could handle herself. *You're the best rider we' got.* She could outride any pursuit. *You can do it.*

And when the bark came, she did.

Raicha's return to Silvercliff was a dramatic one, f they'd expected her back the day after she left, and h counted her for dead. She told them only that she'd tak several days to get her nerve up to ride the hills again. turned out she was the last; no more came through tho trees, and for weeks the modest industry of Silvercliff ca to a standstill, while miners chafed and drank Rees's a until late in the night, shouting and bouncing their fists one another. In contrast, the hills were silent, with no sound of wolf-call. Raicha found she slept poorly anyway.

Eventually one of the men snuck off to his mine, and then another. The town emptied of them. Soon after, a hardy soul braved the ride to Joinen and back. No one died. No one lost their goods. No one came limping back to town on foot.

And eventually, Raicha stopped watching the hills and went back to being who everyone thought she'd always been. The wolf-kin were well and truly gone, and Pheylan with them.

Early morning, in the pleasant heat of summer, Raicha stood in the shadows of the barn and plaited her hair. She was almost done when she realized she was no longer alone, and whirled around to find Pheylan right behind her. Her gasp of surprise turned into a delighted smile, and just as quickly into a frown. "What are you *doing* here?"

He took the braid from her and finished the plaiting without comment, holding his hand out for the gut string she used to tie it. Then he twitched it back over her shoulder and surveyed her a moment. "Stole a few days to myself," he said. "They're too caught up in searching out some good timber land up north—logging will keep them up in the woods. Revenge finally got old, or maybe they just got tired of listening to me.

"I have to stay with them," he added. "Have to try to keep them out of trouble for a while." His hand went to his neck, where the scar from the silver collar was still brightly pink. "But not forever. There's some part of me that doesn't belong to them anymore."

"Not forever," she repeated, and said, "but why . . . ?"

Pheylan grinned, a cocky little expression that showed a slightly oversized canine tooth. "I just needed to see the look on your face. Very telling, those expressions that slip out in a moment's surprise. Told me all I needed to know, in fact."

Raicha scowled at him. "Showed you I was still silly enough to be thinking about you, is all."

He shook his head, but his expression was fond. "Those moments you consider yourself most foolish, I consider you strongest of all."

There was little distance between them; he shortened it

considerably, while Raicha realized she had nothing to say to dispute his words, for the truth of it was in his eyes. Warm eyes. Golden eyes, full of life, fierce with emotion. The moments over which she had derided herself all her life suddenly turned into nothing more than moments of trust and daring.

Not all the trust was honored; not all the daring had succeeded. But now here she was in a town full of silver, and she'd somehow managed to strike gold.

© 96 danforth

# HIGHWAYSCAPE WITH GODS

## *by Lawrence Schimel*

Lawrence Schimel is an author featured in both literary and genre publications. This particular contribution is not a story at all, but nonetheless echoes the inspiration for so many of us, providing a contemporary counterbalance to Alfred Noyes' "The Highwayman" as it takes you vividly through an all-too-modern night.

*In the dead of night a convoy of giants*
*trucked out of Jotunheim.*

*They drove five abreast, doing eighty-five.*
*There was no place to go when they were*
*on your tail, their headlights shining*
*in your rearview mirror like an early dawn;*
*not even the commuter lane.*

*The vans were labeled in big red letters:*
*The World's Longest Snake*
*Ferris Wheel*
*Midgets*
*&c.*

*Carnival.*
*So simple a fąçade. Unsuspect.*
*They drove down the Pacific coast unimpeded,*
*and the cold, crisp air turned gray in their wake,*
*their mufflers spitting clouds of smoke.*

*They were not alone on the road.*

*On the overnight commute from L.A. was an eight-*
*teen wheeler whose vanity plates read: SLEIPNIR.*
*It was heading north into the redwoods.*

*It hung*
*a right around the base of a massive redwood,*
*and stopped. The driver got out, and began to climb.*

*An hour later, when a half-dozen Dykes on Bikes*
*winged past on their motorcycles loud enough to wake*
*the dead, heading toward the city of angels*
*and a goth club there named Valhalla,*
*they did not look upward to see the lone figure hanging*
*from the branches, with two black birds circling the body.*

*Farther up the road, on the other side of San Francisco,*
*the giants overtook Idun—also on the overnight commute,*
*with a load of apples—and forced her off the road,*
*where a tire wedged into a ditch. She stood at the curb,*
*showing some leg even in the darkness to attract*
*some help until a patrolman shows up. Heimdall jotted*
*down her description of the convoy and the numbers*
*on her plates (registered in Washington). As he's writing,*
*a red Porsche doing better than a hundred speeds by,*
*leaving in its wake the afterimage of its plates: LOKI,*
*and the echo of the stereo, the Beach Boys singing:*
*"This is the way the world ends,*
*Not with a bang, but a whimper."*
*Heimdall CBs help for Idun as he takes off*
*in hot pursuit, sounding his horn.*

*The second patrol car soon shows up and gives Idun*
*a lift to a nearby gas station. A young girl pumps*
*gas while the patrolman browses the Twinkies aisle*
*and the middle-aged woman behind the counter*
*listens to Idun's tale as she absently knits;*
*in the corner, an elderly woman rocks forward and back,*
*a rusted pair of shears in her lap, ignoring the conversation.*

*Heimdall, meanwhile, is still trying to catch*
*the Porsche. He is so intent, he does not notice*
*the convoy, which has stopped at a Burger King*
*pit stop. No matter how he accelerates, he can't*
*seem to close the gap between him and the red car.*
*They're almost at San Francisco, and he knows*
*for sure he'll lose him in the twisting streets.*
*The bridge is iridescent, metal struts reflecting*

*the nighttime lights from the city, and with its many lanes like bands of color, it might be a rainbow, arcing its way into the fog.*

*The red Porsche has stopped in the middle of the bridge,
and Heimdall slows to a stop beside it. The car is empty;
yet another jumper. He CBs a tow truck, and gets out.
He can't help walking to the edge of the bridge
and staring down at the surging waves below.
While his back is turned, the other driver leaps
from behind a support, and knocks Heimdall over the edge.
He gives the patrol car the once over, whatever catches his
eye, and, smiling, climbs back into his Porsche. He drives on.
His radio blares the station's jingle, "Ragnarok and Roll,
all night long!"*

*Heading across the bridge in the other direction
is the eighteen wheeler with SLEIPNIR plates,
outfitted now with snow tires and four-wheel drive.
Flakes are coming down on the other side
of the bridge, and they're sticking. But nothing
will stop him. Into his headlights, as oncoming traffic,
comes the convoy, rested and refueled, five abreast
once again. He doesn't take his foot off the gas.*

©
danforth
96

# THE BISHOP'S COFFER

## *by Janny Wurts*

Janny Wurts is one of those individuals the rest of us hate. On one hand, she's a gifted artist. On the other, she writes long, lush fantasy novels as well. Worse, she paints the covers for her own books (thereby making certain mundane details such as hair and eye color are right!) Though she concentrates on novels and painting (*Cycle of Fire* series, and *Wars of Light and Shadow*), Janny also finds time to write short fiction. Many are contained in the collection titled *That Way Lies Camelot;* she's also contributed to *Horse Fantastic.* I am pleased she made the time to write a new story for this anthology.

The coach rocked, jouncing four summer-sticky occupants against its interior of finest, button leather padding. The aristocrat with his velvet frogged jacket raised bristled eyebrows in forbearance and refrained from mopping his meaty face. Even on his way to visit a mistress kept secret from his servants, he maintained his well-bred propriety. No inconvenient discomfort of the road would put creases in the lace cuffs which spilled like froth from his sleeves. "Deuced washouts," he grumbled. "Ruts don't ever get filled. Not the way they once did when a man had the right to work his tenants for day labor."

Beside him, a lean, gray-haired priest pursed lips like squeezed jelly, too godly to voice his disdain. Jammed knee to knee in the seat across from him, a lady's lanky footman sent out to buy pins stared sullenly through the window. A cynical young man with crafty, tight eyes, he was already too resentful of his station to heed the lord's grumpy comment.

Outside the hazed fields of a lowlands countryside flowed past, broken by the stares of cud-chewing cows and brooks that meandered like spilled coffee. Even the trees looked wilted by summer, too enervated to respond to the light breeze which stirred from the sea.

The fourth occupant of the coach, a half-witted monk, stayed oblivious to etiquette or class boundaries. "Ruts don't hurt anybody." He waggled a thick finger. "Frogs like to swim in them, though, I daresay, some few snails come to drown." He shifted ungainly feet; the nails were rimmed black, protruding from sloppy leather sandals. His mouth closed in a brief grimace as he bashed a bare ankle on the square bundle tied in burlap which rested between his splayed legs.

The coarse wrappings slipped and revealed a magical glimmer of gold filigree.

The coach jounced again. One iron-rimmed wheel spanged over a rock. A chance arrow of sunlight struck through the grimed windowpane, and the box which peeped from its veiling responded: a single blood gemstone flashed a tongue of hot fire through the stifling gloom.

The oddity caused all four of the passengers to swivel or bend heads to stare. The expressions on each face revealed volumes in that moment.

The lord forgot his snobbish rank, deep-set eyes narrowed and suspicious. Fervent in devotion, the priest crossed himself against the temptation of earthly things, one dimpled elbow inadvertently digging into the strained seam of his neighbor's frogged velvet. The servant's first amazement curdled to surly envy, while the simple monk blinked, ecstatically lost in his daydreams.

Whatever their differences, each man in his way longed deep inside to strip off the sacking and caress the jewel inside.

The coach jounced over a vicious bump. A groom cursed outside, and the driver on the box snapped his whip. His four-in-hand team veered to avoid a farm cart, and the passengers were cast up, then down, like lumps tossed inside of a butter churn.

"Blast," swore the noble, too entrenched in gentility to blaspheme in front of two churchmen. He made a studied point of gazing at his rings, while the servant clasped chapped hands to his knee breeches and bent smirking survey upon the monk's incongruous parcel.

The burlap protected a coffer; the bounding sway of the coach had jostled the covering and most of one corner stood exposed. Like the flirted skirts of a maid, the puzzle piece cast into view only deepened the mystique. Given a glimpse of elaborate gold corners and filigree that looked exotic and foreign, the box tantalized until even the most ruthlessly stilled curiosity suffered the lure of its challenge.

The nobleman twitched his shoulders in his jacket. He twiddled his thumbs, then gave way to swift, furtive glances.

As if to oblige him, the monk hiked his habit to scratch a hairy knee, and the box's wrapping slipped further.

Not only rubies, but emeralds adorned the corners. The aristocrat measured their astonishing quality, and settings the size of ripe acorns. The stones' clarity caught the eyes, held them captive. No matter how jaded by wealth or position, no man of intelligence could keep up the pretense of bored sophistication. The settings were extraordinary, and only the simpleton monk had the forthright honesty not to care.

Curiosity also swayed the priest. He abandoned the charade of rubbing his long nose to conceal the fact he was staring. "What have you there, Brother?" At least he had the acceptable excuse of making small-talk with another man of the cloth.

The monk stuck out his lower lip and blew the scruffy fringe of his tonsure off his sweat-sticky forehead. "What, this? It's a box. Once it belonged to the Bishop of Wiltdown."

"Lord bless!" exclaimed the priest. He crossed himself again. Fresh runnels of perspiration snaked down his stringy neck. "Not the one who caused the scandal!"

Gold rings clicked over the jingle of harness as the aristocrat unclasped his hands. He bounced like a fat cork as the coach bobbled over another rise, and tried with raised chin not to appear enthralled as he drank in the priest's every word.

"You can't mean the same Wiltdown bishop who renounced God and was defrocked for devil worship last month!"

The monk nodded. "The same man, Lord rest him, but not the first. Two other churchmen burned before him."

"I heard about them," the aristocrat said. He made no apology as he squirmed on his backside, boot jabbing the servant across from him as he fished a handkerchief from a pocket. While the injured party glowered and rubbed his grazed shin, the lord dabbed his damp double-chin. "Wiltdown was a saint, everyone swore. Wouldn't succumb like the others before him. Went mad overnight, apparently."

The servant looked up, not quite outraged enough to withhold the juiciest gossip. "They said he danced naked each rising full moon, with a virgin staked out on an altar. His secretary found him out when he changed the crucifix under his stole to hang upside down."

"Please," said the priest, long fingers flicked in a quelling gesture. "The event was a tragedy. 'Tis unwise to speak of the devil's damned minions. Wiser to pray for the soul of a man who was most sorrowfully led astray."

The noble cracked a fatuous smile. "That's three men in high office who have succumbed to evil. Who can trust there won't be a fourth? The church coffers must be feeling the pinch. I say it's a risk to give charity to a bishopric riddled through with heresy. The cathedral will likely have to sell off its plate to pay for the costs of inquisition." His porcine eyes surveyed the open-mouthed monk. "And just what would a man with a poverty vow be doing alone with the bishop's jeweled coffer anyway?"

All eyes swiveled as the coach jounced again. Outside, a market-bound cotter raged curses as the wheel horse squealed from too close an encounter with his draft beast. Then the obstruction and its fist-shaking owner drew abreast. The coach window framed a flop-eared chestnut mule doddering along with a swaying pannier of vegetables. Then the pair fell behind. The veering team jostled the coach occupants, wedged shoulder to shoulder and knee to knee, with the mesmeritic box still the centerpin of their attention.

A whip crack, and a shouted reprimand from the driver righted the disparity in the traces. The shaking roused the monk, who had nodded into a momentary nap. He scrubbed at his eyes. Belatedly aware of the expectant accusation of his fellow passengers, he swiped drool from his chin with a sleeve already stained from repeated use as a napkin.

"I'm to take the box out and throw it off the sea cliff," he declared with limpid honesty. "A shame, too. The joinery's very pretty."

Roused from lower-class doldrums, the footman's eyes widened. "You say! Throw off large jewels for the tide to rip up? That's madness! Your pardon, Brother, but even the duchess hasn't got any pieces that sparkle and gleam with such luster."

"The very notion is preposterous! The effects of the late bishop's estate could surely be better used to feed the poor." The nobleman shoved forward and his shining jowls thrust towards the priest's bony nose. "You should arrest that scoundrel for a thief." Cuff links flashed as he stabbed accusation toward the monk. "A man of your own cloth, robbing God's church! That's taking advantage of misfortune, I should say. No doubt you were tempted while the dead bishop's belongings were searched for demonic artifacts."

"If," the servant muttered, "the fellow's a monk at all. Anyone could shave himself a tonsure and don an old habit."

The monk bobbed his cowled head like a turtle confused in its shell. "Artifacts? What's artifacts?"

The priest looked affronted, but the monk brightened up as he unraveled enough meaning to respond. "Demonic, oh, yes! That's the word on this box. Inside holds pure evil." He savored the roll of every impressive word he had overheard from his fellow brothers. "Corruption, pestilence, ungodly practice—that's what my Lord Inquisitor said. He warned us never to touch. Ill comes to even the most saintly soul who dares to meddle with this box." The monk tucked his chin against his nubbed robe, brows lowered as he rasped in a whisper, "Possession! That's what Their Graces said. Possession by Satan, his very own self!"

"God forbid." The priest crossed himself, again jamming the bothered aristocrat in the ribs.

"Aye," the monk said, "but God didn't."

"Well then, how did the church come by this box?" pressed the footman, angling for a story to share belowstairs with the butler.

The monk closed gaping knees, discomfited by the attention. "This box was given to Wiltdown's bishop by a sailor who wanted it guarded by the church. But godly men are no match for its power. One look inside, even saints turn to evil. Three bishops undone by corruption, now, and the last of them was the strongest." The monk planted his sandal on top of the coffer to emphasize his last point. "Even

His Grace couldn't withstand the dark powers locked in this box."

The coach tossed over another rut, jouncing the travelers inside with complete disregard for their station. None noticed.

The priest touched the monk's wrist. "Don't you fear for your soul?"

Listed to the right as the carriage rounded a bend, the monk lit up with a vapid smile. "Nobody worries about me, overmuch. They say I haven't the wit to be troubled by demons or satanic possession." He tapped his shaven head, then chuckled, showing gapped gums where several teeth had gone rotten. "No lights on to darken. That's what my brothers say." His wide smile let another gob of drool string down his stubbled chin. "So that's why I was asked to take Satan's burden, and throw the box into the sea. . . ."

From a concealed vantage on a hillside where the road wound in broad, curving loops through the valley, the notorious highwayman named Butcher Jack leaned his brute forearm on the crest of his blood-chestnut mare. "There," he murmured in his gravelly baritone. "Afternoon coach to Baywinside, and slap on time just for me."

He straightened, loosened bearish shoulders in a stretch. Eyes like sheared steel missed no detail as he checked and cocked his primed pistols. "May the ladies and gentlemen be wearing their best rings." Thrushes fled from his savage, short laugh. The words he always used to seal his luck brought a crooked smile to his lips. "Pearls before I hang, and a night with lusty Rosie."

He sighted along one blued, polished barrel; buffed the ivory stock of the matching gun on his knee. "Hup, Girlie," he intoned to his nervous horse. The reins were already knotted. He liked his hands free if he had to slit throats with the knife gripped between his front teeth. Well primed for mayhem, he clapped roweled spurs to the mare and sent her thundering toward the roadway.

The horse careened downslope, ears flat, and hooves threshing the pale tassels of ripe barley. She knew her course well, had carried Jack, flinching, through two seasons of terror as he held up coaches at random on the roads which snaked from the high country down to the seaports. The highwayman was thorough and ruthless. He

knew well how to choose his ground, to lie up in thick
brush and observe each coach route. He memorized the
habits of the drivers that passed before selecting his prey.
Nor did he ever rob the same route twice.

Steal and fly elsewhere was the code by which he ensured
his precarious survival. . . .

The Baywinside coach careened on its way, unguarded
before pending disaster. Its occupants at that moment
tayed engrossed with the monk and the unholy coffer
pinned under his dusty foot. None of them noticed the
hoofbeats bearing down from the crest of the hill. The first
alarmed cry from the groom roused the driver, who swore,
and hauled the lines to steady his team. His whip snapped
to quicken their canter. The corner was sharp. He should
have chosen a trot out of prudence, but the rider sweeping
down with pistols and knife was a sight to strike fear before caution.

"Stand and deliver!"

Inside the carriage, the shout overcame the passengers'
ascination with the box.

The priest offered worried advice. "Good Brother, you'd
best cover that."

The monk agreed, but did nothing, his beatific smile
nshaken.

The coach swayed, almost tipped, while the footman
crabbled to secure a firm handhold. Urbane as he was, he
preferred not to slide and risk touching the Satan-ac-
cursed coffer.

A bang rattled the glass as a pistol discharged. Scarlet
prayed over the reeling view of green fields.

"God save us!" yelped the priest. "That's a murdered
man's blood!"

The coach lurched, swerved; the liveried groom cried out
rom the box as the corpse of the driver slumped into him.
Heels banged the lacquered frame of the carriage through
his lunge to secure the team's dropped ribbons.

Inside the carriage, the aristocrat sucked on his knuckles
and wrestled off his tight rings. A commoner's brutal death
scarcely moved him before the imminent threat to his
wealth. His furtive glances shot left and right as he stuffed
his stripped valuables into the cracks between seat cush-

ions. He fussed to free his diamond stickpin when the sun on the grimy window pane darkened.

The highwayman reined his mare alongside. Flecked foam from her bit streaked the glass as he spurred her abreast of the coach's whirling, spoked wheels. He kicked free of his stirrups. The leaf springs dipped to his weight as he caught the groom's handle, then hauled out of the saddle in one brute pull and clambered upward out of view. A storm of thumps ensued as he battled for control of the swaying box.

"No!" the groom begged in a breaking soprano.

Jack's knife stopped the noise. A thump jounced the carriage. Then a second in succession as two limp bodies were thrown off on the verge.

Inside, the air had grown stifling. Eyes squeezed shut, the priest crossed himself, pale lips murmuring swift prayers. The aristocrat stashed his final jewel and his purse.

Unruffled in his arrogance, he laced plump hands on his belly as though privilege of birth could hold his life and limb sacrosanct.

The servant looked on with cynical disdain, while the monk craned his neck, cheek pressed to the streaked glass to gawk.

"Get down," urged the priest, all but thrown from the seat as the coach bucked over a rut. The springs squealed again, as up on the box, the highwayman dragged the team from their stampeding panic.

Thrown side to side in the careening chaos, the priest strove to rescue the simpleton brother from folly. "That's Butcher Jack, and may God's goodness save us! He kills without thought. Anyone who gets a clear look at his face gets shot or knifed, lest an honest man's testimony should bring the authorities to hang him."

The coach rattled, sashayed, then jounced to a stop. Th blown team stood with heads hanging, too lathered to stra when the lines dropped slack in the terrets. The creak a the murderer stirred from the box sounded loud in th fallen stillness.

His pistol appeared at the window. A dead man's bloo splashed the knuckles which gripped the stock, and a ja of the barrel smashed the glass.

"Turn your backs! Now!" the highwayman demande

"Step out the far door, or I'll blow your liver and lights straight to blazes."

The scramble as the passengers surged to comply jammed and stopped against the monk's rump. He alone had crouched on the floor, determined to maintain his dutiful custody of the coffer he was charged to destroy.

"Never mind that!" the aristocrat snapped.

The priest grabbed two handfuls of stained habit and delivered a merciful shove. "Brother, go on. Best worry for your life and soul!"

The footman callously stepped on the seat and clambered over the obstructing body.

The monk grunted, undeterred. Neither words nor blows could shake his complacency. Nor did he look aside as the door on the other side of the carriage wrenched open, and the coach rocked to the highwayman's boarding weight.

"Get out, I said!" Jack's boots grated on the iron footrest. He slung his huge frame headlong through the interior, smelling of sweat and hot horse. His brass-tipped knife sheath scored across leather upholstery and hung up on a button. He cursed, jerked free of the snag. While the passengers tumbled outside in disarray, he grasped the looped handle and pursued. Blood smears left from the fallen driver dripped over gleaming brass and lacquerwork, not worth his time to avoid. He leaped down. Crowded on the heels of his scrambling victims, he demanded, "Lie down on the verge!"

The monk lacked the wit to respond to any urgency. He mumbled in monotone, shambling along with the coffer clutched to his chest.

Delays made Jack nervous. His impatient dirk had spared him from arrest more than once. He accomplished his robberies with hair-trigger brutality, and a temper which brooked no obstruction.

"Get along, you!" He jabbed the laggard on with his discharged pistol, while the primed one stayed raised in steady threat.

The monk stumbled, hooked his sloppy sandal on a rock and scrambled back upright.

Jack flushed dark scarlet. His furious step kicked up spurts of dust, and his roweled spurs chimed in hot sunlight. "Lie down, every one of you! Press your sorry faces in the dirt. Do as I say, and maybe with luck you'll be able to leave with your lives."

The chubby aristocrat was first to crawl flat, discreetly upset for the distress to his velvets. The surly footman was unmoved by bruised dignity, while the priest cast a glance of fish-eyed concern toward the monk.

The good brother stayed oblivious. Crouched on stork legs, he debated the best way to squirrel an unwieldy box underneath the hem of his habit.

The priest dared a frantic whisper. "Save yourself, Brother."

"Shut yer gab!" Jack's predatory gaze shifted target to the monk's skinny rump, up-thrust since the simpleton had resolved his dilemma by sprawling on top of the coffer.

The burlap strained under punishment. A red splinter of reflection caught in the sun as the edge of a ruby winked through.

"What in hell are you hiding?" Jack's vicious kick spilled the half-wit off the box he flailed bony elbows to protect.

Abused burlap tore away. Noon's stabbing brilliance raised a bright flare of a scarlet, then a teasing cool wink from the emeralds set in the dazzling flash of goldwork.

Jack whistled. His brow furrowed underneath the unwashed fringe of his hair. "Fine haul." He laughed through bared teeth and just for good measure, kicked the prone monk once again. "I'll just tie that lovely treasure to my saddle." A wave of his pistol swept the other victims, trembling in prostration on the verge. "Never mind your rings and small purses. There's booty enough in that coffer to keep me content with six whores for a year."

"Sir!" The monk sat up in appealing protest. "In God's name, for peril of your very soul, you must lay no hand on this box. It once belonged to the Bishop of Wiltdown and—"

*"Shut yer gab!"* Jack shouted. "I'll do just as I please Let the devil fan his fires all the hotter for the hour whe we meet face-to-face in hell."

"That's the problem," said the monk. He snatched a Jack's trouser leg. "Take this box and you'll be damne beyond hope of salvation."

"I should care?" The cocked pistol lowered in a blu flare of steel. Its shattering report as Jack pulled the trigge startled the gleaning blackbirds in screeching alarm from the barley.

The importunate monk toppled and crashed on the blood-wet ruin of his face.

Jack suffered no remorse. He hurled the twitching carcass aside, bent, and hooked up the gore-spattered burlap which held the dead bishop's coffer. Gemstones sparkled like uncanny fire as he rewrapped the wet cloth and veiled them. His victims stayed cowed as he stamped in ringing strides and caught the reins of his grazing mare. Another moment saw him mounted and gone. The sound of her hooves had long faded before any of his traumatized victims raised their heads.

Flies already sucked at the body of the monk.

"Lord keep his poor soul." The priest wrung his hands and paused, frowning as he suddenly struggled to recall the proper words of the requiem.

The servant slapped dust from his livery and looked about. His nerveless curiosity deserted him all at once as he viewed the remains by the roadside. Never squeamish before, he bent double in the ditch, undone by his heaving stomach.

The snobbish aristocrat straightened his soft spine. Moved to an unthinkable break from class character, he murmured, "Poor boy! Let me help." He scrambled to his feet and ripped his fawn breeches on the briars to comfort the suffering servant. Knelt over a commoner's heaving shoulders, he never noticed the priest's simultaneous panic.

The churchman stood in mortified suspension, shaken to realize how terribly he fumbled his benediction for the dead. Just barely, he stopped his hand in the act of signing the cross upside-down. "Lord and saints preserve me!" he gasped, his voice and knees trembling with shock. "Holy Mother, avert! Forgive the work of Satan's black hand!" For he knew he must be fallen under the influence of the bishop's unholy box.

He swallowed, regrouped. "Pray God, give me strength." He gripped his wooden crucifix then made himself resume the last rites for the departed.

Minutes later, the shaky servant was helped from the ditch by the lord's solicitous, soft hands. The priest was surprised to be offered the velvet frogged jacket to cover the monk's mangled corpse.

The aristocrat insisted. "The poor brother died for his duty to God. My jacket will grant him small dignity." The noble's contrition went more than skin-deep. "Keep the jewels I hid in the coach for a mass to be said for his soul."

The footman, still queasy, gave his sincere promise to attend.

All three surviving victims agreed on one point as they started their walk to seek succor. The wretches on the next coach to be robbed by Butcher Jack would fare far worse than they. The highwayman was certain to fall prey to demonic influence since he carried the Wiltdown Bishop's evil coffer.

"The man is the devil's spawn already," sighed the priest. "Who could imagine what his crimes will be now?" This time, with merciless concentration, he managed to cross himself correctly.

The next night, a loud knock rattled the wrought iron gates where the newly ordained Bishop of Wiltdown took up residence.

A cowled penitent shuffled his feet outside. His shadowed features were downcast, and his huge breadth of shoulder slumped in meek, almost cowering diffidence.

The church porter raised his lamp. He cursed the chilling fine drizzle as he peered through the grille into darkness "What's your business? You know the hour's too late to come here begging for alms."

"I wish to see His Grace, the Bishop, if you please." The penitent cast an uneasy glance side to side, then shifted his grip on something he held masked underneath his plain cloak. "I am a sinful man newly wakened to God's grace Show me pity. I need to make my confession."

"At this hour?" The porter looked back in sour surprise "Why not find a priest?" Still clad in his nightshift, and shivering against the biting, wet gusts off the river, he decided he spoke to a lunatic. "Go away!"

But the stranger only rolled fearful eyes at the gargoyle which snarled above the stone arches. He made no move to leave.

"His Grace is asleep," said the porter, exasperated "Why risk his displeasure? It's the middle of a miserable night." He spun on his heel to stalk off.

The penitent shot a fast hand through the grate, clamped

the porter's arm and detained him. His grasp was well callused and his fingers still wore the cinder-black marks of fresh powder burns.

"You must listen," implored the penitent, gruff now, even desperate. "My sins are terrible. Don't make me wait until morning! Were I to suffer mishap and perish before then, my soul would be damned for eternity. Good sir! Please! You *must* listen!"

The porter redoubled his efforts to pull free, to no avail. "Very well, then." he grumbled. He thought if he humored his strange visitor's request, he could pry loose and return to his bed. "Who should I say has called when I roust the bishop from his sleep?"

"Bless you, sir, my Christian name is Jack." The man at the gate slipped aside his veiling cloak. The fluttering lampflame lit the extraordinary jeweled coffer tucked underneath his muscled arm.

Torchlight raised sparkles off rubies, and emeralds, and exotic, wrought filigree in gold, whorled in knots like fine thread. The porter stared, transfixed, scarcely aware of spoken words as the stranger expressed tearful gratitude.

"I ask nothing except the bishop's blessing in return for some act of contrition. Perhaps His Grace knows of an abbey where I might swear holy service as a monk."

The porter rattled his keys, seized head to foot with uneasiness. Such jewels could be paste, and the story a knavish trick to make him unlock the gates at night. "Surely the bishop will be pleased to hear your confession in the morning."

Eyes that once were steel hard and without mercy gazed back, unearthly enough to be a saint's. "Kind sir, I beg you," wept the penitent who once had been a marauding highwayman. He thrust the jeweled box through the gap in the bars, determined to make good his intent. "At least restore this stolen coffer to its rightful place in the Bishop's treasury, for I am a godly man, now."

danForth 96

# THE ABBOT OF CROXTON

## *by Melanie Rawn*

Melanie Rawn has only recently begun publishing short fiction, after swearing it was impossible for her to write anything less than 200,000 words on any given subject. However, she has proven she is as talented at writing short as she is at writing long; one need only read her contributions to *Ancient Enchantresses* and *Return to Avalon.* Fantasy novels include trilogies called "Dragon Prince," "Dragon Star," and "Exiles." She also collaborated with Kate Elliott and this editor on *The Golden Key.* For this anthology, Melanie selected probably the single most famous highwayman in popular legend: Robin Hood. Not only did she find an angle heretofore unexplored, but she presents it with lovely subtlety and matchless irony.

> *Being overtaken by a grievous sickness, and so incapable of making a detailed disposition of my goods, I commit the ordering and execution of my will to the fidelity and discretion of my faithful men whose names are written below. . . .*

"Too fast for you?" he asked of the tonsured monk they'd sent to be his clerk.

"A–a little, Your Grace," the boy admitted.

"For me, also," he agreed. *Too fast, my death—and too slow my tongue for the ordering of my will. Not that I expect it to be obeyed. When did anyone in England ever obey* my will? *Always Father, Mother, and Richard—Jésu, even Geoffrey, even big brother Henry the Young King—*

*But still I outlasted them all, and England is mine. I survived.*

*Until now.*

"We resume," he said, and the clerk dipped quill to inkpot. There was the tiniest rattling noise, as if the boy's hand shook with trepidation, to be acting as scribe to his king.

> *. . . without whose counsel, were they at hand—*

And where were they, his trusty and well-beloved counselors? Off somewhere betraying him, *sans doubt.*

> *. . . I would not, even in health, ordain anything; and I ratify and confirm whatever they shall faithfully ordain and determine concerning my goods, in making satisfaction to God and Holy Church for the wrongs I have done them, sending help to the Holy Land—*

There, that sounded good and contrite, didn't it? And who gave a damn about the Tomb of Christ, in anywise? *He* was the one about to go to his tomb, leaving behind a kingdom in turmoil, a wife sure to be stolen back by her former lover once she was a widow (and well worth the stealing, as he knew, having stolen her himself), three little daughters—the youngest scarce a year old—and two sons, the elder of whom would be the next King of England. A boy of nine.

Henry The Third. He'd named the boy a-purpose, knowing it would infuriate the shade of Henry the Second. Everyone thought he honored his father's memory with the naming of his eldest son and heir—and how that honoring would have infuriated Mother—but he'd done it in truth to wipe out all memory of The Young King. Poor big brother Henry. Crowned in Father's lifetime to spite Thomas à Becket; eager for Father to die so the real crown and real power could be his; dead before he could do more than snarl a few times in true Plantagenet fashion.

But now there would be a true King Henry the Third, the hope of his House. How glad he was that Mother had died before the boy was born. She'd fretted and carped at his lack of legitimate children—concerned not so much for England as herself, the continuance of her sacred line. Pity that his sons Henry and Richard were her grandchildren, with her venom in their veins.

> *. . . rendering assistance to my sons for the recovery and defense of their inheritance—*

"Your Grace—I beg pardon, but—"

"Well? What is it?" He shifted in the vast bed, cursing the tangle of sweat-clogged sheets around his body.

"If my lord the King could perhaps speak just a little more slowly—"

Fixing the boy purposefully with a narrowed gaze, he said distinctly, " '*Rewarding those who have served us faithfully*—' "

The clerk gulped and took the hint, and wrote faster.

> *. . . and distributing alms to the poor and to religious houses for the salvation of my soul. And I pray that whosoever gives them counsel and aid in the endeavors may receive the grace and favor of God Almighty, of the Blessed Mary, and of all the saints.*

Enough pious mouthings. He'd wasted enough words on such treacle to satisfy even the pestilential Pope. He drew breath to begin again when movement at the half-open door snagged his attention—just as quickly seized by the griping in his bowels that permitted no notice of anything but pain. There was nothing left in him to purge, but the rot in his guts twisted until he writhed. He held back his gasps; such were unkingly. They said Richard never cried out once, not until the fever of his wound overtook him and he ranted the way Father used to do even when perfectly healthy. . . . The Plantagenet temper, unrestrained and ungovernable. Richard had possessed Father's fire and Mother's brilliance and everything best of them both—leaving nothing for their last, unwanted, unwelcome son but to rub along on their combined cunning. A formidable heritage, withal—though he could never decide whether it had served him well or ill. He had indeed outlasted them all, but. . . .

A smooth, quiet voice bade him drink. Cool water mixed with a little wine slid down his throat. He swallowed noisily, hoping there was something in this drink for the pain, and fell back on the tapestry pillows.

"Better, Your Grace?"

Not the clerk. Someone taller, leaner beneath the religious robing, the face shadowed by a dark cowl. He regained his breath and gestured to the quill and vellum lying on the table.

The head within the cowl turned slowly in negation. "I regret I'm no hand at scribing, Your Grace, to serve you in this."

Peering up at the monk—no, a priest; he recognized the signs of higher office—he frowned and said, "Recall the clerk. I'm dying, and would have my will completed."

"You'll last a while longer yet, Your Grace."

"Is that meant to comfort? How much pain must I suffer ere I finally die?" Though in truth that pain had subsided to a dull queasy ache; there'd been something in the water after all, something that detached him from the agony of his dying—and from the world, a little, with a cushioning softness. He'd heard that they'd sent for the Abbot of Croxton to attend him here at the Bishop of Lincoln's castle at Newark, for the Abbot was a man reputed skilled at healing. As if anything could heal him now.

"God's will is supreme in this as in all things, Your Grace."

"And you're one of those who think me deserving of the worst He can offer!"

"No. Not anymore." A soft sigh. "I did, once. It seems a long time ago now."

He began a retort, but there was something about the voice, about the poise of the long body—

"Your face," he rasped. "I would see your face."

After a brief hesitation, the fine, war-scarred hands lifted and the cowl was pushed back.

No abbot, this. Saxon-fair still, the years having silvered his goldenness; there were lines on weathered skin, but in the dim candlelight he looked well-nigh as he had half their lives ago.

"Robin," said King John. "Robin of Locksley."

A short bow, but he had no illusions that it was a reverence given *him;* only what was due a king, any king. Even him.

"We missed you at Runnymede, my lord Earl," John said at last.

"It is a far distance from Nottingham, Your Grace."

"And so? Why are you here, and in abbot's garb? Never tell me you've taken Holy Orders!"

"I would not presume to tell the king what he so earnestly desires not to hear." But a sudden glimmer in the eyes, Lincoln green and bright as ever, gave John the lie.

Richard had always found this man amusing. John had never seen it, himself. "Holy Orders. Who would ever have thought—" Then his voice sharpened. "My cousin the Lady Marian must be dead."

The light was extinguished. "The day you were at Runnymede . . . that day, I buried her."

"Next to your Richard, I suppose."

"Yes," Robin murmured. "Next to our Richard."

"He was—what, eighteen?"

"Near nineteen."

The drug cushioned him from his own pain, but not from the Earl of Huntington's. He felt the man's anguish like the embrace of a passionate woman. Lovely drug, allowing him his vengeance after all this time. "Bouvines, wasn't it? Died slow, did he, of a French swordcut?"

"Enough!"

"I'm not one of your bandits," he jeered, "to tremble at a command from Robin Hood."

"One would think your own many losses would have taught you compassion for the griefs of others."

And with that one sentence, Robin sliced into John's heart as surely as John had into Robin's. Henry, Eleanor; Henry the Young King, Richard, Geoffrey—all his brothers but for William of Salisbury, the bastard Longsword; his sisters Matilda, Eleanor, and Joan; even his own Geoffrey Fitzroy, the bastard son dead these ten years and more, whose death still hurt. Everyone was gone but his own legitimate sons and daughters—and Joan, favorite of his children even though bastard, far away in Wales, married to Prince Llewellyn who dared call himself "the Great." Of griefs and deaths he had had more than enough; not that he'd loved any of them very much, but that was only because they'd never loved him. He would have, if they would have. He sorrowed for them because when they died, what they had never given him could never now be given. He mourned what they ought to have been to him, what he ought to have had of their love. All England was his—and all England loathed him.

Robin had picked up the vellum page after all. But not to obey his king by writing. " 'Fidelity and discretion'?"

"I never had any, so none was shown me—is that what you say?"

"Something to that point." Robin sat in the bedside

chair, adjusting the folds of his robes, an action reeking of the same casual grace with which he used to draw a bow. A small golden cross hanging from a leather thong caught the candlelight, hurting John's eyes in the dimness of tapestries and bed curtains. "In answer to your first question, Your Grace, I've come to hear your confession."

John laughed aloud—warily at first, because his belly was sore, but when the pain did not come back, he let the laughter come as it would. The door swung open again, and another fair Saxon head poked through; Robin immediately drew the cowl up to hide his face. John, in the midst of a coughing spasm, waved the servant away. When the door shut and he regained his breath, he eyed his "confessor" sidelong.

"I'm to have absolution from *you?* Of all men?"

"From me, of all men, yes." Robin paused. "I think I shall even forgive you, if only for the lifting of the Papal Interdict. It hurt the people, not to hear the bells."

"They'll hear them loud enough when I'm dead," John replied, the laughter turning to bitterness. All England forbidden the comforts of the Mass for six years—and all because of that whoreson Archbishop Stephen Langton. It was the one sympathy he had for old Henry—they both had troubles with Canterbury. Pity himself, though, for even if he'd quoted his father and asked who would rid him of that turbulent priest, there was no one who would have done his bidding. They hadn't feared him enough, that was it. Richard had been loved, his handsome looks admired, his prowess respected and celebrated. All that had been left for John to rule with was fear. And he hadn't frightened them enough.

"Peal upon peal they'll ring in every church," he rasped, "for the sheer joy of my dying."

Robin shrugged.

"They'll remember you," he went on. "They've already made a hero of you—oh, yes, I've heard all those ludicrous ballads and preposterous tales. Nobody dares say or sing them in my presence, but I listen. I hear. A hero you are, Robin of Locksley, my lord Earl of Huntington—but as for me, I know what they'll say of me when I'm dead."

"Nothing they didn't say of you in life."

"They'll say worse, once I'm gone. Madman, monster, Softsword, Lackland—traitor to father and brothers, mur derer of my own nephew Arthur, who should have had the crown—"

"They exaggerate my deeds. They'll do the same with yours. The truth is known to you and to God. What matters else?"

"Don't prate of God to me! I am a king. A *king!* But I'll be remembered only because of an accident of birth, because I was the son of a king and inherited the right to sit on a throne. You, though—you insignificant Saxon bastard, skulking about an insignificant corner of *my* realm—a few miserable years of so-called great deeds that any king must needs term treason—" He felt a twinge of renewed pain and gasped for breath to finish what he'd always longed to say. "I was a king for seventeen years, and a better king than my brother, the worshiped and adored pervert! They loved him, yes—because he was never here! What do you think they would've said of him if he'd really *been* King of England?"

He coughed then, and not even the cushion of drugged water between him and the suffering could separate him from the cramping spasms. Robin waited him out.

"Richard had faults and failings, as do we all," he said at last, shaking his head as John scowled. "And I dare to say you'll be remembered for more than the accident of your birth."

Robin had done it to him again, and with the very words *he* had spoken. John had indeed been an accident, a mistake. Mother had hated the sight of him all the years of her life—because he was a living reminder of the days she had carried him, the days of Father's first fascination with Rosamund Clifford. King and Queen had come together one last time—not in love as they had made their first children, nor even in lust as they had made the two sisters born before him. Mother had been forty-four—Jésu, what an age for childbearing, the old cow!—and Father had undoubtedly been drunk.

And *he* was the result. Unwanted, unloved, unnecessary—for they had Young Henry, and darling Richard, and even Geoffrey, and surely a fourth son was a redundancy. But he had outlived them all. Damn them, he *had* been necessary, and he'd survived all of it—

—only to come to this.

As if hearing his thought, Robin asked, "How did it happen, my lord?"

"Lynn," he said wearily. "It was at Lynn—they feasted me grandly, after Lincoln—"

"Yes—which Nicola de la Hay held for you. A remarkable woman."

Oh, that was it—grind in the salt, to have one of his most cherished and important castles defended by a woman! It had never seemed to bother Robin that his Marian had done the same for him time and again—first defending the castle of trees in Sherwood, then the ramshackle old ruin at Locksley.

"I had them," John said stubbornly. "In September I had them at Windsor, I cut the country in two and drew off the Scottish King, and relieved Lincoln—and then the news came from Dover Castle—I never know if they tell me the truth," he complained. "Is Dover in such a state that it cannot be held? Or do they lie to me, and have they gone over to the rebels—or is it a false message from my enemies, wishing to draw me south once more?"

"What matter now?"

John felt the roiling in his belly begin anew. Damn the people of Lynn for poisoning his bowels with their feasting. Damn all England for exhausting him unto death before he was even fifty years old.

No, nothing mattered now. Almost nothing.

"Send me the clerk," he said when the spasm passed.

"I'll write as you wish, Your Grace."

"That, I doubt." Cocking a sardonic brow at the Earl-in-Abbot's-clothing. "But perhaps you're right, 'tis better not to commit such things to writing." Let him puzzle *that* one out. "Send me the captain of my guard."

"One thing first."

"Not even a 'my lord' or 'Your Grace' when you ask a boon?" But scorn died aborning when he saw the glitter in Robin's eyes. "Favor for favor, then. Mine first, I am the king. What happened to them?"

"Them?"

"Your subjects, King of Sherwood." He knew the peasant names as well as he knew those equally traitorous noble names listed in the Magna Carta. Will Scarlet. Alan of the Dales. Little John. Brother Tuck. Much the Miller's Son.

The fair Saxon face closed in on itself, retreating into the cowl. "Gone. All gone."

"How?"

Reluctantly, but honoring the request of favor-for-favor—oh, he was ever an honorable man, the people's Robin Hood; all the songs and stories said so—he replied, "Alan died of fever. His two daughters are my Eleanor's ladies. The good Brother was called to God four years since. He . . . missed hearing the bells. John, Will, and Much were at the Battle of Bouvines with my Richard. None came back." After a brief silence, Robin bestirred himself. "And now *my* question."

"I'm tired," John said brusquely. "Tomorrow."

"No. Now." Robin leaned forward in his chair. The cowl shadowed his face so that only his green eyes blazed within. "Where is it?"

John didn't pretend to misunderstand him. "The bottom of the Wash."

"How did it happen?"

"What matter now?" he jeered, echoing Robin's earlier words. "Or are you planning a salvage?"

"You left Lynn and reached Wisbech before dusk on the eleventh of this month," Robin insisted. "The rest of the army ferried the baggage over the River Nar and made for the banks of the Wellstream estuary, and there your soldiers stayed the night."

"Yes," John snapped. "And the next day all was lost—jewels, plate, goblets—"

"—the coronation regalia, and your grandmother the Empress Matilda's crown, robes, gold wand—*and* the Sword of Tristram," Robin finished. "But *how* was it lost?"

"Why do you want to know?" John sank deeper into the pillows, thinking of all that lovely gold and silver and knowing his shrew of a Grandmother-the-Empress would make him answer for it when he saw her in hell. If, that was, Mother and Father and Richard didn't get to him first. But what did they know of the England he'd had to rule? They had never been beset as he had been, with the barons and the Pope and the commons and everyone *at* him. He didn't look at Robin. He glanced over at the tapestried wall instead, and found momentary comfort. King Arthur, riding to Camelot. John was also King of England—but not for much longer. Suddenly the tapestry brought to mind his nephew, Arthur of Brittany—a stupid boy, who would have made a stupid king.

John said, "I'm told low water was at noon on the twelfth. They didn't want to keep me waiting, so they started across the sands too early. But the packhorses were too heavy—Jésu, I can see it as if I'd been there, the animals sucked into the sand, men likewise when they went to help the beasts—"

"But the others, the ones not caught in the original mischance, made their way to the other side."

Bitter laughter escaped John's throat. "You should have seen them when they came to tell me." But they hadn't been frightened enough *not* to tell him. Some would have said they were brave, to come and tell the king of such calamity. Bravery only came when one was well and truly frightened. Richard, of course, had never feared anything at all.

John had shouted and ranted, of course; it was expected. They'd cringed some. But he'd already been too ill to make a convincing Plantagenet show of it. He'd scarce been able to sit his horse on the ride to Sleaford. Then had come the nightmare journey here to Newark. Yesterday, that was. And they had sent for the Abbot of Croxton, reputed skilled at healing.

"And so it is all gone," said Robin.

"And my strength with it."

"The strength of a king lies in the support of his vassals—not, as you suppose, in his treasury."

"You dare lecture me on kingship? Me, son of the greatest king this realm ever knew?"

"I was once a monarch of sorts, my lord—as you yourself have said. The King of Sherwood Forest."

They were silent for a time. Then John said, "If you will not write for me, nor send for the clerk, then give me the pen."

"To what purpose? You seem to have dispensed with all the formalities," Robin said, gesturing to the vellum.

"It is the dispensation of my body I am concerned with now. Write, damn you."

Robin picked up pen and vellum, and wrote as the king bade him.

*First, then I desire that my body be buried in the church of the Blessed Virgin and St. Wulfstan at*

*Worcester. Next, I appoint as ordainers and executors of my will the following persons—*

"No," he interrupted himself, "there is one thing else. I command my intestines be removed before my body is taken to Worcester for burial."

The shining green eyes regarded him from within the darkness of the cowl. "My lord?"

Grimly, John smiled. "I give them to the Abbot of Croxton, to fulfill a vow he once made. To make bowstrings of my guts, wasn't it? It's not as if I'll be needing them, and in truth they betrayed me just as you did. Appropriate, do you not think?"

Robin shook his head. "I'll not."

"I order it."

"No."

"I *command*—" But the coiling pain like serpents in his belly deprived him of breath. Robin helped him swallow more water. "Do it," John rasped.

Unwillingly, Robin nodded.

He collapsed back into the pillows. "Leave me. Send the clerk."

"I have yet to hear your confession."

"I'll go to my death unshriven rather than confess to you."

With a sigh: "As you wish, my lord." Rising, he continued, "No more than a swallow of this every hour, for the pain. It is powerful."

And John knew that Robin was leaving him with a means to end the pain forever.

Taking one's own life was a sin. What matter now? He was bound for hell anyway. In truth, he preferred it so; he would see every member of his appalling family there and match them sin for sin for vile sacrilegious sin. His priest-killer of a father; his arrogant adulteress of a mother; his perverted sodomite of a brother—

"Rest peacefully, my lord." said Robin, and left him.

The clerk came in, and John roused himself to finish naming those he would entrust with his will, his sons, and his realm. When it was done, and he had signed and sealed the document, he asked for one of his guard to be sent to him. The man came, and received his instructions, and bowed double, and departed.

* * *

In the early morning hours of the eighteenth day of October, in the Year of Our Lord Jesus Christ One Thousand Two Hundred and Sixteen, the soul of John, King of England, was given up to God.

When word filtered through the castle of Newark, a rider immediately left the stableyard. His first task was to kill Isabelle d'Angoulême, Queen of England. "*Hugh de Lusignan will steal her once I'm dead,*" the king had told him. "*But she is mine forever. Mine.*"

His second task was to be likewise the death of Eleanor Plantagenet, Maid of Brittany, daughter of John's dead brother Geoffrey. "*No one,*" the king had told him, "*must ever come between my line and the throne.*"

Four miles from the castle, the other man who had listened to these instructions fell upon the rider in the early morning rain, and slit his throat.

"It wouldn't have done at all, you know," he murmured as he cleaned his sword on the man's cloak. "The Queen will live, for she did not love John as he thought she ought, and may return to her true lover as she wishes. The Maid will live, for she is no danger to young Henry, being but a simple child and content to spin and weave her years away."

Slapping the dead man's horse toward a nearby farm, he mounted his own mare and rode thoughtfully through the misting rain.

"And *I* will live yet a while longer, for there is much to be done with the yield from the Wash."

John had told him what everyone believed. For the time it took to say the words, perhaps even John had believed it. But Robin knew better.

And he made his way back to the castle at Newark, to claim what John had ordered given to the Abbot of Croxton. Reputed skilled at healing, he performed the operation himself, and alone, with the door barred. When the grisly task was completed, and a leather bag sewn up to be later burned, the Abbot shoved aside a tapestry of King Arthur riding to Camelot and from the recess it concealed took a locked coffer into his arms.

The rest of it—plate and gems and goblets and pendants and candelabra and basins and flagons—all that was well and truly lost in the Wash. But not this. The device o

Empress Matilda was sunk in gold into the wooden lid of a box as long as a legendary sword and as tall as an Empress's jeweled crown.

Robin knew the king. John—not for familial pride or royal duty, but for the sheer grasping possession of the things—would never have let this treasure out of his own keeping.

Robert of Locksley, Earl of Huntington—Robin Hood—took it now into his own keeping, for those who could not but prove more worthy than the dead king he left behind him.

Note: John's movements through England preceding his death from dysentery are accurately described here; his will reads as presented; his intestines were indeed taken by the Abbot of Croxton; his body was escorted by armed mercenaries to Worcester Cathedral for burial; a priest who went to Newark to say a Mass for the dead king's soul told the Abbot of Coggeshall that he'd seen men leave the city laden with loot, and assumed John had been robbed on his deathbed.

# THE DOWRY

## *by Kathy Chwedyk*

Though relatively new to this audience, Kathy Chwedyk is not a neophyte. She has published two novels, both Regency romances (which makes her ideal for this anthology!), but also claims several short story credits, including anthology contributions to *Warrior Enchantresses* (cowritten with Laura Resnick), and *Alligators in the Sewers.* Humor is always a difficult and dangerous aspect for authors to tackle; Kathy handles her foray with subtlety and panache.

N*ew Netherland, 1660*

The master was in an unusually good humor. The rustic inn was comfortable, the simple meal was hot and excellently cooked, and the lean and hungry countrymen in the taproom regarded the master's fine clothes and ample purse with open-mouthed awe.

A little *too* much awe for my taste.

I had been flirting with a handsome, brown-eyed rogue who watched the goings on at our table from the corner of the room, but when the master hefted a bulging sack of golden coins onto the table, he lost all interest in me.

"My daughter's dowry," Petyr Von Auken declared as he put a pudgy hand into the bag and drew out a few of the gleaming coins for emphasis. He must have been drunk, indeed, for highwaymen were known to ply the dark roads between the country villages on this side of the Hudson, and we would have to travel through the night if we hoped to reach the bridegroom's townhouse in the city in time for the formal dinner that would introduce Miss Krista to her future family.

My master was not kind to his dependents, and the thought that he might be robbed secretly pleased me. *I* had nothing to fear, for I had no personal possessions to interest a robber. Except for my virtue, of course, and I certainly would not mind losing what was left of it to a virile, dashing thief in the night.

A famous highwayman, Jan Huysmann, raided along these roads; I wanted to see him, for it would be something to boast about belowstairs when we returned to Peekskill. The journey had been extremely tedious. My master had relieved his boredom by pinching my backside until it was black and blue as we rumbled along in the expensive traveling coach he had bought to impress his daughter's future in-laws.

"Nicholas Von Tepple will know I am a man of substance when I place this in his hands," the master boasted. His fat jaws quivered with emotion.

Nicholas Von Tepple was the richest burgher in New Amsterdam, and it was the triumph of Petyr Von Auken's life to marry his only daughter to this powerful man. He didn't care in the least that the prospective bridegroom was ten years older than the master himself, while Miss Krista was just turned seventeen.

A more subtle man might have paid the dowry with a draft on his bank in New Amsterdam, but this was not showy enough for Petyr Von Auken. No. He had to carry his great, clanking bag of coins with him so he could lay it at the gouty feet of his future son-in-law.

"A toast to the bride!" a reveler shouted, tilting his tankard in my direction. Several others joined him in saluting me, but the master put up his arms to stop them.

"That girl is one of my servants, not my daughter!" the master said in a haughty voice. "Do you think I'd dress my own daughter in plain brown wool?"

I felt an indignant flush stain my cheeks. He made my best traveling costume sound like a rag, which it certainly was not. It was one Miss Krista had worn herself a year ago. As Miss Krista's maid, I was often given the discards from her wardrobe. I had been especially glad to get this one because it was still quite new when Miss Krista grew too plump in the hips to wear it any longer.

"The servant girl is fair enough for me," the brown-eyed one whispered, seating himself at the next table, but turning his chair so he was close enough to touch me.

I jumped at the sound of his voice so close, for I hadn't seen him approach. Smiling, he took a pitcher from a serving girl and poured more ale into the tankard in front of me. I glanced to see that the master was not looking my way any longer and drained the tankard. I liked ale, but I didn't often have the opportunity to drink so much of it in one sitting. Although he spared no expense to impress the neighborhood, the master considered it an extravagance to provide too lavishly for his household.

The man who had proposed the toast to the bride pointed at the hooded feminine form seated next to the master at the table.

"Is she too ugly to show her face in public?" one of the men asked.

"For a treasure like that," shouted a man far gone in drink as he gestured toward the bag of money, "I would take a sow to bed. Good sir, let's have a look at the bride. Don't be shy, now, sweetheart!"

"A *sow!*" shouted the master as the men guffawed. He staggered a little when he stood. "You call my daughter a sow? My Krista is the most beautiful girl in the colonies, and I'll prove it!"

Krista had been sitting at the table with the hood of her cloak hiding most of her face. Her eyes had been demurely cast down, and, like any well-brought-up young lady, she had taken no part in the men's conversation. Instead, she ate all of the food on her plate so daintily and gracefully that no one—except me—noticed how fast it had disappeared.

Now her father took her by the arm and made her stand up from the table. He pulled the cloak away and smiled with satisfaction when the men gasped and sighed.

Krista endured this passively. From the crown of her shining, flaxen hair to the soles of her dainty kid slippers, she was perfect. Her pretty gown of blue silk had been designed to display the girl's charms rather than for comfort or warmth. It was still very tight across the hips and waist, which the men no doubt found alluring. The dress had been far too small for the girl's plump figure when it had come from the dressmaker's. The master had flown into a rage and forbidden his daughter to eat anything but bread and thin soup for a week. Miss Krista lost enough weight so that she could wear the dress. But lest she split the seams of the expensive garment, her stays were laced so tightly that there were welts on her skin.

I should know, for I was the one who laced them. I took pleasure in it, too, because I knew the meek, stupid creature would endure the pain without complaint. It was no wonder that every servant in her father's house despised her, and none of us paid the least heed to anything she said.

From morning till night all the year long, Krista embroidered, she sang, she played the harp, she practiced complicated dancing patterns with the instructor the master had hired for her, and thus she acquired all the accomplishments her father deemed necessary or desirable in the wife of an important man. Any young man who dared turn his eyes to Petyr Von Auken's heiress was sent off with a burr in his ear, and Krista was punished for having encouraged the hopeful swain.

The brown-eyed rogue took my hand and I felt my heart beat faster. He had a face like a hawk's, all clean, elegant angles in the firelight; his dark curling hair was a perfect frame for it. A close-fitting black leather jerkin encased his lean but broad-shouldered torso, and the fine, knee-length leather boots sheathing muscular legs added to the general suggestion of virility and dangerous excitement that surrounded him.

He was flirting with me, and doing it charmingly. But I was not fooled. His eyes were on Krista, and they were glazed with the usual expression of lust and adoration.

"And what is your destination, my dear?" he asked, rubbing my hand sensually between his long fingers. "Where do you stop for the night?"

"We drive straight through to Nicholas Von Tepple's house," I said. My voice was higher than usual from excitement. I couldn't help it. I knew he was thinking of Krista's charms rather than mine when he caressed my hand, but he wouldn't be the first man who turned to the nearest woman for consolation because he was denied the girl he really wanted. I had had a number of satisfying encounters with Miss Krista's would-be suitors. I hoped the brown-eyed man would join their number.

"A pity," he said, dragging his attention away from Krista. "I would have stolen through your window in the night if you had been stopping at the inn. What is your name, my pretty one?"

"Maude," I said. My voice cracked on the word because he had leaned closer, and I could feel his lips against my cheek. I knew very well that in his imagination it was Krista he kissed, but I enjoyed it just the same. *Let the master see,* I thought, defiant with ale. *I care not what he thinks. My backside could not be more sore than it is already from his attentions.*

"And where," the stranger asked, twining one of the curls that had escaped from my bonnet in his strong fingers, "is Nicholas Von Tepple's house?" He gave the curl a sharp tug, which was exciting—and slightly painful.

"In New Amsterdam," I answered. I would have told him anything when he touched me like this.

"You'll be traveling north, then," he said.

He looked speculatively at the master and his bag of gold. His gaze lingered on the master's daughter, and I saw that she was blushing.

*Stupid cow,* I thought. It was a struggle to keep a sweet look on my face, just in case the brown-eyed one *happened* to look my way. I comforted myself with the certain knowledge that the beautiful and richly dressed Miss Krista, for all her ladylike accomplishments, would be lying passively under a great, sweating old man like the master in a month's time. I suppressed a grin as I thought of that worthy old man's dismay when Krista, released from the master's iron control, began to gulp down all of the pastries she craved without her father's interference.

The men would not gaze at her so lustfully when she had a treble roll of fat beneath her chin, and weighed enough to sink a barge.

The rogue gave my hand a final squeeze and favored me with a melting smile as he stood. Disappointed, I looked up at him. I had hoped he would keep me company until it was time to leave the inn.

"What is your name?" I asked, wanting to delay him.

His teeth gleamed white in his tanned face. "Jan," he said.

The same name as the highwayman's. I gave an involuntary squeak of excitement. Could he be . . . ?

" 'Tis a common name hereabouts, sweetheart," he added, blowing me a kiss as he swaggered out the door.

It was getting on nightfall by the time the men in the taproom finished drinking toasts to the master's health, and I glanced into the amber sky beyond the yard with apprehension.

There is something about the way the sun dies over the Kaatskills that makes nervous folk think of the vengeful spirits of the old Indian warriors who once lived in these mountains. We could see the glimmer of a strange orange-and-purple haze in the distance as we resumed our journey.

We had clattered along the ghostly foothills of the mountains for no more than an hour when we heard a commotion outside the coach, and the vehicle swerved, throwing Krista, the master, and me into one another.

"Clumsy girl," the master said, giving Krista a shove.

Suddenly we heard the firing of a gun, and the clatter of hooves in flight.

"The coward! Damn him to hell!" the master swore. He knew, as did Krista and I, that the outrider he had hired to protect us on the journey had abandoned us.

The door to the coach was wrenched open. "Show yourselves," demanded a familiar voice.

I peered out of the open door. The horseman was tall and clothed in shadow. In the dying light I recognized the glint of deep brown eyes through the slits in his mask. He was an intimidating sight with his sword hanging by his side and two pistols in his belt. The three of us leaped awkwardly out of the coach.

"Broken axle," the master muttered angrily, looking at the wreckage of his expensive carriage.

Krista let out a faint scream when she saw the coachman on the ground, lying in a spreading pool of blood. Obviously he had tried to defend us, for the gun he had carried beneath the seat was lying beside him.

"Shut up, girl," the master said viciously to his daughter, drawing his hand back as if he might slap her in his fit of temper. It was his own fault that he was about to be robbed of the precious golden dowry, but he would never admit it, the stubborn old fool. Not even to himself.

"Shut up, old man," the highwayman said to him. "You, girl," he added to me. "Throw the gold out of the coach."

"Maude," barked the master. "I forbid you."

I had no intention of defying an armed highwayman to obey any order of the master's. I managed to scramble back into the coach for the gold, and I pitched it out onto the road.

"Your ring, if you value your life," the highwayman demanded of the master.

"You were there, at the inn!" the master said accusingly. The ring was a valuable one and had been in his family for several generations. He scowled at the highwayman. "I'll see you hanged."

"Perhaps. Hand over the ring, and be quick about it! As you can see, I have another pistol primed and waiting." He gestured toward the gun in his belt.

The master removed the ring and threw it on the ground with a contemptuous gesture.

"Unwise," the highwayman said. He looked at Krista.

"Pick up the ring, sweetheart," he told her. "And the bag of gold."

"Krista!" hissed the master.

Krista gave a little whimper of fright, but did as ordered.

"Very good," the highwayman said approvingly, as if the little idiot had done something clever. "Bring it to me."

Krista started to obey him, but the master let out an infuriated cry and grabbed her by the arm that held her dowry. Panicked, she fought him.

"Let go of the gold, you stupid girl," the master snarled. "How dare you disobey me!"

The master dealt her a ringing slap, and she fell to the ground next to the fallen coachman.

"Worthless, stupid girl," the master shouted, giving her a shove. "You'll do as I say!"

Krista, true to form, began sniveling and weeping. The master slapped her again.

Suddenly a shot rang out. Krista screamed as the master dropped at her feet. I knew he was dead, because he wasn't swearing anymore. I looked at the highwayman and saw the smoke curling from his other pistol.

"He won't bother you again, sweetheart," the highwayman said to Krista, his voice hard. "You're coming with me. From the moment I saw you, I wanted you. And you want me as well." His tone grew suggestive. "I saw that look you gave me at the inn."

Krista's lips parted and she looked at him with indecision written all over her pretty face. In her place, *I* would have been on the back of his horse by now.

"Bring me the gold and the ring," the highwayman said to Krista. And the coachman's pistol."

"The pistol?" she repeated, as if in a trance.

Instead of cuffing her in disgust at her stupidity, he grinned. His eyes were alight with desire.

It was all I could do to restrain myself from baring my teeth at the both of them. They were going to ride off to some cozy love nest in the mountains and *leave* me here with two dead men, and it was all her fault! I had been ashamed of my impoverished childhood spent on my parents' farm, but I was grateful for it now. At least I knew I could get one of the horses unhitched from the damaged carriage and ride it back to the inn.

Krista and the highwayman stared at one another for a long moment. Here she was, about to be swept away in the strong arms of the most handsome man I've ever seen, and she was just standing there with her pretty brow all puckered like that of a perplexed infant.

*He probably thinks she looks adorable,* I thought bitterly.

"Come," he said. There was a note of impatience creeping into his voice. Good, I thought. Maybe he will take me instead. "Bring those things and come!"

Krista set her jaw and dropped to her knees as if they'd suddenly grown too weak to support her weight. She reached a shaking hand toward the coachman.

"I can't!" she cried, looking as if she were on the verge of swooning. "I can't touch him." She covered her face with her hands.

Apparently well-pleased by this maidenly performance, the highwayman dismounted, swaggered over to the distraught girl, pulled her into his strong arms and kissed her as if he had all the time in the world. When they drew apart, I could see the sheen of blood on Krista's lips.

"You're mine now," he said. For all that she stared at him like a frightened doe, I was willing to wager she enjoyed it just the same. How could she not? I was certain I saw a sly, secretive look on her face when she half turned away from him.

"You and the gold. All mine," the highwayman gloated.

His possessive tone sent a thrill of jealousy through me.

He picked up the bag of gold and gestured for Krista to pick up the ring. She turned her back to him and bent as if to obey him. But when she turned around again, she had the coachman's pistol in her hand.

"That's right, sweetheart," the highwayman said, holding

his hand out for the gun. "Give it to me. I don't want you to hurt yourself."

Krista raised the gun and pointed the barrel at him.

"I said, give the gun to me," he said as the smug smile left his face. "Now!"

The gun went off. Krista watched impassively as the highwayman clutched his shoulder and sank to the ground. He had a look of utter disbelief on his face. Lips working, he held his hand out to her. She bent down and picked up the bag of gold.

"You are fortunate," she told him. "I aimed for your heart."

The master's daughter and I exchanged a long look.

"You've always wanted everything I had, Maude," she said. "I wish you joy of him. But the dowry is mine. I've earned it."

She took the reins of the highwayman's horse and hefted the bag of gold to its back. Then she mounted, settling herself astride. Her lacy petticoats gleamed white, and her silk-clad ankles were exposed to the rapidly chilling air. Those thin kid slippers would be worn to tatters if she tried to walk a mile in them. She was already shivering in the silk dress, for her cloak was still in the coach.

"If you don't freeze to death in the night," I told her, "you will be lost in the mountains before morning. Do you think you can survive all by yourself? The mountains are full of thieves and desperate men. They'll kill you and rob you of your gold."

"But until they do," she said, stretching like a cat and shaking her head until the golden hair I had arranged so carefully that morning cascaded down her back, "I'll be free!"

She lifted her chin proudly and threw the ring at me. Then she hesitated and dipped into the bag for two gold coins, which she threw after the ring.

I didn't watch her ride away because I was busy scrabbling for the valuables in the dirt. Once I found and hid them safely within the folds of my dress, I looked down at the man at my feet.

As usual, I would have to be content with Miss Krista's discards. He would probably stay with me until the gold and whatever money I would get from selling the ring ran out. If he didn't die from his wound first, I thought dispassionately.

He didn't look so virile, now, as he lay in the dirt with his mouth opening and closing like that of a landed fish.

My hands were stiff and clumsy as I went about the unaccustomed task, but I managed to unhitch one of the horses from the team and lead it over to highwayman. He stayed conscious long enough to mount the animal with my help, and then he slumped over its neck. I got on the horse behind him and started guiding it down the road, back toward the inn from which we had come.

©
danforth 96

# THE REST OF THE STORY

## *by Bruce D. Arthurs*

Bruce Arthurs enjoys the vast varieties of life. In his "real job," he is a mail carrier (but he promises never to "go postal"). In his other life he writes, and publishes. His short fiction has been featured in three volumes of *Sword & Sorceress,* in *Marion Zimmer Bradley's Fantasy Magazine,* and, more recently, in *Heaven Sent.* But he has also made his bones in the television industry; Bruce sold a teleplay to *Star Trek: The Next Generation,* which was broadcast as "Clues" during the fourth season. The story he contributed to this anthology is both poignant and surprisingly appropos, for it tells the tale of an infamous highwayman all too often overlooked in twentieth-century literature.

Levi the hosteler was shaking dust from a blanket when the Samaritan returned. From the khan's roof, Levi could see most of Jericho and the groves of palm and balsam around it. The mid-morning air was warm and fragrant. Even doing work that had formerly been done by his wife, Levi had been taking satisfaction in his simple task. The rush of Passover pilgrims to and from Jerusalem had died to a trickle, and the frantic pace to keep up with travelers' needs and demands had relaxed with it.

He stared at the distant figure leading an ass along the dusty road from Jerusalem. He recognized the man leading the animal. The Samaritan, a frequent user of the khan, had departed in the indigo light of early dawn with his supplies and goods tied onto the ass' back. Now, returning, there was a man's body added to the beast's burden.

Levi's satisfaction drained away. He gave the blanket a final shake and draped it over the parapet. There were others to be shaken and aired, but they could wait; the last travelers who had used the roof as their campsite had departed and he need not worry about theft.

He climbed down the ladder set against the khan's inside wall, careful not to catch his robe on the rough-hewn wood. He looked around for Mordecai, then remembered that his son had volunteered, much to Levi's surprise, to clean the rooms they shared at the back of the khan. Since being widowed, Levi had managed to keep the khan clean and in repair, the work distracting him from his sorrow, but his and Mordecai's own quarters had become deplorable. Mordecai had been stoking the fire under a large pot of water when Levi had left to air the used bedding.

Levi went out the khan's gateway. The Samaritan was closer now, and raising a hand in greeting. "Hello, hosteler. An unfortunate discovery has brought me back."

Levi returned the greeting. Even if the man was a Samaritan, a heretic despised by proper Jews, his money was good, and Levi could not afford to discriminate among those he serviced. Had Levi been wealthier, he would have hired a girl to air the blankets and perform other women's tasks.

For that matter, the heresy in Samaria meant that more people took the longer route north through Jericho, rather than travel through Samaria, where violent incidents between Samaritans and Jews were far too common.

The body slumped over the ass was naked, bruised, and scraped. Moist cloths were tied around several limbs. A wider one around the man's chest was stained pink with oozing blood.

Levi spat in the dust, angry and disgusted. "Road brigands?" he asked. "Is he dead?"

"Not yet. Perhaps not at all, with care. I washed his wounds with wine and oil, but he may yet die without rest and healing."

*True enough,* Levi thought. *But* . . . "Who is he? Had he any belongings?"

"None. Whoever beat him robbed him as well."

Levi looked at the naked man again. "The rooms of the khan cost nothing to travelers," he told the Samaritan. "You know that. But my living, poor as it is, is by supplying those travelers' needs. A cot, blankets, food, water, firewood, those I can provide. I cannot *give* to strangers. I am sorry."

The Samaritan stared into Levi's eyes for a long moment

then reached into the girdle of his robe. He passed several bronze coins to Levi. "Here."

Levi, surprised, took the coins. He had expected the Samaritan to proceed on, to look elsewhere for aid. He felt a measure of discomfiture and embarassment, as if he had failed to properly answer one of the questions the rabbis had asked him and other students years before, testing their knowledge and understanding of the Talmud.

But it would not be proper to show his feelings. "As you wish," he answered, taking the rope and leading the ass through the gateway. The Samaritan followed.

They entered the large inner courtyard. A few people, not yet having resumed their journeys, stared as Levi led the ass toward a vacant room.

"Mordecai!" Levi called in a loud voice.

The door-curtain of Levi's room was swept aside a second later by a gangly dark-haired youth, close to his full growth, with a thin scattering of beard across his chin. He set his broom against the wall and loped quickly across the courtyard.

He stopped abruptly as he saw the man across the ass' back. Face paling, he asked, "Is . . . is he dead?"

"No," Levi answered. "Fetch a cot and blankets." Mordecai continued to stare. "Now, boy!" Levi's son looked up, eyes wide, and ran off toward the storeroom.

Levi tried to put his annoyance aside. His son had been moodier than ever since Ruth had died, going off with friends at inopportune times, long silences when he *was* home, leaving work half done. Levi sighed, remembering what a willing student of the Talmud Mordecai had been as a younger child, and his own hopes that his son might eventually become a rabbi. What had happened to those happier days? Had he ever disappointed his own parents so?

Yes, he admitted to himself, he probably had. The job of hosteler, keeper of the khan, was not highly regarded, usually given to non-Jews. But Ruth had been big with child, and Levi had been desperate for a reliable, even if meager, source of income. He had filled the post all these years without complaint or any attempt to better himself. It was, he supposed, one of the reasons for Mordecai's sullen moods.

Some of the travelers approached as Levi and the Samaritan waited for Mordecai to return. Levi turned to them. "Will one of you fetch the physician from the synagogue?"

"I'll go!" A boy with intense dark eyes, part of a Galilean family returning from Jerusalem, raised a hand, only to be cuffed by the gray-bearded man behind him. "No, you won't," the boy's father growled. "We've already lost three days' travel because of you running off to the rabbis."

"The Romans will need to know about this," one of the onlookers said. There were noises of displeasure at mention of the Romans.

"He speaks true," Levi answered. "We need one person to go to the synagogue, and another to the Roman fort." A woman said she would fetch the physician, and she hurried away.

The boy, with a careful glance at his father, slowly raised a hand again. "I know where the fort is. I'll come straight back. I promise."

Levi caught the father's eye. With a reluctant scowl, the father nodded his acquiescence. The boy ran off, sandals slapping in the dust.

Mordecai returned, dragging a heavy rope-strung cot under one arm, blankets under the other.

When the cot had been placed inside the room, Levi and the Samaritan eased the injured man off the ass and carried him in. As they lowered the naked man onto the rough-hewn bed, Levi asked, "How did you recognize him as a fellow Samaritan?"

The Samaritan looked up and into Levi's eyes. After a moment, he answered, in a quiet tone of voice: "I didn't. I don't. When I found him this morning, he was half-con cious, and muttered of others—even a priest—who hac passed him by yesterday eve, ignoring his moans, and leav ing him to lie alongside the road during the night. But o himself he said nothing."

Levi felt a flush rise to his face, and was grateful it woul not be visible in the room's dimness. If he had been a lon traveler, on a road notorious for thieves and robbers, h might not have stopped to help an injured stranger. Eve if recognizable as a fellow Jew, Levi would hesitate. Suc a stranger might be bait, to lure unwary travelers aside fc other, hidden, robbers.

The doorway's curtain lifted to one side. A shaft of ligl shone on Levi's face as Mordecai leaned into the roor

Levi, afraid his flushed face was evident to his son, rose to his feet, casting his face into shadow again.

"The . . . the healer is here," Mordecai said. Levi went to the doorway and invited the physician in, with all the proper respect and veneration due a synagogue official.

The physician examined the man on the bed as Levi and others watched from the doorway. He changed several of the Samaritan's bindings for cleaner cloths, turned him, and was examining a deeper wound on the man's back when the Romans arrived.

The crowd of onlookers drew back as a Roman officer and two escorting centurions—it was not safe for Romans, even Roman soldiers, to walk alone in Judea—approached. The boy who had gone to fetch them skipped along in the dust beside them. The boy's father reached out and yanked his son to him by the collar of his tunic, shushing him to stay still.

The crowd glared sullenly at the Romans. Since the burning of the Imperial Palace by Zealots, the Roman garrison at Jericho had been more than doubled. The resentment of Jews and other Judeans had also increased, and there was little love lost on either side.

Leaving the two soldiers outside, the officer entered the room where the injured man lay. "My name is Marius," he announced. "What has happened here?"

Marius was of medium height, but wide of shoulder. His face was sun-weathered, and a white streak ran through his light brown hair. As he spoke, his deep-set eyes roamed intensely over the room and everyone in it.

The Samaritan answered. "Sir, on the road between here and Jerusalem, I found this man, robbed and beaten. I bore him here to be cared for."

Marius leaned in to peer over the shoulder of the doctor, ignoring the physician's frosty glare. He peered at the wound on the man's back. Dried blood was crusted around the edges of the cut, and a trickle of fresh blood moved down the curve of the skin. There was a streak of discolored skin next to the wound.

Marius reached out and pressed against the discolored area. The wounded man gasped and stirred on the cot.

"Stop that," the physician said, the chill in his voice matching his eyes. "This man is in enough pain."

"This man has been stabbed." Without touching again,

the Roman waved his finger above the discoloration. "With a narrow blade, entering at a shallow angle and catching short on the rib, here." He indicated where the discoloration stopped. "Touch there, physician, and tell me what you feel."

Levi bit his lip, knowing the Roman's statement had not been a request. The physician locked eyes with Marius for a moment, then turned back to his patient and gently prodded against the area. The doctor's eyes widened as the injured man moaned again. "There is something there."

"I thought so." A look of grim satisfaction was on the Roman's face. "The tip, I suspect, of the knife used to stab him. Can you remove it?"

Once again, the Roman's words had not been a request. The physician knelt and unrolled a cloth, revealing iron hooks and lancets, small tongs, several short knives with finely sharpened blades, and even a valuable bronze needle, along with a length of fine linen thread wound on a wooden pin.

The physician took the pliers in one hand and a short-bladed knife in the other. "I will have to cut into the skin," he said. "The patient must be held still."

Marius looked at Levi and the Samaritan. "One of you take his legs, the other his arms and shoulders."

Levi knelt to wrap his arms around the injured man's shoulders, regretting he hadn't told the Samaritan to take his burden elsewhere. The Samaritan held the man's legs. The physician leaned over the patient and lowered the blade.

The man cried out, his eyes snapping open as the physician cut. "Robbers!" he cried as Levi and the Samaritan restrained his struggling body. "Help me! God, help me!"

Marius laid a hand gently on the victim's head. Levi looked up and saw concern in the Roman's eyes; he was not, then, unfeeling toward the man's pain.

Beyond Marius, in the doorway where onlookers crowded, Levi saw Mordecai, face still pale, turn away and leave.

"I have it." The physician lifted the tongs into the light, revealing a splinter of bloody sharp-edged bronze. He dropped it into Marius' cupped hand.

The physician prayed over the injured man as he pressed a clean patch of cloth against the new wound, calling on

God to ease the man's suffering and to allow him to heal quickly and fully. Levi added his own silent prayer. The injured man fell back into his earlier faint, his gasps slowing.

"We must turn him, so that I can bind this—" The physician held up a long, narrow piece of cloth. "—around his chest. It will hold the smaller piece against the fresh incision, and help staunch the bleeding."

Levi and the Samaritan shifted positions, then rolled the man onto one side. The injured man gasped, but did not awaken or cry out again, as the physician pulled the long cloth beneath his chest and tied the two ends together.

The man's face had moved into the light as he was turned. Levi saw Marius start in surprise, then quickly set his face back into a stolid imperturbability.

*He knows this man,* Levi thought to himself.

Levi turned that thought over in his mind as the Roman spoke to the physician. "Will he live? And when will he be able to speak clearly?"

"If his wounds stay clean, he will live. As for regaining his thoughts . . . perhaps this evening. Perhaps tomorrow. Perhaps a week. I cannot say more clearly than that."

Marius frowned, then turned to Levi. "Hosteler, I will leave one of my soldiers here, in case this man should awaken and be able to describe his attackers. I will return this evening to see to his condition. I expect you to care for him as you would your own family."

Levi remembered nursing his wife months before, and his inability to cool the fever that had taken Ruth from him. But of this he said nothing. The Roman, he was certain, was leaving the soldier for more reason than as witness to whatever the injured man might say. He was leaving the soldier as a guard. But why?

But of this, too, Levi said nothing. He merely nodded his head. "As you wish."

Marius turned toward the Samaritan. "Can you again ind the place where you discovered this man?"

"Certainly," the Samaritan replied. "I should like to reume my journey. If I walk briskly, and my beast wishes to ooperate, I may yet be able to make the gates of Jerusaem before night."

"We will accompany you as far as where you found this ian." Marius went outside, motioning to the two centurions. After a moment of whispered conversation, one of the soldiers returned to the doorway and took a stance beside it.

Levi and the Samaritan also went outside. The Samaritan's ass waited, flicking its ears at flies. "Thank you for your assistance," the Samaritan said as he began to rearrange the bundles on the animal's back.

"This is something more than just a man robbed and beaten," Levi said to the Samaritan, keeping his voice low. "I pray that you have not placed me or my family in danger."

The Samaritan glanced around. "I know," he said. Surreptitiously, he removed several more coins from his girdle, passing them quickly to Levi. "Take these. It is all I can do before I leave. Take your best care of the man, and may God and His angels watch over him, and you, and your family."

Levi fingered the coins in his hand. "It might have been better had you reserved your charity for fellow Samaritans."

The Samaritan's smile was ironic. "Our holy writings may differ, but the same God rules over us. We have no choice in the matter, however much we disagree or our priests call the other heretic. I felt I had no choice this morning."

"It is too bad you are not a proper Jew, Samaritan. I think you may be a better man than I."

The Samaritan took up the animal's lead. Marius and the other soldier were waiting in the shade by the gateway. "I must go. But you may misjudge yourself, Levi."

Levi watched as the three men left on the dusty road to Jerusalem. Other travelers, excitement over, were also preparing for departure.

The physician, his instruments rinsed and rewrapped to be purified later at the synagogue, exited the room where the injured man lay. "You will be caring for this man?" he asked Levi.

"Yes."

"Give him as much liquid as he can take. Mix water with wine, first, and dribble it into his mouth by small spoonfuls. When he awakes, a meat broth. When he is more fully recovered, a thin porridge."

"I understand." The Samaritan's coins were still in Levi's hand, and he fished forth one of them. "May I ask you, or your way to the synagogue, to have the butcher send a fresh chicken here?" The coin was far more than the cost of a chicken, but Levi knew the remainder would be considered recompense for the physician's time and service.

"Certainly." The physician accepted the coin and left.

Levi nodded to the centurion by the doorway and, after a nod of acceptance back, looked into the room again. The injured man lay on the cot, his breathing heavy but regular.

Levi lowered the curtain. "I will be preparing a broth, but will return soon with some watered wine for him. Call for me if there is any change."

"As you wish." The Roman's voice was bored. This was just a task assigned to him. He was unconcerned about pleasing his land's subjects.

Levi crossed the courtyard to his quarters, calling "Mordecai!" as he entered. But there was no answer, and a quick look showed that Levi's son was not there.

*Where has the boy got to now?,* Levi wondered. Some progress had been made on cleaning their quarters—belongings and storage pots had been straightened and arranged more neatly under the raised sleeping area—but other parts were still in disarray. *Another job half-finished,* he thought in dismay. Since his mother's death, the boy—*no, the man,* Levi thought, *he's old enough*—had been more distracted and unreliable than ever.

At least the water Mordecai had started heating that morning still hung over its small fire in the corner. As soon as the chicken arrived, Levi could start the broth. They might even add some of the cooked meat to their own meal of boiled grains and fruits.

Then Levi noticed no bubbles were roiling from the water's surface, nor even any vapor of incipient steam. He held his hand over the water for several seconds, then dipped a finger into it.

The water was, just barely, uncomfortably warm. How could that be, over a fire for more than an hour?

Levi went back outside. "Mordecai!" he called again, this time much louder. Again, there was no answer, although the Galilean boy, departing through the gateway with his parents and their donkey, turned at the sound of Levi's voice and waved.

Levi looked around in dismay. *Where has Mordecai got*

*to?* No sign of him in the khan. Had he gone into Jericho proper?

Levi climbed to the roof. From there, he could see most of Jericho. Standing close to the khan's parapet, he shaded his eyes and peered, but did not spy Mordecai's tall, thin figure.

He lowered his head, shaking it in annoyance, then stopped and stared.

At the base of the outside wall, on this least trafficked side, was a streak of dark-colored dirt. Of *wet* dirt, lighter at the edges where it dried, such as might have been made by emptying a pot from where Levi stood.

Had Mordecai carried the water to the roof, emptied it, then gone back to start a *second* pot heating? But why? It made no sense. Why throw away a pot of clean, hot water? Why the roof, instead of across the road and into the bushes, as they did with their pisspots? And where had Mordecai gone afterward?

Levi could find no answers. Slowly, he climbed back down to the courtyard.

The butcher's boy had been sent with a cleaned and plucked chicken. Levi thanked the boy and took the chicken inside.

The water was beginning to simmer now. Setting the chicken on a cloth—he would have to remember to scrape the table clean; it was one of the tasks he and Mordecai had been leaving too long undone—Levi took several small bags from a box and added measures of cumin and dill to the water. Replacing the spices, he took out the salt bag.

It was almost empty; only a smidgen of salt remained. Another neglected task. *Could Mordecai have gone to buy salt?* But Mordecai had not known about the broth.

Levi added the salt to the simmering water, knowing it would be weak without more. But he had no choice for the moment. After he cut up the chicken for the pot, he would have to take the injured man some liquid.

The knife used for meat was not in its place. *None* of the household knives were where they should be, though Levi searched, even lighting a lamp to cast light into shadowed corners.

He sat quietly for a moment. His heart was heavy with dread, a growing fear that somehow the discarded water his son's disappearance, and the missing knives, all tied in somehow to the injured man.

After a time, he stood up. The chicken went into the pot whole; it would take longer to simmer, but that could not be helped. He fetched jugs from under the beds, mixed wine and water in a bowl, and went out.

The injured man stirred as Levi's entrance admitted a bright spear of light. The curtain fell back, and the room dimmed again, but the man's eyes stayed partially open, semifocusing on Levi.

"You must drink," Levi said gently. He pulled a low stool next to the bed and sat. His hand lifted the injured man's head. "A sip at a time."

The man choked and spluttered on the first mouthful, but took the second gratefully before leaning back, eyes closing.

Levi stared down, then leaned in close and whispered, "Who *are* you?"

The man's eyes fluttered open, alarmed.

"Who are you?" Levi repeated. "Why were you robbed? Who robbed you? What was taken?"

The man's eyes widened. "No," he whispered. Again, more urgently: "*No.*"

"I have to know." Levi's face almost touched the other's. "Tell me. *Please.*"

"I . . . I *can't.*" The man's voice was a weak whisper. "You'd . . . you'd . . ." He scrunched his eyes shut and turned his face away. *"No!"*

Levi glanced over his shoulder, fearful the Roman outside might have heard. He looked back at the frightened man, uncertain.

"All right," he finally whispered. "When you are willing to answer, I will listen. For now, drink. Just drink."

It took nearly an hour to empty the bowl, minutes silently passing between each sip. But the man's color looked better, and he slept quickly when done. Levi stared down for a moment, unanswered questions still racing through his head, before leaving.

Mordecai was still gone. Levi checked the broth simmering in his quarters and added a knot of wood to the fire.

He filled another container with more watered wine and left it in the injured man's room. Then he checked and swept out the rooms vacated since Mordecai had vanished.

By now it was late in the day, the western sky streaked with rose and purple as twilight approached. Levi looked in on the injured man again, but found him still sleeping.

Several new travelers, Sudanese desert-dwellers by the dark-skinned hands that jutted from the sleeves of deep-hooded robes, arrived for a night's lodgings. They needed little and said less, paying Levi only for a jug of wine.

Back in his rooms, the broth had grown rich in color, its scent redolent with seasonings. With a long spoon, he lifted the chicken onto a platter, where he could pull the meat from the bones when it cooled. Waiting, he sampled a sip of the broth.

"Still needs salt," he muttered.

The curtain over their doorway was pushed to one side. "Hello, Father," Mordecai said.

Levi stared. "Where have you been?" he finally said, working to keep his voice even.

Mordecai held a rolled cloth. He set it on the table and opened it. "I took our knives to be sharpened." Inside the cloth were the several knives of the household, including the narrow-bladed one reserved for cutting and boning meat. "I am sorry it took so long."

Levi picked up the knife he had wanted earlier that day, brought it close to the lamp's flickering light. "I am not surprised," he said after a moment's examination. "The blade is narrower than the last time I used it. It would take some time to grind off so much and apply a fresh edge."

Levi looked up to see alarm in his son's eyes, and knew the boy was about to bolt. He leaped up and grabbed Mordecai's tunic, pulling him close with an iron grip. He waved the knife in front of his son's face. "Is this the knife that stabbed that man? *Is it?*"

Mordecai stared back and forth from the knife to his father's angry face. "Don't ask me that, Father. If you love me, you'll not get involved."

Levi stepped back, aghast. He stared at the knife in his hand. "It is, isn't it? That's why the second pot of water this morning. You'd tainted this knife with human blood, purified it by boiling, then had to discard the polluted water."

He looked at his son in anguish. "Why? You are my son. Your mother and I raised you under God's laws, as a proper Jew. Why would you rob and beat a stranger, and leave him for dead?"

"Because I *am* a Jew! Because it is no wrong to rob a robber!" Mordecai's voice flashed with anger.

"What?" Levi felt stunned by the sudden confession, confused by the words themselves. "What are you saying?"

Mordecai was trembling with emotion. "I've said too much. If I told you, you would become part of it, whether you wanted to or no. And the Romans would not hesitate to crucify you with us."

Levi clutched at his head. Blood pounded in his temples as a mad whirl of thought and emotion rushed through his mind. "*Us?* Who? Who else is part of this?"

"I'll say no more. I can't put you in dang—" Mordecai's words were interrupted by a loud outcry from the courtyard.

Levi and Mordecai ran into the courtyard. In the near-darkness, Levi saw the centurion who had been standing guard sprawled on the ground. A large chunk of brick lay on the ground next to him.

Beside the centurion was a man in Judean robes. The Judean was fighting for his life, waving a long dagger frantically in front of himself. The two Sudanese from the nearby room were attacking with swords.

*Roman swords,* Levi realized, just as one of the Sudanese' hood fell back, revealing a head of light brown hair—definitely non-Sudanese—and a familiar face. Marius, his face darkened with pigment.

The Judean had no chance against the two swordsmen. A blow from Marius' sword knocked away the dagger, deeply slashing the Judean's arm and giving the other swordsman clear opening at the Judean's chest.

The Judean screamed as the sword entered his belly. He fell to the ground beside the centurion.

"Elihu!" Mordecai cried.

*Elihu, the blacksmith's son?* Levi thought, suddenly certain that the collapsed figure was indeed Mordecai's closest friend.

The two swordsmen turned toward Mordecai, stared for a second, then broke into a run across the courtyard.

Levi's chest was tight with terror, certain that he would see his son cut down in seconds.

"Run," he whispered. "Run, Mordecai."

Mordecai turned. His eyes fastened on his father's for a second. Then he suddenly lashed out with a fist. Levi felt the blow against his face, and found himself falling to the ground.

"No!" shouted Mordecai, breaking into a run. "You won't stop me, Father!" He grabbed the ladder rungs and scrambled frantically upwards.

Marius' soldier reached the ladder and began to climb, but Mordecai swung himself up over the roof parapet, turned, grabbed the top rung, and heaved. The ladder twisted, and the centurion, one hand gripping his sword, lost his hold and tumbled back to the dirt.

Mordecai pulled on the ladder, and the lower end rose into the air. Marius jumped, but missed as Mordecai pulled the ladder up onto the roof.

The ladder vanished from Levi's sight as Mordecai heaved it toward the other side of the roof. Mordecai followed, and likewise vanished.

"After him! Alert the others!" Marius cried, sparing only a glance at Levi. He and the soldier ran toward the gateway, hallooing loudly. There was suddenly another centurion in the road, and another. The disguised soldier pointed and shouted; the others split up in different directions, the disguised man going with one.

Marius had stopped beside the fallen centurion. The man stirred as Marius shook him, pushed himself weakly up on one elbow, raising his other hand to his head. Marius stood and rushed out the gateway after the others.

More shouts, and the sound of running feet, rose from the streets and alleys around the khan. After a moment, they grew more distant, fainter.

Levi pushed himself to his feet, touched his aching jaw. Mordecai's parting words had ensured the Romans would not accuse Levi of complicity in his son's escape.

Levi walked slowly toward the two men. The centurion was sitting up, shaking his head gently. A trickle of blood oozed from the side of his head.

Elihu would never stand again. His fingers clutched at his stomach as his life leaked between his fingers. He was trembling and gasping.

Levi knelt down and placed a hand gently on Elihu's shoulder. "Elihu, why?" he softly asked. "What were you and Mordecai doing?"

Elihu looked up into Levi's face. Somehow, he managed a weak smile. "Rebels, Levi," he whispered. "We were attacking . . . the Romans . . . where it would hurt them . . . the most."

"I don't understand. What does that man you robbed have to do with the Romans?" In his mind, Levi was offering a prayer: *Lord, have mercy on this young fool, and on my son.*

"He was . . . seen in Jerusalem. Recognized. Word came that he would be . . . traveling alone . . . toward Jericho. He's . . . he's . . ."

The centurion had tottered to his feet. He kicked weakly at the chunk of parapet that had struck him down, then looked toward Elihu and Levi. His face contorted with rage. "Jewish bastard!" he cried, drawing his sword.

"No!" Levi shouted, but the soldier thrust his sword into Elihu's breast. Elihu spasmed, coughed blood, and went limp in Levi's arm.

The soldier waved his sword weakly. "Get back to your own rooms, Jew," he muttered. He stumbled back to the doorway and took up his position. His breathing was heavy and slow as he leaned against the wall.

Levi set Elihu down and stood again. It was fully dark now, the stars bright points in the clear sky. The sounds of pursuit were distant now, and fading. With a heavy step, Levi returned to his quarters.

It was nearly an hour later when Marius drew aside the door-curtain and entered. Most of the pigment had been wiped from his face, although there were still some streaks.

He stood silently, watching. Levi sat silently at the table, eyes focused on the flickering flame of the lamp.

Finally, Marius spoke. "He outran us."

Levi could not restrain a small smile. "He has long legs."

"And narrow feet," the Roman replied. "When the Samaritan took us to the place of the robbery, I found footprints behind bushes close to the road. One set was from very narrow feet, and I realized I had seen those same narrow prints in your courtyard's dust. Your son was the only adult here tall and thin enough to have left those prints."

"Ah."

"If the victim had, indeed, been carried into his robber's domicile, then the robber would either flee, or murder his victim to avoid identification. When I returned to town, I sent out watchers who observed your son at the blacksmith's. He was not running. That left only one choice of action."

*Mordecai, you fool. Why didn't you run at the first opportunity?*

"To reach his victim, he would have to dispatch the man on guard. So, after arranging to have others nearby, I and my second centurion disguised ourselves and took a room where we could watch the first. When your son returned, nonchalant, I was surprised. I didn't expect that a second man—his accomplice—"

"His name was Elihu. He was the blacksmith's son."

Marius continued. "—would climb the outside wall and drop a chunk of masonry from the rooftop."

Levi interrupted again. "You put the guard by the injured man's door before you suspected my son, or that there might be an attempt on the man's life. Why? *Who is this man?*"

Marius stared coolly for a long moment before he responded. "He is one of the *gabbai.*"

Levi drew in a long breath. "You mean," he said slowly, "that I have given a bed to . . . cared for . . . *fed* . . . a, a—" He had to swallow before he could say the next word. "*—tax-collector*?"

Things suddenly made sense. The *gabbai* were considered on a level with robbers and murderers. Heretics like the Samaritan might be misguided, but the *gabbai* betrayed their beliefs, and heritage, and people, for Roman coin.

"Had I known that," Levi told Marius coldly, "I would have spat on him, and sent him seeking aid elsewhere, and wished him ill-luck finding it."

Marius was silent for a moment. "You Jews run both hot and cold in your hearts. A difficult people."

"As it should be. As our Lord wills it."

Marius stood. "I will send a litter in the morning to move the *gabbai* elsewhere. But I came to tell you your son had not been captured or killed. It may yet happen, but not tonight."

The coldness in Levi's breast warmed slightly. The Roman had a measure of mercy in his heart, though Levi doubted it would serve Marius well in his career. "For that, I thank you."

Marius departed. For a long time Levi sat unmoving, lost in his thoughts. He picked up the knife again, felt its freshly sharpened edge.

All Levi held most dear had been lost to him. First his wife, and tonight his son. Oh, Mordecai was still alive, and might remain so, but as a fugitive from Roman law he was, for all practical purposes, dead. Levi would, almost certainly, never see him again.

He stood and began to gather together what he would need.

As he crossed the courtyard, Levi saw that Marius had replaced the injured centurion with a fresh man. Elihu's body was gone, but dark stains still showed in the moonlight. For a second, Levi thought about how he would have to spread fresh, dry dirt over the stained ground in the morning, then remembered there would be no morning for him.

"What have you there?" the guard asked.

"Broth," Levi answered, showing the plate-covered bowl in one hand. The soldier lifted the plate slightly, sniffed, and waved Levi on into the room.

The *gabbai* stirred as Levi entered. His eyes, more focused and coherent now, reflected the dancing flame from Levi's lamp. With a grunt, and a small gasp, he pushed himself up on one arm. He stared at Levi for a long moment, then lowered his head.

"You . . . know what I am," he whispered.

"Yes."

"And still you bring me sustenance. The Lord has delivered me to a man kinder of heart than I."

Levi drew a shuddering breath. He felt the weight of the knife concealed in his sleeve, and knew he would not use it. He was not a murderer, or a rebel.

"I am Aaron of Phasaelis," the injured man said. "A . . . tax-collector."

"And I am . . . I am Levi of Jericho, hosteler." Tears ran down Levi's face and fell free, making small splashes in the bowl's contents. The broth would be salted properly, after all.

©danforth 96

# WATCH FOR ME BY MOONLIGHT

## *by Lois Tilton*

Lois Tilton is a prolific short story writer, contributing frequently to magazines, collections, and anthologies; last year alone she published fifteen stories. Her specialty is vampires—and so it will come as no surprise to discover this tale is a deliciously dark look at the highwayman as one of the Undead. Other works containing her fiction are *Time of the Vampires, Urban Legends,* and *100 Vicious Little Vampire Stories.*

The moon sailed the night sky like a ship of the dead with tattered sails of cloud, driven by the rushing wind. Its light turned the road to a silver ribbon, winding through the heather-covered hills.

But on another night, three years earlier, the moon had been the color of blood, casting its baleful red gaze over the Westphalian battlefield, over the dead who lay there and the wounded, bleeding into the torn and trampled ground, waiting helplessly for dawn to know if they would live or die. This was the situation that every soldier feared above all, for there were creatures that followed the great armies from battle to battle, preying on the wounded and the dead: looters, and worse. They cared nothing for a man's uniform, what side he fought for, officer or common soldier, living or dead—it was all the same to them in their search for plunder.

I lay pinned under my dead horse with a French musket ball in my ribs, coughing up blood. Overhead rose the moon, washing the field in a sanguinary light. All around me, men moaned and cried out in a dozen languages—for aid, for water, for the mercy of God. But as the shadows of the clouds blew across the face of the moon, other shadows crept onto the battlefield to prowl among the victims of war, and one by one, the voices grew silent, sometimes in a scream, sometimes in a gurgle of blood.

I knew what was happening. I tried to hold my breath, to feign death. But pain and exsanguination can alter a man's perception, distort a shadowed face into a thing inhuman. I thought I felt the cold breath of a shadow on my face, and I couldn't help myself, I opened my eyes to see *something* bending over me. . . .

The moonlight was running down its face, like blood.

They had taken me for dead. I lay all day among the stiffening corpses, the mingled fatalities of the allied armies. But after the moon had risen again, I stirred, and some of the soldiers heard my groans.

They carried me to the surgeons, and in defiance of the odds, I survived their attentions. Yet blood loss had made me pale and weak, and even after my recovery the force of the sun overhead made my head throb with blinding pain, so that I was unable to go out onto the parade ground without fainting.

I admit that my entire motive in joining the army had been to absent myself from England, either to America or the Continent, as far as possible from my creditors. I'd raised the money to buy a lieutenancy in one lucky night at the gaming tables, but since joining the regiment I'd fallen behind on my mess-bills, and my attempts to make up the difference at dice or cards had only brought me new debts. My hopes of fortune on the battlefield had come to nothing; all my prize money amounted to only a few guineas, long since spent. When my brother-officers forcibly put the matter of my regimental debts to me, I had nothing left after the sale of my commission.

So I found myself back in London in even worse straits than before, my only hope that I could somehow recoup my fortunes at play before my creditors learned I was back within their reach. Returning home was impossible, even in my new guise as a wounded war hero. While my mother had been alive, I could count on a grudging welcome and a few guineas slipped into my purse, but the day after her funeral—he had at least granted me that much grace, to see her buried—my brother turned me out with these fond parting words: "If you ever set foot on this estate again, damn your eyes, I'll set the dogs on you!"

If there was a gleam of hope my situation, it was this: the strange malaise that still afflicted me in the sunlight always seemed to lift shortly before nightfall, to be succeeded by a vigorous rush of energy and well-being. It was a heady sensation, something like strong spirits, that left me feeling as if I could fight a duel against a dozen opponents at once or leap from one rooftop to the next. As long as the night lasted, I could sit to hand after hand of cards, and my wits never faltered or grew dull. There was a new quickness to my perceptions and calculations that afforded me a distinct advantage at the table.

It was not a bad life, for a time. I won enough to live on, to maintain myself in a decent pair of rooms, to keep myself outfitted like a gentleman—I admit that I'd always liked to cut a dash, and indeed one of the attractions of the military as a profession had been the scarlet coat. But inevitably the news of my return came to the ears of my creditors.

It was a waiter who warned me—I'd tipped the man well—that the bailiffs were lying in wait for me outside the front and back doors of the establishment. So. It had come. I felt, almost, a relief.

I stood up from the table, carefully pocketed my night's winnings, and bowed to my companions. "Gentlemen, you must excuse my departure, but there are some persons below awaiting me."

There was a sharp, restless energy flowing through me. If the bailiffs were waiting at the doors, then I would take my leave by another way. That much the army had taught me: to always ensure a route of retreat.

I strode across the room and unlatched one of the tall windows. Outside, the moon was high and shone like a new shilling, illuminating the night with a silver tint. I stepped up to the sill, turned, bowed to the company, whose eyes were all on me now. *If you die,* I thought, *die game, and give the crowd a good show.* "Gentlemen, I bid you good night."

I leaped. I thought, for an instant, that I flew. Almost effortlessly, I cleared the space between the adjoining buildings, scrambled lightly up to the peak of the neighboring roof, and down the rain spout on the other side. Then I walked briskly down the street, like a man with urgent business ahead of him, not one pursued by the Watch. In the next street but one there was an inn, with a groom coming out from the stable leading a gentleman's saddled horse. It seemed a fine, sound animal, exactly what I required.

"Where have you been, Hostler? I've been waiting this quarter hour!" I exclaimed in a furious tone, and seized the reins, throwing the fellow a penny as I swung up into the saddle.

"No, sir! Wait!" he called after me, but I was already gone into the night, and only the words followed me: "Stop, thief!"

Indeed, this throw of the dice had placed me well on the Rubicon's far bank, and there was no crossing back to the other side. I was now a horse thief, and when they took me, it would be to Tyburn, not to the Fleet for debt. But I had always rather be hanged than rot away in prison, and as I realized this, I felt a great weight lift from my shoulders, and I laughed aloud for joy, free, at last.

I was not dressed for riding, but in the pocket of my coat I had always carried a small pistol against footpads, and near Highgate Hill I entered in earnest into my new profession by relieving a mounted gentleman of his breeches and boots, as well as his purse. It was a revelation to see how he waved his pistol blindly at the shadows, calling out, "Who's there, damn you? Show yourself!" when I could see him in the moonlight as clear as if it had been day.

So that I could only wonder: besides a highwayman, what else had I become?

The Black Bull was an ancient establishment located close enough to the Humber that it had often taken part in the smuggling trade over the centuries. I was known in this country, and I am sure the innkeeper suspected what my profession might now be, but he made no question of my habit of keeping my room by day and riding abroad at nights, since I had recently done him a great service.

Before my arrival, a troop of soldiers had been quartered at the inn. These were rude fellows, the usual type of common soldier. It happened that I was seeing to the stabling of my horse one evening when I came upon one of these men in the act of molesting a young woman. I drew my sword, I ran the blackguard through—not killing him, though, as I did not want the investigation that a death would cause.

Then I turned to the fair creature I'd rescued—and

aught my breath. Not one of the artificial beauties of Lon-
lon had been able to trap my heart, but she did, in a single
owered glance from her dark eyes. Hair like midnight fell
oose over her breast—torn from its ribbons by her assail-
nt. She flushed to see me watching her as she tried to pull
ogether her torn garments.

"If he harmed you—" I burst out, unable to bear the
hought of the filthy brute's hands on her.

"No, sir. You were . . . in time."

"Then I thank Providence for that." I offered my hand
o help her to her feet, and after a moment's hesitation,
he took it—so soft and white a hand!

I brought her safe to her father, then saw the wounded
niscreant taken by the law. And on the strength of this
ncident, the landlord was able to successfully apply to have
he troops removed from his house, whose presence had
urtailed some of his other activities besides the keeping of
n inn. So he prospered, and we soon fell into a way of
usiness together, for an innkeeper always has a good noon of what wealth his guests are carrying on the road.

But it was Bess who took me by the hand and led me
o the secret door behind the cellars, who said, "You can
lways hide here, sir, if you are hard-pressed." It was in
his place that she first untied the dark-red ribbons that
eld her hair and let the waves of it fall free. The darkness
ould not hide the blood that rose to her face when she
ressed her warm red lips against mine.

I thought once to make a little light sport with her, and
o I said, "Well, Bess, if they take me, you know what you
nust do. You must go with a dozen other maidens, all
ressed in white, and plead to the King to spare me from
he gallows if I will marry one of you." For tales said this
as an old custom of the country.

But instead of laughing, she struck me across the face.
Never say so! I could never bear it if you were to hang!"

I replied lightly, "Then, to please you, Bess, I must never
t them take me."

But her feelings for me were not light. "Oh, sir, Jemmy,
on't you know? Every night, when you ride out, I watch
r you to return. I know the gait of your horse, and the
t of your hat, and the gleam of your sword hilt at your
de. I watch for you and I fear that one day they will take
ou and hang you, and I will never see you again!"

Then I was ashamed of my levity, and I buried my face in the thick, fragrant mass of her hair and murmured, "Never watch for me by daylight, Bess. Wait until moonrise. Not even the King's entire army could take me then—not by night. This I promise: I will always come back for you, even if all the forces of hell should try to bar the way."

"I'll hold you to that promise, then, sir."

The kiss she gave me then made my blood run hot in my veins, and indeed, I would have promised her anything for just one more touch. Oh, if she had asked, I would have promised to give up the road, to put up my spurs and pistol and sword, to put on an innkeeper's apron and try to live like an honest man. But she never asked, and inwardly I was glad, for there was one piece of business that I had to conclude before I could willingly consider giving up this life. It was for this reason that I had come back here, to the country where I was raised, where my father's estate had been.

As I explained to Bess, "I was the younger son, and my father sent me to Oxford because he wanted me to enter the Church, but I was never suited for it. I was a fool. I fell into bad company—living beyond my means, playing Hazard for high stakes. When my debts became more than I could pay, I was ashamed to apply to my father for help. I went to London, where I thought I could win back what I'd lost at the tables, but of course I fell into the hands of card-sharpers.

"When I finally had to tell my father how much I owed, it broke his heart. He had to mortgage part of his property to raise the amount, and I agreed that this would be all my inheritance, that I could expect nothing more from his will. I swore to him that I would reform all my ways, and I meant it, but before he could repay my creditors, he died of an apoplectic stroke.

"My brother blamed me for his death. My father had already altered his will, so that I got nothing from his estate, but Fitzhugh refused to pay a penny toward my debts and told me I could go to the devil." Then I laughed. "And so, as you see, I have."

But brother Fitzhugh had not heard the last of me—tha I had vowed. I knew that he went every year to Parliament and I intended to meet with him on the road and reliev him of some of the gold that should have been mine, or my creditors', at least.

I was still a fool. For gold, for petty vengeance, I was willing to risk all my new-found hopes of happiness with Bess.

By that time, I knew the highway well—every rut and turning and muddy ford. On the night when Fitzhugh's coach came rattling on its way south to London, the darkness favored me. A thick branch on the road where no branch ought to be, crossing the bleak moorland, served its purpose. A wheel cracked. The carriage halted. And as coachman and postilion sweated and struggled with the repair, I made my approach through the dark and pointed my pistol directly at my brother's heart.

"Stand," I said softly, "and deliver."

Of course he knew me, by my voice if not by my face in he darkness. "You would never shoot me, Jemmy. You would never dare. They would hang you for it."

I laughed at him. "They could hang me ten times over or what I've done by now, but I would rather die for shooting you, brother. In the war, I put a pistol ball through the eye of an Austrian grenadier, and I had less reason to hate hat man."

He swore terribly, and vowed that he would see me hang, ut I relieved him of his gold, and the ring and seal that ad been my father's, as well. Then I rode off into the ight, back to the Black Bull where Bess sat waiting for ne, watching from her casement overlooking the road. I wept her into my arms, and kissed her, and her black hair owed over us both, like a cloak, and I thought I was a appy man.

But in my heedless pride, I had set events in motion hich were to destroy us. My brother had sworn to see me ang, and it was no idle oath. He was a magistrate in the ounty, and a man of influence. That next morning I was oused from my bed by an urgent Bess, who cried, "Oh, r! Jemmy, you must hide, quickly! The magistrate has lled out the Watch, and they mean to search the inn!"

I spent the day down in the smuggler's hole, keeping mpany with some barrels of French brandy avoiding the cise man, as I was dodging the hue and cry. Once the archers left, I thought I was safe again, but Fitzhugh was implacable enemy, and he soon joined forces with a

Captain Wilkins, who commanded the local soldiery. It was Wilkins' troops who had been quartered at the Black Bull, and some of them soon recognized me from Fitzhugh's description. These soldiers had no more love for me than my brother, and they marched on the inn with a good heart for revenge, for their fellow had, after all, died of the wound I gave him.

This time it was the innkeeper who came to me, saying, "Sir, I'm afraid I must ask you to leave."

We understood each other well, and I knew he was afraid his own illicit enterprise would be discovered if the soldiers continued to tear apart the place in search of me. I mounted as quickly as I could, but I could see the anguish and yearning in Bess's eyes as she leaned from her window, and I was afraid to leave her there, with no protector now from the rough attentions of the soldiers, for they knew I was her lover.

I rode to her casement and stood in my stirrups to give her a farewell kiss. "Never let them take you!" she whispered fiercely.

"I'll come back for you!" I promised. "Watch for me by moonlight and be ready to leave with me!" Then I rode off with a clatter of hooves across the cobbles of the inn yard, just as the soldiers appeared at the crest of the hill A troop of mounted men spurred after me, but my horse was a good one, and night was coming on, so that I knew I could lose them in the dark.

But while I fled, and while they pursued me, the foo soldiers had arrived at the inn. They knew I meant to re turn to my Bess. Her father could do nothing. They pawe her with their black, powder-stained hands, and kissed he lewdly on her face and breasts, mocking her: "Are yo waiting for your lover? Are you waiting for your sweet heart? Let us wait with you, then! We'll meet hir together!"

They took her to her chamber overlooking the road, an they gagged her so she could not cry out to warn me.

What happened then, I will never know for sure.

My pursuers had pressed me hard, but I'd shaken the off at last, and I was returning across the bleak, heathe covered hills, with the moon sailing the sky overhead lik a ghostly ship. Below, the road winding through the hil shone like a silver ribbon (a silver ribbon for Bess's mi night-black hair), and at the bottom stood the inn, with the light reflecting from her casement, the window where I knew she was waiting, watching for me to come to her.

Then—a single shot!

And—had I heard it?—a woman's muffled scream.

*Bess!* Without thinking of anything else, I spurred my horse, I raced toward her, crying out her name.

As on cue, the soldiers fired from their places of ambush. I saw the sharp orange flash of their powder igniting, and an instant later, as I was struck, the boom of their musket fire. The balls tore through my body, I fell from my horse, and my lifeblood ran out onto the dust of the highway. Her name was the last word I uttered as I died.

The soldiers claimed afterward that she had turned the musket on herself, that, unable to call out and warn me in any other way, she seized the trigger of a musket and fired at her own breast. Because of this, she was buried as a suicide at the nearest crossroad, in unhallowed ground, with a stake through her heart.

My brother claimed my own body, but not for burial. As a magistrate, he declared he meant to have me gibbeted and hung in chains at that same crossroads, as a warning to other highwaymen.

But that night as the moon rose, I stirred where I lay in the irons the blacksmith had made for me to wear in death, awaiting the erection of the gibbet. I stirred, and opened my eyes, and I felt a terrible thirst. Then I looked about me, and realized that I was in the cellar of the inn. Above me, the soldiers slept, Bess' murderers, in their former quarters.

I rose, I tore the irons from my body as if they had been tissue. I fell upon the soldiers who had killed my Bess, and in the moonlight their blood was dark crimson as it flowed from their torn-open throats—as dark and as sweet as wine.

The landlord was gibbering in terror behind the counter of his inn, but I did him no harm, only asked him: "Where is she?"

The stake through her heart marked her burial place. I lifted her from the ground, and when I brushed aside the dirt from her face it seemed that she was sleeping, her face so pale, her lips still red. But no living soul had ever slept so still, without breath.

I drew out the stake from her breast. Then I bent low and kissed her, and Bess licked the blood of the soldiers from my lips as she opened her eyes. Overhead the moon sailed across the sea of night, driven by the wind in its tattered sails of cloud. A ship of the dead for us.

"I waited for moonrise," she whispered. "I watched for you."

"And now you see I came for you. Though hell barred the way, I came for you."

# THE FOREST'S JUSTICE

## *by Josepha Sherman*

Josepha Sherman is a fantasy novelist and folklorist whose latest titles include historical fantasies *The Shattered Oath,* and a sequel, *Forging the Runes.* Recently she collaborated with Susan Shwartz on a Star Trek novel titled *Vulcan's Forge.* Josepha has also written folklore books such as *Trickster Tales,* and, with T.K.F. Weisskoppf, the euphonious and evocatively titled *Greasy, Grimy Gopher Guts.* Short story credits exceed 125 publications for adults and children, including this very nice tale of Russian resolve.

How did it all start? Fittingly enough, with the forest, or rather, with my father getting lost in the seemingly endless *versts* of it. At first he would have had no reason to think it anything more than his own carelessness that had separated him from his party. Father had been returning from a successful trading mission in royal Kiev, after all, and it would have been easy enough for a man to ride too far ahead of his heavily laden merchant caravan.

But he must have quickly seen how the trails were closing up by themselves, the tree branches quietly interlacing themselves about him. And when the mysterious figure in its green, leafy hooded cloak stepped out before him, there would have been no doubt at all in Father's mind that he was dealing with the supernatural.

Sure enough, the figure bargained with him: "I will put you upon the safe, direct path to your home. But in return, you must give me one thing. Give me the first to greet you when you return."

Why did Father agree so quickly? Surely he thought it would be nothing more important than one of his hunting hounds, glad to see its master, who would come running out to meet him. Surely he had never realized it might be his son, his six-year-old Danilo—me—who might shake off the servants and go scurrying to be the first to greet him.

I dimly remember that much time after that was spent in weeping and wailing, and in trying in vain to bargain again with the Forest Lord. But a bargain made with magic is unbreakable. And so at last I was given up to the forest and its mysterious lord. I was not to return to the world of men till I was grown, nor were my parents ever to seek me out; that was the way the vow was sworn.

Of course that wasn't the end of me. No, the Forest Lord, whose name I never learned, treated me well enough. He (she? it? again, I have never been sure) told me that the rules of such things demanded that once in every generation a human must be chosen to learn the forest's magic.

The lot had fallen on me.

Now, I won't deny that it was sometimes lonely in the forest, away from my own kind. But if there was loneliness, there was also wonder as I grew, if not wise, at least clever in the Old Magic, discovering in myself an unexpected talent that made me suspect my selection hadn't been merely by lot after all. There was also a growing delight in the everchanging, ever constant forest all about me. As the cycles of seasons passed, my strange yet sympathetic tutor rarely scolded or praised me, merely took it for granted that I would want to learn.

Which, rather to my surprise as I grew through childhood to adolescence to young manhood, I did. Also rather to my surprise, the Forest Lord tutored me as well in the ways of my old world, the human world. I was not, it was implied, to be forever exiled from my kind, though I had as yet no idea what I was going to do with my life and learning. That as much time as possible would be spent in the forest I had by now come to passionately love was the only constant.

Only two things was I forbidden:

"You must never use your magics to harm the forest."

"Of course not!"

"And," the Forest Lord added, "since you are human and bound by human laws as well, you must never use your magics to destroy another of your kind."

This I wasn't so quick to swear (though at last I did). What good, I thought, was magic if you couldn't use it against enemies? Not that I *had* any enemies, but my father (I dimly remembered) certainly did: all noble, successful merchants did. There was one in particular . . . cudgeling my brain, since I'd been so very young when I left the human world, I finally came up with a name: Mikael Andreovich.

A name only. I don't doubt I would have forgotten it again and chosen to stay in the forest, for all I was (though at the time I didn't know it) my father's only heir. But change comes to all mortal men. And change came to me, in the form of a dark, stunning thunderbolt of a dream. I woke with a cry, knowing only that something terrible had befallen my parents. I must return home; both I and the Forest Lord agreed on that.

"Remember," were his parting words, "you must not use your magics to destroy another of your kind."

Well that he had cautioned me. For what lay ahead was terrible, indeed. My first sign of wrongness was the guards stationed about my father's estate—the guards wearing crests I'd never seen before. They stopped me at the gate.

"Turn away, beggar. This is no place for you."

Hoping against hope that my dream had lied, I said, "I wish to speak with Alexei Nestorovich," which was my father's formal name—only to be greeted with harsh laughter.

"Then you'll have to go to hell! He's dead, beggar!"

Bit by bit, struggling against my shock, I won the whole story from them. Mikael Andreovich, my father's chief rival, had, indeed, attacked his enemy, not with overt weapons but with vicious subtlety. Andreovich had turned Prince Vassili's mind against my father, making it look as though he plotted against his liege lord. So simple for Andreovich's men to intercept royal messages! So simple for it to look as though Father were deliberately ignoring those royal commands, as though treason were, indeed, being worked.

So simple for my father to be, at last, hounded into suicide.

"And his wife?" I gasped out, shaking.

One of the guards took pity on me. "She is in a nunnery," he said, very gently for his kind. "That of the Blessed Virgin. It would be best not to seek her out."

How could I not? But I was met at the nunnery gates by a kind-eyed nun who showed me my mother from a distance, a woman robed and veiled like any other nun, and told me, "Do not go to her." At my frown, she added in sudden comprehension, "You are a relative. Her . . .

son, is it? Are you Danilo Alexeiovich?" At my nod, the nun added sadly, "She cannot know you. The poor lady has fled for sanctuary into her own mind. She believes she is Sister Sophia and no more than that, and it would be both cruel and perilous to her mind to deprive her of the delusion."

What was there for me to do? Mikael Andreovich had as good as murdered my father and destroyed my mother's sanity. He'd destroyed my family's honor, owned their estates and fortune, and I . . .

. . . could not use my magics to destroy another of my kind.

"There are other ways," I said, and returned to the forest.

The Forest Lord was waiting, and I turned on him as I never had before. "Why didn't you let me go to them?"

"Why?"

"Well, I could have done—I could have—"

"Been slain. What good would that have done you or them?"

"But you—why didn't you do something?"

"I know almost nothing of what happens in the world of humankind. How should I know?"

He was right, of course; he wasn't human and could not be judged like one. The Forest Lord said nothing more, but I sensed a slight, alien move of head and body that might have expressed sympathy. His gaze told me, *Do what you must.* And then he vanished into the trees.

And I . . . I at first thought I could not truly grieve, not having known my parents for so many years. Yet grieve I did, for them, for the lives destroyed so easily, grieved a bit, too, I think, for the child I had been.

That night, I wrapped shadow about me and paid Andreovich a visit, looking down at him in his bed. Odd. He didn't look villainous. Fleshy, middle-aged, snoring gently, Mikael Andreovich looked like nothing more than any other merchant.

"Why?" I asked him softly, magically prodding him to speak. "Why ruin a family's lives?"

His answer sounded almost surprised: For profit, of course! Oh, revenge against a rival was part of it, but the thought of winning all my father's riches at the same time—well, that, Andreovich told me sleepily, had been the true temptation.

Temptation. Tempting to stab him where he slept, that

arrogant, self-satisfied villain—no other word for it now—who had wrought so much harm. But no. He must *know* who was attacking him, and why, or it was no revenge, merely murder. Instead, I did the only thing I could without a real plan and left him a message that I hoped would at least disturb his awakening:

"Set your affairs in order."

I signed it, in a surge of whimsy, "The Forest's Friend."

Returning to the forest, alone in the night with no sign of the Forest Lord, I sat on a mossy rock and pondered what to do next. Bring justice to the murderer, oh, yes. But how? The letter might unnerve him, but he would probably wave it off as the foolishness of some discontented servant. I needed more than vague threats. Go to Prince Vassili? Useless! If he had so easily believed my father a traitor, he certainly wasn't going to trust anything I had to say! No. I must bring the battle directly to Mikael Andreovich. But what would hurt him the most? He surely had a family—*no.* I was not about to harm them; to hurt the innocent would be just as evil as the hounding of an innocent man to his death and an innocent woman to madness.

Hounding . . . no. Something there, though . . . he'd done what he'd done to my father and mother merely for gain. No higher purpose. He'd slain one and banished the other for profit.

Indeed. And the lack of profit should be my weapon. I sat bolt upright as the plan came to me. Did I dare? Could I actually achieve it? Yes, and yes again.

Maybe I couldn't use magic to destroy my enemy, but I certainly could use it to scry out his affairs. In the days that followed I learned, after much peering into a quiet forest pool, that a shipment of rich sable pelts belonging to Andreovich would soon be transported through the forest.

The wagon and its armed escort was met by a mysterious stranger, his body shrouded in misty green, his face disguised by mist as well: I doubted anyone would recognize me after so many years (the nun had guessed only by deduction), but wanted to take no chances. I saw hands tighten on sword hilts and bowstrings and waited for the inevitable rough shouts of, "Get out of the way!"

"I think not. I think it is you who must leave."

Amazing how menacing one's voice could be if one merely pitched it low and kept the tone level. The guards stirred uneasily, not quite ready yet to attack, wondering, I knew, if I was merely a madman or the vanguard of thieves.

"Get out of the way," they shouted, "or we ride you down!"

"I think not," I repeated. "I am The Forest's Friend, and I give you leave to go."

No need to harm them; I had no quarrel with men who were mere hirelings. Instead, I sent an illusionary wave of fear around them, over and through their unshielded minds, so strong a fear that they never even thought to fight back. They ran, urging their horses into wild flight—

—leaving the wagonload of sable pelts behind. I opened one pack, ran my hand along the dark, silky softness. What to do with this treasure? I grinned in sudden inspiration. That night, peasant hut after hut received a mist-cloaked visitor.

"But we don't dare wear such valuable furs!" I heard again and again. "It would brand us as thieves!"

And again and again, I replied, "Yes, but no one but you can know if your families sleep warmly all winter under such nice, cozy coverings!"

These were free men, not serfs, and they were not at all fond of Mikael Andreovich, who held them in contempt. They saw the irony in my luxurious gifts, and I left with their laughter and blessings ringing in my ears.

Akh, but this one loss was only a slap in the face to Andreovich. As was the similar loss of a wagonload of silver bars (which became a fine donation to the poor) and of coin (which found a home at the Convent of the Blessed Virgin). The Forest's Friend was, so far, more of a nuisance to Andreovich than a true peril.

So far. I chose a sigil for The Forest's Friend, a lone oak, and signed it to the message I left pinned one night to Andreovich's door:

"This is but the beginning. Walk warily."

That caused a stir among his servants in the morning! Andreovich, though, merely hired more guards, better armed, to escort his shipments. These men were not so easily frightened away, and indeed I was the one who had to flee a few times, once with a graze from an arrow stinging along my ribs.

But The Forest's Friend was hardly about to surrender. Maybe I was only an army of one. But there were so many convenient small things living in the forest: voles to gnaw

owstrings, gnats to sting men and beasts, no major danger
gainst which a warrior could fight, only unending nuisance
o lower his will.

And *then* fear could drive the guards away. A new night-
ime visit to Andreovich's estate told me that folks there
vere beginning, most satisfyingly, to whisper that their mas-
er was plagued by sorcery. I left a message pinned to his
illow:

"The Forest's Friend was here. There is no safety for
ou anywhere till you confess your sins." And I signed it
vith my oak tree sigil.

But Andreovich wasn't as weak as his servants. I must
ave frightened him with the realization that he wasn't safe
ven in his own home, but he quickly countered with a
rice on my head (illegal for a mere merchant who was not
rince to do so, but who would go all the way to Vassili to
omplain?) and hunters, men skilled in forest ways. They
night, indeed, have snared me. But what had they to track?
left no traces for even their sharp eyes to find, and of
ourse their hounds could not trail what they'd never
cented!

There was, of course, no way for Andreovich's wagons
o avoid passing through forest, not with all those *versts* of
t surrounding every estate. The day after the last of the
unters gave up the quest, I took yet another wagonload
f pelts, casting onto one fleeing guard's saddle the sigil of
The Forest's Friend. I had to sit and rest after that; the
ever-ending war was beginning to take its toll on me.

But I could hardly stop now. I knew I was making defi-
ite inroads on Andreovich's trading ventures, and on his
ecurity as well. Word was spreading among his business
ssociates that deals they made with him never reached
afe conclusions. More and more of them, I learned through
ny scrying, were avoiding him, dealing with more secure
ssociates. More and more of them were beginning to
vorry if the amounts due them from Andreovich would,
ndeed, ever be paid!

I added to that insecurity, stopping the shipments of
ther merchants who traveled through the forest but bla-
antly *stealing nothing,* seeing that they took with them the
nessage that The Forest's Friend gave them leave, taking
vith them as well the unspoken message that it was easier,
nore economical not to deal with Andreovich.

But my increasing success in cutting every strand of my enemy's financial web was making me uneasy rather than cocky, for I was finding it more and more difficult to recover my strength after each attack. I needed rest, a serious, steady rest, badly. Yet I knew there could be no letting up, since Andreovich would—*must*—fight back. And I was beginning to guess what his next counterstrike must be.

I was right. He sent men with torches. If there is one thing the forest and the Forest Lord both fear, it is fire, and none of my magics, forest-based as they are, could work against that element. I watched in growing panic, seeing the line of smoldering danger, trying and trying to find a way out of peril. Fire arrows . . .

. . . don't burn too well in a downpour. I had nothing to do with the sudden rain, I have no such weather magic. And I almost got myself speared by standing transfixed with shock. Racing away into sodden shelter, akh, but I was grateful to Whoever had sent the storm just then! And of course, of course Andreovich couldn't know it wasn't my doing. His wariness of my magic must be verging on awe by now.

"Wonderful!" I gasped. "Wonderful," and nearly choked on a mouthful of rain.

"Lucky," said the Forest Lord, and I turned so sharply I lost my footing and slid to my knees in the loam, blinking up at the dimly seen figure. "No more than lucky. You must never use your magics to harm the forest."

"Was it luck?" I asked daringly. "Or was it proof that my cause is just?"

"Your cause would have burned the forest and me together."

"Forest Lord, I . . ." But there was nothing to say against the weight of his anger except a humble, "I will take my war directly to him."

"Wise."

He was gone once more into his realm before I could reply, leaving me shaken and uncertain. For a time I stood, already so wet that shelter made no sense, and thought. The Forest Lord was right, of course he was right. I had already taken my war of slow erosion against Andreovich as far as it could go without endangering all I held dear. Why had I persisted? Because what I did, these nipping little raids, was relatively safe? Was I truly seeking revenge for my parents—or merely enjoying the power I held over another?

So. There is a time for safety and a time for greater risks. I spent the rest of the day in deep meditation, drawing the forest's strength in and through me till I felt refreshed. That night I roused myself, seeing truly into my heart with magic's aid. Yes, I had enjoyed the easy victories and the feeling of triumph over an enemy; I was human underneath the magic. But yes, there was still the strong sense of justice wronged that must be righted, of harm done to the innocent that could not be ignored. My father's name, his honor, must be cleansed of that untrue stain of traitor. That flame, too, I was relieved to find within myself.

So I visited Andreovich once again, and found more guards ringing round his estate and his own rooms than might be in a prince's palace. No easy thing to get past so many, but I did, sliding past them like wary mist. Standing over my sleeping enemy, I saw worry about him like the faintest shadow, worry and anger: He would not surrender.

"Neither," I told him softly, "will I."

Inspiration struck. Just as my father had been, so was Andreovich a vassal of Prince Vassili. I silently rummaged through the room till I'd found a nice supply of blank parchments; taking only a few so that none would quickly notice the theft, I also found and tucked away some samples of Andreovich's own writing and signature. My last theft of the evening was a quick, careful copy of his seal ring, using wax, not magic.

Then off I went to one of the peasants I'd aided, a man who was clever in metalworking. He took the wax and the scrap of metal I offered, and soon enough had produced a more permanent copy of the seal. I sat me down in the forest with the parchments for some writing, silently thanking the Forest Lord for insisting I learn human ways.

So it was a few days later that Prince Vassili received a message from his loyal vassal, Mikael Andreovich, claiming that, most regretfully, there could not be any payment of the royal taxes this year, since said taxes were far too high.

So it was the same few days later that the more insistent of Andreovich's creditors received messages stating that there would be no payment of accounts due "since the royal taxes are so unjustly high."

And me? During those few days, I took advantage of the

quiet before the storm to do nothing but sleep, eat, and wander the woodland.

Which meant that I was fully rested and ready when the storm broke. First to arrive at Andreovich's gates were the creditors (who miraculously made it through the forest unchallenged by The Forest's Friend). A bewildered Andreovich met them at the gates, insisting over their shouts that no, he had *not* penned those letters and yes, that did look like his handwriting but it couldn't be because—yes, that did look like his seal, but it couldn't be because the seal ring was right here on his hand and he knew he hadn't set seal to letter or written anything or—

At that moment, with a timing I couldn't have improved by magic, Prince Vassili himself and his royal entourage arrived.

What a lovely roar of chaos followed! I watched and bided my time, swathed in shadow. The prince was hardly a patient man, and I listened with a good deal of satisfaction as he raged at Andreovich, calling him fool and liar, everything short of traitor.

Enough, I decided, and stepped out of shadow. "Do you see?" I asked, and all heads swiveled in my direction. Ignoring the suddenly raised weapons, I continued, "Do you see how easy it is to bend reality? Make a man seem a fool or a liar?" I let my voice ring out as hard and sharp as I could make it. "Make an honest man seem a traitor when he is not?"

"Who are you?" Vassili snapped.

"The Forest's Friend," Andreovich hissed, for I was still half-hidden in my misty green disguise. "Guards!"

I stopped their rush more by the drama of sudden upflung arms and their expectation of a spell than by any actual magic. "More than that," I said, and let all illusion fall. "Prince Vassili, I am Danilo Alexeiovich, son of the most foully slain—"

"I never slew him—" Andreovich snapped his mouth shut before he could say more.

"Ah, no. Merely saw that he was hounded to take his own life—"

"I never did that, either! Prince Vassili, I must protest! I acted only as your loyal vassal, as I always do!"

"—by your doing," I continued quickly, not giving him a chance to think. "By your stopping five royal messengers, five messengers bearing edicts my father never saw, commands he never knew."

Akh, yes, it worked, the flood of words overwhelmed him and he started, "There weren't five—" Again, Andreovich stopped short, this time with the color fading from his face.

"Indeed?" Vassili asked, voice smooth as any silk. "How many, then, Mikael Andreovich? How many *did* you stop?"

"None, my liege! I—"

"How many?"

I watched Andreovich redden, pale, redden. "It's a trap," he said at last. "This young *thief,* this *brigand,* this—this foul *sorcerer* has been against me at every turn. Tricking me, robbing me. Ask *him* how many he's slain!"

"None," I said coldly. "Most surely not for gain."

I saw the prince's cool eyes calculate my worth, saw him digest the information that I'd been a robber and weigh it against the evidence that had slipped from Andreovich's own mouth. Quickly I continued, "If I were what Andreovich has named me, that and only that, would I be stupid enough to come here before you? Prince Vassili, I admit to having declared a private war against this man to avenge my father and my mother. I could very well have continued it. And were I only interested in *profit*—" I spat the word out—"I would have done just that, bled him dry. But I cry out for justice! How many messengers *were* there, Mikael Andreovich? And how many messengers failed to return, Prince Vassili?"

That creased the royal brow ever so slightly. A ruler hardly could be expected to keep track of such petty things. But he asked me, "Can you tell us, then?"

Akh. Could I? Glancing at Andreovich, I saw triumph glint in his eyes. And I knew then what he had ordered done—and what I must do. All at once, there were even more lives to avenge.

"I use the forest's magic," I said formally, "to bring the forest's justice."

I sincerely hoped that pose of noble sincerity hid the fact that my heart was pounding. No easy thing, indeed, to let one's mind drift into helpless trance in the midst of enemies. But there was nothing to do by now but do as I'd uttered, and hope to princely honor that all went well.

I found them, three poor souls murdered for no reason other than they'd been the bearers of news Andreovich hadn't wanted delivered. His servants had neglected to strip them; decayed though bodies and clothing were, there was still evidence enough to mark them royal messengers. The hastily dug graves were so thickly overgrown that even Andreovich couldn't accuse me of having newly created them, nor could he, for all his blustering, convince the cool-eyed Vassili that it had been I, not he, who'd slain the men.

I heard Prince Vassili pronounce sentence there and then: Andreovich would die for murder, false witness and treason. And I . . . felt nothing, numb at the sudden ending of my war. But there was one matter yet to be resolved:

"My father's name, Prince Vassili."

"Ah, yes. He was no traitor."

"Proclaim it."

He raised a brow at my tone, but I repeated savagely, "Proclaim it!"

The smallest of wry smiles quirked up a corner of his mouth. "It shall be so proclaimed, my royal word on it. Does that," he added in delicate warning, "suffice?"

"Not quite. There must also be a royal grant made in perpetuity to the Convent of the Blessed Virgin."

He most certainly did not like *that* tone. But after a moment, the prince nodded. After all, charity to the church was always politic for royalty.

"And now," Prince Vassili said, eyes narrowing, "there is one more issue: And that concerns you, Danilo Alexeiovich." Now he meant to take his own revenge. "The issue of thefts, multiple and deliberate. The issue of deeds which can only be those of an outlaw, no matter what the motive. I cannot turn title and honors over to a robber, Danilo."

"Of course not," I agreed. "This way the crown takes both my father's and Andreovich's riches. Very tidy." As he gaped in shock, I added quickly, "I never wanted them, only justice."

I swirled illusion about me in a mist, raced back into the forest before he could order his guards to move. Safe in the shelter of the trees, I dropped illusion and called back to the fuming Vassili, "Farewell, oh, prince, and thank you! Justice has been done. But from this day on, know that the forest shall be watching!"

With that, feeling suddenly wonderfully light and free, I went, whistling, off into the green and living world that was my home.

96
danforth
©

# HIGHWAY TO HEAVEN

## *by Laura Resnick*

Laura Resnick has published stories in approximately thirty anthologies, including *Return to Avalon, Ancient Enchantresses, Dragon Fantastic, Dinosaur Fantastic,* and others. But she is also an experienced novelist; as Laura Leone, she published more than a dozen romance novels. Now she joins the f&sf field as a novelist with the epic fantasy *In Legend Born,* and its upcoming sequel. Several years ago Laura won the coveted Campbell Award as Best New Author. This story, with its broadly painted characters and amusing dialogue, proves why.

She was a pretty little thing, no denying it. Slim, blonde, young—maybe a little overdressed for the job, but, hey, who am I to tell a dame what to wear? Still, I gotta say, that skirt was so short that no daughter of *mine* would've been allowed out of the house in it. And now this girl would be wearing that skimpy orange thing through all Eternity. Just goes to show you: parents can never be too careful. But then, according to the Boss, this girl's parents had been a couple of real polenta-eaters, anyhow.

"Excuse me," the girl said to some guy riding by on an elephant. He ignored her. "*Excuse* me," she repeated. "You're going to have to stop and wait your turn. As you can see, this lady got here before you." She pointed to an old broad in a wheelchair.

"Out of my way, woman!" the guy snapped, urging his elephant to keep going.

"Aren't we done here *yet?*" The old woman sounded kind of pissed off.

"Oh, pardon me for doing my job." The girl sounded pretty pissed off, too. "*Hull-o-o-o!* I've already explained to you how this works. Now, are you going to hand over—"

"Onward! Onward, Maia, onward!" cried the guy on the elephant.

The girl, whose name (according to the Boss—who's never wrong, after all) was Mimi, waved her clipboard at the elephant. It shied away from her—and backed straight into a buggy. No, not a baby thing; I mean one of those horse-drawn things. The horse squealed and made a mess all over the highway. The man in the buggy started shouting. So did the old lady *and* the pansy on the elephant.

I rolled my eyes and decided it was time to step in and take charge. No *wonder* the Boss had sent me here to straighten things out!

I pulled out my piece and fired into the air. That got everyone to shut up *real* fast. Then I pointed it straight at the guy on the elephant. "Yo! Hey, you! Yeah, *you* . . . Get this elephant under control right now, buddy, or you're going straight back to Purgatory. In a *box*. You know what I'm saying, pal?"

He sort of foamed at the mouth, then demanded, "Do you know who I *am?* Do you have any idea whom you're speaking to, peasant?"

"Yeah," I said, "a guy wearing his girlfriend's silk pajamas and riding a gold-trimmed elephant."

"My girlfriend's pa— pa—" He sputtered. "How *dare* you!"

"Take it easy," I warned. "You'd be one of them marijuanas, wouldn't you? I seen one before."

"Mirages," Mimi corrected me.

"Maharajahs!" the guy screamed.

"Whatever," Mimi said. Her voice was kind of nasal. I could see where it might get on your nerves if you'd just spent a few hundred years in Purgatory. "But now you're just another pilgrim on the Road to Salvation, mister, and you're going to have to wait your t—"

"The road to *where?*" he bleated.

"Sal-va-tion," I said, real slow and clear to help him understand. He sounded kind of foreign, and Mimi talked faster than a welsher promising he'd cough up the dough *next* week.

The maharajah frowned and looked confused. "No, no, that can't be right. I was . . . on my honeymoon."

"You honeymooned on an elephant?" I asked.

Mimi made a face. "How romantic—*NOT!*"

"I was *hunting,*" he snapped.

"You went hunting on your honeymoon?" Mimi scowled.

"I was trying to bag a tiger. As a gift for my bride."

Mimi went a little pale. "Gross!"

"My father told me that sort of thing impresses women," the maharajah insisted.

"Haven't you ever heard of Greenpeace?" Mimi demanded. "Don't you know that wearing animal skins is retro, as in *very?*"

"So you died hunting on an elephant," I said. "Personally, I'd rather be blown away by a .45 in the middle of a good meal on Mott Street, but, hey, who am I to judge?"

"Blown away by forty-five *whats?*" he asked, looking really confused now.

"Maybe that's a little before your time," I suggested. "When did you buy the farm?"

"What farm?"

"He *means,*" Mimi said, shoving past me, "when did you die?"

The maharajah clutched a hand to his throat and went all pale and sick looking. "Am I . . . I'm . . . Are you saying this is . . . I'm *dead?*"

"Oh, give the maharajah a low-tar cigarette," Mimi said. "*Hull-o-o-o!* This *is* the highway to Heaven."

"No one talked to you about this in Purgatory?" I asked.

"Didn't you read the instruction manual?" Mimi asked.

"Ah, half the people coming through Purgatory *can't* read, kid," I pointed out.

"Well, they've certainly got plenty of time to *learn,*" she said, kinda snotty-like.

"Just ignore her, Mirage," I said. "Kids, today—whaddya gonna do?"

"That's *Maharajah,*" he said through gritted teeth.

"Kind of a mouthful, dontcha think?"

"*Excuse* me." Mimi poked me. "Who *are* you?"

"I'm Vito the Knuckles Giacalone," I told her, "and I been sent by the Boss to get your operation running more smoothly."

"The Boss?" she repeated.

"Yeah. You know: the Big Guy, the Head Honcho, the Big Kahuna, the *capo di tutti capi.*"

The old broad in the wheelchair rolled forward. "Wait a minute! Are you saying you've been sent by . . . God?"

"Hey, that's *Mister* God to you, sister!" The Boss don't like no disrespect.

"Are you trying to tell me that the Supreme Deity sent *you* to tell *me* how run my station?" Mimi sneered. "As *if!*"

"I say there!" The guy in the buggy that was stuck behind the elephant hopped down and came running up. Yeah, *everybody* had to get into the act now. "See here, my good man! What's the delay? What's the hold-up, eh?"

He sounded a little foreign, too, and kind of girly. "Get back in your buggy, buddy. This don't concern you."

He got all uppity. People are pretty impatient to get on with their journey after cooling their heels in the Purg for a couple of centuries. "I'll have you know that's a barouche, not a— a— Never mind. And this does concern me, damn your eyes! Do you know how long I've been trying to get to—"

"That ain't my problem, buster!" I pointed the business end of my rod at him.

"*Excuse* me," Mimi nasaled at me. "I do *not* like guns at my station. The operations manual—which Saint Peter himself gave to me, I might add—specifically states that no—"

"Yeah, well, I'm writing a new rule book, kid," I told her.

"I can't be dead!" cried the maharajah. "I just finished adding a new wing onto the palace that will hold three hundred concubines!"

"Can I go now?" asked the old broad in the wheelchair. "I wouldn't have bothered going to Church every single Sunday for ninety-three years if I'd known it was still going to take this long to get to heaven."

"Park it, sister!" I said.

Mimi was flipping through the charts on her clipboard. "I don't have a maharajah listed," she said. "There must be some mistake."

"That much is obvious," said the buggy guy.

Mimi blinked at him. "Are you on staff, too?"

"No, of course not."

"Then what do you know about it?" I said, shoving him aside to read the schedule over Mimi's shoulder. She was right: no maharajahs. "He don't belong here," I agreed.

"My point precisely," said the buggy guy.

"Who are *you?*" Mimi asked.

"It's not his turn till you're done with me!" the old broad snapped.

"Until you're willing to hand over your Impatience and Hostility," Mimi said, "you're not going anywhere. How many more times do I have to explain this to you?"

"I," said the buggy guy, "am Sir Leslie Collingsworth-Pickett."

I took a quick peek at the shedule. "Okay, pal, you're on the list. But the old broad is right; she was here first."

Sir Leslie cleared his throat and took me aside while Mimi and the old lady went back to bickering. "Now, see here, my good man . . . There's obviously been some mistake."

"Didn't Mimi and me just finish saying so?"

"I *mean* . . ." He looked over his shoulder at the others. "A foreign chap? And a woman who is *obviously,* if I may so, a member of the lower orders." He made a *tsk-tsk* sound and shook his head. "I was under the impression that I was headed for an entirely different sort of place."

"That can still be arranged," I warned him. "Mister Lucifer gives me a cut of every pilgrim I send him, and the Boss looks the other way as long as he gets his—"

"No! I meant . . . That is to say . . ." He looked over his shoulder again, like he thought anyone else on the highway actually gave a shit what he thought of them, and then whispered, "I was under the impression that there were . . . you know . . . *two* Heavens. One for . . . *their* sort. And then a more exclusive Heaven, one for only the *best* sort of people."

I stared at him. "You're kidding, right?"

He scowled. "You must know what I'm talking about. I mean . . . *surely* you don't imagine that *I'm* going to the same place as *they* are, do you?"

"Ahhhh," I said at last. "I see what you're saying."

"I thought you would! There's a good chap."

"Yeah. And don't worry about nothing. You come to the right place."

"I don't see how—"

"See, this here is sort of a way station on the road to your Eternal Destiny."

"A way station.

"Uh-huh."

"But I don't see how—"

"You will. Now get back in your buggy and wait your turn."

"But—"

"*Do* it, Leslie."

He eyed my gun. "May I remind you, I'm *already* dead."

"Getting shot will hurt plenty, even so."

He sighed. "Oh, very well, I'll get back in my barouche. But *do* let's try to pick up the pace, shall we? I don't want to miss the start of the Season in Heaven. Understood?"

"Yeah, yeah, yeah." I watched him mince back to his buggy.

"What's wrong with him?" Mimi asked.

"I dunno, kid. Maybe that's just what happens when you name a boy *Leslie.*"

The old broad in the wheelchair rolled away and continued on down the highway, having finally given Mimi all her Impatience and Hostility. It was an important job Mimi had out here; the Boss don't like no one showing up at the Pearly Gates loaded down with extra baggage. Heaven just wouldn't be Heaven if everyone was allowed to bring in all their vices, sins, and faults. So, at all the way stations along the Road to Salvation, the Big Guy's soldiers gotta make sure they take away everyone's bad habits and character defects before letting them continue their journeys.

Now, I could see Mimi was dedicated to the job. The kid just lacked experience, refinement, training. She just needed an old pro like me to help her get things under control. Some pilgrims was getting through here without giving up their most coveted sins and most cherished flaws; others was complaining real loud about the long wait at Mimi's station. The traffic jam we had here today was bad for business. The Boss had sent me here to clean up the operation, and I wasn't going nowhere until the job was done.

"Now about this guy on the elephant," I said.

"Is the Supreme Deity upset with me?" Mimi asked. "Am I, like . . . going to lose my job?"

She had dropped the tough act and was looking kinda scared. Yeah, she seemed like a good kid. We'd work this out. "Don't worry, kid. Mister Yaweh is very big on giving people a second chance," I said.

"So what do I—"

"Enough dawdling, woman!" shouted the maharajah. "I am not accustomed to waiting!"

"Let me handle this," I told Mimi. "Mister Mirage, look at me. Look right at me. Good. Now tell me: where have you been for the past few centuries?"

"I, uh . . ." He screwed up his face and thought about it. "It's all very vague . . . I think it started with an 'L.' "

"Oh, boy," I said. "Talk about your mix-ups."

"L?" Mimi repeated blankly. "That means something to you?"

"You're too young to remember," I said. "Hey, buddy, was the place called Limbo, by any chance?"

His face brightened. "Limbo! Yes! That was it!"

"Good grief," I said. "We're gonna have a *ton* of paperwork on this one."

"Limbo?" Mimi repeated.

"Yeah. Before your time," I said. "The Boss closed it down a while back." The recession hit us, too; we're downsizing like everyone else these days.

She looked at the maharajah. "But where have you been since then?"

He was rubbing his chin, trying to remember. "Lost, I think . . . I remember a road. It was paved with good intentions."

"Ah, I know the one," Mimi said. "Look, I'm afraid you're going to have to double back and go to Purgatory."

"But—"

"I'm sorry, but those are the rules."

"I *refuse*—"

"The lady said you're going back to Purgatory, pal, so that's where you're going." I waved my piece at him. "One way or another. Understand?"

He harumphed and folded his arms. "I just want you to know that when I finally meet the Supreme Deity, I fully intend to complain about the service here."

"That's your perogative, pal. Meanwhile . . ."

"Here," Mimi said, thrusting a handout at him. "That's got a list of 1–800 numbers on it, in case you get lost again. On the other side, there's a map which should help you find Purgatory without further delay."

"Back in the Purg," I added, "they'll assign you a final destination and plot your route for you."

"Any questions?" Mimi asked.

"Don't ask him that," I said. "Now beat it, buster!"

"He *might* have had questions," she argued as the elephant trotted away, the maharajah cursing all the while.

"You got too much of a traffic problem here to go around answering everyone's questions for all Eternity," I told her. "You're gonna have to start doing things different around here, kid. No more Miss Nice Guy. No more letting people talk you into letting them keep some of their faults and vices. No more debating with the pilgrims."

"But how am I—"

"From now on, you gotta relieve 'em of those sins and defects *fast.* Chop-chop. No frills, no spills."

"People aren't exactly *eager* to hand them over, you know," she said defensively.

"And that's why the Boss sent *me.* To show you how to *take* 'em away, whether people want to give them up or not."

Sir Leslie pulled up in his buggy. "I say! Are we finally ready?"

"Don't bother looking up this one," I said as Mimi starting thumbing through the schedule.

"Yes, I know he's on the list," she said, "but I need to find out what's in—"

"I can *tell* you what's in his baggage: Vanity and Snobbery."

She gasped and pointed to Leslie's manifest. "That's right! How did you know?"

I shrugged. "Experience."

"That's amazing!"

I could tell she was gaining a little respect for me now. "Okay, go to work, kid. I'll give you a few pointers as you go along."

"All right." She licked her lips and looked a little nervous. "Sir Leslie, at this way station on the Road to Salvation, you're going to have to surrender your negative baggage if you want to continue down the highway to Heaven. Now, as they may have explained to you in Purgatory—"

"Never mind the speech, kid," I said. "Just get the goods!"

She looked uncertain. "But surely—"

"I say, I'm not handing over *anything* to you, young

woman!" Leslie snapped. "What the devil d'you take me for? Some lowly—"

"Look how many people are lined up behind Lord Mimsey here," I said to Mimi. "We can't waste all day convincing him that this is the right thing to do. Especially not when you consider that more than half these sojourners is gonna be bringing Stubbornness here with them!"

"Oh, I hadn't really thought of that." Mimi bit her lip. "But what should I do?"

"I *certainly* don't intend to begin the Season in Heaven without all my baggage!" said Leslie, starting to get a little pink with rage. "The very *idea* of—"

"Hand it over, Leslie!" I pointed my rod at him.

"What?" he blinked.

"You heard me," I said.

"Mr. Giacalone," Mimi said. "Are you sure—"

"Trust me, kid. I been at this for years. Who do you think cleaned up the Road of Good Intentions for the Boss, huh?"

"That was . . ." She breathed real deep and her eyes got wide with awe. "That was you?"

"None other."

"Now see here, my good man!"

"Hand over your Snobbery and your Vanity, Leslie, or I'm gonna blow your brains all over the highway. And with things being so busy in Purgatory, it could be centuries before anyone gets out here to clean up the mess and take you back to square one. Am I making myself clear?"

His pink mouth worked furiously for a few seconds, like he tasted something real bad. Finally he said, "As crystal."

"Then hand 'em over, Leslie," I advised.

"Oh, very well, damn you!"

"Smart decision," I said as he fumbled through his soul for his most cherished defects. A minute later, he handed them over to Mimi, who put a big green check mark next to his name on the schedule.

"Okay, Leslie," Mimi said. "You're, like, totally cleared to proceed on to your final destination."

"Splendid!" he cried, driving off.

"So that's how it's done?" Mimi asked me.

"That's how it's done."

"It seems a little . . . harsh."

"Hey, salvation's no picnic," I told her.

She mulled this over for a minute, then I suggested we get back to relieving pilgrims of their worldly baggage. She watched me hold up a few more sojourners, then said she thought she was ready to try one on her own.

"Whoops! Not this one," I said, seeing the next pilgrim coming round the bend.

"Why not?"

"This one's a friend of mine."

"But surely—"

"Don't argue, kid."

"Who is he?" she whispered as he approached.

"This guy was my boss before the Boss became my boss."

"Oh . . ." She frowned and watched him approach.

"Vito!" he exclaimed.

"Mr. Corleone!"

"How the hell have you been?"

"Real good, sir. And you?"

"Oh, fine. Can't complain."

"Got outta the Purg real fast, I see, sir."

"Yeah. Word is, the Big Guy wants to talk to me about a job."

"That's good news, sir."

"Thanks, Vito. Well, guess I'll be seeing you around?"

"I guess so."

As we watched him continue down the highway, Mimi asked, "Do you think he'll be after my job?"

"Never can tell. But, hey, competition is what keeps us sharp, am I right?"

"I suppose . . ." She looked a little nervous again.

"Don't worry," I said. "By the time I'm done with you, you're gonna be one of the best soldiers the Boss has got working the highway. Trust me, kid."

"Here comes another one!" She glanced at my rod. "Could I . . . Do you think I could use that? I really want to do a good job here, Mr. Giacalone."

"Sure," I said. "No point in trying to do the job without the right equipment." I handed her the gun and took a look at the schedule. What I saw made my blood run cold. "Hey, we got a real tough case coming up next, kid. We're gonna make quite a haul here."

"What's the baggage?" she asked, hefting the gun in one hand.

"Greed, Narcissism, Sloth . . ." I flipped the page and kept reading while a white Cadillac came round the bend. ". . . Gluttony, Lust, Dishonesty . . ."

"Wow," Mimi said, taking aim, "that looks just like . . ."

". . . Ignorance, Vanity, Hostility . . ."

"*Excuse* me," said a strangely familiar voice as the car's electric window rolled down. "Is this the— Oh, my God!"

"No," I said, "just his faithful servants. Now stick 'em up, sister!"

The dame inside the car ignored me. "Mimi?"

Mimi's eyes went wide and she dropped the gun. "Mom!"

I could see it was gonna be a long day in Eternity.

FABRICUS DANFORTH
E.T. KENSYN

# ROGUE'S MOON

## *by Teresa Edgerton*

Teresa Edgerton has published some of the finest and most unique fantasy in this generation, including novels such as *Goblin Moon* and *The Gnome's Engine,* which inspired the setting for "Rogue's Moon," her contribution to this anthology. She has also published short fiction in *Weird Tales From Shakespeare, Enchanted Forests,* and *The Shimmering Door.* I am pleased to present this story here, which amply exemplifies her gift for evoking atmosphere, character, and dialogue, and for making the impossible seem tangible.

*The wind was crying like a lost child up among the rocks on Deadman's Tor. In his hiding place in the graveyard at the foot of the hill, the pale gentleman cursed the wind and covered his ears with his hands. "Don't trouble me tonight, you angry spirits," he muttered under his breath. "I am here on* your *business as much as my own."*

*He removed his hands from his ears, but the wind continued to wail. A cold sweat broke out on his skin, his heart beat raggedly, and the breath caught in his throat. He was—as he had proved again and again—the man for almost any desperate enterprise, but the weeping of small children was the one thing he could not bear. Their shrill voices haunted his every nightmare, dismally crying out for reparation.* Our tiny bones were buried deep, yet we cannot rest. Not while *other* innocents suffer as we did.

*The wind died down for a moment. Over the voices in his head came the clamor of approaching hoofbeats on the carriage road leading past the cemetery. Though there was little light to see by with the moon so new, he was just able to make out an immense brute of a black stallion, and a dark, powerful figure in a many-caped riding cloak and a wide-brimmed hat.*

*So . . . the highwayman would keep his appointment.*

*Hastily abandoning his hiding place behind a tombstone, the pale gentleman pushed aside a rusty iron gate, and whisked inside an open mausoleum. It would not do to be discovered skulking like a dog among the graves—nor did he wish to be caught outside when the wind rose again.*

This was a queer place for a meeting, thought Ned, as he tied up his horse and moved cautiously across the graveyard. Nor did he like the business that had brought him here. Yet he thought of Mary—Mary who had endured so much over the years, Mary who was waiting for him to come back home and make her happy—and he was not even tempted to hang back.

An icy blast lifted the edge of his dark cloak as the wind came shrieking down from the heights again. A flicker of light appeared briefly in the darkness ahead, over by the monuments at the center of the graveyard. Ned moved in that direction, picking his way carefully past overgrown mounds and tilted tombstones, and finally came to a halt outside one of the mausoleums, under the baleful gaze of a dark winged Fate who surmounted the tomb with pinions outstretched.

Clearing his throat, Ned spoke in a low, hoarse voice. *"There's a black ewe caught in a bog t'other side of Grimley, and she's like to die of the cold."*

*"Unfortunately, she* will *stray from the flock,"* came the answering password, in a light, pleasing baritone. "But do come inside, my dear fellow. There is no one here but ourselves and the hallowed dead."

Ned had to remove his hat and duck his head in order to pass through the open gateway. Inside the tomb it was not much brighter than it was outside, but a dark lantern was slowly uncovered by a small white hand, bringing up the light gradually, so as to not dazzle Ned's eyes. "I'm obliged to you, sir."

"On the contrary, it's very good of you to meet me here." The stranger moved forward, surveying Ned with evident satisfaction. "You are larger than I expected. Indeed, you look stout enough and strong enough for anything."

*And you ain't much bigger than a minute,* thought Ned. But he did not speak the words out loud. The little gentleman was dressed in satins and laces, under a fine cloak, but his figure was square and capable looking, and there was a determined glint in his eye. No, this one was not a fop or a weakling . . . though perhaps it might serve his purposes, sometimes, for others to think so.

It was very still in the tomb, with the thick stone walls muffling the voice of the wind. Ned spoke up to break the silence. "How am I to call you, sir?"

"You may call me Hawkins . . . Emmanuel Hawkins. It is not really my name, but I have been known to answer to it. My business, I believe, you already know. I have a great interest in the subject of free-traders."

Now Ned spoke from the heart. "They are the wickedest rascals, the most black-hearted scoundrels that ever walked this earth, sir."

Mr. Hawkins raised a delicate eyebrow, as if astonished at such vehemence—especially from this particular source. "But this is fascinating. I've always found in the past that smugglers inspire a certain amount of sympathy and support in the surrounding countryside. Yet am I to suppose that is not the case here?"

"That is not the case here. If it was just tea and brandy, folks would be sympathetic just as you say—the duty being so high. But these ain't ordinary smugglers. There's plenty of reason to suppose they've been up to . . . darker things."

For a moment, Hawkins seemed to hold his breath. "What sort of . . . darker things?"

"There's a circle of black witches over to Blagmoor—no one knows who they are, but we know that they're there, because of their mischief—and there's reason to believe them smugglers is providing that coven with crocodiles and grave dust out of the East"

Ned leaned up against a clammy stone wall, and crossed his arms over his broad chest. "But that ain't the worst. It's not what them smugglers is bringing *in,* it's what—or who—they been taking out. There's too many disappearances of young boys and young girls from the villages hereabouts."

Hawkins narrowed his eyes. "White slavers!"

"Yes, sir, we fear so."

"And you'd be willing to help put an end to this pernicious practice?"

"I would," said the highwayman, "under the conditions I discussed with your friend, Mr. Evans."

Mr. Hawkins reached idly into a silken waistcoat pocket and produced a tiny box made of gold and ivory. "I will tell you, then, that I am working with the government of Mawbri—though I am not regularly employed by any government—and I am here, among other reasons, to entrap and capture these smugglers. But I require a local man on the inside of the ring, to help me set up my trap."

He gave Ned a keen glance. "But I am told that you are . . . I believe road agent is the term which gentlemen of your calling generally prefer?"

"What I am is a bridle-cull, plain and simple," said Ned, with a grim smile. "It's not something I'm proud of, but I won't deceive you, sir, nor try to make the thing sound any better than it is. And my name is Edward Talbot. Like yourself, I've used a number of different names over the years, but I reckon you'll need to know the real one so you can write it down proper on my pardon."

"Your pardon . . . yes." Hawkins flicked open the lid of the tiny box he held in his hand. It did not contain snuff, as might be supposed, but a pale, crystalline powder. "I've been empowered to offer you a full pardon for all your past crimes, providing you prove to be useful. But this pardon is offered to you on the assurance that you have never killed anyone in the entire course of your felonious career."

As he spoke, he took a tiny pinch of white powder between his thumb and forefinger. "I mention this because it's very important for you to continue to restrain yourself from killing anyone. Otherwise, I can't help you."

"I'll make precious certain that I *do* restrain myself. That pardon means everything to me, sir. I've a second chance at happiness, a second chance to make things right with the sweetest girl in the world—and I don't reckon that I'll be offered a third opportunity."

As Hawkins inhaled the white powder, the highwayman made a grimace of distaste.

"Yes, it is sleep dust." A faint, cynical smile played across the pale face. "An unfortunate habit of mine, but one I'm no more likely to abandon than you are to give up this woman of yours. But I wonder which of us has formed the more dangerous attachment?"

"You don't care much for females, I take it."

Hawkins closed the box and replaced it in his waistcoat pocket. "Not for the grown ones, no." The smile faded, the gray eyes became suddenly very earnest. "For the young ones, however—the innocents carried off to spend the rest of their lives in shame and despair in Eastern brothels—in their welfare and rescue, I have the deepest and most personal interest."

Ned unfolded his arms, stood up a little straighter. "I'll do what I can for you, sir. Them free-traders is careful who they lets in, so everyone says. And it may be—for all my years on the High Toby—they don't regard me as a suitably desperate character."

"Well, well, that we shall see," said Hawkins. "Meet me here in three days' time to report on your progress." He reached out to dim the lantern. "In the meantime, a word of caution: if you should think you recognize me loitering about the neighborhood in any other guise, please be discreet and do not speak to me."

Now it was Ned's turn to smile. "I do most of my own loitering after nightfall. And I think you can rely, sir, on my eyesight being very weak, once the sun goes down."

*Now here's a queer start,* thought Ned as he mounted up. *And he's an odd little gentleman to be sure.*

This Mr. Emmanuel Hawkins (so-called) was a strange combination of cynicism and idealism—though what business he had being cynical, with his fine clothes and his soft white hands, Ned could not guess. *Let him try living rough, as I have, out on the moors, with never a decent roof over his head and every man's hand turned against him.*

But there was no use bewailing the past or feeling ill-used, Ned reminded himself as the stallion carried him down the road. Especially when it had been his own blamed fault to begin with, him being fool enough to trust that devil Elijah Fitch, despite the fact they were both in love with the same girl, despite that Ned knew that Fitch had some vicious habits about him, and was no-ways so respectable as everyone thought.

*"Just you take this watch and these other things of mine over to that goldsmith in Braddon, and I'll make it worth your while. I've arranged everything in advance, but I don't dare be seen with the man myself. People would ask questions, and if my father knew that I'd gambled away a quarter's rents and had to borrow money just to live on . . .*

*Come, be a good fellow, Ned. And if you don't trust me to keep my word, why, I'll pay you two guineas in advance."*

*And there was Ned, needing money himself, and so he had made the biggest mistake that he ever made in his life. Even the two guineas he had in his pocket when the lawmen stopped him had counted against him. "Two golden guineas, a watch, two buckles, a ring, and a snuffbox. The very same items that was taken from Mr. Fitch at gunpoint . . . and how did you ever imagine, Ned Talbot, you wouldn't be recognized because of your size?"*

*Naturally, Ned had protested his innocence, naturally neither the bailiffs nor the magistrate had believed a word. Not with Elijah so apparently respectable, and not even hurting for cash, as it turned out. Ned had originally been marked for the gallows, but the sentence was commuted, at the last moment, to transportation.*

*But the ship that was meant to carry him to Nova Imbria had run into a storm and wrecked herself on the rocks near Brantley. In the confusion that followed, Ned and two other convicts had overpowered a trio of guards and escaped in the very boat those guards had meant for their own salvation.*

*Once on shore, the convicts had split up. Penniless, ragged, outlawed, Ned had known it was impossible to find honest work. His first theft, accomplished from ambush with the aid of a cudgel, had gained him a pistol and a suit of clothes. His second had provided a horse and set him up properly in business as a highwayman—a trade, as he later learned, that conferred considerable honor among thieves, and was generally regarded as more respectable than that of footpad or "scamperer."*

*So he had continued for fifteen years, with occasional secretive visits back home, to see how his family was doing, to pass a few coins on to his widowed mother. On one of these visits he had learned that Mary had married Fitch. Not of her own choice, for the devil had found a way to purchase her father's debts. By that time, Elijah had dropped even the pretense of respectability, and a miserable life he had led her, so everyone said. Many was the time that Ned considered going back home, and putting a bullet through Fitch's skull; he was never quite certain what prevented him. He hoped that it wasn't cowardice but his faith in Providence—or perhaps just an unshakeable conviction that a fellow like*

*Fitch, who was reckless and dissipated, would do for himself one way or another, given enough time.*

*Six months ago, Elijah had obliged by getting drunk, walking off a roof in full view of his friends, and breaking his neck. "And I'm certain sure that Mary still thinks of you," said the cousin who gave Ned the news. "And if you was to ask her to leave the country and start a new life with you, she wouldn't say no."*

*But Ned had been adamant. "From all you tell me, she had a hard life tied to that rascal. And now that her troubles is all behind her, she won't hear a word from me . . . not until I've got something more to offer her than what I've got now."*

*At the time he had reckoned that was the same thing as giving her up. And he had put all hope of a reconciliation right out of his mind—until the mysterious Mr. Evans had spoken of a pardon, and promised an introduction to the man who could provide one.*

"And more than likely I'll end up dead," said Ned aloud, as this reverie came to an end. "If I do, I only hope someone will bring her the word, and she won't spend the rest of her life waiting to hear from me."

Yet the thought by no means discouraged him. Without Mary, the long years stretching ahead were completely meaningless, and he would gladly risk his heart's blood for this last chance at happiness.

The tavern was located far out on the moors. It was a scowling, sullen, ramshackle old place, and its appearance, quite as much as its remote location, caused respectable people to shy away. For that reason, it had become the resort of thieves, poachers, smugglers, and all the scaff and raff of two counties.

In a smoky corner at the back of the house, where the eaves came down so low that it was sometimes possible to hear the mice chewing on the thatch, Ned sat in close conversation with a man he suspected of being one of the smugglers. Tankards of ale sat on the scarred table in front of them. Though there was usually someone on hand who was willing to stand the highwayman a drink, tonight it was Ned who was buying.

"It just ain't profitable anymore. And I'm getting on now. A fellow remains on the High Toby too long, he ends on the gallows with a noose round his neck. What I need is to start putting a bit aside for my old age. I'm willing to do most anything, no matter how desperate bold, so long as there's plenty of money in it."

"You thinking of free-trading?"

Ned refreshed himself with a sip from his tankard. "That I am—but I don't know how to get in with the right people."

His companion hesitated, gazing darkly down into his own stoup of ale. "I don't say that I know who the right people may be, but from what I heard, they don't let anyone in without he proves himself first."

Ned leaned forward and lowered his voice. "But how *does* a fellow prove himself if he ain't in already?"

The smuggler, otherwise known as Jem, hemmed and hawed. He scratched his head and looked up at the low, smoky ceiling.

"I may know of something in another few nights," he finally admitted. "Something as won't be profitable, but it *will* be dangerous, and a fellow who had the nerve to take part, it *could* be that he'd show himself fit for . . . other work."

"Then I'm in," said Ned, offering his big rough hand. "Supposing, that is, you're the one to arrange it."

"Then just you keep yourself ready," said Jem, clasping the hand in return. "When the time comes, we'll let you know. I won't say nothing more than that."

After another bumper of ale, they parted on the best of terms. Jem left the tavern at once, but Ned lingered on for another half hour. He was lounging by the fire in the sooty inglenook, with a third and final tankard in his hand, when he thought that he spotted someone he knew.

A man from Blagmoor had just slouched in, in company with a seedy-looking clergyman: a square little fellow with very white hands, somewhat threadbare and dissipated for a man of the cloth. Ned was in the act of approaching the pair, when he suddenly drew back.

*Blister me! What ails me that I was ready to make such a mistake? I don't know him, and he don't know me.*

In any case, the highwayman reminded himself as he returned to his place by the fire, the hour was late, and his eyesight was likely to be at fault.

* * *

Several nights later, Ned found himself, along with Jem and two other men, outside an abandoned tin mine, with a horse and wagon. As the vein had played out long years ago, the shaft had been boarded over.

But it was not so now. Several of the planks had been removed, and Ned was obliged to help the others lift, by means of a rope and pulley, a long black box like a coffin, and manhandle the thing into the wagon. If it was a casket, it was the biggest that Ned had ever seen, and its weight was so great that it slipped out of Jem's hands as it passed over the side, and landed in the bottom of the wagon with a loud crash.

"Now see, you've broken the bed of the wagon," someone muttered. On inspection this proved not to be true, but there was a place on the side of the coffin which had split open.

Jem, Ned, and one of the other men took their places around the box, while the fourth man drove. A bloated Goblin moon was rising in the east, and the road they traveled was all silver and shadows.

"Wouldn't choose to do this with the Hag so bright, but the roads has been crowded with excise men these last ten nights," said Jem. "And our friends has arranged a little distraction over to Brantley. We should be able to win through to Blagmoor with this little shipment."

In his place near the back of the wagon, Ned cast sidelong glances at the long box. Through the crack in the side, he thought that he caught a glimmer of gold.

"Don't you worry none," said one of the others, with a chuckle. "*He* won't disturb us. They say he was a Gyptian prince in his time, but he's been dead these fifteen hundred years. Reckon he won't sit up in his coffin and wish us the time o'day."

So . . . they were transporting a mummy to the Blagmoor witches. Ned felt genuinely sick at the thought that he was taking part in anything so wicked. Let alone, if he was caught with this lot on his hands, felon that he already was, he would never escape the gallows. Suddenly, he had very little trust in Mr. Evans or Mr. Hawkins, or in their fine promises.

The wagon creaked on across the moors, while Ned brooded in his place at the back. He reached inside his coat where he kept his pistols stuck into a belt round his waist, and he slipped his fingers around one of the stocks. There was something reassuring about the solid weight of the pommel.

Around midnight, they turned off the road and onto a narrow track, leading uphill between immense rugged boulders. They continued on for a little longer, and then paused in front of a wooden gate. Jem swung over the side and opened the gate, so the wagon might pass through. At last they stopped outside a lonely farmhouse.

The farmer who came out to greet them seemed concerned to assure himself that the shipment was exactly as promised, for he climbed up inside the wagon and began to pry open the lid of the coffin with a crowbar. Ned recognized him as the man from Blagmoor, the one he had seen talking with the seedy clergyman several nights past.

The nails came loose with a screeching sound. The farmer lifted the lid of the box, and examined the gilded sarcophagus inside. "Well enough," he grunted, and climbed back down.

The driver took him aside from the others, where they conversed for a while in low voices. But Ned's ears were amazingly keen, and he was able to hear most of what passed.

"I hear you've been thinking about getting your bodies from somebody else," said the driver reproachfully. "And after all these years we've done business! I call it mean, and I expect that the boss ain't too pleased neither."

The farmer only laughed in response. "Churchyard bodies—fresher than this one but not so fresh and lively as them *other* bodies you deal in. Never you fear. We know you're the cheapest and best source for these *old* dead'uns, and you can be sure of our business for a long time to come."

That seemed to satisfy the driver. He climbed up into the wagon and drove if off to the barn. He was to bring it back innocently empty by daylight, but the others would go home on foot. By cutting across country instead of following the road, it would be possible to shave several hours off of their journey.

The farmer sent them off with a brief warning. "Whatever you do, don't go back by way of Grimley Water."

Taking this to mean that the Blagmoor witches were abroad and up to mischief under the full moon, the smugglers assured him that they had no intention of going that way. At the foot of the track, Jem and the other man agreed to split up. "You'll come with me," said Jem to Ned, heading off in the wrong direction entirely.

And as soon as the other fellow was out of sight, he turned to Ned with a broad grin. "Do you want to see a bit o' fun? We'll go round by Grimley Water and spy on them witches. You ain't afraid, are you?"

Thinking it might be another test of his nerve, Ned reluctantly agreed.

By now, the moon was so high, it was almost as light as day, but the shadows were deeper and darker than they were at noon, and the silver light which painted the landscape gave everything a wan, sickly look. With Jem in the lead, they descended a slope, and so came down to the stream. This time of year, it was only a sullen trickle between the rocks. After trudging along the bank for a quarter of a mile, they detected a red glow of firelight in a field on the the far side of the rivulet.

By moving from stone to stone, they were able to cross without getting their feet wet. Then, keeping as low to the ground as possible, and by dodging behind boulders and scrubby bushes, the two men were finally able to reach a good vantage point.

What they saw when they got there caused a cold thrill to snake down Ned's spine. He had always been told that witches danced naked. These did not—though some of the women were scantily clad—and they were all wearing grotesque masks: hags, gargoyles, death's-heads, animals. They cavorted in the firelight, savage, shadowy figures, each one with something horrible clutched in a bloody hand.

And it was what they were holding that made Ned sweat and wish to be sick: wings . . . claws . . . hoofs . . . trotters . . . and here and there a severed limb that appeared to be a human arm, leg, or hand . . . all of these things the witches held aloft and shook at the Goblin moon.

Ned reached blindly for Jem, who was crouched on the ground beside him; it was impossible to tear his eyes away from the figures around the bonfire. "This ain't magic, it's madness," he whispered. "Come away now. We've seen enough."

How Jem might have answered Ned would never know, because just then a ghastly shriek ripped across the night.

One of the young women, who had been dancing in an ecstasy next to the fire, had gone into a fit. What could be seen of her face under the mask was wildly contorted, and froth was bubbling out of her mouth. She flung herself about in a weird parody of her former dance, beating frantically at her own chest, her arms, her belly.

The moon went suddenly behind a cloud. The fire seemed to burn suddenly redder. The girl collapsed on the ground, where she continued to twitch and to howl. Ned thought he saw something small run out from under her skirt; then he did see something, the size of a mouse, then another, and another. As he watched, horrified, a whole army of skittering, squeaking, frantic field mice came out in a black wave from under her skirt and scurried across the ground.

The mice were all over Ned before he even realized they were moving his way. He beat at them, crushed their tiny bodies with his big fists, ripped them off and cast them to the ground. Beside him, Jem lost all caution and leaped to his feet, and began to dance around in his efforts to rid himself of the mice. The witches spotted him and sent up an enraged howl.

Knowing he was a dead man if he stayed where he was, Ned jumped to his feet, grabbed Jem by the arm, and ran for his life, dragging the smuggler behind him . . . through bushes that caught at him, over rocks that cut him, down to the stream and splashing through the water. When he thought that Jem had the right idea, Ned let him loose and ran on by himself, covering the ground with his long strides. He could hear the witches gibbering and howling behind him.

A long time later, when the hue and cry had finally died down, he stopped and stood panting while Jem caught up with him. "Lost them, did we?" he managed to gasp.

"For now," said Jem, equally breathless.

Ned thanked Providence that he and the smuggler had been fresher than their pursuers, and he started off again at a slightly slower pace. His heart was beating so hard, it threatened to burst his chest right open and he had a cramp in one foot, but he would not stop.

As the moon continued to hide behind a thin veil of clouds, the way was dim but not absolutely black. Ned pushed through a hedge, scrambled over a fence, and landed in the road. It was there that several dark figures leapt out to catch him and pull him down.

By what unholy power had the witches gotten ahead of him? Ned twisted, struggled, bashed two heads together, and staggered to his feet. He groped for one of his pistols and pulled it out, but his assailants were moving about so much, that it was impossible to get off a good shot.

Behind him, he could hear another scuffle going on. Then there was a blaze of light as someone uncovered a lantern, and he heard Jem calling out in a stunned voice. "Burn me if it ain't the *customs house men.*"

The humor of his own situation struck Ned forcibly. To escape from witches only to be captured by excise men! The pistol dropped from his suddenly slackened grip, and he bent over double, gasping with laughter as much as with surprise.

It was an hour before sunrise, two nights later, when Hawkins and the highwayman met again at the mausoleum. The tomb was particularly damp and chilly at this hour, and despite his bulk, Ned shivered under his cloak.

Hawkins, however, appeared unaffected and even amused. "I hear that you recently fell in with some friends of mine. It is just as well that they didn't catch you doing anything illegal. If they had . . . well, I might have used my influence to get you off, but what would that have done to your credit with the smugglers?"

"It don't bear thinking on." Nor did the memory of how close he had come in his panic to ruining everything by firing his pistol. To kill one of the excise men would have spoiled his chances of getting that pardon—and the worst of it was that he hadn't been in danger of getting arrested to begin with.

"But them smugglers have let me in now," Ned continued. "I'll be there when the next boat comes in . . . though I can't say yet where they may land her. There's a dozen of us to meet at All Seasons churchyard in six nights' time."

"Very good," said Hawkins. "But I want to catch all of them red-handed. My men and I will be concealed in the vicinity of All Seasons and we'll follow you down to the beach. But we dare not follow too closely. In case you lose us along the way, you had better give me a signal just before they land."

Ned did not care for the sound of that. If he gave any sort of signal, he would place himself in danger of being discovered as a spy. Still, he understood that without that signal Mr. Hawkins and the revenue men might have to wait another four weeks, before catching the smugglers at their work. And who knew what might happen in all that time?

"I'll fire off one of my pistols," he said at last. "I reckon that ought to be sufficient."

The night was dark, the dying moon reduced to an icy sliver of light, but the sky blazed with a thousand stars. Ned did not know this stretch of beach. He and the smugglers had ridden for what seemed like hours since the meeting at All Seasons, and they had reached the shore by a circuitous route. He could only hope that Hawkins and his men were following—perhaps somewhere along the white chalky cliffs which towered above the beach.

The beach ended abruptly where the cliffs jutted out into the water. But that did not stop the man in the lead. He urged his mount into the shallow water where the waves came curling in, and the other riders followed his example. Near the end of the line, Ned did the same. A faint breeze played on his face, the black stallion fought the bit, but Ned was firm and they entered the water. There was a light sucking undertow as the waves retreated.

Once they rounded the point, the smugglers arrived in a secluded cove. Here and there, the sandy expanse of the beach was broken by some great, upthrusting, pillar of stone, like an ancient pagan monument. In the shadow of one of these natural pillars, the smugglers dismounted, and began to swarm around on the beach. Was this the place they were to meet the boat—or had they merely stopped to rest and to stretch their legs after the long ride? Ned hesitated, uncertain whether the time had come to give the signal.

Just then, he heard the sound of approaching oars. One longboat . . . two longboats . . . then a third appeared dark shapes blotting out the stars reflected in the water. Gathering his nerve, Ned pulled out one of his pistols and fired it into the air.

The men nearest to him jumped at the explosion. "What was that for, you great looby?" hissed Jem.

"I thought I seen somebody up on the cliffs. But it was just a bush moving in the breeze."

"I thought you had the nerve for this, but I guess I was wrong." Jem scowled at Ned in disgust, but the highwayman knew that when Hawkins and the revenue officers finally arrived, the smugglers would quickly realize that a signal had been given.

As the first boat came in, half the men went down to pull it out of the shallow water. While everyone was engaged in unloading the one boat and in pulling the next one ashore, Ned faded into the absolute darkness at the base of the cliffs.

Only moments later, Hawkins and a troop of men came riding around the point. Shots rang out on both sides; a man pitched from his saddle onto the beach; another fell out of one of the boats and landed in the water. A fierce battle followed, with firearms, cudgels, knives, oars . . . anything that came to hand. Men shouted, horses milled about, more shots exploded in the salt air.

Ned watched it all from a distance. He had been promised a pardon on the grounds that he did no harm to anyone; he was not certain whether this extended to aiding the customs house men, but he was taking no chances.

And as it turned out, he was not even needed: the government agents outnumbered the smugglers, and they were better armed. In half an hour, they had killed a third of the smugglers, wounded most of the rest, and were tying up the few able-bodied ones and carrying them away on horseback.

When Ned finally ventured out of his hiding place, he found Hawkins on the beach, taking charge of the injured prisoners. Ned stood back for a few moments more, watching in sheer amazement. The fastidious little gentleman had made a fire, and was busily cauterizing wounds, binding up bloody limbs, and easing the pain of the dying with the contents of a bottle he drew out of his coat pocket.

"Blister me!" said Ned, walking out to meet him. "First you was an excise man, then you was a clergyman, and now damme if you ain't a doctor! But what are you when you're at home?"

Hawkins did not answer. He had an abstracted look, like a man who was sleepwalking.

But as the first light of dawn was staining the sky, he

finally left his patients and, along with Ned, went down to the tide-line to inspect the bales and boxes, and to learn what sort of contraband the raid had netted.

"Brandy and silk," said one of the revenue officers, indicating a bale and a barrel. "But none of those other things we were hoping to find. And something that we weren't expecting." He threw open a large wooden chest, which was seen to contain hundreds of small linen bags. He untied one of the bags and poured a fine, crystalline powder into his palm. "It is sleep dust, you see. Which, as you know, has a very high duty."

*"But my dear Francis, how remarkably chagrined you must have been," said a certain young gentleman who stood very high in the confidence of the Crown Prince of Mawbri. More than a week had passed since the raid near Brantley, and he was entertaining the hero of the day at a private supper at his country estate. "Of course, you can still get the drug . . . but the expense, the expense! Your smugglers, it appears, had cornered the market on duty-free dust. By shutting down their operation, you have driven up the the price of the legal drug many times over."*

*Francis Skelbrooke—otherwise known as Emmanuel Hawkins—made an impatient gesture. "Do you really think that is why I'm so bitterly disappointed? It's a most damnable inconvenience, I will admit, but one I am likely to survive."*

*His friend gave him a sympathetic look. "How much of the drug must you take before it sends you to sleep?"*

*Skelbrooke shrugged. "There isn't enough of the dust in Mawbri to give me a good night's rest, the drug has such a hold on me. I use laudanum to sleep at night, the dust to hold back the horrors during the day."*

*"And the nightmares?"*

*"Perhaps one night out of every three. I doubt they will ever leave me entirely. I still see the children . . . especially the two that I unwittingly lured into Lucinda's clutches."*

*There was a momentary silence, broken at last by his host. "But, my dear boy, doesn't anything you've accomplished soothe your conscience at all?"*

*"I accomplished so very little at Brantley. There were no girls being shipped out, no mummies or magic scrolls coming in . . . you'll not be able to charge the surviving smug-*

*glers with kidnapping or black magic. The common scoundrels will almost certainly hang, but as for the others . . . a bribe here and a bribe there, and the ringleaders will go to prison, but not forever. You know how these things go.*

*"Besides, I wanted the Blagmoor witches as well. But no one has named anyone but the farmer we already knew about. When we went to question him, he was found dead. Do you know . . . this was my third attempt to enter and destroy their circle? They will be cautious for a long time. I will have to turn my efforts elsewhere."*

*"In any case," said his friend, "you've made the Blagmoor and Brantley countryside a kindlier place for people to live. The honest fishermen, ploughmen, and farmers will rest easier for many years to come."*

*He offered Skelbrooke a glass of brandy, which was accepted.*

*"Duty free?"*

*"Of course. There was no need to hold it all for evidence. But stay . . . what of that romantic highwayman of yours? Surely you did that fellow some material good."*

*"Romantic?" said Skelbrooke. "He was a great clodhopper in a frieze coat, and not a young man either. I hope that woman of his proves faithful. It would a sad thing if he returned to his village and found that she hadn't even waited for him."*

*He gave a bitter laugh. "Most likely she hasn't. This is a wicked world that we live in, and it seems that every time I try to do anyone any good in it, I fail miserably."*

But for Ned, with the pardon safe in his pocket and the black stallion burning up the miles beneath him, it was a night full of promise. The moors were a hundred miles behind him, and he had finally arrived in heartbreakingly familiar territory: the countryside where he had grown up.

So it was over a fence and across a bridge, then down a winding lane, and at long last, the cottage of Mary's father, where she had retired after Elijah's death, finally came into view. Ned pulled up under an oak tree, about thirty yards from her door.

The stallion had carried him valiantly over a long distance; he could not abandon the brute now, though his heart was pounding and his breath came quickly. Ned led the stallion into the stable and did all that was needful, before proceeding on to the cottage.

There, grown suddenly apprehensive, he peeked in at a window. He saw Mary sitting alone by a small fire. She looked older, to be sure, but he still recognized the winsome, dark-eyed girl he had loved so many years before. Gathering his courage, he pushed open the door and entered without knocking, but he paused shyly on the threshold as Mary started up from her seat.

"You had my letter?" he asked gruffly. She nodded her head, her eyes filling with tears. "And your answer?"

"It is yes, Ned, yes. Could you really doubt it?"

Then he crossed the floor in a rush, caught her up into his arms, and there he was with his own dear love resting her head on his shoulder, alternately laughing and crying for joy.

Fifteen years of exile, loneliness, danger, all melted away in an instant. For Ned Talbot had finally come home . . . and the world was a very fine place indeed.

# GHOST ROT

## *by Jo Clayton*

Jo Clayton is one of the fixtures of fantasy and science fiction. For nearly two decades Jo has entertained us with exciting and imaginative novels such as the "Diadem" series, the "Drinker of Souls" series, the recent "Drums of Chaos" trilogy, with a total of nearly thirty books published. But Jo is far more than "just" a writer. She's also a dedicated, loyal, and generous individual. As one of the authors early on offering up suggestions for various incarnations of the highwaymen, I intended from the outset to feature a Jo Clayton story. For a while, however—after a diagnosis of multiple myeloma—it seemed she might be unable to contribute a story after all. Except that *Jo herself* never once thought she'd miss out. And she didn't. I am extremely pleased and honored to present a wonderful new Jo Clayton short story, written longhand in the hospital and typed by friends. Under such circumstances, many authors might be beaten by this enemy. Jo wasn't. And here is the proof.

1

A small brown woman sat in an alcove at the back of the taproom of the King's Hand, a limp purse and a hot brandy punch on the table in front of her. The name she was using at the moment was Rosamunda Harmony, a euphonious invention meant to suggest a round-eyed femininity that was a threat to no one.

There was a growl beneath the table and a stirring that set the coarse, woolen folds of her skirt scratching against her legs. "Hush up, Demon," she murmured. "You're my reserves; better no one knows you're here." She reached down, drew her forefinger along the delicate round of her companion's skull. "Wait a little longer, then you can go hunt."

A cold nose touched her leg and slid down it till the pseudo-dog's jaw rested on her instep; through the worn leather of her boots she felt rather than heard a long wet sigh.

To the eye Demon was a large black puppy, friendly, happy, exuding intelligence and charm, but in essence he was what Rosamunda named him—a demon from that eerie uncertain non-place that spawned his kin and kind, a place that had many names and neither location nor a specific nature. One way or another he'd been part of her life for so long that she could not remember any time when he was not beside her or ready to come when she called him.

Rosamunda leaned over the brandy glass and sniffed with pleasure at the twisted threads of steam rising from it. Lifting the glass cautiously by the handle of its tarnished silver holder, she sipped at the amber fluid, savoring its taste and warmth as it trickled down her throat. At the same time she used the fingernails of her other hand on the drawstrings of her purse till she'd loosened them enough to fish out one of the coins inside—a broad copper penny turned brown by tarnish but with a faint ruddy shine where pressure from her thumb had polished away the dullness.

Brown and ruddy. Her colors.

"My sweet brown girl," one of her marks called her with a fond vacuity that irritated and thoroughly deceived her. "My lucky penny," he repeated over and over till she was ready to drop a brick on his tongue. Half a dozen times she nearly walked away from the game, not from compassion or the sudden acquisition of scruples, but from sheer boredom. His wealth stopped her; the reality and rumors of that treasure held her with chains of greed, a binding material stronger than steel.

She winced as she remembered the day she'd set to clean his account. A day when a soft and ineffectual fop was suddenly frightening. When blue eyes as empty of thought as they were of malice turned shrewd a breath too soon, giving her a few seconds of warning, all she needed to scramble out of that trap, seconds she stretched into an hour, then several hours, enough time to elude the pursuit that again and again threatened her neck and her freedom.

Groy Mathurin, King's Enforcer. Spider using himself for bait. She'd been careless and had milked coin from a few too many Friends-of-the-King, had started too many stories circulating about her activities.

One by one she worked the coins free of her purse and lined them up on the table in front of her.

Five pennies. One penny to buy her a ride in a farm cart—if she could find someone willing to carry her. Two for another brandy punch. One might consider that waste, but what was wasteful about a moment's warm pleasure? A penny for a bowl of stew tonight and the last for a cup of tea come morning.

And then I'm down to lint and luck.

The King's Hand was the first posting inn north of the Cantus River and the midway stop between Helgarth Market in the southland and Woollery Wheel in the north. It was supposed to be teeming with patrons, so many that the innkeeper stacked the ordinary merchants like cordwood in his dozen fine platform beds, and he still had room for the nobility and nabobs in the private rooms that lined the walls. When she had to run so suddenly and leave behind most of her emergency funds, Rosamunda had counted on the crowd at the Hand and the deftness of her fingers to replenish her resources. But the inn was nearly empty, and the miserable lot scattered so sparsely about the room weren't about to replenish anything.

Rosamunda sighed. She reached for the first of the pennies—and froze.

A man stood holding the swing door open, his body a shout of arrogance and self-importance. He wore a white halfmask and white leather trousers, a black silk shirt flounced and ruffled to the point of absurdity. A whip braided from silver wire hung from a loop on his left wrist. The King's Whip.

Groy Mathurin stepped into the doorway, stood with his head turning slowly toward her as he inspected the taproom. The set of his shoulders and the tight smile that bunched the muscles in his cheek told her that he knew precisely where she was, but was savoring the slow approach of the moment when their eyes would meet and she would understand that this time there was no escape.

Demon stirred. Her foot felt cold as he lifted his head away from her boot.

"Not yet," she whispered. "Wait my word."

Mathurin's eyes passed over her as if she were one of the chairs and nothing more.

He'd sworn to hang her the moment he set his hands on her.

But his eyes slid over her without acknowledging her presence. He strolled across the room, easy, unhurried, stripping off his gloves as he moved. Trying to match his ease, Rosamunda turned her head and glanced at the window behind her.

A man's face floated in the darkness beyond the glass, cut off at the top by flat black hat of the King's Guard and at the bottom by the black silk kerchief that marked a special detail.

No escape? Despite his ring of guards, Mathurin had a surprise or two waiting for him come moonset.

She scooped up the pennies, returned them to her purse and pulled the drawstrings tight. When she looked up, the Whip was standing beside her, his lip curling at her meager hoard.

"He wants you upstairs. Now."

"I don't roll on my back for any man. Not even the King—as you have reason to know."

"Now and then when I had nothing else to do, I've wondered about your price. And why any sane man would bother to pay it. You can walk or I'll have you carried up."

## 2

The King's Enforcer was stretched out in a bulging, stuffed leather chair, his unbooted feet resting on a stool pushed to the edge of the fire smoldering in the grate. He was a pale man, his skin a chalky pink, the scars that marked his face and the backs of his hands knotted lines of blue-white keloid.

When Rosamunda came in, he pointed at a hassock near the door between the sitting room and the bedroom. "Over there. Sit. Answer fully and with truth anything I ask you."

"Of course, Enforcer Mathurin." She settled herself on the hassock, arranged her skirt in neat folds about her knees, and clasped her hands in her lap.

"No *of course* about it. You'll lie every chance I give you. But you had better understand something. I know more about this than you think. I'll know when you're lying, and I'll have you beaten each time you try it."

Rosamunda lowered her eyelids and spread her hands in a gesture of mild acquiescence. At the moment she was thoroughly confused and inclined to walk very warily indeed.

Mathurin filled the wineglass at his elbow, emptied it in three gulps, and patted his lips dry with a crumpled square of lace-trimmed linen. "You lay ghosts."

It wasn't a question, so there didn't seem to be any suitable response. She said nothing.

"I want an answer."

"Ghosts are subjective phenomena in the eyes of most Garmaltese. So to say I lay ghosts has a certain truth to it. I quiet disturbed minds and the manifestations that disturb them vanish."

"Clever. Don't try that again." He squeezed his lower lip between thumb and forefinger. "During the last three years how often have you come north of the Cantus?"

"I haven't. Why should I? I don't care for the sort of austerity they prize up here. And they hold their coin in such a tight clutch the aiglon screams and dies of base metal poisoning before they'll even consider parting with a halfpenny bit." She snatched a quick look, lowered her eyes. She'd enjoyed the snip at him, but his face told her she'd better not try it again.

"Describe your connections with the Pycariot Privateers."

"Connections? In any real sense I have none. I've met the Totum Haggiah and one or two of his sons, but who hasn't?"

"Have you used your arts for them? If so, how?"

"Whatever arts you mean, the answer is no. I have no interest in them or their notions."

"In any sense in which the phrase has been or can be used, whether it is by skill, art or consistent good luck, can you lay ghosts?" He turned his head toward her, the pallid, irregular profile stark against the dyed leather of the chair; his cold blue eyes held a warning that this question was the most important of all those he'd asked and that his patience was limited.

Rosamunda hesitated, her hands closing into fists, nails cutting into her palms. Mathurin had the authority to hang her any time he chose, but an honest answer to this meant death by fire, something that frightened her beyond reason. "Yes," she said finally. "What you call laying a ghost is draining off those surpluses of force that allow a phantasm to assume form and gain sufficient mass to manipulate the mortal world and to give expression to the malice, rage or whatever other feelings are driving them from their rest."

"I wonder how much I should believe you. You sound serious, plausible, not glib but knowledgeable. But that is your true art, isn't it—the flimflam played at the highest level. Half a year I watched you. Half a year. And I never knew how much you believed of what you said. Was it *all* a game? Even now, I don't know what you're thinking or why you answered the way you did." He emptied the bottle into his glass, the pale green wine glowing jadelike in the light of the silver lamps. He held the glass and brooded a moment, then he tossed the wine down and turned his head toward her again. "Not that it matters. I have my orders. The North Highroad has acquired a ghost." Lines cut deep between his nose and the corners of his mouth and his voice went flat. "You'll earn a full pardon for theft, swindling, and any other crimes you've committed against the King and citizens of Garmalta if you rid us of this haunt."

The depth of the loathing in his voice as he spoke of the pardon convinced Rosamunda that the offer was genuine, so she felt safe enough for the moment to indulge her curiosity, but she knew too much about the duration of a Prince's gratitude to rely on any Prince's promises. "Where does this ghost usually appear?"

"Anywhere along the North Highroad, from the bridge across the Cantus to the Gate City, Kerma-in-the-Karpanne."

"Is there any specific place where the manifestation seems strongest?"

"The site where it last appeared."

"Growing stronger?"

"Yes."

"How? What does it do?"

"Rots to dust whatever it touches. Two or three have witnessed this. Mostly we find the piles of dust it leaves behind." He touched fingertip to fingertip and spent several moments contemplating his starred hands. "Two thirds of Garmalta's trade enters the country along the North Highroad. And two thirds of the King's annual income is derived from taxes on that trade."

"So who pays my fee?"

"Cross your palm with silver, Coromany Queen?"

"Ritual has its place, Enforcer."

"Not when I'm paying for it."

"Are you?"

"No. One hundred silver pennies and I put you across the border at Kerma-in-the-Karpanne. Personal Delivery. King's guarantee, no haggling, no right of refusal. Due after the ghost is laid."

"And your solution?"

"Hostage. You have a daughter. . . ."

"No. And my son has friends."

"A secret child conceived three months before your husband died and put out to fosterage once she was born. I have her, and I will hold her until the ghost is gone."

*Pearl* . . . Rosamunda forced her fists to unknot, set her trembling fingers on her thighs. This changed everything.

He watched her closely, his face relaxing as he saw how strong a blow he'd dealt her. "Now that we have that settled, what else do you want to know about the ghost?"

She pulled a hand across her face, scraping away the fear sweat, scraping away anger and distress with it, searching for the composure she needed to deal with this man who'd proved more dangerous than she'd expected. "His history, as much of it as you know. I don't understand this rot business. I've never heard of anything like it."

She was pleased to find her voice steady and the turmoil inside her calming.

"He was a notorious highwayman who rode this stretch of road back in the reign of Harkemer V. One of the few that Harkemer didn't succeed in hanging."

Rosamunda wiped her face again, using the edge of her palm to scrape away the sweat. Her body still reacted to the dry poison of his voice. "Why?"

"He ran into an ambush on his way to spend the night with his woman of the moment."

"Turned him, did she?"

"Her father. The girl was a beauty and he had ambitions." He rang the bell and waited till a maidservant brought a clean glass and a full bottle of the local green wine to replace the one he'd emptied. Rosamunda hung onto her patience as he peeled away the wax and pulled the cork, then poured the sparkling yellow-green fluid into the glass. He sipped at it, enjoying her frustration—she didn't dare protest, knowing he'd simply take longer to finish.

He patted his lips dry with the ornate handkerchief, tucked it back in his sleeve. "Banalities," he said. "All of it. She was bait, set in her window to reassure him, but the Highroad Patrol squad who had sense enough to tie and gag her so she wouldn't warn her lover by shouting were stupid enough to let her get her thumb on the trigger of a musket. The shot killed her, but he was gone as soon as he heard it."

"And when he found out, he went after patrolmen?"

"Dead as mutton two days later."

"Tchah! Romantics, both of them. Believe it or not, they're tougher and harder to put down than the hairiest of cynics. And having two poles complicates the problem. They reinforce each other and help conceal who's where. Looby booby, who's got the needle? Pass it on and let old goose go chase her tail. Tell me about the girl."

"Nothing much to tell. Innkeeper's daughter. This inn, if it helps to know."

"It helps. Oh, yes. Knowledge is power. And power is sweet on the tongue."

He scowled at her. "What's wrong with you? I need you sober and thinking straight."

"No, you don't. Straight line think gets you dead too fast." She yawned. "I'm tired. Better I get some sleep and leave the thinking to you and the Whip." She giggled, but sobered as she rubbed her eyes and got slowly to her feet. "There's nothing in that story that explains anything. I'll look round for the Daughter Node, but I don't expect to find it."

"We ride with the mail and a pair of packtrains tomorrow. Heading north. Be downstairs and ready to leave with us one hour before dawn."

3

The room Mathurin hired for Rosamunda was high in the rafters, a finely carpentered jewel box of a chamber, meant for the darling of a doting father. It was bare and dusty now with a hard narrow cot, a shaky table and on that table a single lamp.

As soon as the manservant who brought her there left, Demon oozed from under the cot. He shook himself vigorously, nipped at a pseudo-flea on his left flank, then went nosing about the room, growling at things she couldn't see, even with her witchsight.

A stab of anguish.

A pillar of light—square—transparent—floor to ceiling.

Inside the pillar, the distorted image of a young woman—darkness for eyes—mouth stretched in a silent scream—hands clawing—

Demon lifted his head and growled, a faint sound at first, then louder and louder. He bounded to his feet and flung himself at the image trapped in the light.

Black light snaked into white light—tearing—clawed into fragments—pseudo-dog—screaming girl—whirling—inextricably mixed—

A sudden flare of light nearly blinded her.

When she recovered, she was alone in the small room. The apparition and Demon were both gone—she had no idea where—and at the moment she didn't particularly care.

She pulled off her boots and stretched out on the cot. The draw-sack over the tester was damp and smelled of mildew, the pallet was dusty, leaking the black, slippery seeds of its stuffing through rips in the seams, but none of this kept her awake for more than half a dozen breaths.

Sometime later a cold nose touched her face and Demon crawled up onto the cot beside her. An unhappy whine in her ear brought her into a twilight awareness where she knew that the apparition had eluded the Pup and in doing so had managed to frighten him. Her arm was so heavy when she reached for the cold and shivering body that she nearly gave up trying to comfort him but once she touched the velvety hide over his ribs and she felt his wobbly damp sigh of pleasure, her hesitation vanished.

Dreams. Silver eyes. Glowing. Molten. Faces part beast, part not-human-not-beast, but stamped with a fierce and alien intelligence. Cubist illusions. Incompatible aspects impossibly visible. Multiple. Never single. Never isolated.

Over and over, dreams that had lived at the back of her head since she was aware of herself as an individual, dreams her mother never attempted to explain.

*Daughter,* the demon forms sang to her, multiple voices, never single, never unmixed. *Sister, don't forget us. When you need us, we will fill you.* The sound of their voices ebbed and swelled, sang through her body. *Child of our soul, you will know the time when you touch it. Listen and call for the Shuttle of Unweaving.* Rosamunda stirred in her sleep. She knew the Shuttle. She had used it before though it was very heavy and exhausted her by the time she had finished stripping away the layers of a spell that threatened her. This was the first time, though, that Demon's demonkin had offered their help. The words fell like rain on her needfulness, soothing even when they grew too broken and blurred for her mind to understand them.

The voices faded with the dream. She slept.

## 4

The moon had set long ago, but the sky was so clear that starshine gave everything a ghostly gray glow, even the dew that sparked and shimmered on every surface. The six horses hitched to the mail coach shifted feet and flicked their ears, then went back to the last handfuls of grain in their nosebags. A short distance off, the mules of the two packtrains were nipping at the tender new growth on the muckle brush and the gorshem, or teasing out blades of grass from the rubble and sand of a pair of hillsides near the Highroad.

Rosamunda's boots, legs, and the hem of her of her cloak were sodden by the time she reached the Whip and the mare that Mathurin had waiting for her. With exaggerated clumsiness, she got her leg across, then sat watching as the Whip brushed his hands of her and with a panache as exaggerated as her awkwardness, rode over to Mathurin and the four men waiting with him—King's Guards, the most heavily armed of the lot.

A tankard of ale in one hand and the ragged remnant of a mutton and onion sandwich in the other, the coachman came striding ponderously from the inn. He stuffed the bread and meat into his mouth, washed them down with the last of the ale, and tossed the tankard to the servant who'd followed him from the taproom. After a mistrustful glare at the Whip, he climbed to the driver's seat, nodded to the sidegun, and planted himself among the horsehair cushions that braced his back.

Rosamunda closed her eyes but forced them open again immediately because wave upon wave of sleep washed over her and she found herself perilously near falling off the horse.

Mathurin and the Whip were arguing about something with a low-voiced intensity that showed no sign of abating. The coachman watched this with an increasing nervousness, his impatience reaching the team through the reins he'd distributed among his fingers, translated into head tossing, angry squeals, nips at the other horses, stamping and sidling. The mules ignored everything but graze and browse and the muleteers either slept or hunched over minute fires, smoking crooked black cigars and drinking turgid kaf from battered pots.

Her mare bent her long skinny neck and whuffed with suspicious gusto at Rosamunda's knee. After she dealt with that, Rosamunda glared a last time at the Whip and Mathurin, settled herself more deeply in the saddle, and whistled, a single note repeated three times.

Demon came trotting around the corner at the south side of the King's Hand. One moment he was a faint shadow, barely visible against the dark bulk of the Inn. A breath later he'd acquired an eerily flickering outline of sulfurous light. Ignoring the off-on light that laid multiple shadows around his feet, the pseudo-dog watched Rosamunda's hands a moment, then circled wide about the mare and headed for the arguing men.

The Whip's gelding squealed in terror, nearly threw his rider as he reared, then took off at an all-out run, his hooves throwing out wide spurts of gravel, the Whip offbalance and struggling to retain his seat. Better trained and ridden, Mathurin's horse tossed his head about but kept his feet on the ground, though he, too, was white-eyed with fear.

"HEE YUP!" The coachman's whip cracked, the team dug in, and the coach took off after the Whip, the four Guards assigned to protect it scrambling to reach their stations without knocking into each other or losing control of their mounts.

A moment later all that was left of the Demon-born chaos were a few yells and a settling film of dust.

Rosamunda whistled again and Demon's flare poufed out. Tongue lolling, silver eyes cool as the starlight, he trotted beside her as she rode to join the King's Enforcer. She kept wanting to grin at Mathurin, to celebrate the triumph of absurdity over reason and the futility of his terribly sober and stifling view of the world, but as long as he had Pearl in his bloody hands, she was constrained to put on any face he wanted to see and to take great care not to push him too hard.

His usual pallor intensified until it had a greenish tinge to it. He stared in horrified fascination at Demon as Rosamunda stopped in front of him.

"Ser Enforcer," she gave him a small tight smile, "we seem to be wasting a lot of time. Wouldn't it be better to use what protection daylight offers?"

"WHAT IS THAT THING?"

"My dog."

"Dog!"

"Shall I have him fetch for you?"

"No!"

"Yes, you're right. It would waste more time." She looked away from him. He camouflaged it expertly enough so she would not have guessed it, but he was clinging to the King's Hand like a baby boy to his mother's skirts, using the Whip's vanity and arrogance, the nervousness of the guards, the sullen stubbornness of the muleteers, every opening he could grab to postpone his departure. He was shamed by his need—and deeply angered by anyone who forced him to look clearly at what he was doing.

"Wait here," he said. "Control that creature or we'll be wasting a lot more of your precious daylight."

## 5

By midmorning the day was already hot, the air dry enough to suck water out of wine. A few distant raptors' cries served only to emphasize the stillness as a silence heavy as the black stone that dominated the land settled over the road, the mules and the riders. Rosamunda struggled to stay awake enough to react if something came at her. Now and then she felt a thing *looking* at her—and it wasn't just her imagination because each time this happened Demon growled and ran off after whatever it was—only to return tail-tucked and whining with frustration when what he was chasing disappeared.

An hour after noon the pseudo-dog came yipping down a precipitous tumble of black rock. He hit the Highroad in an explosion of gravel and the superficial dust of the hardpan base, ran half-a-dozen excited circles around Rosamunda, then took off down the road, disappearing when it curved around a slant-topped tor.

Rosamunda kicked the sluggish mare into her jolting trot, meaning to get around that bend and out of sight before Mathurin woke from his heat-daze. She had a feeling the Enforcer would be adamantly against leaving the road and would waste both her time and her energy arguing the point.

Demon was waiting for her in one of the vallescas, pacing back and forth in front of a fluffy gray mound half-concealed by thorny gorshem bushes and spearpoint munga fern, stopping occasionally to rear up on his hind legs and bat angrily at things invisible to her.

The mare snorted, set herself, and refused to go one step nearer to the mound. Rosamunda echoed the snort; if the horse were hers, she'd have to deal with this refusal, but after this ride was finished, she never wanted to see the beast again, though she'd have lasting and painful memories of the mare pounded into her tailbones.

She slid from the saddle and walked cautiously closer to the mound. This was crofter country and in most of these narrow but lush vallescas the sheep were usually thick as maggots on a dead yearling doe. This vallesca was empty and had been left untouched long enough for the tender tips of the gorshem to darken and harden. She took another step and found herself standing at a line where healthy plants began to turn stunted, bulbous and rotten at the heart.

She hesitated, nose wrinkling from the musty smell, mouth thinned with distaste at the distortion of the plant forms. "Demon, come! I want to get out of this."

Head low, tail down, he crept across the misshapen plants, a picture of frustration and misery. He pressed his shivering body against her leg and whimpered—but when she reached down to catch hold of him by his neck fur, he leaped away from her, moving so swiftly he was beyond reach before she had time to react.

Head tilted, round droopy ears lifted, glowing colorless eyes fixed on her, he yipped. The sound needed no words to be a challenge. *Follow me if you dare.*

Rosamunda sighed. "You win, Dee. So show me."

## 6

"Uh! What was that?" When she looked down, she shivered. She'd kicked into the hub of a coach wheel, still fairly intact and able to bruise the side of her foot even through the leather of her boot; she took another step and nearly trod on something jagged and white.

A fragment of bone. It had probably belonged to one of the wheel horses. She squatted and scanned the tangle, saw bits of leather and fragments of metal, most of it eaten away by rust, more bone and a long snaky blackness that had once been the coachman's whip.

And she understood at last what the ghost-rot was.

The Highwayman was a time sink. He stole duration from his victims. With their lifespans sucked away, the coach body had turned to dust, the horses were not only dead but reduced to fragments, the coachman and sidegun had lost all shape and definition.

Sweat popped out hot and sticky on her brow, her stomach churned, and for a moment she was more frightened than she had ever been. One touch and her life was stolen from her. One touch!

For several moments she stared at the faint gray smear of dust that marked her palm, then a short sharp bark woke her from her horrified contemplation.

Demon trotted round the mound, carrying the coachman's hat in his mouth. By some chance it had escaped the fate of the rest and was intact except for dirt stains and the marks of the pseudo-dog's teeth. She took it from him and began turning it around in her hands, wondering how long it had been lying beside the rotted remnants of its owner.

Her hands went suddenly still as the buckle came into view and gave her an answer that she'd didn't particularly want.

Two nights ago she had ridden the night mail north from Helgarth Market to the King's Hand, the sole passenger in a mail coach driven by a coachman with an unusually elaborate buckle on his hatband, a solid circle-brooch with a triangular bit broken off the upper left arc.

She stared down at a wide hatband and a solid circle-brooch with a triangular bit broken off the upper left arc. "Two days," she said aloud, as much wonder as fear in her voice. "Only two days." She tossed the hat onto the dustmound. "Demon!"

The pseudo-dog thrust his head around a gnarled and blackened bush, one ear lifted away from his head. He surprised a grin from Rosamunda and growled at her.

"Come on, let's get out of here."

## 7

Mathurin waited in the middle of the Highroad, stony-faced and deeply angry.

Before he could spew that anger on her, Rosamunda started talking. "How long has the Highwayman's ghost been riding? Does he ever hit in daylight? When did the dust-rot start? What did he attack first, and how long did it take for the rot to get going?"

"You could have called him down on us!" Mathurin's effort to control the shake in his voice turned it shrill as a castrato in a snit. "You and that THING of yours."

"Wouldn't need a call. He's already out there, watching us. Never mind that. How long has this ghost been active?" She urged the mare into a slow walk, forcing Mathurin to break his rigidity and ride after her; he was too good a horseman to be anything but easy in the saddle. The familiar movement also drained some of the anger and fear out of him and left him more willing to listen to her.

"The first complaints came in two years ago," he said, pitching his voice so he could be heard over the noises of the road. "Several coach horses with broken legs and a plague of broken straps. No reports of rot, but the horses were shot and the straps burned so there's no way to say for sure. The first dead men and horses, seen and reported six months later, coach had all straps and leatherwork missing. Coach body was discarded, was discovered as a dust heap two months on."

"I see. And daylight sightings or attacks?"

"None till now, if you count what you're reporting as a sighting."

"What about inside the post inns or other houses?"

"None." He scowled. "No. That's not exactly right. The ghost has been seen in the taprooms of several of the post inns, especially the King's Hand, but has never done any damage inside."

"I see. When was the first report of such sightings?"

"Around two months ago."

"Hm. When will the mail coach reach Woollery?"

"Close to midnight. If it lasts that long. If any of us survive past sundown."

With a mental shrug Rosamunda dismissed the Enforcer's pessimism. She couldn't afford that sort of negative thinking. Getting ready to use the Shuttle took concentration and time, especially when the spell she had to deal with was as distorted and dangerous as this one.

Someone had raised the Highwayman as a covert attack on the King and on rich and powerful Germalta, an adept who pretended to necromancy but didn't know enough to get his spells right and who was a fool besides. A hireling of the Pycariot Privateers and the Totum Haggiah, at a guess. Mathurin wouldn't be wrong about that sort of thing. She pressed her lips into a grim line. After this is over, if I'm still alive, Pearl and I will go visit Pycarios and a certain misadept. Give him a few lessons about his place in the world of the arts. Tchah!

"Midnight," she said aloud. "So there's no way we can save the mail. The best we can do is get as near as we can and use it for bait."

"We?"

"You, your men and me. Oh, I won't want you near enough to interfere, but I insist on witnesses." There was a loud, assenting yip from round the region of her heels. She looked down at Demon who was pacing beside the mare. "My dog agrees."

Demon lifted a leg, shot a stream of urine at a dusty

spearpoint fern growing beside the highroad, then trotted faster till he caught up with the mare.

Rosamunda laughed. "Yes, indeed, Deedee." She glanced at Mathurin and pinched her lips together to hold in another laugh because he looked affronted as if he'd taken Demon's act as a direct insult to him. Quite soberly she said, "You have what is precious to me. I will take the utmost care to preserve you in good health and contented with my actions."

The King's Enforcer was staring blank-eyed past her at the distant peaks of the Karpannes, fear and confidence fighting across the uneven planes of his face. He wasn't listening to her, hadn't taken in her last words.

"The packtrains are closer to us." She spoke each word clearly and distinctly until she saw awareness return to his face. "If we catch up with them and get them under roof before sundown, they should be safe enough. I'm his prime target or so I think. He'll take the mail to taunt me and pull me from cover, make me come after him." She yawned, stretched it out and out until she ended the grimace with a snap of her teeth. "Moon's Child, I'm tired. I need a couple hours of sleep, then a pair of fast horses so I can catch up with the mail and be ready for the ghost."

Silence for several breaths—then he said, "That can be arranged."

"Good. Tonight I'll either drain the ghost or I'll fail and add the sum of my years to his store."

## 8

Swaying in a precarious stability, skittering from iron-clad wheel to iron-clad wheel, the mail coach bounded over the highroad, spraying gravel from the pounding, driving hooves of the six-horse team and sparks from the iron tires as the coachman ignored the angry shouts of the Whip and the guard who rode in his dust and raced his nightmares into Woollery Wheel.

Woollery was a dark blotch covering the slopes of the twin mountains Bandersic and Bondery, cut in half by the curving silver sheen of the twenty-bridged Breedonna. The only lights in the city were the lamps on those bridges, twenty shallow arcs of blurry stars reflecting off the water and the walls of the wool warehouses that lined the river. Except for a few rowboats tied to the pillars of the bridges, there were no boats or barges because the river cut across the North Highroad and went nowhere useful to traders.

Riding far enough behind the guards to escape their notice, Rosamunda felt the growing hope in the coachman as he drew nearer and nearer to the gates of Woollery, and she tensed with expectation. Where there was hope, the Highwayman would find the opportunity for malice and taunting.

Invisible in the darkness, black Demon growled his own warning, then turned the growl soft as a reminder of the dreamed promise repeated that afternoon.

"I hear, Dee. I'm ready to bear the weight." She slowed her mount to a quick walk, letting the coach draw farther and farther ahead.

As Rosamunda had expected, the ghost appeared at Woollery's South Gate, then came charging up the long slope. First a huge stallion crafted of white phosphor, vividly present against the darkness of the city, then his rider—a man with a profusely curling periwig and a floppy hat with exotic feathers riding the brim, pistol in hand, musket tied across his back. Finally a young girl of great beauty and passion riding pillion behind him. Though her face was mostly obscured by the Highwayman's body, Rosamunda caught fleeting glimpses of her laughter and excitement.

"STAND AND DELIVER!"

The words boomed out from everywhere and nowhere, filling the space between earth and sky.

Rosamunda slid from the saddle, slapped her weary and frightened mount on his flank, and sent him racing back along the road.

The mail coachman sent his whip dancing along the flanks and ears of his weary team, squeezing the last surge of speed from them. At the last moment he tried to turn them and pass the ghost, but the Highwayman did not permit this.

The two forces merged. The Highwayman slid into and through first the team then the coach itself and as he did so, everything he touched fell away from him in a cascade of dust as fine and fluid as thrice-milled flour, the guards and the Whip as swiftly as the rest.

Face twisted with triumph and hate, the Highwayman charged at Rosamunda.

She lifted her arms, holding them rounded and tense as if she balanced a massive weight on her head.

Demon danced round her knees.

Demonkin poured in from the place without a nature, multiple and strange, blending in a wheeling dance around her body, chanting words of power, unknown to any but them.

A Mandorla outline leaped away from her head, rising up and up until like the Highwayman's SHOUT it reached from earth to moon, an almond shape greater than any she had created before.

Horse and riders crashed into her, but she was demon-locked and mandorla-anchored to the earth; her body shuddered an instant and was still again while the horse and Highwayman phantasm flared into shapeless light . . .

One cusp thrust deep within the flare, the other rising to touch the near-round of the almost-full moon, the Mandorla began to turn—slow—ponderous—unwinding the weave of the spell—stripping away the phosphor threads before the Highwayman could force form back onto the duration he had harvested so greedily.

The shuttle spun faster and faster until all that was left was a slowly evaporating pool of phosphor writhing on the gravel and hardpan of the Highroad . . .

The sky shone as bright a silver as the moon and the stars with the unwoven duration plucked free of form and malice . . .

The phosphor on the road shrank yet more . . .

Distorted features glaring at her, twisted lips cursing her, losing definition, melting into the pool . . .

Fist . . . a final, feeble attempt toward shape but the hand that emerged from the pool drooped back into liquid as soon as it formed . . .

A worm of light in the dust.

GONE!

The Mandorla thinned and wavered, dimming until it, too, was gone.

The demon dance melted away, leaving her standing alone in the middle of the road, and gravel, tired and triumphant, but not done yet. The gratitude of princes ends when the emergency ends and Mathurin would be coming for her.

She couldn't wait for that.

Catching the remnants of the Shuttle's spin, she used it to power her body and whirled round and round until she was the heart of a funnel of roaring wind. "Mathurin," she cried. The wind echoed her. "Mathurin, be here!"

The King's Enforcer crashed heavily to earth beside her. Before he could catch his breath and scramble to his feet, Demon was beside him, one large paw in the center of his chest, its massive weight pinning him where he was.

Rosamunda moved around his shoulders and put her foot beside Demon's paw. "Mamera tamera spinner the Orb," she chanted, her voice ringing out to fill the night around her, her hands moving delicate imitation of an orb spider spinning its web. "Web the wit with cords of steel. Spinnera minnera splatter the matter, delve in the depths for the house of the daughter."

She smiled when his chest leaped under her foot, smiled again as she saw him struggle against the harsh pull of the minor spell she'd laid on him. In the brilliance of the light from the slow dispersal of the ghost's hoarded duration, his face was contorted with hatred. At the same time his mouth kept opening and his tongue moving as his body forced him toward speech.

"You can't fight me now, Mathurin, so you might as well relax and answer the question. Where is my girl?"

"At Haymere Croft in the Karpannes. She thinks she's waiting for you." He looked appalled as he heard the words flow so easily from a mouth that no longer answered to his will. The scars and lines of his face shifted and strained as she held him as easily as an angler would play a perch, then she loosed his mouth so he could speak as he wished.

"What are you going to do?"

"Ride with you to Kerma-at-the-Karpannes, take the silver pennies and my daughter."

"To me! What are you going to do to me?"

"Ah! I haven't decided that yet. Right now, I'm going to cache your body under Woollery's wall where I hope the rats won't nibble at it, acquire some horses, and spend the rest of the night in a comfortable bed with clean linen sheets and goosedown pillows. You can contemplate that if you wish." She grinned at him, ground her heel lightly into his ribs. "And tomorrow we'll ride for Haymere Croft."

## 9

Pearl mounted beside her on one of the Highroad Patrol's finer geldings, Rosamunda watched Mathurin trudge back along the road to Kerma. Pearl was a thin dark child not quite twelve with intelligent bronze eyes and a touch of irony in her voice that made her seem older than she was. Rosamunda often found her disconcerting.

"Why leave him alive, Mama? He's not going to forget what happened."

"I know. But he'll never stop being afraid of me and that's the worst punishment a man like that will ever endure." She shivered. "Sometimes I appall myself, young Pearl. Better you forget all that and concentrate on what we've got to do in the Pycariot Archipelago."

danForth © 96

# FOR KING AND COUNTRY

## *by Deborah Wheeler*

Following her debut in Marion Zimmer Bradley's first *Sword & Sorceress* anthology in 1984, Deborah Wheeler has proved herself a gifted short fiction writer with more than three dozen published stories to her credit, as well as a short story Nebula Award contender for "Madrelita," and now "Javier, Dying in the Land of Flowers." Yet far from being a short fiction specialist, Deborah also writes novels, including *Jaydium* and *Northlight.* I suspect much of Deborah's inspiration and versatility is derived from her equally talented family. She lives in a house full of artists, musicians, scientists—and, of course, cats.

The night of Lord Marchwell's spring ball, the high-ceilinged hall resonated with the music of viols and oboes, with a new harpsichord filling in the basso continuo. Five hundred candles sent glitters through the crystal pendants of the chandeliers. The satin and brocade of the ladies' dresses glowed like gemstones, ruby and sapphire and amber; ceremonial swords flashed as bright as the gentlemen's eyes as they met those of their partners in the intricate steps of the minuet and sarabande. A king's ransom in ropes of pearl hung about powdered, pale necks. Servants, as immaculately stiff as the glossy-polished furniture, watched expressionlessly from the sides.

A late arrival paused at the entry way to survey the glittering assemblage. Even in the shadows, his figure drew the eye, the subdued richness of his coat, the dove-gray silk cut close to the body to accentuate the breadth of shoulder and tapering leanness of hips, the silken hose revealing the sculptured curves of knee and calf. He held himself with the relaxed alertness of a swordsman, but with an air of natural grace that bordered on arrogance. Now his eyes narrowed as he spotted his quarry. He moved through the room with the deliberate grace of a tiger. Ladies gazed after him, noting the unpowdered coppery-gold hair drawn back with a single ribbon of black velvet, the controlled sensuality of the mouth, which gave an amused response to their attentions, and the dark lashes framing eyes as hard and opaque as steel, which did not.

The young noble came to a halt beside an older man, dressed in opulent claret-colored brocade, his long waistcoat embroidered in gold thread, cascades of Flemish lace at his throat.

"James, what an unexpected pleasure," said the older man. "I wasn't expecting you until tomorrow."

"My lord." Sir James Sandys executed a bow impeccable in its courtesy and grace. "Your letter said *urgent.*"

"Good, then." Lord Marchwell excused himself and his companion.

As they made their way through the crowd, the young man's gaze rested for a moment on a young woman, caught by the pale face made paler still by the glossy wealth of jet black hair and the proud lift of her chin. Even in the rigidly corseted gown, she moved like a flame. Nor did James miss the way her eyes flashed and then turned dull, like tarnished silver, as the perfumed, periwigged dandy at her side led her away.

As quickly as could be done with decorum, the two men retreated into a small withdrawing room at the far end of the long corridor. Although the spring night was mild, a small fire had been lit and two glasses of fine port sat ready on a silver tray. Lord Marchwell locked the door behind them and held out one glass of wine.

"Yes, well. Please do sit down." Lord Marchwell threw himself into one of the two cushioned chairs drawn up by the hearth. Firelight flickered over the beautifully carved marble mantle. "These new shoes with the high tongues were my wife's idea. My feet are killing me. And by the way, banish all thought of young Lady Elinor Ashcroft. Word has it her family plans to betroth her shortly to Lord Baldridge. A pity, since he's buried three wives already, and her father's let her ride wild over half the country. But it's the girl's lot to obey and yours to turn your eyes elsewhere."

Visibly suppressing a smile, James took the second glass of wine and lowered himself into the other chair. A long moment passed. When Lord Marchwell spoke again, his voice had shed all traces of the fussy, overdressed old fop.

"The King has proposed a summer progress through the county."

A royal progress involved huge amounts of advance preparation, James thought, not to mention expense on the part of the lords hosting the party, but was hardly reason to interrupt his mission to France. His absence endangered the entire network he'd worked to establish within the Versailles Court. And the French king's expansionist ambitions would scarcely await his return.

"The Privy Council has determined to quell the recent increase in highway robbery. The local magistrates can deal with ordinary thieves," Marchwell went on, as if reading his thoughts. "But of late the stretch of road between Byrne and Teasford has been beset by a particularly villainous knave. They call him the Red Feather because of his hat ornament."

"He must be more than ordinary, this Red Feather, if he's the reason you called me back."

"He laughs at every attempt to catch him. The courts have sent out band after band without any result. He seems to know when they're coming. I sent my agent Carter and he came back tarred and feathered. Robbed, of course."

Privately, James thought this only proved the highwayman had a sense of humor.

"And the King insists upon following that route."

James was not a man given to ready oaths, but a flicker of darkness passed across his eyes. "I'll catch him for you, my lord."

"If you can't, no one can. You're the very best we have. But we've discovered his Achilles heel. He has, shall we say, a weakness for the gentler sex. He stopped Lady Carrisford's carriage a fortnight ago and released her without harm. Apparently he played quite the gallant, even returned her mother's pearls to her when she wept." By the look on Lord Marchwell's face, the rogue had stolen the lady's heart instead.

Lord Marchwell heaved himself to his feet. "You swore an oath to serve your King and country."

"I did," James said, rising. It was a source of pride that he had never yet failed or refused a mission.

He began to seriously reconsider as Lord Marchwell explained his plan.

Two days later, a coach made its way along the lonely stretch of highway between Byrne and Teasford. Far from the nearest manor house, the road wound on between steepening hills, climbing, descending. The countryside grew wilder. The last night's rain had left ditches of mud on either side of the elevated road, and a sweet moisture still hung in the air. The road passed through the southern outreaches of the ancient forest preserve. The driver clicked encouragement to the matched bay geldings. The near horse snorted as a pheasant took flight a few feet from its nose. The coach jerked and rattled over the paving stones.

A moment later, a treble voice emerged from the coach's shadowy interior. "Oh, dear heavens, what is it? Are we being robbed?"

The single footman leaned toward the window. "It's nothing, m'lady. A bird startled one of the horses."

Within the coach, the lady settled back against the cushions, easing the tightness of the corseted bodice, and rearranged the folds of the skirts. Despite the rings of gold and topaz, the hand was large for a woman's, the fingers thick and strong as they touched the flintlock pistol hidden there.

"Damn," Sir James Sandys muttered under his breath, suppressing the desire to cross his legs. Confined within the stuffy interior of the coach, unable to scan the passing countryside, bounced and jounced until his teeth rattled, half-suffocated by that damnable corset, he'd count himself lucky if he was able to stand, let alone draw and fire one of his two pistols, when and if the coach was stopped. The paint so liberally applied to his face itched abominably and the powdered wig sat on his head like a beehive ready to explode. Why had he let Lord Marchwell insist on this idiotic, impossible scheme?

Someone shouted up ahead and the coach lurched, then slowed. Raising his voice in pitch, he called out, "Footman! What's happening?"

"Stay back, m'lady—"

A pistol shot cracked the air ahead. The coach lurched to a halt. Rough voices called out, two, no, three of them and not the best class of men either. James positioned himself by the door, his own weapon still hidden but ready. Each pistol could fire but a single shot, and how he could fight or run or even get down from the coach in a hurry wearing these damnable skirts, he didn't know.

The door flung open. A man's head and shoulders, dark against the watery brightness of the day, appeared. James noted the weatherbeaten skin and a grin that revealed uneven teeth; one badly chipped. The battered felt hat did not bear a feather of any sort. The pistol pointed straight at his heart.

"Good day to you, m'lady." The ruffian swept off his hat with his free hand. "Allow me to introduce myself and my rough companions. I be called Robin Hood, and those two are my merry men."

James suppressed a desire to punch the reddened, bulbous nose. He dared not give himself away, or risk losing his disguise. With a vow to extract many favors from Lord Marchwell, he fluttered one hand to his chest.

"Whatever can you wish with me?"

With another grin, the robber replaced his hat on his head. One grimy hand whipped out and snatched the necklace of red-colored stones from James's neck. "Nothing you'll miss, my pretty miss." He guffawed at his own joke.

The next moment, the robber hauled himself into the coach, grabbed James by the back of the neck, and pulled him close. James felt the wet, hot lips slide over his own mouth. The man's breath smelled as foul as the rest of him.

Anger, red and furnace-hot, spurted through James. All he had to do was reach up and twist the pistol from the man's grasp . . .

And then the true Red Feather would be warned.

He must find some way to endure. For his King. For King and country.

"And a solid handful you are, too!" The man drew back. "Come on, give us another!"

There were limits to what even a king could ask. Tawny brows drew together in warning.

"Harry! Let's go!" Another man's voice called from the road outside.

"Dream of me!" With a final caress, the ruffian departed.

James scrambled to the ground, nearly tripping over the long skirts. The coachman held one upper arm, where blood oozed over his fingers, and the footman, no more than a boy himself, looked ready to faint. James could easily have bound up the coachman's wound, but a lady would not do so. He allowed the dazed footman to help him back into the coach, where he closed his eyes and waited for the fire to drain from his veins. The villains who'd robbed him got only paste gems. They were clumsy, inept. He could have killed all three a dozen times over. They would be caught and hanged. They were not the problem. He must keep his eye on the true target . . .

A week later, the road had grown no smoother, but James was becoming accustomed to the coach's lurching rhythm. He'd been back and forth a dozen times, each time with a different driver and footman. There had been no more robbery attempts, and the trio from that first day were already rotting on the gallows at Byrne. He wondered for the tenth time that afternoon if the Red Feather hadn't somehow been warned of the trap. The skin over his ribs was raw from the rubbing of the bodice stays and the tight high neckline.

For King, he reminded himself as he peered out the window into the gathering gloom. For King and country.

They neared the wood. The trees reached branches lacy with new leaves to the darkening sky. A wet, wild, earthy smell rose from the undergrowth. A hush fell on the earth and even the horses' hooves seemed muffled, expectant. A nightingale called somewhere in the distance, then grew still. Listening, James heard the horses' *clop-clopping* slow.

"Oh, footman!" he called in that voice which was becoming disgustingly familiar. "What's happening? Is anything amiss?"

"Just lighting the lanterns, m'lady."

They went along. James stayed by the window, unable to relax. The skin along his neck prickled.

James caught a sudden burst of hoofbeats on the road ahead, heard the coachman's, "Whoa, easy!" and then words spoken, hushed and urgent. He couldn't make out the words, but there was no disguising the cultured velvet of the voice. He eased himself back on to the seat, arranged his skirts, and waited.

Conversation aloft, the coachman's grating rumble. The coach springs creaked. Then came the patter of the foot man's boots on the road. A familiar silvery thrill shot up his spine. He curled his fingers around the hilt of one pistol.

The handle clicked and the door swung open. This time, no weapon pointed at his heart. He leaned forward, peering into the gloom. By the light of the coach lanterns, he made out a figure of a man in a short, broad cloak and a hat whose jaunty plume glowed like a live ember. Beyond, James glimpsed a second ruffian, aiming two pistols at the coachman and footman. A tall black horse blew through its nostrils and pawed the ground. By the gloss of its coat, it was a finely bred beast.

"Dear lady, have no fear." The voice, so close now, reminded James of honeyed wine. It grated on his nerves and filled him with instant suspicion. How could women trust such a voice? But Lady Carrisford certainly had, so he must pretend.

A gloved hand extended, palm up.

"Oh, sir." He forced himself into the role. "Harm me not, for I am a maid alone."

"The young and innocent at heart have naught to fear from me. Come, will you descend and join your protectors? They fret for your safety."

James placed his hand in the highwayman's and allowed himself to be handed down from the coach. The touch was firm but surprisingly gentle. James wasn't tall, but he looked down upon the other man, caught a glimpse of the straight nose, firm chin, sensitive mouth. Eyes like pools of colorless light glinted back at him from under the shadowed brim of the hat, but James read no malice there, no deceit. Before James could pull away, the villain raised their joined hands to his lips. James felt the touch of that soft warm mouth lingering on his skin, the whisper of a breath. His heart pounded and his mouth turned dry. Something quivered in the pit of his belly.

"A sweet lady, indeed. And a maid by the lack of a golden ring. What thinks your father, to send you traveling alone through this wild country?"

James freed his hand. "You said I had naught to fear from you, bold sir."

"And spoke truth. But I never said your jewels did not run the same risk." The Red Feather held out one hand and gestured. The coachman started to lower his arms but, at a barked command from the second robber, thought better of it.

"And your purse as well."

James reached up to unclasp the paste-pearl necklace. He wondered what would happen if he refused. He did not think the second robber would hesitate to shoot a woman. He could pretend to reach into a hidden pocket and take out his pistol instead, blast the highwayman away and take his own chances, but something held him back. Perhaps it was the kiss, or the twinkle of merriment in those steady gray eyes. He had seen hangings enough to imagine that face congested with blood, the tongue swollen and lolling, the eyes bulging, those legs jerking in their final throes.

There might be another way. This highwayman was no common sort, but a cultured gentleman. If James could bide his time, gain the highwayman's trust, learn his identity and secure his contrite repentance, Lord Marchwell could arrange for restitution instead of hanging.

When the second robber had finished divesting the two servants of their own purses, the Red Feather signaled them to resume their places. James lingered. He wrung his hands, as he had often seen women do, usually when they were trying to convince him of something he didn't want to do.

"Oh, sir!"

"Why, what ails thee, maid?"

"Oh, sir, you have done me most grievous harm! It would be far better to end my poor life as we stand."

Taking a deep breath, James launched into a tale of piteous woe, of a girl threatened with betrothal to a man she detested, of how she had taken the few jewels which were hers by right and fled, hoping to seek shelter with a distant cousin, how without the money for decent passage, she would be left with no alternative but vagrancy and prostitution, death by pox or hanging.

He could see the subtle shift in the highwayman's posture, a tautness here and a softening there.

"By all the saints and sinners, I will help thee." The highwayman pressed the necklace back into James's palm. "Here, take thy inheritance, but know well that it cannot buy protection from thy father's will. Instead, let the coach go on alone so that thy father believes thee dead."

"But what shall I do? Where shall I go?"

Strong gentle fingers tipped James's head down and again he felt the touch of those lips, warm and tingling, this time on his forehead. "All in good time. For now, I swear upon my soul that no harm shall come to thee from me. Will thou come with me now?"

What was happening to him? James had always trusted his impulses, but had never before had his thoughts jumbled together with the unmistakable aching of his body. Ever since he had known the difference, he had been a man for women. But this Red Feather, he who had touched James with no more than a feather brush of lips or fingertips, now sent him into a dizzying spiral of confusion.

Was it lust? Was it love? Was it a curse from God for taking on women's clothing?

Was this what women felt when a man swept them off their feet, even as he had so often done?

The coach had gone on, rattling down the road, its lanterns swaying wildly. The highwayman helped James to mount, sitting sideways across the black horse's back. Then he took the reins and followed his mounted comrade into the night.

They came out of the forest. A moon rose over the hills, painting the world in shades of silver. The sweet, earthy scent sent a reckless music all through James. He no longer knew who he was or what he was. He only knew that he never wanted this night to end. But end it must, and he had duties beyond the calling of his heart. He had an oath to keep.

To King. To country.

Leaving the main road, they followed a track that was no more than a ghostly thread. They stopped before a cluster of buildings, silent and dark, huddled together against an imaginary chill. James made out a ramshackle barn and a house that was more ruin than standing timbers. The highwayman helped James from the saddle and went aside with his comrade.

"Distribute the money as usual. I will meet you at the appointed place."

"What about—" The second ruffian inclined his head to where James stood beside the black horse.

"I will see to her safety. There is a hidden story here,

one she may divulge if she comes to trust me. Good night and Godspeed, old friend."

After the second robber departed, the Red Feather led the black horse to the barn where a weathered door led to a sloping underground passage. James had heard of such hiding places, usually for smuggled goods or safe hiding during Cromwell's time. The horse went down readily, as if accustomed to the enclosed space.

The highwayman held out his hand and led James down the passage and then through a side door. He glanced up and down a passageway. The highwayman pressed the lantern into James's hand.

"There is a room aloft. Wait for me there. I must tend to the horse."

Pulling his skirts away from the cobwebs which draped the corners, James climbed the rickety stairs. No doubt the room would be filthy and riddled with vermin.

But when he reached the top and swung open the door, the lantern showed a narrow chamber with no trace of the industry of spiders. The bare wooden floor was recently swept, the covering of the bed faded but unstained, a simple pitcher and bowl sat upon a table. James put the lantern down and lowered himself to the bed, which creaked and gave off a faint smell of lavender. He slipped out the pistol, cocked it, tucked it within the folds of his skirts, and waited.

But not for a long. A quiet knocking sounded at the door and a hushed voice called out.

"Come in."

James waited until the highwayman, still in his hat and cloak, closed the door behind him and stepped into the room.

"For tonight, rest here in safety. On the morrow, I will arrange for—"

Silver-gray eyes widened as James brought the pistol up.

"In the name of the King, I arrest you on the charge of highway robbery."

"Thou—You are no maid!"

True, he'd used his natural voice. With his free hand, James swept off his wig. He caught a flicker of unreadable emotion on the highwayman's face and his stomach twisted. "Sir James Sandys, royal agent."

"Royal? Is't royal to betray one who risked much to help you?" The voice rose, whetted like a knife.

Loathing every word, yet seeing no other choice, James riposted with the words he had heard so often. "Those who break the King's peace deserve no mercy—"

"Then grant me none!" Such fire behind those words, those blazing eyes. "If I cannot live free, I have no wish to live at all!"

The Red Feather, with a final challenging glare, turned and reached for the door.

James fired.

Whether by instinct or luck, his hand swerved at the last moment. The ball went low and to the side, missing the highwayman's hand by a hair's-breadth. For a horrified instant, each stared at the other.

James threw down the discharged pistol and hurled himself at the Red Feather. The heavy satin skirts tangled his legs. He reached out, falling, and grabbed the highwayman around the knees. They went down in a jumble of flailing arms and legs. Something hard and bony caught James on the side of the head. The world spun, but he kept struggling. An opening appeared, a glimpse of the clean fine line of the ruffian's jaw. James connected with a hard quick punch. The highwayman's head snapped back and his hat went flying.

James hauled himself upright, pinning the other man's legs under his own, and drew back for another punch. His fist froze. The hat gone, a tumble of glossy black hair spread across the bare floor. The cloak had been thrown back, and the form revealed under the ruffled shirt was much too sweetly rounded to be a man's.

Silvery eyes met his own.

"I know you now," came a voice which, though low, was unmistakably a woman's. "From Lord Marchwell's ball. The hotspur who thought so much of himself. I remember praying heaven bless any maid who loses her heart to such a one."

"Lady—Lady Elinor?" James scrambled to his feet.

The lady in question held out her hand and allowed herself to be helped up. She rubbed her jaw and regarded him sideways with those light-filled eyes.

"What—why—?"

"Why take to such a lawless path? What desperation drove me when I had everything a woman could desire—wealth, breeding, and a suitably noble and utterly repulsive suitor? Oh, yes, once I was willing enough to marry at my family's behest, to be a dutiful wife to a husband who would care for me in return. Well! You have seen Lord Baldridge, three wives buried now and ten children, too! 'Tis said they died of a pox he caught from a French whore."

"Why," James repeated in a quieter voice, "why this? Why risk hanging?"

"Because at least it would be my own fate! Or if I be pardoned, no man of my father's choosing would have me to wife. Certainly not His Lordship!" She paused, chest heaving, then grew calm.

"Alas, the adventure is finished now. Would't please you to exchange clothing before you take me to be hanged? I fear your own reputation will suffer a great deal more than mine were we to appear as we are in public."

After a few awkward moments, backs turned to each other, they managed the change. James pulled off the loathsome, constricting dress. Elinor's shirt with its ample gathering fit comfortably, although the breeches were loose and the cuffed riding boots too tight. The fabric was still warm from her body and carried the faint clean scent of lavender.

He turned around, for a moment stunned. Her body filled the satin dress in ways that sent his heart pounding, but there was nothing of submission or duty in her eyes. She held her head proudly, her hair falling over her shoulders like an ebony mantle.

Any prince, he thought, would kneel at her feet.

And a woman who could fool even him, who could ride and shoot with the best one moment and carry herself with such poise the next . . .

Scrambled wits suddenly came clear. James bowed to her in homage and lifted her hand to his lips. "To hang such beauty and such courage would be a waste."

"What should I do then?" Elinor cried, pulling away as if he'd stung her. "Take to the road, a penniless vagrant? Return home in disgrace, to be locked in the farthest tower until the moon falls into the sea? Far better to hang and be done!"

"Join me. Use your gifts in service of the King and England."

She blinked in surprise as he explained. He knew he was taking a terrible risk, placing his identity, his very life in her hands. But as he asked her to trust him, he must offer trust in return. It would take some convincing to arrange matters with Lord Marchwell, but James had never before asked for any special consideration or appealed to the gratitude of the Crown for his years of service. He made no promises to Elinor now, no protestations of undying love. He told her everything about his mission to France, and nothing of what lay in his heart.

After he finished, a long moment of silence passed between them. Silvery eyes regarded him evenly, measuring him. In them, he saw a mirror of himself.

A month ago, James would have taken her into his arms simply because she was beautiful and he wanted her. He would have thought nothing more of it. Now, as if emblazoned in fire in those steady gray eyes, he saw the unspoken cost. One false move and he would be no different from the rogue on the highway, or her father, or that philandering idiot Baldridge. She would never look at him this way again.

He waited, for the choice was as much a test of his honor as it was of her courage.

"My lord, your offer seems to me both bold and generous." She granted him a swift, flashing smile, like a shared secret. "Shall we go forth together, then, as knights of old to do battle with the French for England and St. George?"

He took her hand again, but did not lift it to his lips. Her fingers closed around his, direct and firm. Something bright and singing soared inside him. As for the rest . . .

He would leave that adventure for the future.

danForth©96

# A SLIGHT DETOUR ON THE ROAD TO HAPPYLAND

## *by Ashley McConnell*

Ashley McConnell's most recent novels comprise a trilogy: *The Fountains of Mirlacca, The Intinerent Exorcist,* and *Courts Of Sorcery.* She's also the author of several of the Quantum Leap books as well as *Scimitar,* a novel set in the Highlander universe, and contributed a short story to *The Ultimate X-Men.* But the story to follow is unlike any of those worlds. It's a bizarre but highly entertaining contempory tale of futuristic possibilities, the interstate freeway system, orange barrel men, and conspiracies. Ashley says she spent four years in Nevada but never stopped to talk to the highwaymen. As you'll see in this story, that was definitely her loss!

Three o'clock in the morning, ninety-four degrees, twenty minutes to get to the airport. And orange barrels.

Not gonna make it.

Summertime in Las Vegas, they do road work at night. It's too damn hot to do it during the day. Even though it never seems to get below miserable, at least at night you don't get the glare from the sun on white concrete and white sand.

So I see the barrels—waist-high, horizontal orange-and-white stripes, little reflectors on top of about half of them—and I stomp on the brake and slow down. And keep slowing down, as the lane between them narrows and turns. Nobody's out working. Only a few yards of concrete have been broken up, but there're a couple of hundred barrels out there off the highway.

So I'm nearly at a dead stop when I finally see somebody wearing a yellow hard hat, waving his hands around right in front of me. I'm trying to negotiate a particularly awkward corner, using language that a lady shouldn't, so for a moment I can't see where he's popped up from.

"Popped up" is the right word for it; he's actually inside one of the orange barrels.

I stand on the brakes and give up any notion of getting to my plane on time.

He looked hot, she thought, in more ways than one. He was wearing jeans and a denim vest with no shirt, but it wasn't enough. Long dark hair, however luxurious, wasn't the best choice for Nevada in August; he yanked off the hard hat and ran one hand through the heavy mass. The full moon glistened in the sweat on his forehead. He had a neatly trimmed mustache and short beard, large dark eyes, heavy brows, a high forehead.

And a gun in his other hand, she noted. Wryly, because it was obvious by the way he waved it around that he hadn't the first clue about how to use it and was more than a little nervous. That made her nervous too. All she needed was some idiot—

He put his hands on the rim of the orange-and-white barrel and lifted himself out, moving too quickly for the heat. She couldn't see how he'd managed with the gun. It didn't seem important just now.

He was saying something she couldn't quite hear. She shrugged and calculated her chances of reversing out of the maze; not good, but her hand crept to the gearshift anyway. He saw it, and suddenly the gun was pointed more or less at her head, from less than three feet away.

The odds were not, as Jimmy the Greek had been fond of saying, good.

He was jerking the weapon around awkwardly, telling her to get out of the car, and abruptly the situation proceeded from merely annoying, straight through silly and directly into terrifying. This was one of the empty stretches of desert in between developed areas; blank, pale desert, spotted only by patches of dried-up weeds, black in the moonlight. The sound of gunfire would carry, but the occupants of the houses a mile to the south weren't likely to wake up at this hour unless the bullet smashed a window. They'd just ignore screams, huddle deeper into the air-conditioning and tell themselves it was a trick of the wind, nothing to get worked up about, nothing to go check about, nothing to worry about . . . Just another big winner celebrating. . . .

* * *

"Are you going to actually *use* that thing, or are you just waving it around to make sure I know how big it is?" I can't quite believe the words falling out of my own mouth, but these things happen from time to time. Rarely, fortunately.

"Uh—" The gun actually droops. If there were light enough to tell, I'd bet that he's blushing. "Oh, hell. This isn't going to happen, is it?"

He's got an English accent. That makes me believe it; there's something about that accent, so no matter how vile the actual words are, one always expects them to be accompanied by an offer for more tea. And it doesn't matter whether it's the BBC version or Geordie or Liverpool or the deepest slums of London; it's an *English* accent, and for some incomprehensible reason it always sounds elegant and cultured and faintly apologetic to American ears. Well, except when it whines, of course, but this guy isn't whining. If anything, he's despairing. The tone goes well with drooping. And his particular version of the Queen's is elegant, cultured, and completely at odds with his appearance and situation.

"I sincerely hope not," I say, with as much tartness as I could muster. "What on earth were you thinking?"

His name was David, David Wiscomb. His was a sad tale, but not uncommon; he'd lost everything, had no way to get home. "Not a nubbin," as he put it. In this case he'd lost it in a burglary of his hotel room rather than at the tables, which made a nice change of pace. For various reasons he preferred not to go into, he had no one he could call upon for a loan, and so had decided to cast his fate to the winds, or at least the highway. The gun had given him the idea, in fact; he'd found the damned thing.

"And it never occured to you that there might be something a trifle *odd* about finding a gun just lying around on the ground in the middle of Las Vegas? Is the damn thing loaded?"

He winces. "Ah, I don't really know."

I look at the dashboard clock. Three-thirty. Above us, planes lift over the lights of the city, heading east, west, south, north. My plane is one of them. I am irretrievably late for work. I need to find something else to do with my day.

"Oh, for heaven's sake. Give me that."

The idiot offers the weapon barrel first, which convinces me (as if I still needed convincing) that he's either an utter innocent or has spent far too much time in the noonday sun. I push it to one side and removed it gingerly from his hand. It's a revolver, a S&W 686 with a four-inch barrel to be exact, and sure enough, the chamber holds three bullets. I really don't want to know where the other three might be, any more than I want to think about the fact that we now have our fingerprints all over it.

"I really am terribly sorry," he says, watching me. I look up at him and for a second our eyes meet. The realization that my highwayman manque has just handed over his holdup gun to his proposed victim, and the roulette wheel has come up double zero, dawns on us at the same time. If we'd been playing another game, he'd have crapped out.

His eyes are large and dark in the moonlight. He swallows visibly and closes them, giving every impression of nobly awaiting his fate.

What the hell. I've already missed my plane. And I'm still shaking, a little, from the scare he'd given me in the first place. It's his turn to suffer a while.

"Get in the car."

The large dark eyes pop open again. "Huh?"

It sounds every bit as inelegant in Oxfordian as in Nevadan.

"Get in the car," I repeat, waving the revolver in a meaningful fashion. Unlike my failed criminal, I know what I'm doing, and it shows. The part that didn't show, of course, and which he seems to be completely blind to, is my removal of those pesky cartridges.

"Are you going to—to turn me in?" He sounds as if that wouldn't be the worst thing that could happen to him. He's right, as it happens.

"No such luck, sweetie."

He slides in beside me, shutting the door and leaning back against it to put as much room as humanly possible between himself and the gun he'd just threatened me with. "Where, then?"

"We're going where all good visitors to Sin City go," I inform him, keeping the gun trained on him with one hand shifting gears with the other, and steering with my knees. They train us to be ambidextrous, where I come from.

He dabs at the skin above his mustache and swallows again. I snickered to myself. Payback's a bitch.

Did I mention that's my last name? Payback. Amanda Payback. I *love* living up to my name.

The red convertible swept past the valet stand and into the parking garage, pausing only to pick up an automated ticket. She slid the gun into her purse, smiling at him as she did so. "Have I mentioned I can pull the trigger by squeezing the purse in just the right place?" she inquired. "And trust me, I do know the right place to squeeze. Get out of the car."

"You're mad," he said, as if making a momentous discovery.

"Only nor'norwest. Hawks. Handsaws. You know the drill. Stay close. You really, really don't want me to get lonely."

He nodded quickly, lifted himself out of the car, and paused, long fingers wrapped around the top of the door, as if thinking about running away. By the time he had glanced over his shoulder, measuring the distance between himself and the casino entrance, she had exited the car, slammed the door, smoothed down her long skirt, and waved him onward.

A cluster of Japanese tourists, festooned with cameras, exited as they approached. "Bow," she said through clenched teeth, following her own advice.

The tourists bowed back, several of them unlimbering their cameras to take pictures of the parking garage and the friendly *gaijin* they had met therein. She smiled and bowed again, herding her prisoner past the line. He glanced at them desperately, clearing his throat.

"Don't bother," she advised.

His shoulders slumped a little as they marched down the hallway toward the fluorescent lights and the chime of coins striking stainless steel.

They passed row upon row of display windows filled with jewelry, furs, tacky souvenirs, all perfectly designed to lure in those who managed to avoid the siren song of metal upon metal and the cries of winners; set perfectly to muffle the sobs of losers. And there were always losers, of course; the house always took its percentage.

*Well, perhaps not always,* I think smugly. The poor man walks onward, helpless without understanding why. He has a nice walk. Nice butt, too.

He pauses at the entrance to the casino, uncertain of what I want him to do next. There are multiple possibilities, but we're in public, so I dig into the purse, feeling my way around the bulk of the gun for the change in the bottom, fingering out five quarters.

"Video slots," I tell him, indicating with the loaded purse.

He looked at her for a moment. He did have dark eyes, clear crystal brown, vivid against the pale skin as the dark, heavy eyebrows, neatly trimmed mustache and beard were vivid. The long-discarded hard hat had left dents in his hair, and there was a red mark on his right cheekbone she hadn't noticed before. But his hair was clean, and the vest was only slightly grubby, and with any kind of luck they could get in and out again before hotel security decided no shirt, no shoes, no service.

"Video slots," she repeated, holding out the coins.

He closed his eyes and shook his head slightly, as if denying that any of this could possibly be happening. "You seem like such a nice person."

"You have no idea how wrong you are," she responded promptly. "Go. The machine on the end."

"And after I lose them, then what?" he grumbled, but she lifted her purse and he moved off obediently to take the empty stool in front of the poker machine. "One at a time, or can we get this over with all at once?"

She paused, as if considering. "Well, it's not as if I'm in a hurry."

He nodded, fed one quarter into the machine, and tapped the Play button. "I thought you were. Considering how you were driving."

"I was *trying* to get to work."

A pair of jacks; he got his quarter back and arched an eyebrow to her. "Unusual shift. And you're not trying to get to work anymore." He put the quarter into the machine and waited.

"Plane's gone by now," she said absently, reaching past him to hit the Play button. "No point."

"You fly to work?" He sounded politely incredulous as only the English can.

She glanced at him quickly, then smiled. "You'd be surprised how many people do."

Four of a kind. He stared at the quarters clattering into the metal bowl. "Good God," he remarked. "That's never happened before."

"You must have really lousy luck, then." She picked up one of the quarters, paused. "How far from home are you?"

He smiled wryly. "Farther than twenty dollars. How about you?"

"*Lots* farther. Still, if you get a nice supersaver fare, maybe a discount, it might get you as far as New York." She picked up one of the quarters and fed it in again. Once more, four of a kind.

His lip curled.

"I take it you don't live in New York."

"Please!" He was scandalized at the very thought.

"Thank you." This time she fed in two quarters.

"Why does it keep coming up four of a kind?"

"Because it likes you?"

He looks at me as if I've lost my mind, and picking up a fistful of quarters, stuffs them into the slot and punches the Play button. He loses, of course. All the handsome boys are lost without me, but none of them seems to figure that out. You never get brains and looks in the same package. Never, never, never. Talk about crummy luck.

At least he seems to have forgotten about the gun, which is nice; what, he thought I was going to pull it out and shoot him down in the middle of a casino? Granted, it's as empty as casinos ever get at this hour, but that just means the security guys are looking for reasons not to be bored. I'm surprised there aren't more of them around. I let him put in more coins, rest my hand against the machine. He wins. Again. And again. Never too big, of course.

He's beginning to look at me strangely. I take my hand away, surreptitiously rubbing away the feel of the electricity, and let him lose a couple of times.

I'm a little jumpy, too. Any minute now he's going to

ask me why I brought him here. What am I supposed to tell him, that I feel sorry for him, lust after his accent, and want to help him out? As a holdup man, he's a complete klutz.

Hey, I'm no mud fence myself, you know—deduct intelligence accordingly. I just know all about wanting to go home, okay?

Besides, it isn't as if I have anything else to do today. I'll call in later on, let the worryworts up north know I'm all right. It's a little late to regret this particular impulse.

Down the row of machines from us, a little old lady with blue hair, wearing lavender tights and an extra-large flowered blouse, hunches over the row of buttons, gnarled fingers hovering over the Holds. I eye her suspiciously. A whole empty casino, and she has to pick this row?

"Maybe we ought to change machines," I say. "You broke the luck."

"I never had any luck," he answers. The words are strangely at odds with his tone; he sounds brisk, cheerful. British. Best of British luck. Wasn't that what they said?

The little old lady touches the Hold buttons, withdraws her hand, and then touches them again, as if uncertain. Hasn't she ever played video poker before?

I blink. My perspective is shifting in and out again, as if I'm looking through my own eyes one moment and from somewhere up over my head the next. Unnerving, it is, jumping around like that. In shift, out of shift, in perspective and out again. I don't usually tell people about it; it's considered very poor form, going back and forth that way. Happens to me a lot though. Occupational hazard, they tell me, though how they'd know is beyond me.

"Won't your boss be rather annoyed at you, missing work this way?" my captive inquires.

"It's not like it's my fault," I respond absentmindedly. The little old blue-haired lady is fumbling around in the cardboard tub the casino provides for your winnings. She should be rattling around, finding more quarters to stuff into the machine. Her pale gnarled fingers, dripping with widow's rings, should be making a whispery little chime through the coins. Maybe she has arthritis? That would make it difficult to grasp them. Slippery, slender little things, coins.

* * *

Of course, the pearl inlay on the butt of an automatic presents no difficulty at all. As she pulls it out, I observe two things: first, that the light catches the silver barrel and the diamond rings with equal brightness; and second, that *she* doesn't seem to have any compunction at all about shooting people in the middle of a nearly deserted casino.

Maybe she knows someone on staff.

Maybe my boss is more annoyed about my being late than I thought.

I yelp, push frantically at my captive Englishman, and dodge back, trying to confuse the shooter.

He's substantial, in addition to having a cute butt, and doesn't shove well.

"Hey!" he said, staggering between two machines and hitting the Play button as he did so. The display chuckled to itself and blinked, the cards flipping over one by one as he tried to unwedge himself. "What the devil—"

Amanda was halfway down the aisle between the rows of machines, dodging back and forth in an odd, erratic dance toward the woman at the other end. A sudden explosion over his left shoulder made him duck down, cursing.

The crazy woman had bowled over someone's grandmother and was now wrestling with her. It occured to him briefly that he could run, but Amanda was pinning the grandmother to the floor, pounding her arm. The older woman wasn't screaming, but the poor thing was probably in shock. He had to admit to a certain sympathy.

"Have you gone utterly mad?" He grabbed her shoulders, pulling her away, and for a moment she looked back at him, her green eyes feral, her teeth skinned back.

He couldn't meet that glare; he looked away and down and saw the gun in the old woman's hand. Completely confused, he looked from the weapon to the woman's face, and failed to see the expected expression of helpless terror. Instead, he saw white powder, coral color smeared over tightly pressed wrinkled lips, and hard, glittering blue eyes. With a startled squawk he overbalanced, toppling over them both.

With a shriek of rage Amanda lost her grip on the other woman's arm. The "grandmother" shed several decades, squirming out from under the two of them, but the gun went spinning under the video poker machines; she staggered to her feet, cursed, and fled around the corner and out of sight.

"I don't suppose you'd care to explain that?" David gasped.

Amanda twisted up and to her feet. "Come on. Where there's one, there's probably more."

"More what? Crazed blue-haired grannies?"

"Crazed blue-haired grannies *with guns,*" she reminded him, looking up and down the aisle. "Damn. I can't see *anything* in here."

"I'm surprised we haven't been surrounded by security," he commented, standing on tiptoe to see over the machines. There was nothing there; the cashier's cage in the middle of the forest of slot machines was unoccupied, the blackjack, baccarat, poker, and craps tables were all forlorn. Shoes lay askew on green felt, cards spilling out; the roulette wheels were still.

"Where's the noise coming from?" he asked, straining to see. "This is bizarre."

It was true. The ghostly sounds of dice against wood, the soft slap of cards, the crank of one-armed bandit levers, even the chill, impersonal music of coins falling into metal basins still echoed against the high ceiling.

"Oh, absolutely. Will you *come on*?" She spun around, grabbing at his arm.

"Oh, no," he said. "No way. No thank you. I want to be as far away from you as I can possibly get."

"Don't be stupid. Where there's one, there's more. Always. They come in teams."

"Then they're coming after you, not me. Have a nice life. Remember to duck." He started to pull away.

"I told you *don't be stupid.* You're with *me.* They're going to be after you, too." She pawed at her shoulder, looked around frantically, and discovered her purse lying on the floor. "Look, you're safer with me. Besides, I've got a gun."

"There's something inherently illogical about all this," he observed, allowing her to hustle him to the end of the row of machines. Pushing him behind her, she peered around before scuttling across the open aisle.

"And who was it who was jumping out of orange barrels an hour ago?" she snapped. "It looks clear. Come on."

They ran through the abandoned mall, away from the

ghostly sounds of gambling, and down the empty hall to the parking garage.

"Look," he said as they raced through the garage, "if this is just a very bad dream, I'd like to wake up now."

Shots rang out. He yelped and slipped on a grease spot, and a chip of concrete sliced across his face. "My God, they're shooting at us!"

"No, *really?*" She was on her belly, peering under cars, her purse stretched out straight in front of her as she sighted along the clasp at a pair of running legs. He watched, appalled, as she squeezed, and fire spat out. "Damn. Another purse ruined. And I didn't even hit him."

A large hole rimmed in smoldering leather had replaced one side of the purse.

"Someone could get *hurt,*" he protested.

"You already have been," she pointed out, rolling into a crouch. "And you're a mess, too. C'mon."

"Please. Couldn't you just *explain* all this?"

"This is not a particularly good time for explanations. Let's just say my boss has a really strict tardiness policy, which makes this all your fault, really." She grinned, a startling flash of white teeth against tanned skin and dark hair. "I love it when I can blame someone else for a change."

"I'm sure you always have a lot of candidates," he said, following her at a stumbling run to the little white car. The blood was running freely down his face, collecting in his mustache and beard and dripping on the denim vest. He wiped at it, a useless gesture that merely got it all over his hand. "Christ, all I wanted was enough to get home!"

"That'll teach you to hold people up, won't it? Crime Does Not Pay," she announced sententiously, sliding across the passenger seat and into the driver's. "Come on." When he hesitated, his hand on the door handle, she added, more softly, "Look, they're going to shoot first and ask questions later. You're safer with me than you are doing a duck imitation sitting in a barrel on the highway."

"That's debatable." But he got in, pushing the seat back and lying nearly flat beside her.

"I think you'd better fasten your seat belt," she advised, the softness gone from her voice again. "Things are going to happen fast as soon as I turn over the engine."

* * *

Things happen very fast. I turn the key. Men in dark suits and sunglasses—sunglasses! at night! in a parking garage!—appear all over the place like cockroaches pouring out of the woodwork. Coming behind them, limping and snarling ferociously, is the little blue-haired granny, brandishing her gun and shouting, "Don't let them get away!"

Poor David. He's scared rigid, his hands knotted into fists at his sides, his eyes closed. His beard is very dark against his pale skin. All he ever wanted to do was hold up somebody, get enough money to go very far away—fly across a continent and an ocean, and disappear into a seething mass of people who didn't talk funny. I really can sympathize.

I corner hard, the tires shrieking, and barely miss one of the dark-clad men. Another is standing directly in our path, in a textbook stance, using both hands on the gun. The nitwit doesn't believe I'm going to run him down.

If I were going to run anyone down this godforsaken morning, it should have been David. I'd have been at work now, in the middle of the empty Nevada desert, and some kind soul would have *told* me we were all blown. But noooo. I had to find another stray cat and try to help him out.

All right, I ran him down. He was going to shoot at me. It's self-defense. The jolt as the body flips over the hood and the man clutches briefly at the windshield nearly sends us into the wall. Then the man is gone and we're accelerating up the ramp, through the barrier to a slowly brightening sky, with a fusillade of shots to send us on our way.

Beside me David is keening quietly. I'm right; he's a Celt.

We slow down, blend into traffic on the Strip. It isn't heavy yet, but as far as I can tell they haven't mobilized. They were too sure, once they spotted me in the casino, that they could pick me off there. Their mistake. I let out a long unsteady breath.

Beside me, David sits up, raises the seat back to the upright position and looks around, cautiously.

"If it isn't too personal a question," he says hesitantly, "why are those people shooting at you?"

Poor soul. They'd probably ID'd him as one of us now. He was going to spend the rest of *his* life running and hiding and trying to blend in. With that accent, he hadn't a hope.

"Shooting at *us*," I correct him, running a yellow light

and heading toward the back highways. It's a long way up north when you drive; good thing the gas tank is full. "Were you in a really *big* hurry to get home?"

"Am I being given a choice?"

I shrug.

"I see." A pause. "And something else," he adds.

We're getting to the edge of town now, beginning to get caught up in the rush hour traffic of all the people who work out at the Nevada Test Site. All right, so it wouldn't impress anybody from Los Angeles, but for an apparently empty chunk of desert, there's an amazing amount of activity.

Nevada is deceptive that way.

"What else?" I ask patiently. The poor boy is clearly having some problems with the whole experience. Well, I can understand that.

He remains silent for a long time, long enough that we pass the little Air Force station at Indian Springs and come up on the Mercury turnoff. "I always won when you touched the machines. Every time. Why is that?"

Oh, dear. Perhaps there *are* some brains in this package. "Would you believe coincidence?"

"No, I wouldn't. You did that on purpose. You were controlling it somehow. Weren't you?" The last two words are unnervingly certain.

"Absolutely. And all those men in black were casino security. You think that's bad, you should see what they do to card counters."

He sits back against the door, looking at me. He's beginning to relax a bit. We pass Mercury, the front door to the Nevada Test Site, and the road narrows and traffic drops off. It's just us, now, for the time being, except that there aren't that many routes where we're going, and it's not that tough to cover them. People can pop up anywhere.

I blink. Things are shifting on me again. Perspective, again. Nothing is as it seems.

"At least I got the right one," he says.

Amanda's foot comes off the accelerator and the car begins to slow. The sun is fully up now, and a shimmer of heat is beginning to rise from the asphalt.

* * *

"David," I ask gently, "are you wearing a tracer?"

David laughs.

"You never did say where you work," he observes. "Or what kind of work you do." The car comes to a stop. "Or why your boss is so cranky about your being late."

"Oh, come now," I respond. "This is Nevada. I can't answer those questions; I'd have to kill you."

"Like Grandma was going to? What did you do, show up at the wrong place?" The crystal clear brown eyes are very steady now.

"I have a feeling I showed up exactly where I was expected to." I'm beginning to feel defeated. "Whose side are *you* on, David?"

He smiles. He has a very nice smile.

I look up the long empty road, the highway that stretches almost forever, branches at Tonopah and dives back into the secret places, the hidden nonexistent places lost in the high Nevada desert. The places where we go to work. To hide. The places even the men in black, even the UFO buffs and the TV shows don't know about. Or at least they're not supposed to know about. Not Dreamland; Happyland. "Is there any point in going on?" I ask, beginning to feel shock. When all this started out this morning, and I thought I was being held up, I'd been afraid. When the actual shooting started, I was too busy to be afraid. Now . . . now I'm not sure how I feel. I'm not able to grasp the idea—it's not just me. We're all blown. "Is there anything left to go to?"

The smile is gone, replaced with sadness. "No."

"I'm alone, is that it? Except for Grandma?" Grandma and her pearl-handled automatic.

"And me."

I stare at him. Poor tapped-out Brit, just happens to be sitting in an orange barrel at three o'clock in the morning waiting for someone passing by. Someone driving a back road to the airport to catch an anonymous plane that takes off from a shabby little hangar. "Stand and deliver."

I am an idiot.

"There are people who'd sell this story to Hollywood and make a fortune," I say slowly.

"Don't be silly. Nobody would believe it." It amuses him, but not that much. He brushes at the drying blood on his face, scrubs the brown flakes out of his beard, and looks at them with distaste. "I don't suppose you have any aspirin."

"It doesn't work on me."

"Of course not. Silly of me." He scrubs harder.

"Are you one of them or one of us?" That was what it boiled down to. Whose side?

He smiles. "There's always the third alternative."

"You are bizarre, you know that?"

One elegant eyebrow rises high. "Excuse me? *I'm* not the alien."

"I was born here!"

He nods. "I know. And if we're very lucky, perhaps you have some kin remaining."

"But not at Happyland."

"Alas, probably not."

I nod slowly, put my foot back on the accelerator. The car speeds up.

"Where are we going?" he says comfortably.

"If I told you, I'd have to kill you."

He smiles.

It was nine o'clock in the morning and a hundred and six degrees when the red convertible reached the place the road branched. One branch led to test ranges, places alien hunters called the Nellis ranges and Area 51 and TTR. The other led to cities and dreams. She looked over at her passenger, shaded now that the convertible top had been pulled over. He was napping, perfectly happy no matter which choice she made. No matter which way she went, he was going to stay with her. No matter what trouble she brought him into.

And as yet she had no idea why.

Interesting perspective.

danforth96©

# THOUGH HELL SHOULD BAR THE WAY

## by A.C. Crispin and Christie Golden

Apart, A.C. Crispin and Christie Golden are successful short fiction authors and novelists with twenty-three novels and twenty-one short stories to their credit. Ann Crispin is best known for her *Star Trek* books and her own *StarBridge* series; she has also collaborated with Grandmaster Andre Norton on several novels, and is now working on a *Star Wars* trilogy featuring Han Solo. Christie's most recent novels are *Instrument of Fate* and *King's Man and Thief,* set in her Verold universe; she has also written *Star Trek* and game-based novels. Together they have conspired to present us with a wonderfully imaginative sequel to Alfred Noyes' inspiring poem "The Highwayman."

Mist . . .

Mist it was, insubstantial and barely seen . . . mist that arose above a mound of weedy, winter-blighted grass, hesitating beside the iron-barred fence. Inside lay the kirkyard proper, hallowed ground where headstones bore mute testimony that this one or that had once lived, once loved . . . once died.

Mist it was. Wispy white in the light of the silver crescent moon, incorporeal as smoke . . . Feeble, drifting Awareness awakened, Awareness struggling to survive, to grow stronger, to Know.

*What am I? How and why did I come here?*

The mist moved, in response to a barely sensed need. It flowed onto a ribbon of moon-washed road, gaining strength, coherence, identity.

*I am . . . I . . . was. Was. Dead now, but was . . . I must . . .* Must what?

Unknown. Despite the cold, brutal wind that assaulted it, the mist thickened, steadied. Now it had Substance.

It? No, not *it. She* had substance.

Knowing her sex brought a moment of pride, and in-cluded a vision of herself. A woman, wearing a rust-colorec dress, white apron. Long black hair, wound with a rec ribbon . . . a ribbon tied in a love-knot as crimson as blood

Memory supplied a face . . . large, coal-dark eyes, strong jaw. There was beauty, yes, tempered and honed by strength, and love.

The cold ribbon of road led her, drifting over frozer slush bearing the marks of hooves and wagon wheels, to a town. She knew, somehow, that she should know it. Here a baker's shop, closed and still, about which the aroma o bread still clung. There, a tavern that serviced the garrison that topped the hill.

*Baker. Tavern. I know these things. I. Know.*

The building by the tavern drew her. No sign, only a candle guttering in a hanging globe of red glass. Memory supplied distaste for what transpired within, but she found herself at the window, experiencing a moment's distress a her fingers went *through* the solid pane. Peering inside, she found that, despite the whorls in the thick, greenish glass she could see and hear clearly.

Laughter, drunken singing, and off-key music from a fif and a pennywhistle. Women dressed in chemises and robes their breasts spilling free from their bodices, their hai hanging lank, laughed shrilly as they sat in the laps of me who had discarded their uniform jackets and weapons, an sometimes even their breeches.

*Why?* the watcher wondered. *Why here?* Yet, disguste as she was, she could not move.

Then she saw him. A man, sitting in the corner by th fire. Hate flowed into her, hot as the flames. She wasn sure how, but she knew him. Iron-colored hair, tied bac with a ribbon. Pale, thin features, though a flush of colc stained his cheekbones, and his eyes glittered feverishly. A woman clad only in a scanty chemise brought him a pewte mug, laughing as she handed it to him. Fear and loathin washed through the observer at the window. *Why? Wh him? What is he—or was he—to me?*

The blowsy woman giggled as the man guzzled. "Thirst tonight, ain't we, Captain?" The man nodded and shivere pulling his red coat with its shining buttons and fringe epaulets close. "Sure you wouldn't like a nip of somethin warmer?" she cooed, cupping her barely covered breasts

The officer guffawed, but the laugh turned into a wheeze. He coughed, burying his face in a handkerchief. The whore backed away from him, eyes wide. When he took the white linen away from his lips, it was spattered with red.

The watcher's full lips curved in a cruel smile. *If I could drink, brave Captain, I'd drink to your death. May it be long and painful and but a taste of the hell you are bound for!*

She still did not know *why* her curse was merited, but she had no doubt that it was.

Turning away from the tavern, she headed up the street, misty feet barely touching the cobblestones. A soldier on his way back to the garrison staggered into her, then *through her,* without ever seeing her, leaving her saddened, but not really surprised. By now she knew that she was a ghost.

Barely glancing at the surrounding buildings, she drifted on, drawn by her unknown goal. A large, half-timbered structure loomed before her in the moonlight. She slowed, stopped, and gazed up at the creaking sign.

The Black Mare. Beneath the words, a black horse pranced on the whitewashed wood. She blinked, confused. No, that was wrong, it wasn't The Black Mare, the name of the inn, was . . . was . . .

The White Swan.

With a choked sob, she fell, crumpling into the snow without marring its virgin drifts, or feeling the cold. Sobbing, incorporeal tears pouring down transparent cheeks, she *remembered* . . . remembered the inn, remembered . . .

Names.

*Father. Jamie. Bess.*

She was Bess, the landlord's daughter, and she had stood at that window to watch her beloved Jamie come riding, riding up to the old inn door. He'd promised to come to her, the dashing highwayman, with his pistol butts gleaming in the liquid moonlight, though hell should bar the way.

*Jamie. Bess.*

And hell had come, in the form of King George's soldiers, and—and—

"Oh, merciful God," she wept, now remembering what had happened on that night, the iron hardness of a muzzle pressing the warm flesh of her breast. Now she knew *why* she not been allowed to rest in hallowed ground.

* * *

"Are you certain you can't go on?" Lieutenant Robert Larrimer asked his wife.

Anna, pale, rubbed her swollen belly and nodded, just as the carriage gave a particularly savage lurch. "I'm sorry, my love, but the jouncing . . ." She bit her lip, then, and gasped. "Oh! A cramp, Robert!"

"Birth pangs?" he demanded, frightened. Anna was more than a month from her time.

"I don't think so. But . . . I must stop! Please, Robert!"

He nodded, and leaned out to shout to the coachman. Truth be told, he had hoped they wouldn't have to stop here. They had neither relatives nor friends in the vicinity, and that meant they must stop at a public lodging-place.

There was only one inn in this little northern town—and that place held only bitter memory for him. He gazed anxiously at Anna, who sat braced against the bumps, one hand pressed to her belly, the other grasping the locket with both their pictures that she wore strung on a crimson ribbon. Larrimer's heart swelled with love . . . they had been wed barely a year. He would rather be tormented by memories than see her suffer, or risk their child.

Anna knew nothing of the . . . incident, in fact had wed him after his request for a transfer to another unit had been granted. He didn't want her to find out. Perhaps no one would recognize him.

Larrimer licked lips suddenly gone dry, and shivered despite the cape he wore over his red coat with its bright buttons.

Dawn came, and cock-crow. Bess expected to vanish—wasn't that something that ghosts always did at sunrise?—but she remained.

Her memories had returned, but she still had no idea why she was here, what she must do. Her control over her movements and form was better, now, and she could see herself, even feel herself. She watched the inn, saw a slatternly girl come out to empty slops, and a brawny middle-aged cook bustling about. Tasks that she herself had done when alive. But where was her father? Drifting, she entered the inn and glided through the rooms, familiar, yes, but strangely altered, and not for the better. Dust lay in the corners of the furniture, and dirt and cobwebs had invaded every corner. The floor appeared not to have been swept for a fortnight or more. Bess tried to pick up her old broom from its corner, but, of course, her misty hands could not grasp a solid object.

She drifted past the room where she had died, and, after a single hasty glance, averted her eyes. A dark stain still marred the floorboards before the window.

In her father's room, a man slept in the bed. Not her father. Bess stared in horror at the white face, the closed eyes that mercifully hid the dark, mad gaze of Tim Alcott, the ostler.

Tim was master of the inn now? How could that be? Tim was half-mad, and nigh simple. He was also dumb as a beast. In all the times he'd trailed about after her in life, gazing at her with smoldering eyes, Bess had never heard Tim utter a single word.

Tim stirred, rolled over, groaned, then sat up and cursed, stretching out a kink in his back. *He can speak! Sweet Jesu, what has happened here?*

Determined to leave this place that brought only pain, Bess headed for the street. But she could not leave, she discovered. Some unseen force held her in the vicinity of the inn, and it would not grant her the peace of her unconsecrated grave.

Back in the courtyard, Bess "sat" upon the mounting block, gazing at her surroundings, utterly bewildered. Why was she held here? Who had summoned her? What was she supposed to do?

Memories . . . memories filled her, though she tried to push them away. Jamie, her Jamie, had stood upon this mounting block. He had tethered his horse over there. Over there, in the shadow of the bayberry bush, he had kissed her, long and sweet. Tears filled her eyes.

*Jamie. Oh, my love. I hope you made a clean escape. I hope it was worth it.*

Perhaps that was why she was here. She was a suicide, albeit a suicide in a noble cause—to save the life of the man she loved. Perhaps she had to make atonement, or somesuch?

She wondered what day it was, what year it was, and then she realized, with a jolt, that it was already early afternoon. The light had changed, become robust and golden instead of thin and pale. Time had passed, for her, in the blink of an eye.

Arising from the mounting block, she drifted about the courtyard, then into the stable. As she moved past the horses, it became obvious that, if humans could not see her, the horses could. Their eyes rolled white-rimmed, they backed away, snorting.

Bess came nearer, talking in low tones, but many animals panicked, rearing and kicking. Others simply stood, sweating and trembling.

"Good boy, good girl," she tried to soothe them, but to no avail. She stood wringing her spectral hands in distress.

"They do not understand. Stupid creatures."

Bess whirled. She found her gaze locked with the large, intelligent brown eyes of a shining black mare who might been the inspiration for the inn's new name. No, surely not. . . .

"Yes, it was." The mare nodded her head. The "voice" had echoed inside Bess' head, but it was clearly the mare who had "spoken."

"How . . . why . . .?"

"Oh, in your present state, we can all speak with you if we wished. But they are too afraid. As I said, stupid creatures. Dogs will snarl and whimper, and most cats, save witch familiars, will hiss. Ravens . . . they care not if one is spirit or flesh, they view everything without wings as beneath contempt."

Bess laughed, a strained, shocked sound. "Merciful Heaven," she breathed. "Are you a witch, then, in the shape of a mare?"

The horse whinnied, as if laughing itself. "I hardly think a self-respecting minion of Satan would permit herself to be locked up all day, fed poor hay, and be tended to by the loving kindness of Tim Alcott. No, I am what I seem—a mare, one who pities you, Mistress Bess."

"Tim," said Bess, slowly. "He was asleep in Father's bed. He can speak now. He used to be dumb and simple. How can this be?" She rubbed her arms, feeling a chill not of body.

"Yes, he is now the innkeeper of The Black Mare. As to how he gained his new wit and wagging tongue, I remind you of what they say about those who wager with the Horned One. Great power may be granted—for the gamble of a soul."

"He wagered with the Evil One? For wits and speech?" Bess was shocked.

"And the chance to be master here at the inn. Wager he did, and he got what he bargained for—all except for one thing." The mare snorted, fixing eyes the color of peat upon her.

"And . . . and what was that?"

"Your own sweet self, Bess. You cheated him out of what he wanted most."

Somehow she had known that. Tim's lust for her had been something she'd always avoided acknowledging. She'd been too wrapped up in Jamie, and between Jamie and Tim . . . well, the contrast between them was laughable. Bess drew a deep breath and asked the question that could be put off no longer—though she dreaded the answer.

"What happened . . . to my father?" *And to Jamie?* her mind added, but she could not force herself to ask that yet. As long as she did not ask, she could hope that Jamie was safe.

The mare took a step toward Bess and attempted to nuzzle her comfortingly. The velvet muzzle passed right through Bess' misty form. "Your father died the same night you did," she said softly inside Bess's head. "Found dead with a knife in his throat. The soldiers always claimed that your highwayman did it, but . . ." The mare tossed her mane in the equine equivalent of a shrug, and said no more.

Bess closed her eyes. *Hasn't there been enough pain and death and suffering?* she thought miserably. A memory floated back to her; Tim, listening intently to the captain, then hastening off on some task. . . .

A sudden bustle and clatter in the courtyard distracted her. Bess turned to listen, heard voices.

"Welcome to The Black Mare, young sir. And the missus, I take it." Tim's voice, and it fitted the rest of him. Even dead, Bess felt her skin crawl at the raspy, obsequious tones.

"Thank you," came a man's voice. Young. Earnest. Familiar.

"Here now," said Tim, "don't I be knowin' you, sir?"

Curious, Bess left her equine friend and floated to the entrance of the stables. In the center of the courtyard, a carriage had pulled up. The horses pranced, barely winded, and a young soldier stepped out. He turned to extend his hand to a pretty young woman, probably his wife, whose belly was heavy with child.

"I know him," Bess whispered softly.

"No," said the young redcoat, addressing Tim but avoiding the ostler's gaze. "We've not met."

"Liar," said Bess. "Oh, you liar, you evil man."

Tim's eyes widened, then he touched his forelock in exaggerated deference and gave the soldier a sly wink. "All you soldiers, I s'pose you look the same. Well, I'll give you m'best, for your lady to rest in, sir. Please to follow me."

"You? But I thought the landlord was—" The soldier stopped in mid-sentence, and his shoulders sagged. Bess' lips twisted in a silent snarl. Ah, but he was handsome, wasn't he, with his wide blue eyes and fair hair tied back with a red ribbon. She remembered his name: *Lieutenant Robert Larrimer.*

The innkeep and his guests walked away, and Bess returned to the mare. "That was him! He was one of them!"

"Balance," the mare replied, pawing with one black hoof. "The wheel turns. It has been a year to the day since your death, Bess."

"And he has come, this day of days," said Bess. Her spectral hands closed into spectral fists.

"Now you know what drew you here." The mare's "voice" was intense and hot in her mind. "Larrimer is the reason you rose from your uneasy rest. He is one of those responsible for your death, and the death of your beloved. Revenge is in your grasp, Bess."

"My beloved—merciful Heaven," Bess could scarcely speak. Breath was agony in her throat, and tears sprang to her eyes. "They killed Jamie, too?"

She had given her life so that Jamie might be warned of the ambush, might flee. And her sacrifice had been for naught.

The horse nodded, and her eyes were sad. "The next day, he returned. In broad daylight. He knew only that you were gone, and he couldn't live without you. They gunned him down, Mistress Bess . . . shot him down like a rabid dog, on the highway. He died in a pool of his own red blood, and they buried him at the crossroads, in an unmarked grave."

Bess sobbed, but the horse was relentless as she finished, "And now, his killer is here. It is your turn to kill."

Bess shook her head. "But Larrimer—he didn't—he tried to stop—"

The mare was inexorable. "He was one of them. And he is within your grasp. Heaven is merciful, Bess, for it's given you a chance to win your passage on to the afterlife. Kill the man who killed your love, and the balance is restored. An eye for an eye."

"But I can't . . ." Bess protested.

"Do as you will," the horse said, suddenly indifferent. She reached for a mouthful of hay, began chewing. "You can always stay here with me. I enjoy the conversation."

Trapped here in the inn forever? Bess shuddered at the idea. If she was truly being given the chance to go on, for a real afterlife, hadn't she better take it?

"How do you know all this?" she whispered.

"Beasts know things, see things, that humans wot not of," the mare said, still chewing. "Just as we can see you, where they cannot, we know things."

"I see," Bess whispered. It made sense. The stories always talked about animals being sensitive to otherwordly forces, able to see spirits. She thought of Larrimer again. That handsome young man, alive, married, the father of a child, while her darling Jamie lay in unhallowed ground, trodden on by man and beast alike. *It's not fair!*

"No, it isn't," the mare agreed.

Bess nodded, her mind made up. It could not be mere coincidence. She, dead by her own hand, a ghost returning on the eve of her death, and he, one of those who had killed her, returning as if by fate. Larrimer, the key to her own afterlife. Jamie was dead, yes. But she could avenge him.

Tonight. Please God, she would have revenge tonight, hurt that handsome, sweet-faced youth as badly as he had hurt her, as badly as he'd hurt Jamie. The thought filled her with hot pleasure. Bess turned back to the horse and smiled, and the mare closed one eye in a conspiratorial wink.

Larrimer was appalled to realize that "the best room" was the one in which Bess had died. Anna, tired and drained, had been too distracted to notice her husband's reaction to their quarters. After the midwife had examined her, given her a potion, and prescribed a day's rest, Anna eased her bulk onto the bed, and was asleep in minutes.

Her husband sat in a chair near the window, his head buried in his hands. The memories haunted him at night, lurked on the edges of his consciousness by day. And here, in this room, where the worst of it had happened, they flooded his mind and would not be dismissed. . . .

*. . . . "Is that all the ale you've got?" Captain Jennings bellowed, slamming his empty tankard down on the table in the taproom. The innkeeper, a tall, thin man, shook his head. "But, Captain, you've not paid—"*

*"Bring me ale, damn you," thundered Jennings, and the landlord scurried to obey.*

*Larrimer cleared his throat, "Captain, with due respect, we ought to pay the man for—"*

*"Larrimer, you irritate me," growled the older man. "He's been giving aid to a killer. Taking his ale is little enough punishment. Ha, look how he sends his daughter to wait on us!" His voice dropped. "I've got other plans for her tonight."*

*Larrimer closed his mouth in miserable compliance. Bess, he believed the girl's name was. It was she who had been consorting with the highwayman James "Bonnie Jamie" MacLaren.*

*The girl wore a dress of dull red, and a white apron. Her feet were bare as she walked over the cold stone floor, and her breasts moved with quick, shallow breaths. Larrimer could see she was terrified.*

*"Mistress" he said gently. She turned eyes that were black as coal upon him. "Our orders are to capture Bonnie Jamie, so he can be tried, but he's never harmed anyone. Likely the judge will spare his life."*

*She smiled then, red lips curving hesitantly, shyly. Sweet Jesu, but she was lovely.*

*"Ha! The Colonel said if he resists, he's a dead man!" Jennings snarled, and then showed crooked teeth in a cruel smile. "Mistress Bess . . . I'm glad you're here. Lads, did you know that if you wish to catch the big fish, you need proper bait? I'd say this slut is proper bait indeed!"*

*As Bess backed away, furious but too frightened to defend herself, Jennings made a sudden, deadly lunge. Clamping a hand upon Bess' arm, he dragged her into his lap. She struggled, then froze, a drop of sweat trickling down her suddenly pale face, as Jennings placed the muzzle of his pistol to her throat.*

*Larrimer bolted to his feet. "Captain, this is outrageous! I will not—"*

*Then he, too, fell silent and still as a tiny sound—the almost unnoticeable click as the pistol was cocked—reached his ears. Smith, Jennings' second in command, had drawn his own pistol and now stared down the sight directly at Larrimer.*

*"We soldiers work hard," said Captain Jennings in a deceptively gentle voice. "We deserve a little . . . sport . . . now and then. The girl's a whore, Robbie, and we've got the authority to send her whole bloody family to a very nasty gaol cell if we so choose. All I'm asking is that she help us snare her elusive fox of a highwayman." Without removing the pistol, he tangled his fingers in her hair, tugged her face down to his, and kissed her wetly.*

*Larrimer looked away, sick. He'd accepted the offer of a commission in the King's army, thinking that the life of a soldier would be filled with travel and excitement. He'd had no idea that officers like Jennings even existed—men who enjoyed causing others pain. But Jennings was in command. What could he do?*

*He wished for a moment that he could leave on some pretext—leave and warn the highwayman not to come. That ugly scarecrow of an ostler, Tim, speaking in a voice that sounded rough and somehow unused, had told Jennings that he'd overheard MacLaren promise to come to Bess "by moonlight, Cap'n. He said he'd come t'her by moonlight, though hell should bar the way. His very words, Cap'n."*

*Larrimer cursed silently as he stared at Bess' terrified face. Bonnie Jamie MacLaren had robbed a good many travelers on the road, 'twas true, and had been a thorn in the side of the law for almost four years now. Capturing him would be quite a coup. But MacLaren's glittering pistols and rapier had always been for show. No one had ever been injured by the highwayman—save, perhaps, their pride.*

*He remembered something else that Tim had said. At the time he hadn't understood, but now he did, all too well. "Don't forget, Cap'n. When you're done wi' Mistress Bess . . .*

*"Yes, yes," Jennings had said. "You have my word. Now*

*hurry along and attend to that other matter we discussed, Tim, that's a good lad."*

*The ostler had tugged his forelock, and melted into the shadows.*

*Now Larrimer knew what Tim had meant when he'd said, "When you're done . . ."*

*My God, Larrimer thought, in horror, I can't let this go on! I must do something!*

But he hadn't, had he? Larrimer lifted his head from his hands, not at all surprised that his face was wet. "I should have, damn it," he said aloud to the dark stain on the floor.

He had woken Anna. She stretched, and smiled sleepily at him. Larrimer's heart turned over. He went to her and kissed her softly, sweetly. The shadows had fallen outside as well as in his own heart, and he told her, "It's time for supper, love."

Bess hovered over them as they ate.

The serving wench commented on the strange chill that haunted that corner of the otherwise cosy, firelit taproom. Pale, pregnant Anna shivered and put on her shawl. Lieutenant Robbie Larrimer rubbed his cold hands and glanced reflexively behind him. Bess watched them, excitement flowing through her. Soon . . . soon . . .

The words of the black mare in the stable, who said her name was "Night," spurred Bess on, warmed her. Revenge would win her rest; revenge, and nothing else.

Before retiring, Larrimer and Anna sat beside the fire in the taproom for a while. As the minutes stretched by, Larrimer grew increasingly uncomfortable. Bess drank in his apprehension like wine. He was nervous, nervous about lying down to sleep with his warm wife and baby-to-be in a room where he'd watched a girl die.

"Be nervous, then, Robbie," Bess urged him. "Be nervous while you still can. . . ."

Surely it was his imagination that had him so rattled, Larrimer consoled himself. He didn't believe in ghosts, not in this rational Age of Enlightenment. He was haunted, true enough, but by memories and shame, not by specters.

Despite the diligent application of a bedwarmer, Larrimer was cold. His wife slept peacefully, her breast rising and falling, the swell of her stomach arching up beneath the covers.

Larrimer tossed and turned, watching the hands of the clock next to the bed mark the passage of the hours. It had been a year ago, tonight, in this room, and he had tried, but not hard enough. . . .

*. . . They tossed the sobbing girl back and forth between them, each of them taking crueler and more vulgar liberties. The harder Bess sobbed, the louder they laughed, slobbering and pawing and pinching.*

*Larrimer stood by, feeling wretched. He could no more have stopped it than he could have stopped the moon from rising in a few hours. The lieutenant glanced out the casement at the road that waited in the darkness like a serpent, and found himself hoping that the highwayman would break his promise—that Bess would not have to watch his capture—perhaps his death—in the ambush Jennings was planning.*

*"That's enough, lads," the captain said finally. Larrimer sighed with relief. They'd had their fun, they'd let her go, now, lock her in her little room in the attic, while they waited for her lover. Bess was rumpled and sore from pinches, but mostly unhurt, save for her dignity.*

*Larrimer turned back from the window. They had torn her dress, using a bit of cloth as a crude gag. Chuckling, Jennings took a dagger and slit the chemise that peeked through her torn bodice. The men laughed and slavered as the girl's breasts bobbed free, white and rose-tipped in the candlelight.*

*"Now, watch this," said Jennings. He took a musket and rubbed its muzzle over the girl's nipples, which stiffened in response to the cold iron. The soldiers hooted.*

*"Good God, Jennings," Larrimer protested. "Haven't you done enough?"*

*"You and I will have to have a talk when this is over, Lieutenant," replied the captain, his eyes never leaving the wide, frightened ones of the girl.*

*"Yes," said Larrimer, in a strong voice that shocked even him with its edge. "Before God, we will."*

*Surprised at Larrimer's tone, Jennings turned his head and regarded him. The younger man stood his ground, sticking out his chin. "You and Smith keep watch, then," Jennings said. "See that the girl doesn't escape. And to make you task a bit easier—"*

*He bent and propped the musket up on its butt, wedgin the barrel firmly beneath the girl's heavy breast. "Oh, goo job!" said one of the men, who began to tie the weapo against Bess' body.*

*"Now, keep good watch!" laughed Jennings. He remove the gag and kissed her lips, then jerked back, his hand t his mouth. "You bitch!" he cried, staring at the blood o his hand. "The wench bit me!"*

*He cracked her across the face with his hand. Larrime winced. Bess' eyes filled with tears and the imprint of Jen nings' hand welled up red on her face, but there was n surrender in her expression.*

*Angrily, Jennings shoved the gag back in her mouth. " had half a mind to keep you for myself, and not give yo over to that madman of an ostler. But now, you get wh you deserve."*

*He straightened and glared at Larrimer. "Watch her. And then he was gone.*

*Silence fell. The minutes crawled by. Larrimer and Smit alternately stood by the window, and sprawled in chair. Larrimer tried not to look directly at Bess, sparing her wh small amount of humiliation he could, but once he caug her in the act of twisting her hands against the knots. Whe she saw him looking, she froze like a frightened deer. Tryin to get the blood back into her hands, poor lass, Larrim thought, and he looked away again, wishing he could loose the knots. But Smith would never stand for it.*

*The minutes stretched into hours, and more than onc Larrimer caught himself drowsing. The moon rose like silver ship tossed on cloud-waves.*

Tlot-tlot, tlot-tlot. *Hoofbeats along the road.*

*"Bastard's on his way," said Smith softly. He began prime his musket. "And it looks like we'll have a clear sh at 'im from here."*

*Larrimer realized that they weren't even going to allo Bonnie Jamie the opportunity to surrender. They were ju going to kill him in cold blood. Sickened, he heard Be take a breath, a deep, deep breath, and he turned toward he*

*Afterward, he was never sure what he planned to do- free her, perhaps. But time suddenly seemed to slow as faced her. He realized, too late, that she had managed work a finger free—one finger, placed on the trigger of the musket, and she gave him a blazing look of triumph as she pressed down and—*

"Bess, no!" screamed Larrimer, bolting awake.

"Oh, yes," came a soft, angry whisper. His heart slamming against his chest, Larrimer looked wildly around the room.

She stood beside the open casement, transparent as gauze, white as moonlight, floating a foot above the floor.

"Bess," he breathed. His skin erupted with gooseflesh and his blood went cold as well water. "You've come back!"

She nodded, still floating. "Yes, I've come back. For you."

He would have thought it impossible for his fear to deepen, but it did. He clutched the coverlet. Somehow, impossibly, Anna slept on. Out of the corner of his eye, Larrimer saw the hands of the clock spinning wildly and realized that this moment was out of any time ever known by mortals. Anna drowsed in the true time, but he had been plucked out of it by the vengeful ghost of a dead girl.

"Bess, I tried to stop them—I tried—"

"But you didn't," she interrupted. Now she moved, floating gracefully toward him like milkweed down. "You didn't stop them. You didn't save me. And you helped murder my Jamie!"

Out of the corner of his eye, Larrimer noticed that a pile of rope was slowly uncoiling. It undulated like a snake in the air. His pistol floated upward, as if borne by an unseen hand.

He opened his mouth to protest, but that was all she needed. Her body contorted into a slim thread and she dove down his throat.

*She* was there, inside him, and Larrimer felt the terror, the same terror she'd felt that night one year ago. The pain, the humiliation, the fear, the futile hope that her sacrifice would save her beloved.

And suddenly Bess saw what Robbie had seen, that night one year ago. Through his eyes, through his memories, she saw her own death. The gun exploded, shattering her breast. She convulsed, but she was already dead, had to be dead, with a hole in her chest and back and the red blood trickling down over her pale still face like a red ribbon, like the love-knot in her black, black hair.

With her spirit animating him, Larrimer moved. He climbed out of the bed, and stood beside the open casement, against the bedpost while the rope snaked around him and the pistol pressed close. His fingers writhed, seeking release from the tight bonds, stretching to find the trigger.

*Tlot-tlot, tlot-tlot.* Hooves on the cobblestones. For a wild moment, both ghost and mortal thought the highwayman had returned, as he had vowed, for his black-eyed Bess. But a shadow moved across the courtyard, trotting over to the window; a black horse, riderless. And beside it, a man, a white-faced man with eyes the color of madness, and hair the color of moldy hay.

"Come," said a voice inside his *(her)* head. "Take your revenge, Bess, and let me bear you away to a better place."

And his mortal ears heard the ostler's rasping tones, "Kill him, Bess! He killed your Jamie!"

Blood soaked the bonds as Larrimer's fingers reached for the trigger. *This is justice!* thought Bess wildly inside Larrimer's thoughts. *A life for a life—for Jamie's. . . .*

Larrimer knew he had only seconds to live. Images from his life flashed through his mind—and Bess shared them. She saw Robbie, in civilian garb, approaching the highwayman at a tavern, delivering the sad news with a warning to come not near the inn. Larrimer had wept as he'd spoken to Jamie. And then, later, when Jamie lay dead, Larrimer had challenged his Captain, had dueled with him, rapiers flashing by torchlight—and he would have won, save for the Colonel's interference.

Pity flowed through Bess, as she lived Larrimer's torment, his grief, his guilt and shame. He'd suffered for a year, suffered as much as any prisoner locked in a gaol of his own making.

"No!" echoed words that Larrimer somehow understood came from the horse . . . the mare called Night. "No, do what you promised, Bess, revenge is sweet. . . ."

*More than one life,* thought Bess, even as Larrimer's fingers, under her guidance, brushed the trigger. *More than one life lost and ruined . . . Jamie's, mine, Father's. . . .* She could not help herself. She turned her *(his)* head back over the shoulder, to see the sleeping woman on the bed

*More than one life . . . Larrimer's, and Anna's, and the baby's, shattered by me. . . .*

"No!" shrieked Bess, pulling herself abruptly out of Larrimer's body. The soldier sagged against his bonds, gasping. "I will not do this! I will not ruin more lives because mine was cut short!" She wept freely, and tried to touch Larrimer's face. Her fingers passed right through him. "I forgive you. I forgive you with all my heart."

The soldier staggered as the rope fell as if it had been abruptly cut. He dropped to his knees.

Bess leaned out the casement and confronted the mare, who pranced agitatedly. "He had no part in it, Night. How will killing him send me on to eternal peace? It cannot be right, it cannot!" She glanced over at Tim, who was staring up at her in horror, horror that had nothing to do with seeing a ghost. "Night," Bess said, in fear and consternation, "Night, why is Tim with you? Tim killed my father, he betrayed Jamie and me. He is no friend to either of us."

Larrimer crawled over to the casement, beside Bess' spectral image, and looked out. The horse neighed, a harsh sound that never came from a mortal beast, and then—Larrimer moaned with terror—it began to *change*.

The creature retained the outward seeming of a horse, but its pawing hooves left trails of fire. Its mane and tail erupted in sheets of black flame. Larrimer could feel the infernal heat against his face. The beast screamed in anger, exposing sharp teeth—the teeth of a carnivore. Its eyes became red coals, and steam floated from its nostrils.

A Nightmare, in truth, from the depths of hell.

The creature turned to Tim, who had fallen to his knees and was groveling in fear. "We wagered for a soul, and you wagered that I'd have hers, Tim," it thundered in a terrible silent "voice" that filled the night. "She is proving . . . difficult."

"Take her! She vowed to kill him, and by doing so, damned herself!" Tim gabbled. "Take her, take her!"

"Take her I shall," the beast growled.

Suddenly it grew long arms, black as pitch, and reached for the specter. Bess cried out and struggled. But these hands, unlike human hands, were able to close upon her misty form. She was dragged toward the casement.

"Leave her be!" cried Larrimer. He was determined to fight for Bess, as he had not fought before. His gaze darted desperately around the room, seeking something to serve as a cross.

Nothing . . . but wait! With a gasp, he dragged his rapier from its sheath, and, with one swift snap, he broke it across his knee, ignoring the blood that slicked his fingers. To make a cross, he needed something . . . rope, or ribbon. . . .

"Fight, Bess! Fight it!" he shouted.

In his fingers was the ribbon from around Anna's throat; a the ribbon that held her locket. Quickly, feverishly, Larrimer bound the broken sword into a cross.

Larrimer thrust his makeshift weapon between Bess and the Nightmare, brandishing the holy symbol in the face of the thing from hell. It hissed violently, and drew back, but it did not release the ghost girl. "I am no simple demon, foolish mortal! Think you a *cross* can defeat me?"

Larrimer felt his conviction waver, but he looked at the locket, then at Bess. "And this is no simple cross," he stated. "I have broken my sword, and will never wield it against man nor woman again. And I have bound it with a symbol of the deepest love of which man is capable—my vow to my wife. I challenge you in the name of a God that bade us show mercy and love—as Bess has shown mercy and love to a poor, unworthy soldier!"

The Nightmare cried out, a low, ululating sound, and fell back. "I wagered for a soul, and a soul I shall have!" it shrieked.

Tim was already up and running across the courtyard. The Nightmare was upon him in a single leap, her hooves clattering against the cobblestones, leaving ribbons of fire writhing in her wake.

"Nooooooo!" screamed Tim as the beast, never pausing in her giant strides, swept him up onto her back. He shrieked, but stayed on as if tied there.

A moment later the Nightmare, bearing its damned burden, was gone.

Larrimer's "cross" fell from nerveless fingers, and he clutched the casement sill to steady himself. He drew a deep breath, then another. Finally, he looked up at Bess.

She was not looking at him. Her head was up, cocked, in a listening pose. Then Larrimer heard it too.

*Tlot-tlot, tlot-tlot.* Hoofbeats on the road. Bess smiled, the secret smile that only women in love can know, and began to loosen her hair.

Larrimer could see it now, coming along the ribbon of highway—a man on a horse, a smoky dappled beast that shone like mist in the moonlight. Larrimer smiled, and softly whispered a blessing upon both of them.

There he was: the French-cocked hat, the thigh-high boots, the doeskin breeches. His spurs glistened and jingled. It was Bonnie Jamie MacLaren come at last, as he had promised so long ago, for his Bess.

The highwayman paused beneath the window to fondle a length of hair that had once been black, inhaling its sweetness. "My love," he said in the rumbling, warm burr that Larrimer had heard once before, when he'd broken the news of Bess' death. "My love, I've been waiting. But I could not come for thee until the stain of thy suicide was purged. Had thou killed yon soldier boy, I'd have never been allowed to see thee again."

"Jamie . . ." Bess whispered. "Oh, Jamie."

The highwayman held out his arms, and Bess slipped over the casement sill. He clasped her close, and then bent his head to kiss the landlord's daughter—kissed her with a fierce tenderness that Larrimer understood; had shared with his Anna.

Neither of them looked back as the ghostly figure spurred his spectral steed. Away they went, following the highway until, at last, they were gone.

The cock crowed. The clock chimed softly, marking the return of time's passage. Larrimer slumped against the window sill, his eyes filled with tears of joy.

It was, finally over. He need not carry his burden of guilt a step further. He was free to hold his head high, to love his wife and child, with no secrets between them. For the highwayman, as he had vowed, had come for his love by moonlight, though hell had barred the way.

©danForth'96

# BY THE TIME I GET TO PHOENIX

## *by Jennifer Roberson*

I put off writing my story for this anthology until most of the other contributions were in hand. That's one of the benefits of being editor: one is able to see what everyone else is doing before deciding on an angle or a plot! I had originally expected to write a fantasy or historical story; it's what I do most often, after all. But one early fall weekend I headed out of the city for a hiking trip with friends, and, as driver, had to wend my careful way through ponderous flocks of what we Arizonans call "snowbirds," the retired couples in (exceptionally slow) cars and (exceptionally large) RVs who annually exchange the winter snows of the Midwest for the sunny climes of Arizona. After surviving the trip up north and back down again with teeth only barely intact, I had my inspiration.

I was dead-heading on I-17 southbound out of Flagstaff, swapping pines for saguaros on my way to what the tourist flacks call the Valley of the Sun. Midweek, and quiet: mostly eighteen-wheelers on the road, like mine; one or two RVs; a handful of cars.

Midsummer, midday, maybe 112 degrees, and the mercury headed higher. Waves of heat shimmered into watery mirages stretching across the pavement, but I was okay with a/c chilling the cab, Garth in the cassette player, a waxed cardboard cup shoved into the plastic holder lodged into the slot between window glass and rubber molding. Watered-down cola and melting ice sloshed as I changed lanes, crossing the lumpy reflectors mounted in gummy asphalt. A little to the right and I'd nudge Bott's Dots, those annoying metal implants meant to keep you awake if, nodding off, you ran onto the shoulder.

Dooowwwwnnnn the long hill, the border between the cusp at Sunset Point where dogs and their humans got a chance to lighten their loads, and the desert canyons below.

Curves like LeMans, this road, this place; but not banked for racing unless you were a college student coming down from Flag to Phoenix, stupid enough to put the stick into neutral and let 'er run. I'd done it a time or two myself; but other drivers tend to freeze up when they see a big ol' chrome grille and the bulldog filling their rearview, and I gave up the game. I blame Spielberg for that, you know: for making the truck out to be the enemy in that TV-movie called *Duel.*

Two sets of curves called the Big Hill, a few milder hummocks of undulating pavement and painted lines, Bott's Dots, then the desert flats sliding into Phoenix beyond Black Canyon City. And where pickings are usually good; with forty-fifty miles between Black Canyon and the outskirts of the Valley, drivers stop thinking about the heat, the haul from trees to cactus. Their minds are on the city, not on their gauges.

Beyond Black Canyon City there's Rock Springs; but it's not much more than a wide spot in the road and no one wants to stop there when they're so close to "civilization."

So close. So far away.

Easy pickings, when urgency and impatience lulls them into pushing the car too hard. Some of them do make it to the rest stop; but that's okay, because in high summer people just want to push on. Which means I'm usually at the rest stop alone except for the marks.

All it takes is a few minutes, usually, to fix what's broke or to break what's fixed; or to give them a lift to the nearest gas station forty-fifty miles up the road—and drop them off short. Maybe a mile or two, and about the time they're relaxing, too, thinking about repairs, about calling the road service. Never about robbery.

Easy. Take their cash, leave 'em their plastic, point them to the gas station, and wish them a happy hike. And I'm gone before they can get there to tell the mechanics to call the DPS and report a robbery. By then I'm in Phoenix where the jurisdiction changes, and in the time it takes to describe the truck, the driver, I'm somewhere else. In the truckyard, likely, swapping out the bulldog for a Kenworth, or a Peter.

No real harm done, after all. By the time the day is over they've got their car fixed, and more cash from an ATM. They don't even have to cancel any of their cards.

I squinted out the windshield. Yup, car at the side of the road, chrome blinding in the sunlight. And two ladies there with it, holding sections of tented newspapers up to shade their heads. Poor old gals. Out all by themselves with no menfolk around; they'd be pleased to see me, all right.

I smiled, cranked up Garth, started through the gears. By the time I got the box stopped and climbed down from the cab, they were aflutter with relief.

Bluehairs. Marthas and Mildreds, I call them. Maybe widows, maybe sisters, or maybe just two gals the golf-shirted, plaid-trousered husbands had let out of the house on a summer afternoon. Identical blue eyes, heat-pinked faces. Identical hair as well—too heavy on the rinse, which turned natural silver-gray to a wispy shade of gentian—shellacked into place, and the uniform of their generation: polyester knit tops and slacks, and those cheapo plastic sandals sold most often at state fairs. But nice ladies. Sweet-faced, crepe-armed, road-flat in the butts. And utterly helpless here by the side of the road, unable even to lift the table-sized hood on the big old Caddy.

Land-barges, is what those damned cars are. And I swear, they must card you before you set foot on the lot, because I've never seen anyone but bluehairs and old men driving 'em.

Usually twenty miles an hour in a 45-mph zone.

"Afternoon," I said pleasantly. "Where you ladies headed?"

They exchanged glances, afraid to say.

"Outlet mall?" I guessed; we were maybe ten miles away. "Guess the menfolk didn't want to come."

My ladies surrendered. "They never do," one said rather gloomily. Martha, I decided.

I grinned. "Well, some of them ol' boys get pretty bored when their women shop. They'd rather stay home and watch the golf on TV."

They exchanged glances again, chagrined. Then Mildred straightened her shoulders and put her chin up. "What's the harm in it?" she asked defensively. "It's a way to pass the time. Why shouldn't we get out? They can stay home and watch all the TV they want—"

"—while you two ladies do the outlet mall." I nodded agreeably. "Only fair, I'd say. Now, what seems to be the trouble?"

Martha pointed. I saw the pool of sickly yellow-green antifreeze creeping out from under the car. "Uh-oh. Looks like you blew a hose." I shook my head in sympathy. "If that's so, I'd do better just to take you two ladies on into the nearest gas station. It's only about twenty miles back." I paused. "That is, if you think you can trust me."

They looked doubtful. I didn't push it; let 'em come to their own decision. They feel safer that way.

"If you want," I continued, unoffended by the lengthy hesitation, "I can try to reach the Department of Public Safety on the CB radio. If it would make you feel better."

The ladies conferred. Examined me. Looked at the truck, their car. At the spreading neon ameba.

"Tell you what," I said reasonably, "I'll take you in to the gas station, get the guys going on fixing up your car, and I'll go ahead and take you on to the outlet mall. No reason for you to hang around a gas station bored out of your minds when you could be shopping." I grinned. "Just ask one of the gas-jockeys to come pick you up when you're done. Promise him a tip, he'll do it. Seems a shame to ruin your day because your car's being temperamental."

Hooked 'em. Shopping won out: they're women. "If you're sure . . ." Mildred began doubtfully.

"But only if we pay *you* for your time as well," Martha declared forthrightly. "Seems only right."

"Oh, now, ladies—"

"We insist!"

I gave in gracefully. "Then allow me to help you climb up in my chariot." I gestured toward the idling eighteen-wheeler, then paused as if struck. "You don't mind Garth Brooks, do you?"

"Oh, my, no," Martha said. "He's such a nice boy."

"And rich," Mildred added.

I had to agree with that. Likely ol' Garth didn't do much shopping in outlet malls.

"Here," I said, "let me get that door for you . . . it's a big step up; if you like, I can give you a hand up, each of you."

Martha took a good look at how far up the seat was from the ground, at the inset steps, hesitated, then dropped her purse.

"Oh, here, let me—" But even as I started to bend I felt

the unmistakable bite of a gun muzzle dug into the small of my back.

"If you don't want me to put a bullet through your kidney," Mildred said sweetly, "you'll do as we say."

Martha picked up her purse; or rather, took her gun out of it. Now I had a second muzzle resting against my belly.

I pulled my arms away from my sides. "You gotta be shittin' me."

"Take out your wallet," Martha commanded in her soft little voice, both hands rock-steady on the automatic jammed into my gut. "Strip out the bills; we don't want your plastic."

"No quick moves," Mildred added, prodding a flinching kidney. "We can't *both* miss you."

Likely they couldn't, not with me as a bullet sandwich. With care I dug out my wallet, pulled the bills from it—twenties, mostly, with a handful of tens—held them out.

Martha took them, disappeared them. "Check him."

I felt a deft hand digging into the rest of my pockets. Mildred found them all, all the bills folded over and rubberbanded. A good weekend's take, dammitalltohell.

"That's better," Mildred said in satisfaction. "Go ahead, Sister. The boy wants to keep both his kidneys."

Martha nodded briefly, then climbed up into the cab without any trouble at all. She pulled the door shut, then leaned out. The gun glinted in the sunlight. "All right, Sister, you come on around now. He's mine."

"Wait a minute," I protested, "you can't take my rig!"

Martha smiled sweetly down upon me. "Of course we can."

"You can't even drive this thing!"

"Of course we can."

"My God, woman, it's got more gears than you do genuine teeth!"

"You know," Martha said, smiling, "I find that a pretty sexist thing to say. You just *assume* because we're women we can't drive a big-rig."

"I don't think you can even reach the pedals!"

"Don't tell that to our daddy," she said. "He'd be disappointed that he wasted all his time teaching us a trade."

A concussive hissing of the airbrakes told me Mildred was behind the wheel. "Wait a minute!" I shouted. "You can't steal my truck and my money just to go *shopping*!"

Martha shook her head. "I'm afraid you really are a sexist pig," she said sadly. "Too bad you never met our daddy; *he'd* have changed your mind in a hurry."

"For God's sake, woman—you can't just leave me here!"

"Of course we can." Martha smiled kindly. "But I'd like to be a fly on the wall when you try to explain to the police how you lost your eighteen-wheeler."

Something came sailing out through the open window and cracked against the asphalt: a gift from Mildred. I heard her say something; Martha laughed and repeated it for my benefit. "There's Garth," she said. "You can put him in the cassette-deck there in the car. Give you some company while you wait for someone to come along." She glanced briefly at the sun. "Hope it's not *too* long."

The truck began to roll. "Wait! *Wait!*" I put a hand on the door, and nearly got it shot off. I fell back and dodged a richochet as it whanged off the pavement.

Martha stuck her head out the window. Blue hair glowed in the sun. "Thank you for the grubstake," she called. "It's so much more fun to gamble with other people's money!"

"Gamble—?"

"Casinos!" she shouted gleefully. "God bless the Indians for building them! Dozens and dozens of them!"

Mildred blew the horn, then put the pedal to the metal. The last I saw of the bluehairs—and of my truck—was Martha's waving hand.

# THE LESSER OF . . .

## *by Dennis L. McKiernan*

Dennis McKiernan's most recent novels are *The Dragonstone,* and *Caverns of Socrates.* He's actually written a *lot* more than that, but if I list all the titles, this introduction will be longer than his story.

*Megállni és adni!*” came the faint cry, a cry I could but barely discern above the thunder of carriage wheels and hammer of hooves running upon the hard stone of the narrow mountain road.

I flung aside the curtain and lowered the sash and leaned out the window.

Ahead in the moonlight I could perceive the figure of a man standing in the road; he seemed to be holding something in one hand and waving it over his head.

“*Megállni és adni!*” he cried again, and this time I heard it most clearly, and although my grasp of the language is tenuous at best, still I apprehended what he meant.

Gasping, I ducked back inside and jerked up the sash and slammed the window to. Hurling the curtain across, I clutched my briefcase with its valuable papers to my chest as the coach plunged on.

I thought I heard a pistol shot, but whether or not anyone or anything was struck by a bullet, I could not say. And then there came a most horrid shriek and a sickening thud, and the carriage lurched as it ran over something and thundered onward without slowing.

I collapsed back in my seat as relief washed over me. “Sweet Jesu,” I prayed, “protect us all from evil highwaymen.” As I made the sign of the cross, one or both of the horses squealed as if in pain, and I thought I heard my mysterious coach driver groan . . . and the carriage hurtled onward through the Carpathian night.

# ABOUT THE ARTIST

lizabeth T. Danforth has been one of the mainstays of ie gaming industry for nearly twenty years. Present at its iception with TSR's *Dungeons and Dragons,* Flying Buffa-'s *Tunnels & Trolls,* and many other products, Liz has ot only seen many changes in the field, but helped shape s now-healthy present as magazine editor, game designer, riter, and artist. In 1996 her long-term service resulted in ie sole and unanimous induction into the Academy of aming Arts and Design Hall of Fame, the first artist to e so honored.

Liz is perhaps best known for her black-and-white illus-ations appearing in various game-related products and aps featured in novels. However, her interest also lies in olor work, and she was given the ideal opportunity to iow off this facet when Wizards of the Coast established ie collectible game card market with *Magic: The Gather-g.* Liz has painted many of the most popular cards, and as since gone on to do the same for other companies, icluding the Nazghul cards in Iron Crown's *Middle Earth.*

Contained herein are twenty-three original b&w illustra-ons done specifically for *Highwaymen: Robbers and ogues.*

The artist may be contacted via e-mail at: E.DAN ORTH@GENIE.COM

# ABOUT THE EDITOR

Since 1984, Jennifer Roberson has published nineteen no
els in multiple genres, primarily fantasy and historical fi
tion, and has contributed short stories, articles, essays, an
appreciations to more than thirty collections, anthologie
and magazines; she also co-edited, with Martin H
Greenberg, the DAW anthology *Return to Avalon,* a tribut
celebrating bestselling author Marion Zimmer Bradley. He
works have appeared in translation in Germany, Japan
France, Italy, Poland, Russia, Sweden, and China.

Jennifer holds a Bachelor of Science degree in mass com
munications journalism from Northern Arizona Universit
with an extended major in British history. Prior to becom
ing a full-time writer in 1985, she was employed as an in
vestigative newspaper reporter for a morning daily, and a
an advertising copywriter for a major horsecare produc
manufacturing and marketing company.

Jennifer Roberson grew up in Arizona and used to com
pete in amateur rodeos. Her primary hobby now is th
breeding, training, and exhibition of Cardigan Welsh Corg
and Labrador Retrievers in the conformation, obedienc
and agility rings of AKC dog shows and trials. She is th
Cardigan Welsh Corgi breed columnist for the America
Kennel Club's *Gazette* magazine, and lives near Phoeni
with (for the moment) six dogs and two cats.

Visit the editor's website at www.SFF.NET/peopl
Jennifer.Roberson/